CRA B B AIT

A Gay Mystery

FIRST EDITION

PUBLISHED BY HARD CROSSING PRESS 2023

COPYRIGHT © 2023 JOSEPH BRENNAN

ISBN: 978-0-6455553-3-2

Paperback ISBN: 978-0-6455553-6-3
eISBN: 978-0-6455553-5-6

AUTHOR PHOTOGRAPH BY KIM NGUYEN-VAN ZOEN

THIS NOVEL IS THE SECOND OF MANY STORIES JOSEPH BRENNAN HAS PLANNED.
DISCOVER MORE AT **JOSEPHBRENNAN.COM**

HARD
XING

For mum

O

WEST PIER

IT WAS THE golden age of the gentlemen's club. Felt in every corner of every London establishment of standing. An away place from the gut-fuck of the New World's Gilded Age. So plentiful in the St James's precinct of the West End we know it as "Clubland"—a roll call of handsome venues all competing to cater to the most inside needs of Britain's very best men. Georgian London was the cradle of the club, with *White's* (1736) starting it all during the reign of the second Hanoverian king and the B's of *Boodle's* (1762) and *Brooks's* (1764) being built during George III's tenure. Public establishments at first, finest-bred men soon closed ranks and doors of their gatherings. Meets became private affairs convened in often lavishly custom-built home away from homes, each club creating individual rules and rituals, often secret; like the candle-and-cloak customs of the American education fraternities.

None were as secret as *Sizar's* (1868), however, whose address would never be known in the annals of Clubland, only its scandals...so soiling-ly, ruinously ungentlemanly that the club's name dares not even be whispered in civilised company, certainly never in *White's*. "White" was a living person, believed by those in the club to have been of foreign extraction—Italian likely. "Boodle" was the club's head waiter, so had something of a whiff of tongue-in-cheek behind its namesake. But "sizar" beat the rest in a bow down to boys who serve, being both a more abstract thing of reference and nod to many, many men, taking an ancient root in the lowly tending to better men.

Sizars were given a slot at Cambridge among kings, with food for the belly, knowledge for the mind and lodgings in the colleges along the Cam as compensation for their service. Sizarships offered the loftiest chances at a better life, paid for in the smallest way through menial *bending to*. *Sizar's*, like masters of in-service boys of old, sought to breed the proud college traditions of Cambridge into a world of its own, into boys of the poorest fortunes but the richest flesh; its infamy to-day owes dues to this ambition, having thrashed in the washing-in tide of one frigid morning on the Brighton sands, 1888.

*P*ink flesh pricked with each in breath as Stewart Marsh's nostrils took the sea air in an unaccustomedly vigorous manner...to shake off the demons of an especially disappointing night of one of *Sizar's* rituals—the sorting of boys. He enjoyed the burn; it brought peace to a Brighton-in-winter beach sprint before dawn: the last bastion of a former athletic life and days of pre-sculling sprint-race and hurdling training. Another sole-beach sprinter through a restless sleep was responsible for his burning breath; a faceless but uncannily familiar figure, of whom he had drawn inspiration for this most unusual of activities...to sprint alone and outside of the sport. This figure from his nightscape, bold against the brilliant yellow white of the Brighton sands, merged with boys-sorting disappointments to lead him to an early rousing and carry him down from the Royal Pavilion and to the sea. There was such a chill in the air that morning the sand clumped together as granules of ice. Crunching and collecting on his track-shoe soles. The tide was out. Brighton was known for its king tides. Swells that swept in and up to the dress hems of promenaders at its height. But at its out...well, it receded almost as far as the steamer launch platforms of the town's 1000-foot piers.

The sight of the sands stretched out into the waking morn reminded him of both childhood and man-coming—an odd mixture. But he enjoyed the sight sensation, as queer as the joining of ages was. Piers are provisions for pleasure-seekers to walk out over the waves and the perfect cross-age bridge. A pier walk was a particular thrill for him who, like many in Her Majesty's navy, had the sea in his blood but could not swim it. Sprinting under these iron, into-sea projections was specially stirring of the spirit of the non-swimmer. To thread through the barnacle-covered needles of these man-made marvels. To tread well below where the surface of the ocean had churned mere hours earlier and to see up. Up and into the wooden planking from below. It brought some of the perspective he needed to push out regret over how the night before had played. Fish flapped with land/sea odours at low tide in shallow deposits of seawater and around the corroded bases of the pylons, which added to this push—speaking to the speed with which the ocean rushes away, leaving behind any not fast enough to keep pace with change, even its own.

But what's this? This morning, this hour, there was something larger left there; a mammal, certainly, coiled in a puddle in one of the outer-most crevices of West Pier. Curiosity cut him from a sprint to a gait to an utterly out-of-breath stop. To investigate.

A body!

Marooned, at the turning of dead low. Burning intensified with the discovery. Drawn from nostrils and down his throat, into the lungs and to grip the heart with a deeper chill. And, most eerie, the darkness increased with the investigation, too. The sun itself was blinking. On approach, the pier had appeared softly illuminated, gently outlined with the fore-coming of full sun. But now in its unders, sea-soggy boards of wood above, well…darkness was deeper here. There were sea depths at this point of under-board pier thread. Moreso even it felt than when he had set out from the Pavilion and passed the Grand Hotel little over one hour ago. Through what little light the morning now gave in teasingly flickered illumination he saw the sublime mound. Snagged in the pooled crevice where sand had been drawn away by the tide lay a young man. He felt able to adjudicate the mound's youthfulness by the roundness of boyish bulk, having refereed many a wrestling match in the scouting for *Sizar's*. The weight class of young men was something he knew intimately after twenty years as a club "head," and this one's was a rare weighting, in its own class, and more familiar than any restless dream. The creature was stripped, its skin a pale blue. But still, there was some white and a shade of pink beneath. *Here was a beautiful creature.* Lovely to look upon, even if he had only the back of it to appreciate. Beautiful. Even though flesh was torn in places where the creature had been snagged on the shell-sharpened iron. Beautiful…even with small-shelled scavengers already wide-circling. He brushed the crustaceans away from the creature's wake with care. They were only proceeding based on the natural order. *I will not allow natural orders on the Brighton sands,* he thought. *O no, not just yet.*

Despite the trauma, there was no blood and no damage to the finest features…from his vantage. The side of the face, the buttocks, the genitals— viewable plump from the back between legs. The ripest of English sweet fruits. *This is the freshest and most valuable of morning catch,* he thought. A macabre imagining but he couldn't help himself, feeling the need to touch…to turn the creature over…for air…for the face to be out of the pool…and so he might know this beautiful catch. He curled forward in the manner of the hard-shelled critters circling, acting on this feeling by rolling the sublime creature over. As he did, a voice called shrill through the mist of the Brighton winter——

"Oi there, what th' hell 're you doing?"

The call's authority cut through him like a rogue wave against craggy outcrops, igniting an impulse for a four-legged retreat from the sea, back into the safety of his club's exclusive use of two Brighton establishments. *For how would this all appear to a fellow gentleman?* But the intonation of his haggler held him there. It was…familiar. This voice was distantly known to him. To tr-ace the voice's origin was to shake him back to when his flesh was as fresh as the catch before him—though warmer and less fine-tasting. Before he could arrive at the precise point in the past where the sound could take shape in his mind, the voice through the mist was replaced with heavy breath by his side and a hand to snag him like a crab cage. It was a meeting of before-morning racers, he could tell by the scent of sweat. But after over-shoulder glance, as the voice had suggested to him already…a reunion of old boys, too.

"Oscar?" he said. "I do not believe it! What are you doing here?" The question was absurd. Mute to the salacious scene at their sand-granule feet; but on now having sight and smell as well for this known figure from his past…it was the only sentence construction. *Oscar Glass* of days along Cambridge-colleges riverbanks flinched being recognised, he would later lie-at-all-too-many-more-restless-wakes recall. "Oscar, dear fellow, when did you get in?" he followed fast with.

"Yester-day. Ye—es. Yester-day, 10 am service from London."

Oscar's hairs were dark and his own blonde. Oscar had not aged much and had youthful skin, vital in the cold of morning. His old riverbank mate was almost as handsome as memory could make a man, with big bushy black eyebrows under which peered out round, inquisitive eyes. If any man were born to be a detective, it was this one. Unlike most men of their day, Oscar had no facial hair, which was a requirement of the man's line of work—of keepers of the peace and enforces of law and order, or so he thought he had read somewhere. Seeing how young a fresh blade had kept the fella from his youth, he longed for a cut-throat himself to clear away his own lip growth, so he might be young again with Oscar, too.

"You shouldn't be here, Stew Boy," Oscar said heavy. "Nay. *Quickly!*"

Oscar remembered him, calling the name only Oscar ever had. *Is this equally transporting an experience for him*, he wondered. *To youth-filled times?* "*No!* the poor creature. You get help; I'll stay with…I'll stay…here."

The sands were shifting under their feet. As is the way with the tides in Brighton—especially out there, around the iron of her piers—already the water was rushing back towards the dress hems. Crevices were being swirled into sinkhole softness around the men's grounded bits as had been formed around the pillar that had snagged the creature.

"Insist on staying, eh Stew Boy," Oscar said, stern still, as he remembered the man. "Help m'get 'im up the beach. *Come now!*" The commands spoke of confidence in the matter at hand. A knowingness of what to do.

How anyone could *know* in a situation such as this struck him as beyond the civilised world he'd wished to shelter such creatures from through his club. *It stinks of the outside under the irons.* But to the task of getting the creature back from the sea, keeping perfect flesh from being torn any further, advanced upon by sea undertakers any more…this task formed fast as more than the civilised action—as something dear to him. "Careful with his head," he said, as Oscar took upper portions in capable arms.

There was resistance at first. The creature steadfast, having become stuck fast to the pier. But when the body gave to their tug, Oscar took the creature competently. Caring-ly, compassionately, against adult chest. Committed, they were both, he observed, to see that no further harm came to the creature. He was at the legs himself, where the joints moved supplely still. So too did the parts that made this a man. *The fruits*, full and fragrant up close to the nose and mouth, still soft and responsive to movement. They were, he noticed from recollection of yester-day, untouched by the sharp edge of the sea.

Preserved.

"Put 'im down carefully now," Oscar said, then removed outer tunic to drape over the creature's body, lain flat at the top of the beach.

It seemed a shame to cover the creature, nearly more poetic to have left the sublime thing where it was, bundled at the base of the pier, ready to be consumed by sea. And had he or Oscar not come by, this was precisely what would have happened; the patch of sand where the creature had been discovered was now buried by more than six feet of the rising tide. It was now a watery grave for whatever unmoving flesh was left caught under the pier. "Time to go now, Stew Boy. O yes, mean it now. No sense in you getting pulled into this."

More than twenty years since last seeing Oscar, still the man had the power to pull him into line. "I suppose…yes, very well, I will. But——"

Patience left their bundle with the swiftness of the unpredictable sea: "What d'you want, *Stew-art?*" Oscar said cutting.

"It's just," he said, "you see, I—I—I *know him*."

A face he remembered as a boy being of constant composure flinched for the second time in the space of their morning reunion. "Know 'im, eh? O yes, that does change things. Where're you staying, Stew Boy?"

He hesitated: "The—the–the, at the Grand Hotel."

"Right. Still go—but know I'll be calling in on ya later, Stew Boy."

*T*he crab feeds on carrion, the octopus feeds on crabs. The octopus arrests in its passage any swimming animal, a dog or a man, if it can, drinks his blood and leaves the dead body at the bottom of the water. Crabs are the necrophagus beetles of the sea. Decaying flesh attracts them; they come; they eat the corpse; the octopus eats them. Dead things disappear in the crab, the crab disappears in the octopus...

Clubin had served the octopus as bait.

The octopus had held him down and drowned him; the crabs had devoured him. Some wave had thrust him into the cave, at the bottom of whose niche Gilliatt had found him.

Gilliatt retraced his steps, fumbling among the rocks in search of sea urchins and whelks, as he no longer desired any crabs. It would have seemed to him as though he were devouring human flesh.

VICTOR HUGO, TOILERS OF THE SEA, TRANS. I.F. HAPGOOD, 1888 EDITION, T.Y. CROWELL & CO.

I

PULLMAN

Death had rendered Victoria a black widow. That was
longer than the life of *Sizar's* ago, but death's haunt
continued for the Queen, and into this darkness
the gentlemen's clubs matured to a status of deep
entrenchment. So hard-rooted these clubs were that
lawmen knew to leave them be. They were all-powerful, self-governing
other worlds, you see. Out of reach of the detective mind, and his sights as
well. Although London's detective forefathers in the form of the Bow Street
Runners (1753) predated *Boodle's* and *Brooks's*, Scotland Yard's Detective
Branch was much more the measure of to-day's detective man, and far more
recent as to be David to the giants of the gentlemen's clubs—the branch
only set up in 1842, while *White's* is a year senior to the Bank of England.
And despite the best efforts of novelists the likes of Mr Dickens and Collins
to enshrine through fiction a place for Scotland Yard's detective branch in
civilised thought, *the detective* as an entity moving un-uniformed throughout
all levels of English society is still so shocking an idea, so shaking of the order
of things in the public's psyche that the profession has not the mint to even
attempt to proceed beyond the porters of these premises.

Any with a nose for detection, however, knows these closed societies are
dens of vice as much as they are houses of best breeding. Their exclusive,
beyond-the-law status that breeds manly-but-ungodly transgression. And in

some respects, the more exclusive the club, the more secretive and selective in its recruiting, the higher the criminal stakes. The more in-it-together the men were bound. Even *White's* attracted much ire earlier this century for its gambling traditions, frequently referred to as a "gambling club." As recently recorded as an 1884 edition of the *Living Age*, *White's* forms a key *club gambling of the last century* case study—together with the *Cocoa-Tree Club* (1746), started in a chocolate house and where bribery to pervert the course of Parliamentary affairs is the order of things. Many of the London clubs were canny enough to save slots each year in their books and around their gambling tables for a high-influence magistrate or two, to join in the fun.

The stakes were staggering. To lose £20,000 in a single evening was not unusual, and a 1780 account by Horace Walpole tells a cautionary *Cocoa-Tree Club* tale concerning a young man by the name of Mr Harvey who lost £100,000. "You can never pay me," his opponent said. "I can," the young man replied, "my estate will sell for the amount." The highest stakes were once the order of things at *White's*. On New Year's Eve, 1755, member Lord Mountford, after incurring heavy losses, supped at *White's* one last time and played into the early hours before then courting the company of a lawyer for the writing of his will. After the lawyer confirmed that the will terms would stand were he to shoot himself, the Lord said, "Pray stay while I step into the next room." There was a grim-reaper's poetry in Lord Mountford's self-murder, the man who had placed a bet with a Sir John Bland as to the lifespan of two other club members…both bettors would be dead by their own hands before the victor of the bet placed on the other two could be known.

But among the most famous accounts of *White's* morbid gambling ways was in the regard for the lives of non-members, drawn in as pawns for rich men's pleasure. Probably the best-known tale tells of a man dropping down at *White's* door. He was promptly carried in, but rather than aiding the man, bets were placed on whether he was alive or dead. When the suggestion to bleed the man was put forward, objection was most forthcoming, for fear of perverting the integrity of the bet. Yes, *White's*, *Brooks's* and *Boodle's* were known for reducing once noble men of vast estates to beggary, starvation and blowing out of the brains.

But *White's* is moving to distance itself from its gambling ways these days—there's talk of a history of the club being written, white-washed, of course, it's sure to be. But if it is true that *White's* has turned from its wicked ways, places like *Brooks's* and *Boodle's* are on hand to pick up the players—it's what they've always done. With this whitening up of some of the best-known clubs in decades recent, newer clubs have spored with even greater proclivity for the criminally minded: to court the grey mass of the detective. Clubs with lower standards and less pull in high places, such as the new-to-the-scene *Albemarle* (1874), which weaved the womanly sex into its membership in a decision with only a whiff of what was sure to be a disgraceful world order within its walls...already it has the reputation as a sodomy palace.

Yes, Detective-Inspector Oscar Glass has made it his business to stay abreast of the London clubs, especially what he calls the "catch-all's" like *Albemarle*. Catching all the well-off sinners of the capital. He did this as a means of self-preservation and as a biding of one's time until law might seek to purge sin from such places. As fortune would have it, also of great interest to him were a growing number of underground clubs. Those that were so secretive they forfeited the prestige of a built presence in the West End in favour of *the venue bounce*—pop-up clubs that take only transient residence in the opulent buildings of London's city and county environs. Such a sacrifice of any club front that might allow these worlds, he suspected, to still operate long into the civilised future; to survive as self-governed sin cities, continuing to run even when, in the detective fantasy, vice squads had brought the biggest household-name clubs to their knees. If such secret gatherings went unchecked, that is.

White's and the others of any reputation had chosen their premises quite simply because the St James's area of London was populated by "persons of quality." In its chocolate house days, it was from *White's* that tickets to all the most fashionable London amusements could be had—as contemporary advertisements attest. *White's* reputation as holding the right company in London soon gained beyond-reproach status.

Sizar's sits in stark contradistinction with such as status. Its sought-after membership he learned not from a porter in the West End he could court the company of, but from the whimpering lips of a sludge-smudged boy whore he'd batter-spread under London Bridge. Yes, experience told him his boy under the pier had not drifted to Brighton of an own accord, but on the current of an underground club. And of all the secret gentlemen's clubs, the dead boy must have belonged to the only one he'd ever heard spewed from the lips of London's slums. But what was it that had led the dead boy to end up this way?

Ah! that compelled the detective brain matter with a vengeance.

M urder facts were these… The body was discovered at dawn, around two hours before his arrival on Brighton's to-London platform. This discovery time gave him a slim margin to manage the collection of the body, ascertain Mr Marsh's whereabouts, collect his own belongings, and arrive at the station himself. Learning Marsh's whereabouts included both that while the man had stayed at the Grand Hotel in the past week, Marsh was not lodged there the night previous. From the reception clerk of Marsh's actual place of lodging (the Royal Pavilion), it was learned that luggage was being transported to the station to join an 8.05 am train to London. The case was further complicated that morning by the fact that the 8.05 am service from Brighton was not on the public timetable. Managing all he had in his dead boy's wake, he arrived on the platform with only a few minutes of grace before eight, to be greeted by the growl of the new *Pullman Limited Express*.

It was indeed the age of the engineer. Whose ingenuity all men and their sovereign saw in every rivet, every puff of steam from these marvellous machines. The train awaiting him was among the most marvellous. Having only started running in November just passed: it was specially built by the Pullman Palace Car Co. for the London, Brighton & South Coast Railway, it took on average one and no more than one and a half hours to travel the fifty-one miles from London to Brighton, and ran two daily services each way. The London–Brighton service departed 10 am and 3.50 pm while the return Brighton–London service departed 1.20 pm and 5.45 pm. It consisted of four Pullman day cars; a marvel, for on this train the experiment of electric lighting was underway. The four carriages of the *Pullman Limited Express* disappeared into the steam of the warming engine. They were named "Maud," "Victoria," "Beatrice" and "Louise"—in that seating order from the locomotive.

Maud and Victoria sat dutifully silent while, he noticed, the last two ladies were blushing with a bounty of young men, or mature boys—he hadn't the time before needing to board to cross the steam and find out which way it went or why those carriages were so boisterous; and besides, was distracted by the commotion that he could always count on from a train station in the flush of the morning rush.

Connection to the capital by track for travel to the southern resorts was still the sole activity of those whose work came secondary to opportunities for leisure. Pleasure-seekers, primarily. Yet to the trained eye crime could be found, even in Brighton. Such as in ladies who loitered a-little outside gents' ablutions—to solicit services either quick on site or fuller in one of the town's many inns, their true intent given away by the too-frayed hems and lace of their dress. But he already had a case to detect on, so turned a blind eye to such pursuits of the street crawler, his plain-clothes disguise aiding his cause——

A hand stopped his advance on Maud as his eyes were still fixed on the solicitations of the train-station sluts. The hand that stopped him belonged to a brash, vice trap of a lad. Perhaps his disguise did not function as aptly as it once had.

"Zis is Firrrst Class."

The boy had the crass Eastern way. Tongue-thick speech and body fresh from the slums of some Russian heavy-industry city. And a mongrel face and tight frame to match, the mix of sultry and scoundrel. Brilliant-white complexion, the East boy with bulbous Moscow features would see out any harsh winter—had laddish coarseness, but a rural softness, too.

A snappable quality.

It would take hardly an effort at all to break this scally bent over a man's knee, he thought then barked at the Eastern cheek of a lad with badge raised, "Back off, boy. Scotland Yard."

But the boy did not look at the badge, nor move back to allow him to pass, verifying his right to be there via facial and bodily sizing instead.

"Murder business," he added, "with a suspect pool travelling on this train. So, if you know what's good for ya——"

"Of kourrrse, detective. At yourrr serrrvice." The Easterner spoke low and lazy slow, the roll of each "R" as exaggerated as a to-the-back-pro-jecting pantomime performer—subservient in words chosen, but no manner else.

He pushed the boy aside, entering. But not cutting clear, coming to stop pressed up as a man-boy mash in the iron threshold: "You reckoned I didn't belong. Without seeing any ticket. Why, boy?"

Only using the effort of the lips and cheek of one half, the Russian said: "I kouldn't, niet, vould offend."

"Come, boy," he pressed his body in. "Show the man your work."

"Da, you perrrsist." Russian lips, plump and purple-pink, edge in and to his ear for the reveal: "The suit. Is nice enough, expensive when new, but…is not." Russian hands came into use. "See: vorrrn thrrreading herrre," touching the shoulders.

The elbows.

The knees. "Is too small herrre," touching the dough part of the belly. "Shoes. Is beyond spit polish. And zis," holding up his case—with now boy and man hand at the handle—, "it not shoving of karrreful attention zat zose vith ticket forrr zis karrriage vould have made surrre."

"Good eye, boy."

The assessment did impress, but it annoyed more. The need to keep a low profile, and on occasion, to pass, was *une profession primordial.* The papers called them "Jacks" because they move through classes undetected. To catch their criminals from within.

A Russian runt's seen through m' disguise with a glance.

He went to push through, but the Russian's run-on speech kept him there: "But I be show off vith zat. This is prrrivate serrrvice. Ve don't adverrrtise. Saying it was Firrrst Class was de–eterrrrrrent. I knew men to expect forrr zis karrriage, ve be all given descrrriptions. Niet, you don't match zese."

He remained unsure about the boy, who seemed to sense this in him.

Eyes darting the carriage corridor, the runt added: "Zis train is secrrret."

It made it better, revealed something to get the investigation started. "Ya name, boy."

"Sergei C——"

Stopping.

"Well?" he said.

"Co–ox. Sergei Cox."

Little liar, he thought, but didn't challenge. "Cox, eh?" taking the boy's hand in a grip and pulling them both out of the threshold into the carriage passageway.

"Da."

"You might be 'f some use to me."

"Da."

"Knowing the men on board, if ya get my meaning."

"Da, da."

"Good boy. Stewart Marsh, show me to him."

The Russian kept a resistive stance for seconds more, eyes wandering as if in search of other instances of ill-costume. But once foreign eyes had finished their scan, the mouth—plump and in constant smirk—submitted: "Da."

"Where, boy?"

"He in dining karrrrriage."

"He got a private compartment?"

"Da."

"You'll show me the compartment first."

"Da."

"Then fetch him for me."

"Da, da."

"Good boy."

R ight behind the engine sat Maud, a smoking car made up normally
of three compartments—the main with twenty-six seats, a servant's
section accommodating six, and a guard and luggage compartment.
Normally, as it had been specially reconfigured for this service, shrinking the
main compartment to create private suites. He waited in the suite assigned
to Marsh, where two average-sized suitcases could be found orderly stacked.
The suitcases suggested to him something learned already from his Grand
Hotel and Royal Pavilion visits: that Marsh's stay in Brighton had been more
than one night. Though for a man of Marsh's means and as many reasons
for changing costume, it was an unstable observation without the hotel boys'
testimonies. The temptation to rifle through was there. To rip open those
suitcases of the man who had already lied to him and search for clues to the
curious circumstances surrounding his boy from the edge of the sea, who
Marsh admitted to knowing, and who was found stripped and dead-snagged
under West Pier that morning.

He resisted the rip. The return to London would be brief: one hour plus
little over a third more. He would need to accomplish much in this time and
would need Marsh's help if he was to succeed in securing interviews with any
others with a possible hand in the boy. "Hullo again, Stew Boy," he said when
the Russian came good in the entryway to Marsh's private compartment.

Marsh's wide eyes were all in way of reply as Maud jolted into motion.

"Vill zat be all?"

He nodded with the addition of a "stay close" instruction. *Boy'd make a
serviceable peeler,* he thought.

Marsh was an angular man of face and stature in his very late forties. The
nose and chin were especially enlarged, as was the amber bush of the man's
upper lip—features in contrast with the crew-cut tightness of blonde hair. *Stew*

Boy was once attractive. Striking, even. But is cartoonish now. It's like parts of the boy had grown old while others remained stunted in boyhood. Serious, a statesman (or so he would wager Marsh tried to project in public), but with a glint of gaiety that couldn't be pinpointed to just one aspect of the man's appearance, and which…he would wager, too, found fulfilment in the man's private affairs. "Si' down," he said, palm showing and directed to the bed.

"Pardon?"

There it is. That trace of fire from his memory.

"This is my compartment, Oscar Glass. If any of the two of us are to be telling whom to sit on the bed, it is I." They held strong sight for seconds, half of ten at the most, before both breaking into laughter and drawing into an embrace. "It's been a long time," Stew Boy said into his ear, moustache tickling earlobe. "I thought I might not see you again."

He pulled Marsh back to an arm's length, gripping still. "O dear ol' Stew Boy, surprised you remember me."

"*Come!* don't be modest. Ours was an encounter no man could forget."

"Quite," dropping the grip, "though now's nay the time for any o' that."

"Indeed, the poor boy. He had such promise."

"Did 'e?"

Marsh seemed to close in and on to. Like a flip into frigid seas from an ice floe: the realisation that a detective's interview had begun. His old acquaintance conceded then, sitting by the suite's window where the man prepared a pipe as Brighton's outskirts became smaller in the distance, the sea pushing them away as the boy from his younger days stuffed tobacco into pipe end. "Am I a suspect, detective sergeant?"

"Detective inspector now."

Marsh raised pipe to that, bringing smoke to their encounter as steam plumed outside.

This train was confounding him. Two strongly different parties; a man he knew as a young man and a boy of foreign float in, both who in the space of a single morning already seemed to have insights that were typically the sole mental sphere of men such as himself. "How do you know me? As a man now, I mean."

"Nothing of to-day. I followed your career, Oscar. I feared for you, and I will not deny it. You have chosen a dangerous business. Policing, in London, during these times."

"For men without…means, it's a good profession."

"An honoured one. I'm proud of you, Oscar."

"But the detective part. How did you know?"

Marsh examined the smoking pipe, like a bridge player their hand—the temptation not to show. "*O alright!* I get the London papers. And your name…it appeared in policing matters with enough regularity that I took notice. And then, when mention of you in the papers ceased, and there's all that reportage regarding the London detective force, you know—going undercover, into plain clothes, out of public sight. Well…even I could put two and two together."

He nodded. "About the boy now, Stew."

"What do you want to know?"

"All of it. Yous dealings…the boy's character."

"Character? O no, no way I could speak to that. Truth is, I knew very little. All I did know came from observation. I watch out for talent. He was a remarkable creature."

"*A creature?*"

"A creature *beautiful,*" Marsh clarified, looking back toward Brighton—but the sea was long gone. "He is a thing of beauty."

"You'd best watch ya wording, Stew, when it comes to this boy."

"Creature…thing…" still looking in the direction of the sea. "Alright, Oscar. I see your point, I suppose."

"Beautiful, too."

"Come now, Oscar. That is pure, unemotional observation. You were there…was he not the most beautiful creature you have ever seen?"

"I ask the questions, Stew Boy. But hear my warning."

Marsh turned back to the interior of the carriage, like a child not being indulged. "Have it your way, *inspector.* But if this grisly business is all you're here for, our reunion's a waste of time. I'm not the man you should speak to."

"Then take me to that man."

"That man may not wish to speak. None of the others will." The world outside captured his interviewee's attentions once more.

"Stew Boy," he pressed. "Square up."

"O very well. You best come with me then."

Marsh led the way through a seating area, past what he assumed were further compartments of privileged privacy and to a door at the end. The train was furnished in the American style; loads of heavy fabrics and detailed ornamentations. The New World's fantasy of the Olde. Marsh stopped at the second-carriage threshold. "Before we enter, there are some things you should know. We head a little association of likeminded men, you see."

"Kind of like a private members' club," he said, eyes raised to heavens. "I'm familiar with gentlemen's clubs."

"O not our one."

"*Sizar's* is it?"

Marsh stood bloody-cheeked embarrassed before him. The face resembled a butchered beetroot. Most men of Marsh's standing would have been shocked in the extreme had he slapped them, but the colour in the face was more a beast-sliced-open red than any slap could have coaxed. The revelation *that he knew*. It was like he had slit the cheeks clean off the man with all the brutal confidence of the Whitechapel murders which, that year, were keeping all the other detectives so distracted in London.

His deductions were these... Though many gentlemen's clubs were identifiable by their London real estate; their way of things, their *culture*, was not confined to brinks nor mortar of that central district of Westminster known as St James's. Gentlemen's clubbing ways had their roots in more ancient stone. Namely the clubs known as the "colleges" of the Universities of Oxford and Cambridge. The collegiate cultures of "Oxbridge," they're the true root of clubs for gentlemen. Oxbridge is now by royal charter an institution of two halves: of colleges with universities attached, homes with study theatres adjoined, clubs funding centres of learning. The London gentlemen's clubs simply exchange the theoretical with a practice half; so, clubs became sanctuaries, drinking halls and headrests for those who out of (as well as in) its walls are engaged in the business of being the ruling elite.

The best Oxbridge colleges were just another name for, and a much more ancient iteration of, a private gentlemen's club. Henry VI's *King's College*, Cambridge (1441) came one year after the king established *Eton* for the boarding of boys. Both have become known for breeding the best of men and boys, right up to royal ones. For more than three centuries, *King's* kept its secrets in school by only admitting Etonians, keeping privileged what went on inside its walls. As in life, *King's* men needed to mix in the mornings with men of all kinds, of all intellects, colours and breeding; but after lunch, all the king's men could retire among their own. *King's* men held dear their boyhood bonding, stayed together in sanctimonious seclusion...with gentlemen's clubs waiting to welcome them at the end.

Men who do not know their history might believe that a keeping-pure mission set up the colleges, erecting their walls as reaction to the rising threat of the outside. But intimacy with beginnings finds an obsession with the idea that betterment could be bred into a boy. *Eton* and *King's* were founded as asylums of betterment for the poor of potential. As scholarship centres—a tradition continued in a much more limited sense to-day. He learnt this fact from the month of a *King's* boy many years ago. That boy was obsessed with the possibility of betterment being bred into boys of even the most unfortunate circumstances; now stood beetroot-faced before him. This was his lasting impression of Stew Boy, in fact, in the soggy grass behind a boathouse on the Cam in the aftermath of a *White's* rejection.

"How do yous choose?" he asked. "Nay ballots for *Sizar's*, I bet." It is true, many of the elite clubs were founded on highly politicised or specific-interests grounds. *But!* the brass of the best was that these were social affairs, with entry to the most elite based on a *vouch* from members of the same club, and often the referral of a respected college head. What little he had heard of *Sizar's* told him it was run by kingly arrogance of men strongly disliked by their peers. Stew Boy had the all-important vouching-then-ballot-box-and-blackballing traditions to thank for a *White's* exclusion.

Marsh was too red and raw for him to tell whether this latest, no-ballots deduction came as a shock. "Members are sorted by a contest of manly pursuits," Marsh said with hardly any air. "Open to the poorest of the poor."

"Nay blackballs for m' Stew Boy now. And members get?"

"*O only everything that matters!* The chance to change one's lot in life."

"A motive, then."

"What we offer is tasty and worth killing for. *If!* the boy had managed to qualify. He didn't. So, you see, none of our future residents stood to improve their chances of eventual victory by this boy's death."

"Never said it was one 'f the poor boys that did it."

Marsh ignored the insinuation. "It's sad because he was a true talent. He'd have made a solid member, but for his performance on the day."

"Then why not allow 'im an improved chance, as ya put it. Doesn't sound like a very fair club to me, Stew Boy."

"You seem to know a fair amount, that's sure," red rising in Marsh again. "And yes, perhaps it was not fair. But life is not fair. And every club needs some selectiveness."

"Tell me, then. How d'yous select?"

Marsh took a long drag. "*Sizar's* is a club for future gentlemen. Four houses each named after a home county, each with a *head* who selects sixteen *candidates*. These selected compete to be *residents* in the club, across four rounds, once every two years. *Keep up!* Running every two years means one year in recruitment and preparation of candidates and one year for sorting and a row-race on the Cam. Residents are the eight on the winning team from the Cam. Each house has a *tutor* on hand to assist for the competition, but each head runs his own show, so level of tutor involvement and, for that matter, a head's hand in the club itself varies. The boy on the beach was in the first sorting round in our tenth competition year. So, it's our twentieth year overall. *Got all that?*"

"Cambridge-colleges nonsense, Stew Boy," he said. "*Candidates* bowed to by *tutors* competing for breadcrumbs and rubbing vanity 'f *heads* as *sizars*. I suppose *Sizar's* residents get a chance to enrol in Cambridge—about twenty years since that non-collegiate rule ya used to moan about, I should think. And should they graduate they get ta stay as sizars, and those that don't become *bedders* after a set period or until ya're tired of the sight 'f them, or they get too old. All paths for boys ya fancy leading to bedding, but never heading.

Am I on the money with that, Stew Boy?" That Marsh didn't answer at first told him he had the measure of it. He was particularly proud of the "bedders" deduction. Boys who at Cambridge tended to stuck-up college boys without ever being really part of the "club." But he wasn't too self-congratulatory. The Cambridge set-up was familiar enough in his own memory of both the university and Stew Boy, the *King's* boy—of his days knocking about at the back of the colleges along the Cam.

"On the money? Why yes, actually," Marsh said at last. "You seem to have a lot of information about my little club. *Initimate* information. How was it you came to know so much, Oscar?"

Of course, he had the advantage of those whispering whore lips of London Bridge… "I 'ave my sources, Stew Boy," he said. "Your house?"

"Middlesex, of course."

"And you're known by that name in the club?"

"I am."

"Good ta know. Now the boy, which county head did 'e belong to?"

Marsh drew them back from the inter-carriage door and into seating-area openness, a positioning closer to the private compartments. "We're talking candidates for a life-changing residency. We're talking the height of charity work. Nothing of possession in *Sizar's*. Nothing sordid in this secret, Oscar. All sign up willingly. It is a singular opportunity for a young man, of all circumstance, to better himself. The secrecy helps safeguard our residents, stems a gush-in of mass want from workerboys to take part. That simple."

Frustration crept on: "What we're talking is murder. 'ose was 'e?"

"But I shouldn't——"

He took Marsh's arm in a firm grip, twisting the boy inside like he used to. "Listen and remember," he spat. "I ain't here to protect ya. I want the truth, 'ose was 'e?"

Marsh shook himself free. "Since you knew of *Sizar's* already, I suppose… And we have our own secrets, from when we were boys…"

"Which of yous four had 'im?" he twisted more.

Marsh crumbled under his twist. "Head of Essex House."

"So—take m' ta Essex, Stew Boy."

*B*ent on the truth, he followed Marsh cross carriages and into Victoria, a parlour and restaurant car with bar counter and twenty-eight seats normally, though configured that day for the comfort of just four. A sign in the car reads: *No wines or spirits will at present be sold in the train, but if desired to do so by passengers the conductor or his assistant will obtain for them what they may require from the refreshment room before starting. Mineral waters of all descriptions can be had in the train. Smoking is not permitted in any part of the train except in the smoking car 'Maud.'* Special provision must certainly have been made, for in Victoria sat three men of vastly different form in a cloud of smoke and with both wine and spirits aplenty, filling their bellies with butter curls melted on toast, poached eggs and kippers. Drinking tea, no coffee. Cox was tending to them, at that particular moment lighting the cigar of the most developed of the group, the only gathered that he would consider manly; tall and broad but with a wide-flat nose and eyes closer to the ears than to each other. The features of a bull shark—intimidating, severe; he'd say uneducated if it wasn't for the cut of the man's suit.

There, he thought, *that's Essex. Gotta be.*

There are many qualities that a man needs to succeed as a detective. Stealth, sure; cunning, too; a cool head helps, though the last is not a trait that Glass had naturally. But most of all, the work called for instinct. And Glass would die by his.

"I do not know who let you on here, but this is a private service," the well-built man he took to be Essex said.

"Detective-Inspector Oscar Glass."

"And?" the same man replied.

"And, sir, I am investigating a boy found dead this morning."

"And?"

"*And* the boy was in Brighton under direction of one of you here. In a program that sounds suspicious in itself, and that all yous all run."

The one with the bull-shark features, the only suspect to speak in this carriage so far, turned to Marsh. "I am not sure this is a police matter, Middlesex. In fact, I was not even aware that any of our boys were unaccounted for."

"I am afraid there is no mistake," Marsh replied. "I was with———"

He shot Marsh a cautionary glance.

"I mean, I was…down at the Grand this morning to check on the boys who did not qualify, which was when I met the inspector. And I made a positive identification of the body. By the time I returned to the Pavilion, you all had already left—damn near missed the train."

"Any of you aware of more than one boy being 'unaccounted for'?" he asked.

"Why would you ask that?" the bullish man said while the remaining three shook head.

"An accident, surely," said another present, who continued eating, obviously also unimpressed by the intrusion on a to-London breakfast. This latest man to speak was the most respectable in appearance of the bunch. Buttoned-down. A pastoral sort of businessman, he'd wager.

"Doubtful, sir, I am afraid," he said to the new voice while keeping his attentions on the first to speak; not breaking contact with the man's widely spaced eyes. "Highly smelly circumstances surrounding this body, I can tell you. I need to speak to you all one by one and record your whereabouts last night as a matter of protocol, you understand."

"Tread carefully, detective," the wide-eyed man said. "The men who authorise your salary answer to men who answer to me."

"It's detective inspector, and you do not intimidate me, sir."

"I should." The warning hung in the carriage like herring, with a soundtrack of awkward eating and the rub of iron wheels on rails. The man went on: "After even rudimentary intelligence of the situation, it will become clear to you, detective inspector, that this young man's death is nothing more than a tragic accident."

Bastard's wasting time, he thought, his patience with the scenario at its end. "Even were that true, the boy's a person of interest, so this compels me to speak with any in his association—even men above my pay grade."

"What do you mean, 'person of interest'?" the wide-eyed man replied.

"Well, beyond the fact of *murder!* he has been caught up in...no delicate way of putting it...no women 'ere, so, *body business* for——"

"He was a boy whore, you mean?" the buttoned-down one asked.

"That's the measure of it."

"How do you know any of this?" Marsh blurted out.

"Yes, I'd like to know that, too," the wide-eyed man said.

He felt caged, like he had tred wrong and come into a situation where he would have to now reveal something he didn't want to. *Need to come a little clean*, he resolved. "The boy is *known* to and wider than the police. He is the criminal referred to in the papers as 'the Pipe.' I followed 'im here. To you all."

That year *the Ripper* and *the Torso killer* were key figures of public appetite for gore, but *the Pipe* had a place in the press stages of London horrors, too. A faceless boy-whoring master villain luring workerboys into flesh service to rob the well-to-do. A whore kind of Robin Hood, striking fear into the gentry through an army of boy sluts courting coin in the brothels, running criminal errands for the Pipe and bringing down the powerful through scandal.

That shut the group up...except for the one yet to speak. A gangly, bumpy-faced, sickly of pallor effeminate sort who wheezed, "which boy?"

"It was your first boy," Marsh spat in disgust—the third shock to his instincts since joining the train.

It prompted convulsion of the sickly one. *Seen this one before*, he thought.

"I think you should speak with the inspector, Essex," Marsh added.

"Yes," the rough man agreed. "You should. Clear this mess up."

This case... he thought. *No damn sense in it.* His missed-mark instincts ate at him like a Judas warning, a feeling of unfitness to see things. He pushed these anxieties aside. "I will be speaking with you," he said to the gangly sickly sort. "But first, I'll talk with you," turning back to the well-built man.

Eyebrows were raised in response, but no reply was uttered.

"Unless you would rather me interview you at Scotland Yard, *sir*."

L eading the way to Maud was the one with the bullish features. His
preferred suspect. He had left instructions with Cox for the remaining suspects—Marsh not excluded—to isolate in respective private
compartments until such a time as they were called for questioning. Keeping
the men separate was insurance against the opportunity to triangulate their
accounts, but knowing noblemen as he did and their attitude toward those of
the service classes—especially one of foreign extraction—he knew this would
be a task for Cox. But he had no other choice of deputy and would not risk
any advantage that came from prior dealings with Marsh by enlisting the
man's help so soon.

There were four provisions for accommodation made makeshift in Maud
that morning: two on either end of the carriage, with a shrunken seating area
in the middle. Though the *Pullman Limited Express* was new that year, he was
familiar enough with this weekday express service from London to see these
provisions as of the "special service" kind. His first interview subject had a
cabin located on the opposite end to Marsh's and nearest the entrance. The
man had some difficulty walking, he noticed, dragging the right leg slightly
with each stride. Once in the private compartment, his preferred suspect
settled in at a window seat, firing up another cigar.

"What should I call you, then?" he said. "I have a"——he checked his
notes——"Essex and a Middlesex. You are none of those, so what home
county do you head?"

"Drop the pretence shall we, inspector? Seems like you know enough to
make pseudonyms useless. Benjamin Blunt. You've heard of me, I expect."

He had, of course. The office of detective inspector involved signing off
on many appointments across Scotland Yard and sighting referrals. More
than enough had carried that name for it to be committed to memory.

Blunt went on: "I tell you my name also because I am sure you know how things work in this country. Not just in the City of London, or its greater regions of governance of the Metropolitan Police. I'm not just a man of importance. I'm a man of weight in your own circles."

"No man is above the law, Mr Blunt. Not even you," he said, his tongue a gaff, ready to slice the belly of the shark. "By the way, ya house?"

"Why?"

"Indulge me."

"Kent."

He made a note of it then returned attentions to the interview. "Let's get to it, shall we? Say you start with telling what you knew of Mars Piper."

"Who's that?"

"The identity of the Pipe."

"*Ah!*" Blunt rose palms as if any case against the man had been suddenly put to rest. "You see, I didn't even know the name. What's with boy whores and these strange names?"

"Well, real name was Marty Piper."

"Like that's any better. You should have listened to Middlesex. Essex is your man; it's his poor judgment in selecting the whatever-the-whore's name that's arrived us in this mess. Stop wasting time. You'll get nothing from me."

You'll get nothing from me, he wrote in his notebook. "This may be a waste of your time, Mr Blunt, but questioning you ain't no waste of mine."

"See here, I appreciate your need to explore all avenues. Truly, I do. I, too, on occasion, have been swept up in the twists and turns of a Scotland-Yard yarn. But I only met the boy once――"

"――on the night of 'is murder――"

"――was it, even, murder? Perhaps the boy, full of drink and regret at his failure to qualify, decided to strip down for a swim and drowned. It would not be the first time."

"I examined the body, sir. I assure you this boy's death was no accident. Other hands played a part."

"Well not mine, inspector. And unlike at least one other head of this club, you will find no connection between myself and Piper beyond that night."

Blunt conveyed safety in that fact, which he made reluctant note of. "That may be so. Though that night happens to be the most important night of this case, and you *were* in the boy's company soon before his death."

"I was…together with more than twenty others, inspector. And if that is your only means of tying me to this boy, I think we are done here."

"Almost, Mr Blunt. I am as eager to interview the others as you are to have me leave to see them. I assure you of this. This express service to London"———he turned pages forward and back through his notebook———"it frustrates the in-depth interview. So pl–lease excuse me if I come across as flustered in my effort to collect all the pertinent details."

Blunt seemed to like the sound of that; of him as time strapped and under pressure. But appearing as such was a tactic. One he had employed with success on other cases. Cases such as when, in the space of the short steamer service down the Solent from Ryde on the Isle of Wight to Southampton, interview fluster had helped apprehend a jewel thief. Relaxed by the sight of the pier of the thief's destination, without thinking and in conversation with a detective running out of time, the thief readjusted the crotch. A crotch that, as he had been already observing, was generously pronounced. Adjustment disrupted the integrity of a codpiece fixed to the inside of the thief's trousers. Just enough to allow stolen family jewels—from more than a dozen ladies on board—to tumble down the man's inside leg and scatter out over the deck, allowing all manner of man to see the false measure of the lad's cock pouch. Adrenaline of time shortage yields mistakes on both sides, he'd found.

"O yes," he said in feign of a regain in composure—returning to then stopping the flick through of the pages of his notebook. "The boy was beaten by a"———one more page turn———"by a———"

"———god man. Lewis, yes, what of it."

"One of your boys," he guessed, satisfied with what he'd netted so far.

"Paired with the boy at random," Blunt shrugged off, "and hardly surprising, given Lewis is a champion at the sport."

"A champion, you say."

"A fine wrestler. God man, you're not going to debate that with me!"

The Pipe wrestled just before death. Pressed to the mat by Lewis, a known champion brought in by Blunt, he thought, feeling returned to form. "Yous place bets at *Sizar's* like in the other London clubs, Mr Blunt?"

"Why would our club be any different?"

"And has yous been known to place bets on *Sizar's* qualifying matches?"

"Gentlemen have been known to flutter."

"Did you flutter on the Pipe match, Mr Blunt? Sounds like this Lewis boy would be a lad worth betting on." No answer. "I'll need a Lewis interview."

"Which doesn't surprise me. You have more than demonstrated your eagerness to waste time, inspector. Pursuing avenues that you should be able to rule out on reason alone."

"Still—can you arrange it?"

"No. You need to speak with Marsh. Lewis is his boy now. Might have luck, too, he seems content to tear up all discretion. "

Possessive regard for candidates, he wrote in his notebook. "What about blackmail, Mr Blunt?"

"What about it?"

"The Pipe lived by milking bent men of means." He let it hang heavy. Knowing the man won't respond, "Thank you for your patience, Mr Blunt."

"Yes, well, it was tested."

"I appreciate it. It was…illuminating. And what address can I reach you at in London—should I have any further enquiries?"

"You won't have further enquiries, inspector, not for me."

"I'm not sure that's your decision to make, sir."

"Ah, but you are mistaken again. The incentive is entirely mine. I have shown you a courtesy in speaking. I will not discuss this matter further, and I would have you remember my standing in the capital. I could make your life in service particularly hard, inspector. You can show yourself out."

"Actually, I do have one last question," he said on the threshold of the carriage corridor. "I noticed you walked with a limp here. It appeared to be the result of an injury to your right leg. How did you injure yourself?"

Blunt tucked the implicated limb under so that the satin drapery over the edge of the cushion concealed it some. The tuck clearly pained the man.

He let the silence stay a while, with only the rattle of iron wheels on rails and the in-intervals sound of steam. "Well?" he said at last when the pressure of how little train time he had left took hold of him.

Silence continued for several more rattles until, "detective inspector."

"Yes."

"I assume you are mindful of the timetable?"

"Meaning?"

"We are more than halfway through our journey to London, and you have only spoken to one of us. I daresay you have wasted your time on me."

"I don't think so."

"Still, if I may offer your investigation some guidance?"

"Go on."

"I would suggest you speak with 'Essex' next."

"And why is that?"

"Because I have it on good authority that he was seen on the pierhead on the night of the boy's death. After dinner, when most had gone to bed."

"Which pier?"

"The new one."

West Pier, he thought. *The pier to snag him.* "Surely, then, I should speak with the witness first?"

"And allow the suspect additional time manufacturing an alibi?"

The man infuriated. Such arrogance. He disliked the man. Distrusted any testimony. But unable to resist and conscious of the misapprehensions of his instinct so far on this train, he heeded the suggestion, heading to the opposite end of the carriage and its makeshift private cabins. Later he would tell himself that it was already his intention to interrogate the sickly one next. That this was logical in the method-of-things; that he would have interviewed the para-man first, were it not for Blunt's impactful command in the dining carriage. That this was a good move, from an investigative standpoint—as much as it riled him that the decision matched the suggestion put to him by the man whose testimony he did not trust. *O no*, he couldn't ignore a man spotted at the pierhead. It haunted too much, would distract too much, to interview anyone other than that one next.

U nder-window reclined, the sores-covered aristocrat kicked their interview off in a roundabout flamboyance to second his first impressions. "Your bravado may impress the *Pullman-Express* attendants, detective inspector, but it is wont to much sway me." The window gave a view opposite to Blunt's, the encroaching grime of the capital rising behind the ill-framed man like some statement on Essex's modernity. The aristocrat would not reveal a legal name. That was no matter, though. He would ask Marsh for it. For now, he wrote *the Ponce* in his notebook. He regarded it as more apt than any identifier assigned at childbirth.

"The dead boy went by Mars Piper, legal given name Marty. What can you tell me about him?"

"Wrong off the starting gun! Mars was short for Marsden, I think you'll find. Not much to say beyond that he was talented and finely sculptured…so I made use. I just called him Mars."

The Pipe was a big name among the London beat criminal files. The whore commanded enough with only one name—in the Ponce too, it seemed. *But it's Marty!* he thought. Having recovered from a breakfast shyness— though with no warmer a complexion—Essex now spoke with confidence and sureness-in-statement he did not trust. Men like him, he thought, were able with words and more agile still with performance. Always careful to conceal. Each action is in the public view, especially the eye of a man of the law. It was an art form in passing. "And you last saw Mars when?"

"At the match."

"The wresting match?"

"Quite—though I went looking for him afterwards, too. Following dinner. I was…restless."

"You admit that?"

"Naturally, since it is the truth."

"And where did you go looking, exactly?"

"Up at the dorms of the fallen. Where I thought he might have been."

"*The fallen?* and where are those dorms."

"The losers, detective. And at the Grand Hotel."

"The one on the seafront."

"That's the one."

"The one with a view of West Pier."

"I think it probably has a vantage."

"And?"

"And detective?"

"And…did you find him?"

"No."

"What did you do then?"

"I…retired."

"You gave up your search for him?"

"Ye–es."

Essex was good…generally; had a way of regulating responses with a melodic rhythm that matched the aristocrat's flamboyance. A side-effect defence mechanism of a society man in a world hostile to "men" like the Ponce, he guessed…a man for whom a secret club made all the sense in the universe… But Essex was not perfect in their interview. In the Ponce's final response, he noticed some hesitation. And for this detective, hesitation was when you pounced on a ponce: "You ceased all search for him?"

"Yes," Essex said sharp, back on form.

"What time was this?"

"I do not recall."

"Can you swim?"

The sickly man looked at him like the question was a trick. "No."

"Interesting," he said, dropping his attention to his notebook and thumbing back two pages. The present line of inquiry was fresh to him and thus not scribed in those back pages. But the suspect's interview, as the insights gained from Mr Blunt had revealed, is a form of theatre. Of directing the subject's attention toward the pouring forth of *the truth*, and the detective as documentarian of this truth in all its particularities. The truth, as he had often reflected, was that elusive construct towards which art also aims—except in this profession, where deceptive dimensions of human nature were the dominant mode.

"Is it?" Essex said, carrying ponce eyes to the book, too.

He kept its contents angled out of view. "You visited the new pier yet?"

"West?"

"Yes."

"No."

"Never been to its pierhead?"

"That would require a visit, I expect."

"Indulge me."

"No."

"Not that night when you were up at the dorms?"

"The pier was closed when I visited."

"Indulge me."

"No."

"What if I told you that one of your peers saw you on the pierhead that night? After the rest of the club had...retired? Long after dinner and far from your own accommodation for that night."

"I would deny it."

"You would call this individual a liar."

"I would. *And it was dark!* how would I even be seen?"

It was a fair point. "What benefit would lying hold for this man?"

Essex shrugged. "You are the detective." Sharp and short in responses, the Ponce stayed calm, relaxed, under-window reclined.

"You're not very cooperative," he said, allowing his frustration to heat their exchange. "The boy was in your care, so I'd have thought you would be more eager to speak on the matter."

"Out of concern for him?"

"More for yourself."

"Staying silent is often the best method of helping bring about justice."

He wrote that down.

"Besides it all," Essex continued, a glance to the wood panels partitioning this cabin from the one assigned to Marsh, the scratch of pen on notebook page completing the scene of suspense and self-importance. "Marsh will confide in you intimately, and offer all you need know about me, I'm sure."

"For the club? Out of duty?"

"No, detective," Essex said, eyes locked on his. "Not for those reasons."

It was then, in escaping the knowingness of that stare with a prime suspect, that he saw it: a keyhole in the panelling. A line where a door would be. *The compartments are connecting!* "You keep that locked?" he asked.

"Marsh and I both, detective. We're not connecting doors kinds of pals."

Connecting doors made the mind wander to connective tissues, and contagion—Essex's sores caught his eye. "Your skin, sir," he said forensically.

"Cholera."

Cholera was a new-that-century blight and a nuisance oft discussed in the parlours of the well-to-do; used to complain about the stench of sewage from the Thames but seldom showing up in physician visits. And here was not a gentleman likely to be consuming spoiled water. And so, though the sickly man's pallor made cholera plausible, he had spent enough of his career around prostitutes to recognise on this man's skin a much more ancient ailment that showed itself in the angry sores that hang around London and its slums like Black-Death-bringing rats. Plus, he recognised the man.

"*Sizar's* is not the only club you frequent, is it sir?"

"I have fingers in many things."

"Fingers and other things, I think. Might enterings at 19 Cleveland Street have some things to do with your sores?"

The boy brothel at this London address had become known to him as part of his pursuit of the Pipe. *Surely where I seen this sick one*, he thought.

Queerly, the man's eyes lit at the implication. "It's true then, you were on the trail of the Pipe. But all the King's horse and men protect *that* play pen."

There was a riddle there that would have to be uncurled later. Knowing the man would not divulge further he started his last question: "My first——"

"Benjamin Blunt," Essex disclosed with a shrug.

"He walks with a limp. Have you noticed?"

"Yes, to-day I did."

"Did he have it yester-day?"

"Not that I noticed," drawn to dirty air outside. "It's funny."

"What's that."

"Silence."

More bastard riddles! "What of it?"

"Well...though I deny having visited West pierhead the night just passed—as my other mates implicate me in doing—, I have admitted to being in the general vicinity. Is it not probable that it was entirely innocently? In a town like Brighton, is it uncommon for a Londoner of means to visit the seafront and its bars, at a late hour—or to check on a boy *in my care*, as you put it? No suspicion in that, I shouldn't have thought. Were I to have been there—innocently, you understand—well, from a detective's point of view, I would have thought it would be a cunning line of inquiry to wonder whether I, as bystander, may have seen for myself someone else there who has been implicated in this whole affair. With my views of West Pier, perhaps I saw someone. Someone who, suspiciously, to-day walks with a limp after the discovery of a violent death. In which case, gaining my trust could in fact give you a valuable witness. Hypothetically."

"Do you wish to make a witness statement?"

But Essex had only silence left.

Were the Ponce not the skilled deceptive sort, he wondered whether grief would have seeped through the exchange. As it was, and as advanced as the Ponce was in staying hidden, emotion ebbed their interview...but only in the laps of a bay rather than the beats of a beach like the one on which the Pipe was found. Serrated words and descriptions of the boy's vice were companioned with refusal to name the victim. Angry, jagged words that prevented the sweetness he suspected sickly had felt for a dead boy whore to be laid bare. *Grief's being suppressed*, he thought. Yet still the boy came through in other ways. And he too would suppress what instinct told him was an attempt by this phoney man to lead him into a false intimacy. Though the sored man's statement...however "hypothetical," was noted.

N one interested him less as a suspect than the buttoned-down one—though the man did puzzle most as a *Sizar's* master. At first he had intented to make do with whatever time remained to put routine questions to the man. *But!* the two preceding interviews implicated buttoned-down in some way, changing things. *But too!* time was short, so he would need to act fast. Even as he was finishing up with Essex the picture window at the Ponce's back had mould-ed over with the London city mist, made up of heavy industry smog. The capital now had the train from Brighton. Like the claw at the end of a hand line, it was drawing them in. Blunt's strong-armed, interview-next suggestion together with new knowledge of interconnection between certain cabins left him feeling duped: led by notepad-pen down a particular schedule that would allow for corroboration of facts among suspects. Quiet familiarisation with the carriage layout before confronting his next suspect raised further suspicions. "Damn you, Blunt," he whispered to his investigative self, ear pressed to the wood of the door of the next suspect's cabin, trying to pick out noises beyond rumbling of the from-the-coast express train. *Two voices!*

Sizar's traditions made his job of sifting clues pertinent to his dead whore boy from those pointing to the general secrecy of the club especially difficult. But he would find his truth, whatever it took. Truth called for careful footing. He would not burst in. Other than the pronounced probability that the door was bolted from the inside, he would not give the two voices any satisfaction in seeing his sluggish awareness—that Blunt had succeeded in getting a story straight while he queried the Ponce. Nor would he allow the misdirection to sideline the Ponce from his inquiry, as there were promising possibilities there, too. He had competing witness statements… So, he knocked. But he did so with an ear still nailed to wood, as part of a detective ethnography

that would see him learn from the response, to later record in his notebook…
Voices dropped out of audible range. To be replaced by the rustling of furniture and the
whine of an under-oiled hinge on an internal door.

A shaken voice came in reply. "A moment, pl–lease." After further rustling
the door was drawn open in a rush of air that sent out into the hall the scent
of fine cigars and honeyed pastries. The density of London's outskirts was
like a stage master in the wings, prompting him to progress this interview
with the tightest of formalities, to arrival at the crux of the drama: "No
mistake, I saw Peele leave in the direction of sea," George Cohen, who was
head of "Surrey," replied at that point of greatest concern in his questioning.

Leslie Peele. So, this was the name of the Ponce of Essex, volunteered by
Mr Cohen, probably under the assumption that the name had already been
disclosed; Cohen not seeming the sort to intentionally undermine a peer…
though content enough to speak out on what was witnessed in the context of
a young man's death. *Blunt and Cohen are men acting together.* So certain he was
of this fact that he chose not even to question whether the other had been
in the cabin when he knocked. He knew Blunt had been there, the man's scent that he would recognise anywhere. The Ponce's name was made note of
with the relief that he would need not rely on previous history with Marsh to
find it out. It surfaced in their interview that he was wrong to excuse Cohen
as a person of interest. This man was, in fact, the most interesting so far. As
a pleasure-driven church devotee with the most plainly middle-Englishman
demeanour and appearance—dressed simply but smartly in finely tailored
clothes…how did the man fit with the whore whispers he'd heard of *Sizar's*?

"Quite sure. Yes, quite sure I am, detective inspector," Cohen said when
pressed on whether it was indeed Mr Peele he'd seen on the pierhead. Cohen
gave the impression of becoming calmer through confirmation, in fact. "You
see, I do not drink. And, and always take the air after dinner and before my
nightly prayers, which took me right down onto the sands with a clear view
of the full length of the piers." In addition to being a man of faith, here was
a shrewd railways man, with a controlling interest in the London, Brighton &
South Coast Railway that explained the special attention and reconfiguration
of the service they were on. On the topic of the train service and facts of

Sizar's men and boys' arrival to Brighton—now known to be two days before the death—Cohen had little trouble giving simple-but-precise information. In fact, the death of a boy whore did not seem to trouble the man in the slightest.

"You don't fear disrepute with this death?" he asked.

"I loathe the secrecy, detective. Rather it out. We do God's work here."

"And the dead whore? Was he doing God's work?"

"*Ah!* but you support my point, detective. Desperation can lead even the most pure of heart astray."

"And how exactly does a man of God find desperate boys, Mr Cohen?"

"It's too easy."

"Indulge me."

"Have you never visited a London workhouse, detective?"

He had. Cohen was right—there couldn't be a clearer path to finding such boys. But he had a card to play that just might rattle the man; drawing on knowledge he had retained from a practice of committing the names of key criminal cases to memory, he'd attempt to make Cohen ill at ease, maybe even show an appetite for murder. "As I understand it, Mr Cohen, you have been instrumental in getting the Pullman enterprise established along this line."

"Indeed—I am an advocate."

"Don't be modest. I read *the Times*. You've impressed the importance of adopting the concept to Brighton, at great speed and seems success so far."

"You flatter me, detective inspector."

"Beg pardon my next question, then. Your want for good press. That a cover for fears from the Lefroy murder?"

Percy Lefroy stalked the society papers and struck fear into rail travellers that decade after murdering by way of stabbing Isaac Gold in the first-class smoking car of the LB&SCR express train from London Bridge to Brighton. Cohen went white as an innocent man in the gallows at the reference. "I... fail to see," the man bumbled. "There—there—there is no connection. That was such a time ago."

So, not unfeeling on the subject of murder, he thought. "Two murders, sir. *I wonder* whether this Pullman exercise is all, shall I say...reputation repair?"

"*O quite!* you're right, it is," Cohen said—at ease, it seemed, to be back in a passion realm of all things trains. "And if Pullman does restore faith in our means of transport as not only the safest, but the most luxurious as well, that is a happy coincidence. This train," the man went on, tapping the panelling, "it has been under construction more than twelve months."

Seven tunnels and a superb Sussex viaduct carried the new concept, specially built for the railway by Pullman at their Derby shops. The service had been a triumph so far, making Brighton, truly, London-by-Sea. That the cars were lit throughout by electricity gave the service a buzz of what was to come…but on the case at hand: that Cohen's upset at murder was more evident in the Gold case, long since cold, and the topic of scandal on the Brighton line than in the fresh Pipe death and its impact on keeping a club's secret—a secret the man actually did not seem to want to keep—appeased his detective mind that Cohen was not the one he was looking for. *One man down*, he thought with satisfaction. "What's that there?" he then asked, pointing to an ivory knob by Cohen's leg he only now noticed.

Cohen beamed at the chance to move conversation on to the innovations of the train, perhaps sensing that his intensity had softened. "Passengers who desire the attention of the conductor or his assistant for refreshments during their journey need only press it to call."

"Where are these found?"

"Between every seat, with communiqué to the restaurant, Victoria."

He wondered whether there was any relevance in this, thankful that he had instructed all suspects to leave Victoria for Maud before starting his interviews. At last, something in his investigation's favour, he thought. The rest of the interview proceeded with the comfort of speaking with a man ruled out, albeit a talk cut short by the commotion from the compartment corridor at the final approach to the London terminus. "Did this particular train bring the boys to Brighton, too?"

"Yes," Cohen said.

"And it was specially configured?"

"O no, in fact the service was on the public timetable."

"The 5.45 pm?"

"Quite—with provision made in our booking offices to make sure no members of the public joined it."

"And you're sure none did?"

"O yes, we've quite careful about all that."

"Yes, your attendant was most thorough."

A comment met with a satisfied nod. "In fact," Cohen volunteered, "we were two short." Before he could pose a follow up, the man went on: "As a matter of fact, I believe your dead boy was one of the missing from that train."

"And the other?"

"Also a poor Peele boy, the 'number two' contender. Killen, or was it Keeler? Yes, that's it, I think."

"Did you notice the boys missing yourself?"

"No. Middlesex, I mean Mr Marsh, wanted segregation of the house candidates, to which the four carriages served nicely. But the concern was raised with me by Peele before we left. We delayed a little, but I couldn't hold at the platform for more than five or ten minutes, you understand."

"Did Mr Peele hazard a reason why the boys missed the train?"

"No."

"Did it strike you as unusual?"

"Were it one of the others, it might have. But I have come to expect such——*how shall I word this?*——lack of reliability of the boys Leslie chooses." Again, the man pre-empted a question: "Leslie was in the last car, and I in the second, behind Mr Blunt and before Mr Marsh. I understand that all was good in the end. The two missing came the following morning on the 10 am London service. Well, maybe not so good, now that I state it... Not to tell a detective his business, but perhaps looking into w——"

"And to-day," he said, "for this return journey, what is the story with the remaining two cars?"

"Beatrice and Louise, you mean?"

"Sure."

"Those ladies are our drawing room and parlour cars normally."

"And now?"

"Why they carry the boys, of course."

"The losers, too?"

"I see them more as those who did not progress. Poor souls who must return to resorting to wretched bodily sin in London…but we can't save them all, can we?" The man seemed lost in the smog of the hard-to-breathe outside. "You know," Cohen said, eyes skipping across the bodies of the boys swelling the platform from the ladies at the back, "I also read *the Times*. This Pipe boy has been on the prowl for some years now, reeking all sorts of havoc, bringing all sorts of devil-driven mischief. But I was under the impression that, like the Torso killer, his identity was unknown."

"So?"

"How do you know it's Mars? What gave the dead whore away?"

"More's known to a Scotland Yard detective than *the Times* reports."

"I see. Then actually," Cohen added while gathering luggage, "I think that also you are quite right, detective. My ladies have carried back boys who have lost their shot at God's redemption. Even the worst of them."

" T here's no questions left in that detective brain of yours for me, then?" Marsh said, cutting through his thoughts in the corridor as the train emptied its bowels across the London Victoria platform.

"On the contrary—I have the most for you, Stew Boy. You'll help me make the pieces fit."

"I feared that might be the case. In that instance, I think we better have dinner. How are you placed to-night?"

"To-night is no good."

Marsh looked as if the refusal had come by fist rather than tongue.

He turned down also the offer of a calash share back to London headquarters. "But grateful for a feed to-morrow night," he softened with.

II

ALBION

Every gait of man was indeed changing. The taint of progress was real. The steam engine was racing the unwashed to soil Britain's finest watering holes. The lowest were moving about and into once-exclusive places. Sectarian separation was under siege! Even at the highest levels, a dilution of purity was underway. Gentlemen's clubs offered an exclusory kind of tonic, with processes for keeping numbers low and bans on intra-club membership often enshrined in club law. Only the most select men were entered into the fold of a good gentlemen's club—entered and interned there. By 1813, the Regency era in its strict sense; as insanity gripped the George who had overseen the arrival of *Brooks's* and *Boodle's* as decedent gentlemanly alternatives, *White's* members' book swelled to some 500 under the new management of George Raggett. With Raggett as the club's own Prince Regent, the year also saw the introduction of *White's* first Candidate's Book—a recording-keeping tradition that is now standard in clubs.

White's 1813 Book recorded the candidate, proposer, seconder and, most relevant, the result of the ballot, which showed a rigour-of-sifting-recruitment ethos in the club. This first book recorded the number of "black balls" by which, in each election round, hundreds of proposed candidates were rejected, much to the chagrin of their proposers. Yes, in many cases the clubs were founded on political bents. Tories turned-to by a *White's* position while

Whigs were probably more bent on the company of *Brooks's*. But politics was a surface thing. Certainly so by the age of High Victoria, clubs had become much more circles of style and fashion, subcultures in and each of their own. And of these, the stylings of *Sizar's* were surely the most subterranean, the most acquired tastes. The most mixing of unwashed men in sacred watering holes. O yes, the detective had his suspicions. *Sizar's*, from an unkind eye, could be seen as the kneejerk of the rejected. A less refined *Brooks's* or *Boodle's*. Founded by men blackballed from best clubs. Not for lack of monies, or family-name standing, or manner in life, but a lack of social graces. *Sizar's* was founded, the detective suspected after meeting each of its 'heads,' by deeply unpopular men. And it is from unpopular men that, experience had told him, the darkest desires were often seeded.

*D*eposited in a calash each, when the heads of *Sizar's* had scurried like rats in wheeled boxes into the sheltered warrens of London, he had workhouses on his mind as inspections of the connecting doors between the compartments could now be carried out. A visit to the cabins occupied by Blunt and Cohen showed the interconnecting door to be unlocked on both sides—the door between Marsh and Peele both-side fastened. But otherwise, the carriage was clear of any clues or characters. Save Cox, slipping in and out of the suites the four men had used for the short duration of their direct route to London, bundling fine china and cigar trays to broad-but-boyish chest.

He stood awhile to observe the boy's movements. Here was a fit-bodied ugly boy, with a face hardened by a life out in the cold. Much colder streets than London. The new *Poor Law* 1834 forced those who wanted relief into a workhouse, with purpose-built designs like Sampson Kempthorne's cruciform going beyond being akin to prison, conjuring sanctimonious torture, too. No, he much preferred the poor who kept to the streets. Those with the grit to get by using the one asset they had to their Godforsaken existence to full, gut-filling exploitation, finding hard work in whatever form that would keep their bellies full. Its why he continued to visit the bridges of the Thames, long after his beat days.

Likely aware of the audience, Cox went about china and cigar-tray clearing duties without eye contact, working deeper toward the far end of the carriage, cleaning and tidying until arriving, empty handed, just opposite where he had been halted from entering based on, he was led to believe initially, a sub-par appearance. They met again and, moving more swiftly now, the boy turned upper half to stare straight at him at last. Cox cocked his head to one side in the direction of a door just opposite where he had boarded...just before the vice trap of a lad ducked in. Tucked away from the platform and the pandemonium of London Victoria Station, the crude Eastern boy shut the door with such hurry that it rushed his ears.

He followed. Inside was a watchman's cabin. Practical and plain. For provision of the staff or in this custom carriage, perhaps a valet. It was equipped with a washbasin, latrine and thin-foamed bed. For breaks or for sleep, on sleeper services. He found Cox pressed up, back to the small window that looked onto the iron of another locomotive. Cox was perched in the basin—a bold thing of seduction. The boy relieved the strangle of a bowtie in a single pull and the top two buttons of shirt uniform with the same nimbleness. "Lock doorrr, inspectorrr."

He did lock the door then moved on Cox at speed. Landing his body between Russian thighs and coming to a stop just after their noses had collided. "What is this?" he barked. "I could clap you in irons for this."

"Kould," Cox sighed, extracting what humid air remained between them, "but I zink you von't, not if you vant me be use to you."

From the basin down, both legs of the Russian between the parting of his own, he tore Russian boy rump from the bowl, spun it 'round and push-ed his forearm into the boy's back like he would for arrest. Then, he, bore, down. Lay pressure. Smudged the round Russianness of the boy's features into the glass to fog up the view of a beside locomotive engine. No fear of damage to the boy's facial features—they were too rounded and unpretty for any damage to matter. And he held the Eastern thing there. Testing.

Cox remained limply bent over the basin, the only activeness being an arch of the spine. A backwards arch. It was as if Cox's hips were in tug of the fogged train through the glass, the boy's hips a magnet to the iron opposite. Cox's slender neck reclined then, like the tip of a fisherman's rod, snagged in the London smog. After a while of the boy's arch, he replaced forearm pressure with the grip of two hands at Cox's slight waist and then slid to the seductive sod's tuck point—the creases of cotton where the white of Cox's shirt was pulled in below a buckled belt and black, tight pants. And he rested himself there, at the belt.

Being young, athletic, Cox's hips were narrow, but the arse was big. It took some force to pull belt—and with it the upper quarter of slacks—over that arse and to the knees. Cox stayed supple as he did this, spine arched, chest pressed to the glass, though shaking slightly under stripping. It was unfortunate that he had to do what came next, but it was a natural self-preservation for any man of the suited class who buggered street crawlers. He slid a hand between the peachy pinch of arse cheeks, feeling for lumps. Rubbing coarse in search of any suggestion of sores, with enough force that, if there, they'd rupture and pus-erupt. Nothing.

So spit, self-unfastening and fast lather then insertion was followed and replied to with a sharp cry from the boy. *That* he stifled with a spit-slicked cup of his hand. "That ticket enough for you, boy?" he said in vengeance to their first meet.

No words came from the Russian, only whimpering to his thrusts.

The boy had incited it, asked for it, but in the insertion, was…it seemed… unprepared for it. He liked that—could work with that.

It's warm in here.

Then there was thunder from the head of the beast in which he defiled and a jagged jolt of movement. "What's that?" he said, creating a gap between joined fingers for the boy's breath and a response.

"Ve head back," Cox said, voice high and pain punctuated, "to Brrrighton."

"Well in that case, perhaps I may find use for you after all."

R oyal Albion in Brighton was his waking place the next morning. Dawn
broke on a rare mist-lifted winter's day. But they missed it—he and his
attendant sleeping sound well into the middle of morning, by which time
some of the salt spray from the sea had found its way up from the sand, to
stain their windows and the Venetian doors leading out to their balcony. It
was a rasping at the door that had woken him. The suite was large enough
that the tray with fruits and Danish pastries and cooked food—kept heated
under a lid—could be delivered into the entrance area without fearing any
discovery of the boy who shared his bed. Cox did not stir as breakfast was
deposited; sleeping solid, spread out, like it was all as familiar as Cox's own
soft-home mattress. *No.* Rather, like it was the first soft mattress the Russian
in London had happened upon.

Cox had disembarked with him on arrival in Brighton, the pair remaining locked up in that service-accommodation compartment for the return
journey. Cox was not missed—he learnt between repeated using of the
fleshy sock-point of the boy on the rails back to Brighton. It had been Cox's
intention to change at London Victoria for transfer to a public Southern
Railways service. It had all been arranged, yet that the boy's employ would
assuredly now be terminated on account of failure to front up seemed not
to faze. Upon arrival into the crisp Brighton open air, Cox followed him
carrying one bag, just the one, his bag, the boy having no possessions to carry
down the slope to the sea and into the Royal Albion and a top floor, sea-view
suite. To-day it was the scent of sausages and bacon that lured the boy from
slumber and, sheets-and-all, to the terrace where he had set out breakfast,
where they would eat with their view—a salty sweep of the Sussex scene.

"You be missed, boy?" he asked.

A mouth stuffed with sausage. A shake of the head said Cox would not be.

"What of your family?"

After a heavy swallow, the boy replied: "I have none, not in England. And in RRRussia, zey not miss me. Verrre I die, zey vould not know."

It confirmed his impression of the boy, whose age and bodily currency aided a day-by-day-decisions outlook. Were Cox middle-aged, overweight or unappetising in any way other than in the face, a decision to desert sure income on the morning of a workday, to roll the dice on the chance of better conditions on the curtails of a stranger, would have been clinically crazed. But the boy had bet well on him and the better conditions he was now willing to provide. And, that the boy took the risk...*zis was pleasing*, he thought with a smile. He sat Cox in the corner joint of the suite balcony, with the boy's sights set west towards Shoreham. He searched the shores east, in a heading towards Dover. It was deliberate...a pier each. Cox may well have felt it proper that the youngest and tight-bodied one should take in Brighton's newest West-Pier attraction, while he as the senior had the view of the older Chain Pier. But it did not quite work as he had hoped.

Deliberate positioning only drew more attention to the task at hand, to trauma of discovery, and simply angling West Pier out of sight did not wipe the sight from his mind. Of the beautiful body; of yester-day morning, in the footprint of Eugenius Birch's promenade pier. He wanted to erase the vision, especially here, in the presence of good-bodied, ugly-faced Cox. But Cox's best features only made the beautiful one stay more. Even in his position, of back turned away from West Pier, and focusing on the chain links of the old one while Cox filled belly with breakfast—still on the hot, not yet progressed to the chilled—he could not escape seeing *him*. Finding pools in the foundation poles of the Chain, too, wherein to remember him. "What do you want from me, boy?" he blurted out against the memory.

"Serrrvice position," Cox said, a different sausage stuffed in this time.

"Not sure you're cut out for my kind of policing, boy," he said then paused, expecting Cox to perhaps panic or protest a little; the boy did not, though, seeming sure enough in service potential. "But," he went on, "I will make provision for you, and you will be useful to me."

"As I shown alrrready," Cox said in that vulgar way he hated about boys.

Now robed instead of sheeted, the thick accent only further guttered it up. *Better start stamping that out now.* Grabbing the boy by the throat to come up from seated with a force that flung the robe open and an unexpectedness that spilt spittle and sausage grease down the chin, he then spun the boy 'round and bent Cox over the intricately cast iron that was now all stopping the boy from a tumble to the dozen-storeyed promenade below. Then, he flipped the back of the boy's open robe up in three tight folds and draped the bundle over the curve of Russian back like a bed scarf. Coarse fingers on the train from Brighton had not found any evidence of disease, and visual inspection satisfied him that the boy, despite a potted face, was surprisingly underused. Cox's service lips bloated and bruised blue, showing struggle from taking him in the train. "Serviceable," he said, placing a single sovereign between the boy's shoulder blades.

Cox ceased sausage chew, clawing for the coin like a strangle victim the frays of a tightening rope. Once the boy had it, Cox stayed silent and un-chewing, turning the gold over in callused hands as he yellowed the boy's blue lips with a butter curl and put himself back in. Without fear that he might rupture some buried sore, he hit the Russian's opening with a force that brought puffs of stone dust from the railing's bolts in a test of tension in the iron. But Cox had found numbness through the coin; transfixed and un-chewingly still in the head, even as the body took on the rotations of a top-speed pistol. He hated the boy's indifference in the face of monies. It made him look elsewhere, towards West Pier, where he found figures in seabed debris that had been torn up and pushed high onto the sand by winter storms of recent.

This is why coin comes after, he thought as he approached the end.

So as to not finish hating the boy, who he knew couldn't help being so worthless when it came to coin—he snatched it away. The change was instantaneous. Like a sleepwalker set alight. Every nerve-ending inside the boy's service corridor burnt with each of his butter pumps. The ugly head jolted into motion with the pistol of the torso, and masticate meat spewed forth in the direction of West Pier.

The boy cried.

"Good boy," he said. "Eat your breakfast."

He meant it at both ends, fetching a sausage from the table and stuffing it down the boy's throat. He was on the edge of spewing in the direction of West Pier himself when he got an idea. The whimpering runt was numbing up again, he could feel; still choking on sausage, but chewing a little, too, and looking about in a thrashing, frenzied, insane sort of way...cruising for coin. "You want this?" he said, pressing the gold into the face cheek of the boy with all the power of a coin-minting press. Parts of the coin that had sharpened from drops to the cobbles cut the skin and raptured lengths of the sausage beneath.

The Russian nodded as best as the boy could against the reps of his entering, spittle and gristle specks dangling toward the promenade in the manner of melting stalactites. As swiftly as he had first entered the boy on the train to Brighton, he then withdrew. His member jerked and throbbed at the head— its finish denied. He pressed the coin flat on the boy's swollen arse lips. Like the wealthy would on the eyes of the dead. But the runt was a half cast, a one-eyed beast, not a man. So, there was just one coin, jagged and dirty from the pockets of strangers. Putting enough pressure on the flat side of the coin, the lips eventually gave way, skin succumbing to the pressure of gold, breaking the boy's seal with a force no butter curl could curb. Once in the depth of half his thumb, he pushed the legal tender in deep with his member, beating it inside the boy hatefully fast with all the bitterness of a blacksmith, spitting on the back as he seeded coin deep in the belly.

"You'll get one of those each week you serve me right," he said.

Then he left the boy to drip. Drip, drip. The coin pushed up inside left the runt diluted and running out with him even as he left, taking two tan bags by the door to head into town and make true on his investigation into what had led to the murder of the beautiful Pipe boy he had found. The room had been paid for use for the rest of the week. Though he didn't bother letting Cox know that, leaving the runt to reach for the treasure at the bottom of the boy's rear well with one hand, holding a handwritten address in the other; of a place in London he owned, where the runt could stay sheltered-rough until he found his next £1-per-week use for an ugly Russian.

I t was only a short walk back from the Royal Albion to where he'd meet the Pipe again. Along the promenade then one building's width behind. On the incline toward the train station, to the morgue of the town police station, located in the town hall. The town hall was in the Classical style, its contouring more of a grand palace-by-the-sea like the one he had just come from than a place for serious civic matters. There was a bleakness to conducting such affairs from a building that also served a public-forum function in a beach town like Brighton, he thought, an undercurrent of gassy odours bubbling beneath the surface of the so-called public sphere. He was alarmed on arrival to be told not just that the coroner was already there but had commenced preparation for an inquiry into the death—all standard procedure, sure, but far sooner than he had anticipated.

"Where can I find the boy?" he said urgent to the officer at reception.

His question's receiver was about a generation older than him and with whisker-white muttonchops that said the man saw little active service.

"*Now!* old man," he added, in case the white ear hairs impeded hearing.

"See those steps there," the whiskered man said. "Take them down to the basement and carry on past the cells to the room at the end."

He hurried down the stairs indicated, broad and stone, hoping it was not too late.

Brighton's police force had swollen to 100 strong in the 1880s, as warranted by the sharp upturn in the town's population and popularity—with its direct rail link to London and influential writings on it as an ideal watering place for the reprieve of the London-and-surrounds wealthy in all the tourist guidebooks of note. But with this spike, crime also came in inflated numbers. And if the sensations of the press were anything to be believed, criminality had crescendo-ed to a fever pitch.

The day had dulled as it went on. As he descended into the depths of the town hall substructure, any natural light left got swallowed by the darkness of narrowing stone walls. Like the catacombs beneath Paris, affairs of street-level-daylight living died a little when lit by gas-fed wall lamps alone. Despite their flames, the wall lamps—licking and hissing at the underbellies of the cobbles caught in the street above—did little to illuminate even in-confines brickwork of their immediate surrounds. This only fuelled his own urgency to get there, to see the Pipe boy—however putrid he had become—before dissection, prior to commencement of the invasive, forensic portion of the investigation. This bubbling need to see the Pipe drove him to place speed ahead of careful footing—and twice or thrice he nearly dropped a step.

Down the stairs, past the cells and to the end, he recited to himself, white-whisker's words. When there, he burst through the double-swing door to find the Pipe on a slab. The facility was surprisingly ample, with three rows of stone cadaver tables then four tables for each row. Though his boy was the only resident that day.

"*Ah!*" exclaimed an odd-looking boy-man who he took to be the coroner, welcoming intrusion. "You must be the inspector from London. The one who brought *this one* in. And just in time, too; I'm about to open him up."

"Glad I caught you in that case," he said with an expression as welcoming. "I would like to examine him first. Assuming you've no objections?"

"Of course," the coroner said, dropping scalpel as if it were a pistol in an out-gunned Western. "He's all cleaned up for you."

And the coroner had…*cleaned up* the boy. To a high standard. He'd had dealings enough with dealers-in-the-dead over his years as a detective—from top government-sanctioned coroners to Met Police surgeons, to undertakers, to learned men with university professorships using teaching specimens, and even to grave robbers, harvesting buried bodies for black-market profit—to observe diffidence in these men's dealings. Treatment of their trade on the slab not as once-living, but wholly dead flesh for butchery. Butchers them all, he found, when sprung upon, such as nearly here; at times when they had th-ought they were left to their own devices. But in the cleaning this man had shown care. Compassion, even; tending to a beau rather than a corpse.

After the initial breath-bated burst in, he now approached the slab with trepidation—of step and eye contact—, dreading-for the horror he might find there. Maggot tracks, eaten soft parts and the like—always the eyes, experience said. But his boy, the slain hero of his case, looked every bit as alive as before the beach—only bluer. There was no smell and no visible trace of putrefaction. The Pipe was a fresh and clean catch. In a boy-side basin was, in the bottom, sand. Above that, debris of shell fragment and weed ribbon from the sea collected...like an aquarium at the boy's side, from which the coroner had taken due time—with a soft, non-abrasive sponge, he could see by said instrument's placement at the basin edge—to clean the boy, to remove all trace of the sea, and of that beach that was his hero's downfall. Cleaned so that only boy remained; wiped of death. Marsh was right. The Pipe was, is still, a beautiful creature.

"In remarkable condition," Pipe's grim caretaker said from the shadows. "Truly, I've never seen anything quite like him."

Lain flat on the frigid slab, cleaned of all sand or sign of the situation whence the boy was discovered, the skin was the most remarkable aspect. It appeared soft. All over. There was no rigidity. No grotesque contortion, common from a corpse after as many hours. The Pipe should have been iron now, been twisted, bent, frozen in the postured position that he had landed the boy in after the lift to the upper beach. There was no evidence of imprint on the flesh like fossils, except for the slashes of barnacles belonging to the pier substructure. He shouldn't, but he found himself needing to...to touch the boy, to be sure that Pipe was not just beautiful-creature-sleeping. So, he did. But Pipe was dead. There was no heat off the body. *But!* though touch did confirm death, it also raised more questions based on his experience with all the coming-before corpses.

"Spectacular, isn't he?" the coroner said.

He had forgotten the sponge-wielding dealer-in-dead-flesh was there. He would not have touched the blue so boldly had the transfixing boy on the slab not made him forget himself.

"I've not seen anything like him, either," the coroner confirmed.

The coroner was crooked. Much more junior than he had been expecting but aged by a hunched posture and dress. Ol'-fashioned clothes under a leather apron dyed black with years of stale blood.

"I don't see much action," the coroner said, as if a mind reader. Like the hero in a penny dreadful, sweeping glances 'round the room. "In the summer, this place is full. In fact, we keep the fresher ones—the ones in less need of the chill—in the cells, which, let's face it, are much lower than living temperature as it is. I'm just assisting-to the town coroner then. But he's on holiday. Since most of our deaths are holidaymakers—some drownings, like our friend here, but mostly burglaries gone wrong. Now, without the leisure seekers, without the sun…well, it goes quiet here. And so, it falls to me to care for the few unlucky ones that do come to keep company with me at the underground inn."

The crooked coroner had a clear penchant for storytelling, but he was only interested in the facts. "Drowning, you say?"

"O yes, though not in the traditional way. No—not by the sea alone. In fact, he may well have been dead before he hit the water. Of course," eyes a glassy twinkle, "we'll know for sure once we *open him up*."

"You'd say it was murder. Not a drunken accident?"

"I can't speak for drink; again, we'll need to *peek inside him* for that." The man's bead eyes shone like wetted black stones with the "peek." "But there was foul play here. Definitely. See here," taking his hand, bringing touch to cold flesh again, and tracing it along Pipe's clavicle. "Give the lad a rub. Do you feel that?"

It felt like running one's hand against the grain of newly sawed wood.

Prickly.

Before it had been sanded. "Yes."

"That's acute fracturing of the bone from intense blunt force. I would wager that his windpipe was crushed. If not eviscerated, stripped apart. Notice the more pronounced *fossa jugularis sternalis*—the space between clavicles. How deep it is. I expect, beneath there, we will find our cause of death. If my suspicions are correct, this boy did drown…but in himself. It would have been instantaneous, or near close to, I would think. Something quite extraordinary to witness. Extreme fracturing of the centre part of the neck, causing a concave vacuum beneath the skin that was unstressed and explains the lack of bruising. Into this vacuum, and through the suction of the severed oesophagus, would have been drawn at great speed—as the boy, on instinct, drew for breath—all manner of surrounding blood and tissue—filling him. Drowning...in and on himself. His body was then dumped, or perhaps tumbled, into the sea. But rather than floating out, as perhaps many dead would do. He sunk, heavy with himself. And was lacerated by the iron of the new pier with the tide, or so I have been informed."

Though a lot to take in, the crooked coroner crafted a visceral visual picture of his dead boy's final moments.

"Instantaneous, you say. Would there have been pain? Did he...suffer? Should I need assure his next of kin."

"Pain?" the coroner pondered. "No, unlikely I'd say. The caving would have been rapid. But...and I would refrain from sharing this opinion with any who will mourn him——"

"Speak plain, boy."

"Well, at the risk of contradicting myself...I see credit in a different theory that is most unusual—in my esteemed profession's estimation at least. What I think...inhumanely as the intuition is...is that there was an extreme panic that gripped this boy at the moment of breach, then implosion. So... acute pain. See here—here—here," the coroner said, their hands still joined, the hunched medical man moving their touching parts across various points of the boy's body.

Biceps.

Abdominal muscles.

Upper inner thighs.

"They're like an over-inflated medicine ball," he remarked.

"A sound analogy. These muscle groups are all taut. *Caught* in tension-death, in a petrified state. For his attacker—and perhaps that was the desire of such a violent assault—this boy's death must have been a supreme spectacle. His body would have riled up like a great bull before velvet stimulus. As every muscle in him bucked against the brutal throaty break. It quickened the end, certainly, but made it more monumental, too. And I would expect—as parts of himself flowed into portions that should have remained free of obstruction—that it would be a terrifying end, too traumatic for even shock to soften. Yes—yes—yes, a terror for this boy and any spectator with an ounce of compassion for human life."

"You seem to have an especially vivid image of what happened." "Suspectly" was exchanged for "especially" at the last moment, checking himself in the face of an apparent clairvoyant kind of crooked man. It was natural for him to find the preciseness of the coroner's reconstruction of Pipe's death suspect. For one to be so intimately acquitted with what had happened, based purely on surface review. Even one with medical training. To question how this coroner could know so much was the stuff of even the most amateur detective work. He was no amateur, however. He could have cast suspicion upon the coroner—it was an enticement, the mark of lazy policeman-ship—were it not for admiration for the care this untouched-by-sun man-boy had taken and a knowing that, of course, the assistant-to the coroner during the high season did not kill his boy.

"It's my theory," the coroner said with a shrug, "and one my colleagues would probably not abide."

"But why does he look so…alive?"

"*Yes!*" the crooked coroner exclaimed, an excitement that encapsulated the young man's broad-based fascination in a boy sublime, still, in death. "That plagues, too. I have never encountered anything like it. But I have theories, if you will permit; ones that build on the scenario already set out but that lead us, also, beyond the realms of conventional science."

"I'll bite."

"Self-preservation through implosion!" the coroner said, jumping straight into the outlandish. "Plus, small incisions for nourishment; let us take each in turn. When the boy's fluids rushed into that great fleshy vacuum, natural deposits of gases and pockets wherein gases may form were filled with more accustomed apparel, even if such placement would, in practicality, cease breath and take his life."

Oddly.

Irrationally.

It made sense. "Death preserved the poor sod. *Embalmed?*" he said.

"*Precisely!* You paid attention in Mechanics' Institute history lectures, I see. Gases, understand, so noxious when we cut into a corpse for inspection, these are what accelerate decay. Imagine him as a gas pressure cooker, his body the meat. The gas brings the broth to boil—raging, charring, advancing the meat. We then eat it, of course. But if left on too long the meat spoils, dries out. Goes rotten, which is essentially what happens to a corpse after death. But this boy, essentially, embalmed—to use your theory—himself while he was alive and before dying would even have registered. Meaning preservation was in place, even before any disintegration of organs or interiors or other gas-creating processes could come into play. Here he was ahead of the ancients: not letting any time lapse, any decay commence; not letting himself gas-up and dry-out at all."

His crooked medical authority took a breath and another sweep 'round of the under chamber, and when not finding anything there to cause a stop, continued: "This leads me to my second thesis: Moisture preservation." The coroner let it hang in the cold, stale air before elaborating: "We are, at our essential chemistry, water-based creatures. Colleagues of mine, drawing on ideas by the likes of Charles Darwin, have even put forth the view that we evolved, clawed our way up the order of things out of the sea. I'm not sure I see reasoning where my peers seem to. But we cannot deny two facts: Water is our base element, the largest part of our whole; and second, salt—level with any embalming agent—is our greatest natural means of preservation. We have used it from the earliest records. In fact, even with advances in cooling technology in facilities such as this———"

The medical inquirer was turning slightly mad around the eyes. Twitching, those coal eyes twinkling with the telling of a science-fiction-surely theory.

He allowed his mind to wander and his companion's speech to wash over him...wandering the room with his own eyes, to the suggestion of...cooling technologies. It was dangerous degrees colder here in the morgue. There were gas flames as illumination on the walls, a standard sub-street-level light source. But between gas flames were gaps with extruding brass tubing, out of which cold air was pumped into the double-door sealed room. It was on the same principle as the locomotive that had returned him there. A generator— an internal combustion engine, on miniature—generating energy. But in place of fire in a boiler-powering piston, here a fire-driven machine in a separate part of the building was pumping cold air from the snow-capped streets into the basement levels, emptying into this chamber. He had been so hot-flushed when he made his burst-through-the-doors entrance, so well-heated within himself, that he had not noticed how cold it was. Until it was pointed out to him, that was. A chill over him that probably was in part to blame for his slip out of attentiveness...like the effects on the brain of a drop in oxygen. But he had gotten the gist, returning his attentions—like a caffeine injection mid-matinee—in time for the summation of the second point of the crooked coroner's prognosis.

"——concerning the nourishment, which is an extension of the salt point, I might add." The coroner had gained confidence in his company, having not yet been interrupted. Relishing, seemingly, in bending the ear of the detective inspector in a case for why the boy on the slab looked alive well after slaughter. "These incisions," the coroner's intonation rising and now with a physical dimension: the crooked man tracing the tears across the torso and limbs with the padding of a finger, "they are of—of—*of the sea*, by barnacles. Quick forming even on a pier as young as the one under which he was found. It reminds me of mariners' wounds, from a wholly condemned, and claimed to be no longer practised—though hearsay tells me better—practice of *keelhauling*: where a sailor who had wronged in some way is dragged by ropes across the underbelly of a ship. Wooden ships mostly, as was the heyday of the barbaric—though perfectly British for the time it was used—practice. And the purpose? To rake the back. As would happen on land by lash, off land happens by barnacle. The body is dragged under and through the waves, across the crustacean-sharpened hull. But here is the curious part: Those lacerations, unlike what might happen upon meeting with the barbed end of a whip, or the iron-added improvisation of a disciplinary cane of a college-dorm master, actually—by combination with sea, salt and incisions across the skin—had benefits. Not only did the combination help with healing but, I believe—controversially, admittedly—plumped-up with nutrients the surrounding tissue."

"Outlandish," he said. "But say it was true. Were it deliberately done?"

"No, I don't believe so, though opening him up will help me be certain. In short, to return to your original question: He looks so alive because *he is!* in a manner of speaking. The circumstances of his death combined with his dumping in the sea starved off any commencement of decay. Even your decision to move him up the beach served him in this purpose, caking his lashes with sand, corking in the sea that he had absorbed. Like the way one might slash a beast before roasting it and lather in these lacerations jars of butter and oils that will keep the meat hydrated throughout cooking. It was not done to him; he just happens to be a morgue miracle. *He is undead!*"

"The boy," he said, "if I get your meaning, is still...fresh?"

"O but you don't quite see yet, detective inspector. A fish caught just this morning is fresh. He's much better than that, I'd wager. Like a chicken might race around a farm after the severing of its head—on nerve endings and muscle memory. It does this because it does not yet know. Its body, its tissue, its very motor capillary action has been fooled to think that it is not yet deceased. It does not know it is without facilities conducive to life. And neither, I believe, does he," giving the boy a more whole-bodied rub this time. "Perhaps still."

A boy who doesn't know he's dead! Such thinkings were madness, the superstitions of the fantastic imaginings of horror novelists of the age. "Scientist" and "detective" were, sure, *professions du jour*; but, too, mysticism and mediums were all the rage. He did not subscribe to all of it, most were the fancies of the corseted sex. But like many men his age—with scepticism for the church but a longing for something meaningful after death—he read the Gothic fables. Books about the god-making advancements of medicine, filled with re-animation obsessions and Grail searches across the dark alleys of London for the modern Prometheus. He enjoyed the notion, the age of man-made advancement: of God as science and Science over god.

"Probably not possible…but say it was true, what'll it mean—opening the boy up?"

The crooked coroner seemed to take the question like it were an as-yet-unsolved mathematical equation. "We are in the unknown. But if I'm honest, I'd wager an awakening to decay."

"The boy will need to be sent to London," he said suddenly and with a tone of authority and decibel more elevated than he had yet used for their encounter. Then, after a pause, went on calmer: "For—for—for incision from a surgeon of Scotland Yard, which retains jurisdiction over this case."

"That is most unorthodox. To transfer a body when there are all the facilities here for pathology."

"He will be examined thoroughly, don't worry. And I'll make sure of a full and proper inquiry. Moving him to London is the best thing for him."

"O well, yes, well. If that is your wish. I must say that I am bitterly disappointed! Though you might question me for this…I was eager to—to—to open the boy up. For in cleaning him, removing sand and other sea debris from his wounds…with each layer of grime and residue I removed, he seemed to become *fresher* the deeper I moved over him. As if he had drawn on the sea for nutrients while *down there*, like a sea sponge himself."

"Maybe you might want to help me with one examination needed before London, then—so that my investigations might continue in the interim and while the particulars remain…*fresh*."

"O certainly, that would be something of a welcome compromise."

"*Ah!* Reserve judgment on whether my need is welcome or not until I have explained the inspection that my investigation requires, m' medical mate. Detective work is a grim calling, and this case is of a—a—a sensitive persuasion. Sensitivity to certain facts that, in fact, my decision to move the boy to London for the intrusive portion of his bodily survey services."

"Alright, that's snagged my attention."

He caught himself talking in a manner more put-on class proper than he every day would, probably without complete grammatical correctness. But it went over with the desired effect...and so he persisted: "Here lies a boy prostitute," he spat out—the suggestion of it, venom, like might be sucked out of a scorpion sting. Spat from his mouth because in his mind there was no dignified way to disclose it. Though perhaps a profession more objectively viewed by present company—by a man of Science whose training in biology may inspire more empirical regard for the base functions of boys.

"Intriguing," the coroner said, looking more like one of the London Bridge boys now. "I should not. No, no—no—no truly, I shouldn't assume, of course. And, and—and—and," stuttering and red-growing, "certainly not leap to such an extreme conclusion in present law-enforcement company, either...but, scientifically, on account of his age, attractive qualities, and most crucially, his sex, I would be led to ask: A sodomite?"

He responded to it flat. Swiftly. Stark. "Yes."

"I see. Yes, I see now. And yes, see further that you are correct; London is better qualified to attend to must-be murder of this sensibility."

"Quite...should such details of the boy's ways get into the papers."

"It's just the sort of scandal our vapid press would splash in salacious uppercase letters across their street-corner pulp."

"Quite. And circles of, let's say, *influential gentlemen*, complicate matters."

"I see..."

"Hence...the need, *my need*, for discretion."

"Understood, *and yes!* I am still keen to assist you."

"Your scientific impartiality impresses me, *boy*."

Crooked creaked straighter at the spine and curled at the corner of the lip with "boy." "Thank you. Now to that inspection. What is it with which you require assistance?"

"No delicate way to say it. I need to know if he was *used* prior to death."

"You wish to examine his anal canal for deposits of semen, you mean?"

"*Precisely!*" he said, relieved that the nature of the examination was made plain enough and that he did not need go into further details, "and should evidence of use be found, whether this likely occurred before or after death."

"Or during, presumably?"

"Quite."

"As an act of in-passion aggression."

"Yes."

"*It might have been accidental!* Voluntary manslaughter, is that the term?"

"Now that's a detective-then-magistrate's matter for deliberation."

"Of course, of course. Quite, quite," crooked-again medicine-boy said, eyes blacker-bejewelled with the amateur partaking in a police matter.

"Or a jury," he added.

"*The intrigue thickens!* I will assist you, more certainly this time, if only to have the pleasure that will come from having touched this boy now, to then read about the case later through a veil of the printing press."

He had himself sodomised; boy, not beast. But to take seed was not the same to him. He still harboured some—more than some—self-loathing for seeding boys...but had taken historical comfort in being not-receiving and in being able to conceal his inclination to seed boys from others. The close-to-home discomfort of the Pipe case came as an abrasion, however. By discussing such morally and judicially deplorable displays of the buggering-boys kind, it was as if the veneer of his hiding was being peeled away, like wallpaper to the edge of a blade. But to turn away from it now would be worse. It was a handicap; he was self-loathed aware enough to see. He was also old enough, having lived with it long enough, to see it simply now, to see it as——*how I am. This case.*

Pipe's trade, rather than the custom targeted, disturbed most. Selling of the flesh. The way Pipe self-exploited; the danger it courted, including of other boys Pipe roped in and, too, toward those with whom Pipe consorted. He should be impartial. Of all people, he should have compassion. But no, even so...he could not abide it. Its why he'd planted the coin deep in his Russian with his seed on top. The seeding was a use, but the payment was for the whole boy and works to come, not just the hole of the boy he had come in.

"It makes perfect sense," the coroner added, breaking into his thoughts—showing a hand of desperation to play a part. "And—and—and you are right to look for such evidence here rather than wait until London. Not just to speed up your own investigations and to gather a clearer picture of the killer's character. No, not only those reasons; nor only to narrow your avenues of inquiry during these crucial post-incident forty-eight hours; not just those reasons, but also from a pathology perspective, where the search for such… residue…well, it should not wait." Swept up again by excitable rhetoric, the crooked coroner took a deep in- and exhale. Then said, more calmly: "Mind you, even now our examination is impacted. Though the boy drowned, had he not the death would have surely been ruled as suffocation, strangulation, given the trauma to the neck. Involuntary defecation—that is a voiding of the subject's bowels, it is common in such cases. That is not to say we cannot make the assessment. Merely, I wish to preface whatever we might find with the point that voiding of the canal may have already taken place."

"Got it," he said. "Shall we get to it?"

"Pleasurably."

"I'll look first. Then, maybe, might call on your expert view. Agreed?"

"As it pleases you."

It then dawned on him that he had no iota how to *get to* such an examination. "If you'll"——clearing his throat——"tell me."

"Advise you on how to begin?"

"Quite."

"It is simple," the coroner said, though took a deep drag of the dead-cold air that suggested the crooked man would do whatever possible to tangle the procedure up. "Pathologists ply trade in corpses, but this boy…soiled by his profession as he might be, does not appear as a corpse. If I may explain: A corpse, traditionally, at this interval of decay, would be entirely rigid. Like lumber, any inspection of a cavity such as the anal shaft—that is in part obscured by the buttocks—would require from his—or 'its,' depending on your regard for the dead——"

"His," he said, some compassion swelling for the beautiful-dead whore.

"Very well…required from his inspector would be incision tools and assistance in flipping the body over. He would need to be turned, in short, and would be heavy and stiff thanks to the locking of muscles and the onset of *rigor mortis*, given many several hours have now passed since the death-causing event. And once turned over, incision tools would need to be employed to fold apart his buttocks and have access to the anus."

"Right…" he said, losing his nerve, the procedure now explained.

"Except that in this boy's case we have no sign of *rigor mortis*, no inkling of stiffening or decay of any kind. Not even on the underside, where he has been left to lay. He has the dexterity, is what I am trying to say. Check out this dexterity"——and the coroner unhunched again in excitement, grasping the concavity under each of Pipe's knees and taking them from flat on the slab to face the ceiling, bookending the boy whore's ears with kneecaps to illustrate the point in a swift fold over. The demonstration of Pipe's aptitude for movement was a provocateur's masterstroke: The beautiful boy was opened, showing supreme suppleness, more so even than men the boy's age still with a pumping heart. "Ready for inspection, inspector."

He lent in… Pipe's skin had a blueish hue all over. *Ain't unpleasant a shade*, he thought, more like turquoise with a gentle teal in places, like summer rock pools with perhaps a filter of green all over, like the surface of a tropical ocean. Pipe had no smell, he registered, when up close for the inspection. He pressed a finger into the upper portion of buttock; a part under Pipe that had been under pressure on the slab. He expected it to be flat and hard like hide from congealing of the unmoving blood. But it was supple as the rest of the breathless-beautiful boy. Pipe's buttock bounced back full and round instantly after touching. But it was the lips that caught him. The contrast with the Russian he had brutalised only hours before could not have been starker. He had left his mark on the runt cunt, tore the boy up. Liked doing it.

Nothing could make him hurt the lips he was a breath's distance from now.

"He is ripe," he said, eyes surveying…up to Pipe's tailbone through the buttock divide to arrive, happiest, at the boy's sublime opening. And returned there: "Remarkable," he added.

"What is it? What do you see, inspector?"

"His anus… The…lips."

"Yes."

"They are pink."

"Pink?"

"Yes. Not like any other part of 'im."

"I wish to see, take a knee, will ye?" And with a knee each, pinned opposite Pipe-ears, the whore's more natural mouth was now shared, and they went in close to inspect the anus, the boy back to being a prostitute. "Most extraordinary," the coroner said, more crooked than ever. "And a good thing too that I am here with you to see it. For, were I told that these many hours after death, and being plucked battered and slashed by the sea—not least, in an English winter. After all that, were I told that I should encounter such a sight. I would not have believed it."

"What could cause this?" he said, excited though hesitant to proceed further with his probe. "It is as if there is life in him."

"It appears that way, yes. And perhaps it has happened as so. As wild and unscientific...*as Gothic* as your assessment sounds. I must confess, I cannot readily disagree with it."

"O?"

"'O' indeed, and not as outlandish as it all might seem. There have been recorded cases—obscure, I'll admit, and many not of a reputable lineage, but documented cases no less—of parts of the body...supple parts, shielded parts: underarms and upper inner thighs, mostly. Parts that have lived longer, shall I put it, than the rest."

"What's the cause of such things?"

"It is not accepted science; you must understand. And certainly not something that my superior—the one I stand in for in the off-season—would entertain; but even he would be hard-pressed to deny the possibility when presented with evidence such as this."

"Could..." he said vaguely but homing in on the evidence, which appeared in pinker shades the nearer he got. "Could what's *behind there* be playing a part in the preservation of this extraordinary appearance of life?"

"You mean, that behind the illicit entry point of a boy prostitute—an illegal, immoral and therefore highly life-threatening line of work—there might lurk, inside him, live remnants of heads past, you mean?"

Heads! Word selection struck him. It was irregular to refer to those who solicit the services of sellers of their flesh as "heads," but he supposed that was what they were—that was the end of the cocks that entered as well as the status of the ones with coin to fund whore use. Had he his notepad handy he would have jotted that descriptor down with a note that the bent coroner, who thus far had been wholly insightful, had happened upon a strange-yet-apt descriptor for the users of a whore. It collided with his gut instinct, which was that one of the four heads of the club *Sizar's* to which his dead boy was a candidate were responsible for the slaying. "Yes," he said.

"Well, let us assess," said the coroner, who was feeling to the detective more like a colleague at this point. "The anus acts as a fleshy sealant, that's sure. Compared with the reproductive orifice—the channel through which semen is supposed to travel—anuses are more…adaptable to resist intrusion and retain once intrusion has taken place. In a complete prolapse, as is the definition of death, I suppose such an orifice would be less equipped to expel, even though expulsion of the bowels is a known occurrence after death. The anus, what I am arriving at here, and this is the rawest of research, you must understand…*this anus*, of a youthful, muscular man. This anus is empirically, to finally answer your question, inspector…it is, yes—yes—yes, it is naturally enhanced to retain and maintain life given to it by a donor."

He was comfortable enough in his own lay-science standing—along with a reputation Scotland Yard detectives had for not being backwards in coming forward, however crude to the sensibilities of the time he and his peers' deductions may be—to entertain the supernormal hypothesis. The theory that the still-living essence of a user of this whore, swirling inside the loin-mouth of a plump-from-experience yet resiliently sealed-up entrance, served to keep this boy's down-there lips pink. "You intrigue me, coroner," he said, the crimple-backed boy rising in his estimations exponentially now, as from akin-to-colleague to potential-confidante; and in matters even as ghastly, as fleshy, as these.

"As indeed, I do, myself."

As he moved in to separate the pink lips of Pipe's anus—lips that may hold the code to the whore's freshness, but also death, and the whole case:

rendering as a break in it—he prepared himself to have a stockpile of semen gush forth. Opening Pipe's service entrance was as effortless as the rest
of the boy whore's opening up, which had been in the hands of the coroner's unfolding. Gentleness and thumb-with-index-finger in pincher were
all that was required to peel his way inside. But once open there was...
nothing! No outpouring of trade semen. No pouring out of anything else
either. Not any seawater. So...the boy whore hadn't been breached. No
excreting matter, either. Pipe was empty, cleaned out comprehensively. But,
on lingering, also with pleasant notes. A sweet-smelling scent—thyme with
highlights of rose.

"You seem disappointed," the coroner said in a tone suggestive. Like his
crooked confidante, too, had foreseen fluids spilling forth.

"More confused," he said. "Certain that I'd find him had been used. The
whole viewing's left more troubling questions, needing deeper and harder
lines of inquiry. He is more of a mystery than I thought. But I am grateful to
you, coroner." He thought of but then dropped the "acting" qualifier from
his company's professional title, for there had been nothing diluted in the
detail and attention to the Pipe that had been rendered. "Would you care to
see?" he asked the coroner, who was yet to peer inside.

Coroner looked unsure, like the Pipe was a honey trap or a step beyond
comfort confines.

"Be obliged if you would," he said to encourage. "Want your opinion on
a matter."

"O *in that case!* happy to help." The medicine boy slipped from timid to
enamoured at the sight and scent of pleasantness beyond pink lips.

"See any evidence of disease, coroner? Syphilis most specifically."

The other pulled away like he'd made a direct assault. "*Impossible!*"

"Be sure. Take your time now. I think its spores can be deeply lodged."

But the other needed no time at all to render a decision: "Frankly,
detective, the very suggestion is absurd."

"Stay with me. Say a man is presenting with syphilis sores now...what's
this one's chance, in your opinion and the disease lifespan, that intercourse was
had with the infected man in the weeks or months just passed?"

"There is a gestation period to syphilis, and a latency period, too. And symptoms take some time to show from time of infection. But I would consider recent coitus with a symptoms-showing person unlikely in our boy's case. Out of the question, actually. It may challenge all assumptions of this young man's chosen profession, but I would say that, empirically, what we have here is evidence of discernment in sexual receptiveness. There is only health here."

Though it raised more questions about Pipe's rôle within *Sizar's*, about Peele's motivation for bringing the boy in. Crooked's medical opinion brought some satisfaction. Some increased desire—an itchiness, in fact—to seek the truth about the circumstances leading to death. "I'm pleased by your insights," he said. "In fact, I find myself wishing you were a suspect, as you have revealed more to me than any of the actual suspects I have interviewed so far. I would have Pipe's death well wrapped up in that case."

It was the way that his detective brain ticked that he had to stop himself short of asking what the crooked boy's movements the night previous were. In fact, as the detective mindset started to churn, the medicine boy's interest and willingness to play in the realm of extra-scientific inquiry left him and his detective mind to wander... *The cutting-boy's awful open and keen about the whole sordid situation my Pipe ended his life in*, he thought, caught in a cog of the detective process. "Well, I got to go," he said, stopping the thought line again. "Due on the train to London. But you will arrange for the boy to be sent to London, too, for more intrusive investigation by my offices?"

"I will."

"Good boy. And you will safeguard this one's...ripeness, best you can?"

"I shall, of course. It's important to me." They shook hands on it. "You are fortunate, inspector," the coroner said as he turned to leave, "that the boy died as he did—in deep winter. He will be packed in ice and sent on a meats train to London—one trick of our trade that would surely cause all a ballyhoo should the papers catch wind of it! Though, really, it would practically be as best to strap the boy to the front of the tender and let the snow and ice form over him on his return to London." The coroner pulled out paperwork from a cabinet along the wall and with it a pen, and said: "4 Whitehall Place, St James's, then?"

"No—nay—not to that address, got a different address where I want you to transfer custody. Still within the city, mind, but to m' surgeon there, directly. He'll take possession of the boy."

It was met with a raised brow.

"You see," he said, feeling the need to meet the quizzical expression, "and I ain't mind being straight with you, after the help you've given, and with the complexity of the case, which now, I think you know. You see, there are… hierarchies of power to contend with. Society men, putting it plain. And while them matters should not make my murder investigation hard…alas, I'm afraid, they can. I mean to say: The boy's best chance at justice is to send him to the address I give you."

"Very well, I think I understand, and, I might add, do not envy you in the task that lies ahead: To catch the culprit for the death of a boy whose sexual proclivities make the appetite for any justice for him slim."

"Ya understand the grim realities of police work in this age of rising suspicion of us and the desperate lengths gone to by poor boys. Should there be an opening for a police surgeon within our jurisdiction…certainly, yes, for sure, I'll have a spirited recommendation for your end."

The coroner opened mouth to talk. Detail of their dealings already told him this bent boy would natter him all day, even on the grimmest matters. But he only had the morning; he had a train to London to catch and unlike, perhaps, for that figure from his young years he was going to visit, were he to be late it was unlikely the train would wait. *I need to move!* So, instead of leaving it to an acting coroner to decipher the nuances of his angry-cadenced hand, he spoke the address to which Pipe should be sent along with directions for depositing the boy via a service entrance and had the crooked youth confirm the address and delivery advice twice. Then he left back the way he came, up the steps, through reception and on the continuation of an incline path from the Brighton sea and its piers to the station, which started some way back, in the town. He arrived with hardly a second to spare, a bag in each hand for the afternoon *Pullman Limited Express* bound for London. He would actually alight this time. And relieved to, too. Brighton, he felt, had taken more than it gave in the way of answers in the Pipe affair.

III

PAVILION

The realm's sixth Henry set up *King's College* (1441) as a Cambridge sanctuary for twelve poor scholars. To-day students of all class populate most of the Cambridge colleges, and the "poor scholars" traditions of the ancients are continued in restricted fashions—through the taking on of sizars. Formerly, the rôle of the sizar saw the poor scholar earn his place at Cambridge through menial services, such as waiting on other students and fellows at dinner. For such service, a sizar received his education, food and housing. Most menial services have long since been abolished for the sizars of to-day, though the taint of a sizarship as a lower class of student still stands. Sizar boys are branded differently, you see. Their gowns are marked. Not all colleges accept them and for those that do, their numbers are strictly limited. Many men, unless elite enough to enter as "fellow commoners"—*generally the younger sons of the nobility, or men of fortune, and have the privilege of dining at the Fellows' table*, or so the *Cambridge Calendar* informs—prefer to enter as "pensioners," a student-type capturing much more the every man of the modern world—from boys poor of circumstance but rich of intellect to boys with the parental means to be afforded an attractive yearly allowance.

With no charitable grounds whatsoever, *White's* and the majority of the gentlemen's clubs sit outside of the sizarship concept—membership being among men of fortune. But these clubs are also primarily run on a "vouch for" process. Vouching is a socially complex thing, striking at the heart of the gentlemen's club concept. Above monies, learnings and even status, above all else to be a member of a gentlemen's club is to belong, and to be wanted by other men. Complete unselfconsciousness is what a gentlemen's club offers. Utter freedom to be oneself among peers who are the same. And it is in this sameness that the true test of membership comes. So, the clubs have always been high anti-social affairs among sociable men. To be elite is to exclude. To be a member of *White's* was to be an insider, against a world of outsiders.

To understand *Sizar's* was to understand its founders as unpopular Cambridge Old Boys. Men with god-ordained delusions of setting up a sanctuary for the poor…but desiring an exclusory ethos of their very own. The former desire is slipping out of favour in the wider world. The poor are being put to back-break in search of a "solution." While the latter, exclusory ideals, have never been more popular; to belong in an exclusory sense is a highly prized thing. A womanly King's sort of vanity of the age. Like a Knight of the Templar, to secure a place in *Sizar's* was to be one of the womanly kings' own apostles, one of the chosen few, modelled on the lowliest of Cambridge student types. Why *Sizar's* and not *"Pensioner's"*? Both pensioners and sizars at Cambridge are students who seek out endowments. They are similar in this way. These endowments often take the form of scholarships—of all sizes— given out by colleges, and sometimes from London companies, too.

At Cambridge there is not meant to be a practical difference between sizars and the rest of studently bodies…*alas!* the world is simply not like that. At *that other place*—at Oxford, for the non-Cambridge boy—the sizar finds his root in the college "servitor." The Oxford colleges are not ones to obfuscate! *Over there* servitors are a distinct caste, not mincing with other matriculated men. What to make of *Sizar's*, then? Was it named as such to wipe the stigma from lowest boys in service to fortunate men, seeing no shame in poor men being duly rewarded for service? Or was there something else in it? A more ancient tradition of giving sanctuary to serviceable boys. Boys who, in the vernacular of the gentlemen's clubs, were suitably "clubbable." Or was there much less lofty reasons for it all? And what of the dead whore? *O how that one haunts any chance of honour in such things!*

"Sincerely delighted you came, Oscar," Marsh said atop heavily red-pattern carpeted stairs—the first of several in the grand London residence. "I was—confession...surprised when you declined my invitation for dinner last night. It left me this-afternoon questioning...*will he come true?*"

"I keep my word, Stew Boy."

"I remember much of you, Oscar Glass. My recollection of your finer contouring is vivid. But that quality, I confess, is no portrait in my memory."

Good fuckin' start, he thought. Marsh had left him waiting there in the entry hall for near-on thirty minutes. He begrudged the contempt for the time of professionals. Such contempt was routinely exhibited by the leisure classes. But in this case, having it shown to him negated straight-up any pretension to them being equals. *Need to realign Marsh's attitude on this*, he thought... Though the days they met in the back of the Cambridge boatsheds were well of a different time, he would shake the man back to them. *Nay yet, though*, he thought, patting down having-to-wait resentment into the already ruined space in his contemporary impression of the man.

London residence "Marsh Park" had a Mayfair address most desirable. Notably *not a St James's one*, its close-to-the-palace locale rendered a clean respectability from the outside—unlike the almost-rest of London, which bubbled like a foul stew...noodle streets made up of muck and the trading of tramps. The road the residence rose from was Classic-lined and without smell—other than stench from horse tender. Of the Prince Regent period and therefore new, that same century, when wealth for those in situations like Stew Boy here fattened to their fullest. It was clean-lined and multi-storied in finely polished stone that was smart, austere even. It was neoclassical with something of the ancient Greeks in its sensibilities and what he imagined *Sizar's* to be about. Something of an Old Boy's own model of man in it.

But as with all models, not all was as simple as it appeared, and inside Marsh's London home was an unbridled extravagance of excess. Without manliness nor anything of the classics. Its interior was heavily layered, with bold-patterned wallpaper, curtains and hardwood furniture that had no surface space left bare from trinket. It was tawdry-fashionable flamboyance embroidered into all visible points of the house—its host included. Over a suit of plain respectability, Marsh wore a velvet kimono with samurais depicting a scene of intimate wrestle training of some kind and bound at the waist with golden cord. "*Do forgive* my tardiness, Oscar," the man said at his level.

Marsh spoke as if it were to an assembled group who had been happily mingling. With champagne and appetisers, unaware even, that their fanciful host had not yet arrived. Those crowds instead of a detective, on business, tired from travel and the grim realities of that business. Having swept down to his level, Marsh now led the way to a dining room with eyes over a lantern-lit Grosvenor Park. The man's wife joined them over dinner. She was a fragile, flighty thing. She sat upright and as if strapped to one of the femme man's thickly upholstered dining chairs, like a pale blue mid-flap taxidermy sparrow—slight and wrapped in pastel silks, much duller in colour and lighter in materials but only slightly softer than her husband and environs and with a doll porcelain of a face that told him she could not be more than twenty. A fitting analogy for Marsh's like-a-doll's-house London life…he thought it the saddest outcome of the impacts of a sheltered life on the shape of a man who, while never full of the fire of ideas, had at least some zest as a boy.

"Ask me what you will," Marsh said, arms wide in the manner of telling fire tales and after dismissing the staff and adjourning the wife to needle- or quilt- or anything not-reading work in a parlour room somewhere away from them—dismissed without even the introduction of a name. Now just two long-since-acquainted men, Marsh managed to make an environment of manly things unmanly, taking up the rôle of server—handing him a Cuban cigar and a healthy portion of port in a cut-crystal tumbler. "We can speak freely now. But I am afraid, Oscar—indeed, I am—that I can't offer you a bed for the night! We have the rooms, but my wife has the jealous gene, like many young wives. Had you come last night…I could have invited you to stay."

Marsh had stayed silent throughout dinner, observing how he handled the questions about detective work from the softly excitable, unnamed Mrs Marsh—as sheltered as her husband had become. How exciting it must have been for her to hear details of cases she had read about in the London papers and from the safety of her sparrow cage, he thought. Curiously, by the look of Marsh—playing with soggy duck breast on the proud man's plate—it was from the "Mr" of the married pair that he sensed jealousy.

To Marsh's comment about being unable to extend an invitation to stay—another sharp-tongued statement—he wanted to say that he wouldn't have stayed anyway, even if he had visited last night instead of this one. The detective in him, however, bit the tongue, opting for a polite, thin-lipped smile instead. Seeing Marsh sat there, old and soft, reminded him of first whispers of the club called *Sizar's* that he'd heard from whore lips about some of the hardest boy parts around London Bridge. The club may have been good at keeping its secrets among gentlemen, but for boys of hard trade, there was no stopping a wag about soft men offering a cushy life for boys willing to excel at certain *manly pursuits*. The whispers started in the early '70s when he was a night watchman and would, from dark until dawn, rule over boy whores in his own piece of London real estate. It stuck with him because you never heard gentlemen's clubs come from the lips of a boy whore.

"I suppose you want to know what we were doing in Brighton and what my little club is all about?" Marsh said.

"We can start there."

"*Sizar's* got started by four, including landed financiers and social influencers—you've met us all already. We're a good balance, I think. I and Peele bring the capital and societal connections, Blunt brings the sporting angle and Cohen the church and some good-colleges inroads. Blunt even coaches at Cambridge! We devote ourselves to the club for no greater satisfaction than knowing that men like us: good men, strong men, remain at the top of the societal running of things. But unlike every other club of London, we recruit the best men on merit, not on circumstance of birth or circles of friends. I like to think of it as one big social experiment. The workhouses are failing to combat the problem of the poor. Mostly because they seek to help the masses, they see all men as equal. They what to treat the whole of the unfortunate. We sift through and give opportunity to only the very best." Marsh took a breath as if prepared to field questions. And when none came, carried on: "A secret fiefdom, you could call it. Recruitment is an every-second-year affair, with each of us putting forward candidates to compete *for a chance!* Started this year in Brighton."

The first boy whore he'd caught whispering about a club called *Sizar's* he'd beaten blue, bludgeoned out of action the boy's anus with his truncheon as a form of street-level deterrent to whoring. The whore had coloured Marsh's *opportunity* and the nature of the merit sought with a different shade, but otherwise corroborated the account. He found himself disliking Marsh harder the more the man spoke—much more than the lips of a boy whore under beating. *Healthy that*, he told himself. Would lead to more emotionless detecting. He needed to keep cool, and in Marsh's verbiage were key facts about the structure of the club. "Houses Surrey, Kent, Essex, Middlesex. Get on."

"Given half a chance," the in-love-with-monologue man said. "From sixteen candidates at Brighton, eight of the strongest progressed. Because I hosted the round, these eight will form my 'team,' to compete in the row-race regatta at the end. Winners from this race who will become members."

"Member in-take of eight every second year?"

"Yes."

"Not a big club, then."

"Necessarily intimate," Marsh countered. "Considering that it is only once joining the club that the experiment of *Sizar's* begins."

"Don't do that. Don't make me need to prompt you."

Marsh smiled. "Eight each year is manageable. My sizars are funded by the club and no Cambridge college would have more than eight."

"The Pipe. Was a serious candidate or just Peele's play thing, you think?"

"Right to it! You've patrolled the city alleys, so probably realise that Peele prefers the company of men. Well—boys, to be precise."

"But Pipe was an apt wrestler, well able to pin a fella his size."

"He was probably the finest natural talent I've seen, which makes me even more convinced that he was paid to be there."

"Again; *speak plainly, man!*"

"*Ah!* yes, this is an important bit. Peele populates his teams with boys he's involved with, usually sourced from track teams, his choice sport—if we're being so loose as to include track in the manly pursuit taxonomy."

"Where do you stand on Peele?"

"He's the most susceptible to scandal."

"You don't give 'im enough credit. If any man can dodge a scandal, he can." He looked back over his notes, reading aloud Peele words he'd jotted: *In my experience, detective, staying silent is often the best method of helping bring about justice.*

"Why did you write that down?" Marsh asked.

"The same reason I write anything down: it had the sound of a hint about it. Not a slip of the tongue, not a clue—Peele, I believe, is too clever, too calculated for that. But a hint of something."

"We've too much history for riddles, Oscar. Now I'm asking you to speak plain. Is Peele a suspect or not?"

"Most definitely," he said.

"Am I?"

"No." Marsh beamed at that, though he had not intended it as a compliment. The man he looked for in connection with the Pipe affair was a man more cunning than he thought Marsh capable. The man draped in heavy fabric across from him had softened with age; even the skin seemed smoother. But not in a youthful way; it had taken on greasy translucence. Gone was the boy of some energy inside; gone was any backbone to the fellow. Marsh was too soft for this boy-whore-killing business.

"Good," Marsh said with a demeanour of satisfaction. "Tell me about the case, then. Are you so solemnly certain this wasn't an accident?"

"Quite. The death was violent, Stew Boy. It would have taken a man of considerable strength to carry out. The trauma to the body was severe. It made the boy seize up with spectacular intensity."

"That rules out Peele, then," Marsh said. "Ain't no strongman."

You too, he thought, saying instead: "Not necessarily. Remember them second men of many a crime-fiction fancy…he could have had help."

"Did it happen at the pier? Or is the pier just where the body was———"

"I'm clear on the pier, Stew Boy," he cut in. "It's what came before that interests me and where I need your insights. You understand?"

"I can be of much help to you," Marsh said, ignoring his attempt to keep the man confined to answering direct questions.

In suspect interviews, creating an atmosphere where those under inspection spoke freely, volunteered their information without the need for interrogation, was valuable. Trouble was, he'd no desire to listen to the man ramble in self-importance.

"Have you read Darwin?" Marsh went on. "No, I don't suppose you have. I don't suppose you will. O well, he has some wonderful ideas on 'fit men' rising. At *Sizar's*, we help fit men rise, you know. You should write that down."

That snapped it.

He cast the cut-crystal tumbler into the hearth, which burst in an almighty fireball that singed all the items around it—the lead of the wallpaper bubbling like an ill-advised chemistry experiment under far-from-laboratory conditions. Marsh's mouth opened and shut like a ventriloquy prop…more so as he came up behind the man and put a knee into the dummy's back, sending Stew Boy crashing forward between kimono parting, to land face-plant-cracking the cigar tray. "And what would you know o' fitness, you dumb dandy? I want to know what you did and who you did it with on the day before a body of fitness you could only ever dream of found himself dead under that pier. I'm done hearing about you. You don't matter. I want to hear about *him*, from the moment he arrived in Brighton to the last time you saw him on the night of his death. Every. Pitiful. Detail." Each last word a lift-and-crash into an incentive to speak, an encouragement of hot cigar ash and broken glass. "Every pathetic pass you made, you dirty old bastard. You leave nothing out. You hear me, old man?"

"Ye—ye—yes, *master*," Marsh whimpered, spit flecks of blood and ash.

Keeping Marsh clamped to the cigar and port table with his knee, he lent over the trembling fold of unmanly softness, putting two fingers of his dominant hand in the glass-cut mouth and drawing the cheek back in the action of an archer—to keep Marsh's airways open enough to blood-spit a full and proper story. *Stew Boy can no longer bend the way he once did.*

*E*arly morning back in time on the Brighton sands… He started *Sizar's* '88 round-one proceedings against a backing of bleak sea mist. His speech was shaken by nerves that morning, stirred into showing themselves by the south-coast chill. Candidates were laid out ready for the picking. Pin prick blood bursts clustered high on their cheekbones, over which their skin pulled taut. Breath was seen from prickle-pink nostrils—a sign to him of the warmth that lay inside them. Those pledging for a place in *Sizar's* were always more than boys—recruitment makes sure of that—but they were not yet what he'd call men. *They are my lads.* And they were especially fresh this year, though the white under their eyes was just that little bit muddied that morning. *Mud that marks their English exuberance with shadings speaking to the boisterousness of a first-night rush*, he thought as he stumbled through a rehearsed address. *Age…how mean it has been to me, having diminished my confidence in speaking to fit lads.*

This morning's lad-hoard was fourteen strong. He had counted them while waiting for the right occasion to commence his address. That occasion came mid-morning: a little past eleven am, or half-past, or thereabouts—he couldn't be sure exactly how long had passed since he last retrieved time from his breast pocket. There was no bustle to Brighton the day before the creature was found, not even in the prime of her light. No bustle about a seaside resort gripped by the blister of deep winter. No bustle that made time harder to grasp… Whatever its precise time, his commencement of the welcoming address came later than he would have liked because of the lad count. Fourteen lads when he started, when there should have been sixteen—four candidates for each house…and on reflection, *yes!* the creature was one of the missing.

Of the lads that were there, each fronted-up in their best suits, and although the tatter and cut of candidates compared to the fine tailoring of the heads and tutors set all men apart by class, most were of the finest athletic form. Though nervous, the contents of his welcome were familiar enough, with the usual details of the club's origins among four Cambridge Old Boys. This gave his thoughts freedom to roam. To turn on how he would have liked to have been witness the night before. To the horseplay and hazing of lads bound together for the first time.

At the end of his welcome, he directed those under his feet to ascend the steps to be taken by horse-drawn carriage to the contest venue. The distance to traverse was not far; horses were not, really, needed. If it was more than half one mile from the Grand Hotel to the venue of his choosing, it would not have been more by much. All a dozen minutes of a brisk winter's walk. But still, the services of the Grand's porter—or night watchman, or night manager, he didn't bother to remember which rank or file—had made arrangements on his instructions for the arrival of eight carriages. He'd chosen horse-and-carriage transport as a deliberate contrast with the steam engine that delivered his lads to the town the day before. It was his medieval defiance to anything of a motor or combustion engine. Horsepower would take his first rounders from the sea to the contest venue—a citation to longer histories, with warm fires of the pre-locomotive coaching inns and——

It was sharp in the present... Glass rolled his face in chunks of cigar-ashtray glass. Breathing was made more difficult by the roll, telling him his manner of storytelling was tiresome. It was glass on all fronts. But it encouraged him.

Torn off the digression and back to past facts... The carriages chosen were intended for the comfort of two across extended distances; he had estimated, therefore, that two lads and a head or tutor would make it at a squeeze for a short excursion. As was their instinct, the heads positioned themselves closest to the road, their respective tutors and candidates coming into line behind them. All heads were the founding heads, while the tutors were a more transient appointment; downright translucent a concept for one head. It was this man, Peele, the one with a historically reckless regard for tutors who decided to claim the front two of the four carriages that had arrived thus far.

Marsh Park... "Separation among the heads is like limbs torn from the heart of *Sizar's* at its start," he admitted under the persuasion of glass in cheek. Tearing was perhaps inevitable after such a period, he had reflected regarding the heads, and he do not mind the drift apart from his college-days comrades. *It makes for more salivating sport,* he had concluded. Admittedly a queer kind of private club, Essex House's Peele wore difference more publicly than the others. "The man's soft, and his eccentricities are O so much more accentuated," he spat into bloodied glass shards. "He gets about like one hard done by, easy to pity but difficult to like; the commandeering of the front two carriages…O it was a sign of the man's insufferable vanity. But I've come to tolerate the man because pity is aided by bad luck. Peele's boldness rarely serves in getting him ahead, and this day before the poor creature's discovery destined a display no different."

Peele's initiative to claim the first two carriages for the Essex house was undermined at its outset by quarrelling among the home team over who of the five would ride in which carriage. Embarrassment at the display of dissent evident, Peele sorted the seating in sharp instruction, taking the front carriage with the two finest candidates as company and assigning tutor Tanner——"who you haven't meet, so I'll say is slightly less offensive to look at, though still overlong and stick-like, very tall but often bent over, with skin bearing the scars of some disease"——to the second, sweeping in the remaining two candidates, "much more the mutts."

Glass removed fingers from his mouth, allowing him to breathe better, then come to sit opposite him again.

He went back straight in the chair, face stinging of alcohol and hot ash in weeping wounds but feeling a pleasant sort of pain at being able to please by sharing an intimate account of the day before their pier reunion. He would lean into it, leave nothing out. Give his detective an even better account.

"The dissenting display drew my attention and alerted me to a fact that I might otherwise have missed," he said, pouring port into his unbroken glass and taking a stinging sip, hoping to return them to a civilised meeting of men. "My facts for you, drawn from the Brighton sands, are these: 1. Two of Peele's party had arrived late to the beach, 2. These were the two missing from my headcount, thus delaying my welcome, 3. It was these two who now travelled with Peele in the front carriage, so clear favourites. I knew it to be these two lads on the basis that they were at a physiological cut above the calibre of candidate I had come to expect from an Essex house selection. Two who would have captured my attentions well and truly had they stood before me on the beach... Though my glimpse was just that—a gist of them, in mist, joining the assembled from street level, down in the direction of the Chain Pier—one of the pair snagged me. This lad was, without exception, the most beautiful creature I have yet seen. And now that I had seen this boy, the desire to do anything to get the creature in for nurturing washed over me like a king tide. O indeed, this was no ordinary ol' Essex lad. Yes, that's right, fact four: One of the two candidates that Peele claimed for his own carriage was the very same creature over which you and I would enact our reunion the very next morning."

Glass retrieved a fresh glass; he filled it for the man.

His detective rose the unshattered cut crystal and took a long drag of its brass-gold contents. "Getting tiresome again," Glass said with a sigh.

Eager to please, with shakily stinging port lips: "I don't know what you want to hear about. About the ride to the contest venue, with my lovely Prett *my pretty*, my favourite competitor, so well-spoken that few would believe I plucked him from a royal stable, to then compete in a royal stable. About the 'numbering' at the Pavilion, where each head ranks their four and where I gave my Prett a number one, in paint on his naked body with my house's colours so all would know he was mine? My feelings of excitement undressing in front of my pretty Prett in my bedchambers?"

"We can skip all that non-sense, I think," Glass said. "Just the main event, Stew Boy. Just the wrestle. With all the detail you can manage."

Glad of the direction, his real-man-given cuts were becoming sacred to him. He was learning again, after so many years, how to behave to Oscar Glass' liking. How to give the man what was wanted...

Back in time in the stables of the Royal Pavilion... Sixteen stood white velvet robed and rigid before him, shoulders back in a circular formation. He was at their centre, alone, the remaining three heads and four tutors side-lining the arena floor. "We shall draw lots, for partners," he announced to both the robed lads and the fully clothed men who had chosen them—their tutors, utterly clothed, too. Each round's host had an own-individual manner of convening affairs. One might put partnering for the combative challenge to a vote—among the heads or even the candidates themselves—when another runs a kind of raffle for selection, as another adopts the more personable and perception-based sizing-the-lads up for partner selection. If feeling charitable, a head might inform allocations by how the lads spread before him had been already numbered—numbers that a head would typically record before the challenge commenced, then paint on the body.

He favoured the drawing of lots because it was straight and forward. There was no potential for sleight of hand—or none that he could think of. No suggestion of favouritism based on the fact of a head's own tribute rank, or the rank of his peer, or indeed any preliminary impression of one or two competitors who might have imprinted on the host during earlier encounters. The method was visible to the naked eye. He had sixteen long matches bundled and held up for all assembled to see. Then a galley knife was drawn and taken to the stems of two at a time—except the first two, which were set aside intact. Slicing went two-by-two in thumb-widths up toward the ignition point, until no more than two were alike, and each one was not without a partner. Once the preparation of the matches was complete, he discarded offcuts and bunched the remaining elements back into his hands. Back turned, he then adjusted the matchsticks to different lengths until each length of the sixteen varied in tower reach, before returning to the circle's centre where he held out the jagged, red-tipped bouquet like it were the releasing of a dove. A grand invitation for the lads to come forward and feed for a place from his hands.

"The first two shortest together, the next two shortest together to determine wrestling match-order, starting with the shortest. Agreed?" None answered, though one of the assembled was immediately stirred to step forward—the finest lad of Essex, evidenced by the yellow-painted, three-bladed handle on the creature's chest. O yes! the creature. The emblem was drawn in shaky strokes low between the creature's pectoral muscles and down the first hard bumps of the lad's mid-front...so he saw when the robe was cast away—with all the skill of a magician's sweep of silk covering a trestle of sublime tricks. Honour to Prett kept him from flickering a sight down there right away. Though this determination was not to endure; no devotion could have kept his gaze long from a full and frank survey of the extent of the beautiful creature that had made itself bare before him. Of all the sixteen candidates assembled; many fine at point of looking; the creature was infinite; there was the sublime about this One. He recognised the lad straight-up as the one missing from the beach. The creature, more man–boy melted than the rest, stepped right up—the One from Essex house. Unsmiling, stern, not-tall—shorter than him, and the rugby stock of Kent lads that had become standard. Not strapping, like a Kent man, but apparently as strong as. Compensation for shortness marked by arms that, in comparison to stature, were immense, vital, vascular, but still round and soft and supple to look at. The creature's facial features had comparable contradictions of quality—being hard, sharp, assertive, and soft, boyish, smooth. He did not need to see the creature's back to know the numeral ("I") that would be marked there, in the same shaky hand.

The creature stepped up close, being short enough to have to raise eyes to him but without a break in a stern—*why resentful?* he wondered—expression. The creature looked him in the eye straight and selected a match. It was the easy picking, the clearest of a sure bet: at the tip of where he had configured the matches; at two ignition tips, held in pincher. The short straws. The options one did not mind snatching only if one did not mind going first. As the creature did it, in that moment of selection of a lot that was, for all intents and purposes, pre-allotted, another tribute dropped robe to step forward for a spin at the wheel. This lad's chest painting was red, puffed out, proud; this candidate was taller, though a leaner build than other Kent tributes (known by the colour red, the county colour), and lanky in comparison to the already-at-the-selection-point competitor. The Kent lad stepped up astride the creature and, boldly, took the remaining lot at the tip of his bundle.

Two just-the-tips joined together—confirming a match. They were the first to draw and would be the first to duel. The competition had its first pair, and he made note of it: *Match I: Essex I vs Kent I.*

How curious a procedure...to read lads by markings on newly nude bodies alone, he thought as the drawing of lots played out. But paint aside, reading the bumps and bulges of each candidate and seeing the bold or not-bold actions in their drawing of lots, he felt could know them. He knew that both firsts-to-wrestle, of Essex and Kent, would bear the same mark without needing to see it, both "I," in shades of yellow and red: the colours of their respective houses. "Ones" of each house were always the ones to watch, and by stepping forth first, these lads were announcing their status—in that knowing way that extraordinary boy-men often do. The display of this pair stirred up the circle by way of shifting stances and sideward glances. His Prett was next up to eat from his hand, robe as rapidly dropped, venturing to the centre point. Prett's approach—at first rapid with the unveiling, to then slow in a small stride to the base of his matchmaking bundle—gave rise to a sensation inside him that was not quite describable. *A pinching, was it?* This feeling made him take in his surrounds and the impressions of his peers. Blunt was transfixed on the Peele top pick. Peele was transfixed, too, but on his own number one, who he had poached from the man; *unsportsman of me, I know. But I had to have him.* While Cohen, true to form, avoided any gaze at all over naked flesh. He was both thankful and vengeful that only one of his peers had his Prett in crosshairs.

Prett selected a match with eyes locked on his, drawing unseeing, drawing by chance, the second shortest of the matchsticks. His first, third up, would be second into naked combat. His second candidate, Distler, was up next to the bundle, disrobing in a more disjunctive action. Distler had come from a family who'd fallen on hard times, so was comparatively well-bred and looked at the sticks in his hands rather than him. Distler took time, looking the jagged match-making mountain up. Looking for, it seemed, some slice of a stick in particular. When Distler settled on a choice it was from a cluster, tall but not the tallest, in the furthest reaches of his palm. Distler had drawn a lot that if it were not the longest, it was no less than the second longest, for sure. Were it calculated, and he had no illusion from what he knew of the lad that it wasn't, it was a self-serving manoeuvre, fitting of Distler's station. Others assembled started to stir. A tremor, a signal that soon the grasp for sticks would be swifter; but first one more lad came forward for a private selection: the first of Surrey, he assumed by the shape of the lad.

This was the only "first of" yet remaining to select; an initiative, really, thrust on by a boot in the behind from the house tutor, tenting a buttock-reveal like a stick up a petticoat hem, thrusting the lad forward. Cohen's tutor had sensed too that the mood in the room was turning. The Surrey-house first "Munns" did not stay long, opting too for the Distler directive, drawing a lot from the same recess of his grasp. Choosing a stem that looked to be the longest of them all. But it was deceptive, and its cut-point only just pincered by his hand. A slower study would even have seen it sway some, without any sub-structure support. It was the decoy, the dummy pick, the one stick that a strategic fellow should have seen as too-obviously safe in the bunch. But still, its superstructure was plenty tall enough to place it in the middle of the bundle; something, he observed, that spoke of Cohen's lads overall. Even the Surrey house Ones; not firsts of this man's reckoning.

The drawing was thick and fast after this; even before Munns had found a break in the circle through which to join the other contenders, the lad's nakedness was companied by a tide of the rest, closing in. It was messy. Unsportsmanlike. The frenzy took flight in a flutter of white robes thrown off lad bodies, like the wings of pelicans off a tidal river when a deep water, sub-marine threat presented itself. They flew in at speed. Not to read his palms, not to admire his puzzle put to them, but to grasp indiscriminately. To find a stick for their own; as if getting in before last was the only strategy available to them now; as if it was all a trick, and there were not enough sticks to go around—no credit to the offhanded fact that, by mistake or attempt-at-choice between two, some tried to grasp more than one. But it was no trick. There were precisely enough lots for each lad assembled; this was shown when, after the scavenge had passed, and the lads who had come forth were now moving en masse out of the circle, the next part was carried out with great commotion: the affair of finding one's pair.

He remained at his station through this commotion with a stick left over. But quite right, too, for there was one candidate remaining, still white robed.

What was once a circle was now a dot of last-lad standing, faced off with him. For a moment he thought it was a case of the pull away. A contender, though taut on the line of the private-head recruitment and numbering, and comfortable enough with the initiation, but who when confronted with the ritualistic manner of the sorting challenge, would wish to pull out, rather than put out and be exposed for the assembled contenders, tutors and other heads to see. There had been the occasional one of these in the teething times of *Sizar's*, before the heads had become more rigorous in their recruitment regimes. But that the lad left without a stick could be such a pull away was not entertained for long. When he locked eyes with the lad left, an eerie calm in the chaos of the clamour for clarity over with whom each of the lads would partner, came…and there was no question of commitment there. It was not a cunning—no—but a knowing—a care, a courage. For patience; even as the masses of able lads around this last standing succumbed to hysteria in the push together of his unhanded sticks.

The lad calmly dropped robe. Impulses rose as velvet dropped. Impulses…like to bundle the lad back up in robe and reposition them both somewhere private, where the unrolling of acquainting could occur away from the eyes of all others assembled. He wanted the exposure to himself. Another stellar specimen, painted Essex yellow. *Damn the man!* The last lad closed the path to their joining using sure-but-unassuming steps to collect the last lot. The stick sat small in the Essex-coloured lad's palm, the second smallest of the lots he had cut up. A pain formed as he realised that two of the proudest of the assembled, two of the most befitting of his benefaction, and of a slot in *Sizar's* circle…two who had near-bookended the lot-drawing character test—as he envisioned his method of wrestle pairing—would finish that day with one leaving for certain. As the last lad walked away to partner, the double *numero unos* strewn in yellow paint on lower back led sadness to take him. This Essex "II"—no second he had ever seen. This wildcard favourite from the heat of lot drawing. This lad, named "T. Keeler" according to a hand-written list he now handed Glass, would come into flesh combat with his own, *my pretty*, his Prett.

Marsh Park… "The lots betrayed me," he said to Glass back in London.

*E*bbing unconsciousness, Marsh sat ashen-blood dripping and weeping before him. He'd tolerated much in listening to the story of the day before Pipe was found. Of sorting boys from wretched worlds, naked wrestling for the satisfaction of old men and the slightest chance of a game change. The story had lasted long enough for shadows to float through Grosvenor Park like worm-eaten wood on the incoming tide. *No sympathy for how soft Stew Boy has become.* "Mark the pairs and the victors," he said, sliding Marsh's list across the port and blood and glass-shard table with a pencil on top. Colour numbers on prime-aged chests in rubbed, blurry competition seemed to pass Marsh's mind as the pairings were recalled with powdered graphite on paper. Winners circled, now the Middlesex Crew for the row at the end, wrestle pairs numbered in match order. And the fallen struck out.

Middlesex	Surrey	Kent	Essex
S Marsh (head)	G E Cohen (h)	B Blunt (h)	L Peele (h)
K Porter (tutor)	S Brown (t)	A Underhill (t)	W Tanner (t)
M1	S1	K1	E1
E.M. Pratt	J.J. Munns	S.R. Lewis	M. Piper
M11	S11	K11	E11
W.G. Dexter	J. Bishop	J.S. Whyte	T. Keeler
M111	S111	K111	E111
G.E. Bentley	J. Atkinson	B. O'Connor	H.H. Ingersoll
MIV	SIV	KIV	EIV
E.S. Bates	G.T. Cross	J. Hunt	A.G. Cady

86

The facts were these... Wrestling ended with a confirmed eight-boys-between-thighs for Middlesex Crew: one from Essex house, three from Kent, two from the namesake, and two from Surrey. It interested him to see that through the circle-and-cross exercise Marsh could not strike off two fallen names—Prett/"my pretty" and Piper/"the creature." In these two, left exposed without strike nor circle, a pang of greatest concern seemed to be carried in a weeping frame. Sadness settled on Marsh's messed-up face like silt on a pebbled shore—a same sadness, he knew, the man would have carried the night before Pipe was discovered. *To what action?* he wondered.

As Marsh had circled, crossed out and made connections with the names of the first-round candidates, he reflected on the peculiar details of the account. He knew some parts—such as that Pipe arrived a day later than the rest of the contenders, as he gained from the Cohen interview. Other parts of the account added colour to previous information he had received. The rôle of "Keeler" (EII), Pipe's travelling companion in all this, for instance, who Cohen had also told him arrived late and was rising in significance in the case—being a conflicted source of love/hate intrigue for Marsh, who now had the boy on the Middlesex "crew." Gained were possibly significant parts of the tale he had previously no notion—such as bickering among Peele's boys over the carriages that would transport them to the Royal Pavilion.

Marsh's account was helpful, but he wouldn't let on. "Your pathetic ramble neglected the actual wrestling, you fool! And what of the critical after hours? Stop wasting my time. I want detail on what I ask, you hear? Only my questions. Of the matches, what of the"——consulting the marked-up sheet before him——"first. Detail the Piper and Lewis match."

"The most perfect match," the bloodied-pathetic man said, speaking in a sort of perverse dictation. "Squared up, naked-beautiful contenders; not a sweat shed between them in the exertion, yet sliding off each other like they had been oiled up. Naturally frictionless in the muscle rub up, their bulges fattening to the intertwined-limb touch. It was a solid display. One where the dominance of the Piper climax was clear enough not to cause anxiety throughout, not to need even hope for Piper to end up on top. Piper-the-victor was that certain an outcome, yet with a contender—of Kent—who was able-bodied and aesthetically muscle supple enough to turn a sure thing in all the right contortions. Strong enough to snag interest until the very, inexplicable end, when a sure winner dashed all joy by succumbing to the mat. *Yes!* Piper lost in a final rush of holds. Like a terrible dream—the beautiful creature slipped my grasp."

Marsh's manner was better. Clearer by his roughness. He topped up his own port glass, tracing the rim with a touch that made it whistle, pleased what rough-with Marsh was yielding. It was as he had suspected: The dead boy had deliberately fallen in the wrestling match. Not surprising, really... that a boy motivated by money, to whore out for sums that even the most modestly monied would consider paltry... Would such a boy throw a match for quick money rather than a narrow shot at success in a much longer game? Naturally. It was the street-smart thing to do. And he knew from the train, from Blunt—whose own boy Piper fell to in the final holds—that bets were sometimes placed in the club. It pleased him to have substance for a suspicion of Blunt. "Blunt walked with a limp yester-day," he said, glass whistling. "On the day of the matches, you notice a limp when he went from the beach to the carriages?" Marsh shook head. "Good. What followed the match?"

"Dinner, served was the finest——"

"What you ate doesn't interest me. What of the defeated boys? And what was the reactions to their defeat?"

"It is customary for the eight defeated halves to lodge separately after. Segregated from the victors, who should spend the evening in a more close-knit fraternity. This tradition applied to dinner, too, where the defeated are left with empty bellies, ferried from the match arena via a secret under-Pavilion passage. I never liked that part. Felt it unsportsmanlike to send the fallen off into the night without a feed nor the warmth of the comrades they had enjoyed on their first night. I hated myself over dinner for not ruling against the way things always went, at dinner as well as before. I was questioning the reasoning of sending those defeated back to the Grand, for a night on their own, for a journey—short as it was—in the blister of seaside, deep winter, when there was all the space and warmth of a dining hall and large lodges right there, only one floor above. Dinner-inclusion guilt grew to dreamings of dorm-mateship gropings, too, and an impulse to wind back time and rule against the losses of the creature and my pretty——"

"Fuck ya pretty boy. What of the others at dinner?"

Still sniffling, Marsh seemed to buck up being rough spoken to.

Some bitch pups never grow, he thought.

"The rest ate in unusual silence also, a weight of shock in the air; save for Peele, who seemed undampened. *Peele goes against the room*, I remember thinking, *the rest of us are reeling*."

"Blunt seemed upset?"

"He was melancholy. It made no sense to me. Perhaps he was regretting not saving talent for his own round. Cohen was pensive, but this was not——"

"Mr Cohen is not of consequence," he said, irritated that the wrong head seemed fine with the Pipe boy throwing the match. "Do you know of any bets having been placed on the matches?"

"No."

"Careful now—you better not be lying to me." A tremble of the other's shoulders told him it was the truth. "What happened after dinner?"

"My inability to—to—to settle my own upset and play host conjured a cloud of unease over dinner that stifled conversation and any jubilation after. It infected the after-dinner time," Marsh said, suddenly dropping eye contact. "I—I—I went straight to bed."

He moved with a similar swiftness as at the start of Marsh's testimony. Behind the man, scruff of neck pierced and pulled back by the fingernails of one hand. With the other, still holding his full glass of port, he rested the crystal on Marsh's forehead, now level as a ship's plank. The man convulsed under the promise of further glass shards. Then, *gingerly*, he dipped the middle finger of his free hand in the port and traced the open cheek wound, swirling flecks of glass lodged there in the stinging liquid. Marsh screamed, but his nails kept the man planted there. "And you were doing so well," he said, recoating his finger to find another cut to tease. "But it's alright, *shh shh*. I've got the measure of it, I think. Two of your mates on the train implicated themselves as being down near the Grand Hotel, with the suggestion that one of your lot was even seen on the pier. Peele has been implicated, but you have just as pathetic a frame as he. Maybe it was you. Maybe if you couldn't have the Pipe boy, no one could. You'd hang on that, Stew Boy."

"*No, no!*" Marsh cried. "*Yes, yes!* I was down there, but I went to be with my pretty. I was nowhere near the pier, I swear. Please believe me."

"Ya had the boy bend y'over and bugger ya. Didn't ya, Stew Boy?"

Tears washed the man's wounds, but there was plenty of port in the glass. Plenty that the liquid swished like a swell in a great storm, splashing over the rim and running down the man's face, into the eyes and even the deepest bottoms of the cuts. "*Yes!* alright, yes. Prett fucked me, again and again. Half the night. The bastard owed it to me. He lost to that Keeler boy. And it sickened me that Keeler was liked—the lad jumped forward to tend to an injury and stop cauliflower ear later in the game. Prett had let me down."

"He let ya down. But you'd still get the service out of him—that right?"

Marsh's eyes flickered like stricken-liner morse code. Loss of consciousness was close.

"O no, not sleepy time yet," he said, wiping the man's jagged face with his sleeve, then slapping the cuts to bring the eyes wide once more. "Almost done. It's almost over. You bent your pathetic body over to have the poor lad fuck you as his punishment. And say I believe you—that you're not man enough to have confronted Pipe, who you held no power over. And that even if you did, you haven't the strength to have been able to end him. That you weren't on the pier. But maybe ya saw someone else. Someone who shouldn't have been there. Did you, Stew Boy? *Who did you see?* Tell the man."

Marsh jerked from side to side with such force that the head was ripped free from his fingernailed grasp, and the glass keeled over, spilling port down the flesh-ribboned face of the man. "*No, master!* No, I swear it. I saw no one," and then Marsh was gone, out cold.

"I believe ya," he said to the unhearing lump of the man. "You'll thank me latter for the port. It'll keep ya from going septic," a last slap on the cheek.

Stepping out into the London night, he hailed himself a calash to carry take him across town and to the Thames. To make provision for Cox to lodge in the small apartment he had use of on there. It had taken much longer than anticipated with Marsh, but he had got what he needed.

IV

MARSH

Erecting edge of the Thames, Marsh House rose into white as Thomas Keeler arrived by carriage less than one week the wake of his mate found dead-snagged under a Brighton pier. He had been collected from a station so rural and with a situation in the Middlesex countryside so private halt in character that few would know its name. That was near-on one hour ago, with darkness having arrived several hours before that. He had been left waiting at the station for collection so long that had a train returning to London happened past he would have been sure to jump on it—money for a ticket or not, and this whole shot-at-a-better lot hoo-ha be damned. The weather was dastardly—the mist across the moors. He assumed they must be moors in a place as Godforsaken as this; so soup thick that there was no way of his verifying its makeup or any other vapid assumption he had made about the place. After collection to now being horse drawn across a part of the country unknown to him, the mist made the unfamiliar county feel under threat of being rubbed from England's map. After a time of only wet white the middle front of the manor came clear, its stone a study in the Gothic and with gravel around it. It was lit yellow by the carriage front lighting and spill out from the lead windows, out of which light escaped from the fireplaces within. It was a warm glow like what emulates off the coal remains of a hall fire when covered by a screen and left to die out at the end of a banquet.

The house itself was bleak grey...by design. It had no age to it. In fact, was still under conception—construction seemingly closer starting than complete. But enough was done to make the ethos evident: even the under-building parts being made to look old. Just by the illuminated foundations and frontage that were seeable through the storm he knew the house was vast...biggest-in-county vast. Its façade disappeared into the countryside night like an anchor over a continental shelf, fading through storm shading into parts of itself that the owners would probably never have time to inhabit. It stretched outwards and up into the blizzard night. There seemed no end to its sprawl; the storm keeping its mystery as if it built itself into the bliz-zard; its window lights growing fainter as it rose and crawled into the countryside and sky. There was the odd window illumination in the rise that came to resemble distant shipping in a fog. *Somewhere up and out there.*

"You're late, boy," his new head of house said at the door.

The man was Gothic, too, enveloped like the house in layers of out-dated showiness, and spoke from the shadows. Mr Marsh, Head of Middlesex, was robed in red velvet, heavy as the upholstery of the carriage that had transported him there. This robe was bound at the waist with golden hemp, and emerald slippers wrapped the feet. Marsh presented as eccentricity manifest, warm and in from the weather while he stood shivering on the step, soaked to the bone. His new head was cloaked in darkness that played tricks with the face in its depths, the golden hemp-bound man looking jagged and purple in the shadows.

"Sorry, sir. I ha——"

"You can give me your excuses in the morning. Or never—actually. I detest boy excuses, and it's late. The staff have retired for the night...*so late*. If you require it, I can rouse them to feed you..."

"No, sir. I don' wan' be a bother." The weight of hidden eyes upon him led him to extrapolate: "Any further bother."

"Kind of you, boy," his host said in a way that betrayed the face value of the words. Marsh then handed him a lantern that cast light on his host more. The man wobbled in the shadows, as if rocking on the decision of where to put him, before muttering directions to a room *in the West Wing.*

Up the main flight then left will lead to the west wing. Then continue to the end of the corridor, up a second flight and into the third door on the left, the one past the portico window looking out onto the moor; at least, that was what he thought the directions were, running them over in his mind.

How exactly he would recognise the detailing of a portico from the inside (or more to the point, what a portico was), he was left unsure of as he walked away—not before apologising once more and wishing the master of the manor a good night. He had not dared ask the host to repeat the navigation before setting out into the vast dark of the stately-house-in-the-making. After a few times ending up in a part of the manor so under construction it was without a floor, he stepped inside a room he had only the shakiest of beliefs might be his. It was warm and steamy in there, with glass that was frosted just like the cosiest of Christmas mornings. In the shadows he caught sight of the buttocks of a man, a boy really, but manly-built; half-silhouetted, half-light-emboldened by the window. Brilliantly plump and curved in contrast with the jagged ugliness of the man of the manor.

"Sorry," he said, speaking that word this day three times more than he was accustomed. "I've taken the wrong door."

The bare-buttock boy stayed calm. "I don't think so."

Were the stranger startled it was not shown, the naked boy stepping into full view between the two single beds in the room. "You're 'Essex II,' I remember you. Your wrestle was a standout for me. I'm 'Kent I.' No mistake, my friend—we're roommates."

The nude boy's speech came with movement and opportunity for the fire-light to prick out places of appendage that were easier to discern from the other boys' bodies he had seen at the qualifier. "You're Squire Lewis."

Calling the nude boy—who he could recall from movement of mannish parts—by name was apparently unexpected by the other one. Not to be outdone, Squire replied: "And you're Thomas Keeler."

They stood a while.

Wary.

To rub out the tension, he said: "You wrestled with and made lay on the mat the only"——he hesitated...*how to describe him?*——"the only—the only—the only mate I had coming into all this. That's why I 'member ya."

Squire looked somewhat disappointed in that response. "While I," Squire replied, "asked around about you, after seeing you wrestle. Though you were…elusive—to learn about."

They had clarified their positions. Explained how they had knowledge of each other without formal introduction.

But the wariness remained.

Squire made a move toward him, arm outstretched but naked and with a bob of that same motion that recalled the boy to his memory and that moved now as a wet, hot-from-bathing manhood mass, swaying with advance in step as well. It was unavoidable. Primal instinct of someone so weary, also, from the weather—that that part of Squire is what he looked at.

"I'm sorry. I've forgotten myself. I'll cover up," Squire said, though with expression that did not connote the embarrassment the words did.

Nor should it have, he thought, by the state of the other one's endowment.

Squire resumed coming, hand cupping down there.

Well…it was like a tease 'n' takeaway.

Squire then turned for the bed and the towel that was draped on its edge… but the muscularity of the boy's buttocks was just as stirring of instinctual, unavoidable gazing; they were so…immovable; unswayable by human or much other force upon those muscle groups.

"*No!*" he cried, much too late. Tiredness a contributing factor in the delayed outcry, which was also…much too passionate. His weary eyes much too long spent fixed on another boy's bulkhead behind, and too long after his allotted lodging partner's change of direction to be feasibly interpreted as intended: as a casual, among-boys acceptance of in-lodgings nudity.

Too late since Squire had fetched the towel already and swept it low around the waist. Then returned with hand outstretched once more.

It was his turn to display disappointment: "I mean," he said, subdued by the towel but livened a lot as he touched Squire for the first time; a hand, firmer than ordinarily. "What I meant to say is that…" he let his words catch his thoughts: "Nay embarrassment needed. We've seen *this* all before."

But and *alas!* he put the wrong emphasis on his words, *this* instead of *seen*...
or should it have been *we've?* It was met with a returning sweeping gaze of his
waist area all the same. *We've were meant*, he decided upon. The Royal we('ve).
As in: every boy. Though the linguistic reason outside of instinct was lost on
him; the comfort that every boy should feel in a natural state with another
member of his own sex was what he had been shooting for. Comfort was a
requirement. It was why showers were shared; why urination was a social
enterprise between men, and a sometimes social-too, playful even, crossing
of streams between boys; why defensive, combative sports were at their most
authentic when bodies clashed unclothed. *We've* would have signified this. But
this drew them back to the tournament, to the singular courtship of voyeur
and exhibitionist, as was the nature of the naked circle in which combatants
wrestled for dominance over each other. The place where———

"I'd like be pals." Squire said, slicing his weary inner wordplay.

"We will be. M' pals call me Keely." The air grew cold between them as
he weighed up what pals might mean.

"It really is nice to meet you, Keely. And good to hear you are not a
prude...because I sleep naked."

"So do I."

It was a lie.

He never lied, but he had for his bunkmate.

"Then we will be seeing much more of each other. Though, I too,
remember what I have seen already."

The comfort of a dorm bunkmate set in fast. Though—and perhaps this
was always ever the case with dorm bunkmates—what lay beneath Squire's
towel was ever on his mind.

"Rooms were arranged after dinner," Squire said through his distracted
state. "The other six had already formed as a cluster of chums. So—I was
the odd one out. But I don't mind confessing this: you would have been my
pick, anyhow." Squire took in his look, then proceeded without any prompt:
"The rest are a bore." Another taking in his look was had, before proceeding:
"I saved you the bed by the window. When we arrived, if you will believe it,
the sky was clear and I thought I was doing you a favour."

Now he responded. "Ya got 'ere first…y not take the view for y'self?"

The window scene was now onto atrocious weather, though he knew from the train journey that the day here had likely once been fine.

Squire shrugged. "I felt bad, I suppose. You had missed dinner, and I, being just one of me, had failed to secure a particularly nice room for you to sleep in. Least I could wrangle was a view for you."

"Seems sweet enough to me."

"The room itself is nice enough. It's just its location in the house. It's a bit…remote."

"O I hadn't noticed, m' path up was mostly dark."

"Exactly."

"So where are——"

"The others?"

"Yeah."

"In the opposite wing of the house, where most of the…life lives. We are the others in this house I think, Keel."

"And the other six was already chums, y'think?"

"Funny you should ask about being chummy. Marshy seemed especially keen on those six forming a bond."

"We're out o' his favour, y'reckon?"

Squire looked at him with the contours of the sceptic.

"He gave me the frost-bit 'ullo, is all." This seemed to strike Squire somewhere soft within. There was something in the way his bunkmate looked at him in that moment.

He would later regret not pursuing Squire about what was in this look. What the possibility of their othered status—about why they had been ostracised—might mean…that would plague him into the future.

But for now, towel-wrapped company was too promising for such probes. "Is that where Marsh sleeps, in that wing with the others?"

"No," Squire said; slowly, suggestive of an understanding that he meant to ask something more meaningful about why they found themselves there, but that there was also a need felt to pull back from deeper things. "He's in a separate wing—all his own. To the back of the house; a tail, really. But from my understanding his domain is like the one the rest of our crew are in… more lively."

"Le' me get this straight: we're in the lifeless west wing, empty except for us, our crew-not-chums are in the east where there be maybe some life, and Marsh is———"

"I really can't speak to orientation," Squire cut through in the tenor of a campfire ghost story. "Best not to approach this house with reason."

The blizzard—at an intensity that suggested the snow had piled up; all the way up and over their window—punctuated Squire's statement. In fact, it was just the concentration of wind-stirred winter flakes that gave the impression of being snowed under. Being—buried together. "But we're… alone here…in this wing?"

"Enough of that," Squire snapped———English blizzards, especially those that must-be moorland born, bring out hysteria in even the most level-headed of young men———"we have each other and you're safe enough with me." Seemingly attuned to their discomfort, Squire stepped forward to grip his arms with an authority of purpose.

It was a ripe thing to be told after the only chum he'd ever had was just found dead. Probably murdered given all that "Pipe" had going on in the Pee-le camp—*Pipe*, that's what he had always called his mate, long before "the Pipe" of the papers..

"Good God boy, you're freezing," Squire said, the grip had of him sliding into a stroke. "And to the bone, with a chill that not even burning proximity to our fireplace could remedy. It's out of those clothes and into a steaming bath for you, my new friend."

"You'e probably right."

"By God, I know I am."

"But I needn't ya handholding. It's getting late and you'll wish to be turning in. Just put me in the direction of the baths and a stove."

"*Nonsense!* Boiling water for the volume of a man in your state's bath, at this hour, will require…co-ordination. But to square ya up, chum: I don't fancy staying here alone."

Me don't blame him. There be ghosts in unlively wings of dens like this, he thought.

In the west-wing baths he waited, while Squire wrangled boiling water to pour into one of a line of iron tubs. *Squire*...it was growing in popularity as a name for England boys, though only among the better classes. This was the first Squire he had come across and the medieval connection with a knight's assistant was not lost on him given the generosity he had been shown—the boy was out of place with most of the poorhouse lads in the competition. Chivalrous...that was another one—as uncomfortable as between-boys romance was to a workhouse boy. He was no knight himself—of social standing nor monetary expenditure. Perhaps loneliness underscored his bunkmate's kindness...he could understand that now he was there, alone himself in the baths in a deep-night blizzard, in their solitary wing of an English country house whose extent of expanse was not yet known. The place he waited was one of cold iron and subway tile where in certain angles of the light bouncing off ceramic reflectiveness and joins in the walls...well... he thought he caught glass eyes upon him. Cold eyes watching him. In such a place as this he could understand a desire not to be left alone.

"I hope you have not completely frozen," Squire said while wheeling in a vessel of boiled water for transfer, "it took an eon to heat." Squire lined up the barrel to spill over and into the metal receptacle then said before the pouring started: "now stand clear, it is too hot by far...now. But the iron and chill of this house in a blizzard will soon cool it to a temperature just right to warm you to the core. You are still in your clothes." Squire said that last bit like it was nothing; a mere trinket tucked on only to the last of his bunkmate's statement about the cooling from the boil of a bath.

"Yeah," he said—an attempt at straight betrayed by his own coldness.

Squire stepped up. "We need to get you out of those wet clothes," Squire said after having started stripping him... It was a good way into his nakedness before Squire resumed strip-down reasoning: "It will take a good dozen minutes for the bath to cool to a climate that won't burn you—even then you'll poach a little; but you should not stay in clothes a moment longer—doing so will only cause grief. We've seen all the bits-and-bobs before, remember."

Hands on him was a shock at first but turned out to be of grateful help—a lot less grateful was he for reference to his intimates as bits-and-bobs...like they were the odds and sods kept inside a deceased estate's left-behind-by-the-family hall bureau. Gratitude for the help set in especially when he tried to remove garments himself. That showed just how cold he was—fumbling with the buttons of his tunic, his fingers blue and shaken, unable to unthread his shirt. Squire was swift at it, swiping his attempts at self-undress away like they were an insect nuisance. His boots were removed first, soaked through; these were followed by his woollen socks that dripped all the way off each foot. His trousers and underpants came down and off each leg at speed after. Even if his bits did bob a fair few inches tauter in the cold, once his soaked down there kit was off the relief and warmth from proximity to the steaming tub and Squire's hot, hard hands swatted away any unease he felt being stripped naked by the boy with whom he would spend the night. Having assisted his pants off, Squire moved to making short task of the unthreading of his shirt, stuck wet to his back. In the end of the strip down the much larger button threads of his overcoat were all that he had managed himself.

"It's a queer place, eh?" he said when they were face to face, his body still shivering but warming by the iron tub—like a boiler in the room. The two of them were roughly commensurate. In physique, in weight, in overall contouring. But there was enough——nay, more——that was foreign about Squire to reel him in. Squire had dark hair like charred bark fallen off an evergreen in a forest fire. His own hair, however, was a dull golden. Like the thick-as-pebbles stone sand along the Dover shore—about the only seaside place in England he had visited...before Brighton. The cut of the hair on both was roughly the same. A smart short, neatly parted—though Squire's fringe flopped to the right while his own went to the left. Much that was similar, but different enough. Though he had knocked about with Pipe since they were proper young boys, when it came to sex and what types he was

attracted to, it had never really factored into his thinking. He had frater-
nised, of course—what London dockyard boy hadn't? But he had never felt
for someone much. For certain, not the way he was feeling for Squire now.
"I feel better," he said, in some way just for something to say and while in
a proximity where the steam from a cooling boiled bath was in diminishing
warmness with the breathing of his bunkmate.

"Blue is fading," Squire said, a glance south. "Looking more…yourself."

Red surely then pushed out any blue hue left in his cheeks.

"Still, I'll feel much better once we have you in that bath…to complete
transfer from blueish white to a reddish pink, that's more your colouring."

As eager as he was to be in it, to have the cloudy hot water consume and
cover him, the bath was still too hot by far for him to get in; so instead he
moved closer to it, to warm his nakedness by its steam. Would he have felt
more or less comfortable had Squire been naked with him? he wondered.
"Marsh," he said, again for something to say: this time to break the into-eyed
stare of his bath-time companion who'd also moved closer to the warmth of
the iron. Is this to share body heat? he wondered. It sounded absurd. Yet.
Now. *Yeah!* there seemed more heat emulating from the body in front of him
than the too-hot-to-touch basin at his side. He continued: "What d'ya know
'bout 'im?"

"I know some, I know *of* him," Squire answered with a smile and no
interruption to their present bearing—of room-share proximity to his body
and intensity of staring. "My family are of Middlesex since, well, the Middle
Ages. It's a small county, with the soot smudge of the creeping capital making
it smaller by the year. And though it is per square yard densely populated
by pure toff, most of the bigger estates are well known, and stand out as the
toffiest. Especially estate men as eccentric as to insist on being called by that
county in such a 'club' as all this. I'm here for the chance to go to Cambridge,
being not smart enough to get funds and my family no longer with coffers big
enough to send me on my own steam. Father lost it all in a bet, if you can
believe it. Marsh is obsessed with Cambridge, and——"

Squire should have been named "striker," holding the stance of a rower.
And had all the features of a home-county crewman. But, too, a peacock

quality. Squire's hair was feminine, dainty; it floated over a high brow. But the eyes, lighter than this hair, were a hazelnut. An angularly long nose, ears—protruding, somewhat—and lips that were a confusing concoction of narrow, plump and stiff…when taken together these elements had a suggestion of the simpleton about Squire. Simpleton until downward scan and the row-man's jaw and neck were considered. Stern and thick, respectively, with an ample Adam's apple, drawing together the head of a fine man with a body wholly masculine. The result…when all tied together, was of a being altogether sculptural. The sort that in a fable a father might sacrifice to a god, because this son was too perfect for mortal mesh. Marbled, even, but only after close inspection.

"——as we're seeing now with the building of those faux-Gothique architectural monstrosities across campus, pitted against those Classical revivalists within the same expanse, erecting stitched-up monster buildings… Marshy seems to be doing the same here. At least at Cambridge," the intellect of it all well lost to him now, "these past-referencing-obsessed designers are left to build visions of an earlier period in distinct quarters of the university; in fact, they are quite purposely being kept separate from each other—presumably in case one manages to infect the other with a flight of reference from an entirely different century. But here, on the banks of the Thames, Marshy seems more keen to mix these men together, which is resulting in the monstrous mongrel of competing styles that is this house: and that is not dis-similar to what is happening across the New World."

Though the entire exposition was into his ear, he tuned in in earnest as the tale turned to the story of the manor they were in. A topic that stirred intrigue inside him. Squire enlivened with the interest in his eyes. "But my criticisms aside, it may come good in the end. It is intended, this house—as Marshy explained over dinner—as a revival of the grand country homes of earlier this century, with a twist. With medieval influences, such as a whole-in-stone grand hall with Tudor-inspired gold gilding that, I am told, depicts scenes from Geoffrey of Monmouth's Arthurian story. And why not, given that Marshy has only his imagination as a boundary wall to what's possible."

"That rich, eh?"

"O indeed, much more so than any of the others. This house is being built with the fortunes of mineral wealth; of mining, which has fuelled the expansion of England across the globe. That this folly seems set upon a re-vival, and *rival* of the more romantic of English traditions sits well with all the oddities and flamboyance of its financier. And now ours as well—who by the looks of it, is not opposed to a good rough and tumble himself." Squire liked to talk. Was good with words. Wagging a writer's tongue; and he found this a comfort, a distraction from his nakedness as he returned his body to a comfortable temperature-setting after having stepped in the iron bath while Squire was talking. Squire continued with the story of Marsh and the strange murmurings among the county society-folk while he bathed. It suited him to listen and soak; to be receptive. And with his background, he didn't feel that he had much worth listening-to to say, anyway.

N ow the bathwater had cooled to a point where it started to threaten to undo all the restorative heat work he had been instructed into it for in the first place, Squire summoned him to stand and wrapped a towel around him, carrying his wet clothes for the return walk down the hall and to their room. There was an eeriness to their assigned wing, he thought as they walked back—situated as they were in an especially under-construction section of the manor-folly. Since his arrival he had not yet longed for a room to himself for the night—and with this walk any desire for privacy left him completely. No longer distracted by the immediacy of a need to get warmed, he now realised that there was a rasping chill through the air. An unnatural draft that pricked the hairs of the skin running the length of his spine and made him walk in closer company with his rowing mate; having Squire there felt like the only safe comfort in a near-London country house blizzard, where floorboards seemed to quake even under no human weight.

"O damn!" exclaimed Squire first thing on re-entering their room.

The fire had been reduced to struggling embers on the outskirts of the logs and would take some encouragement to flare up again, but worse off was the bed by the window. The one with the view that had been so thoughtfully delegated to him, the late-arriving guest. It was now as he had been on crossing the threshold into the house: soaked through.

"So…" Squire said in a confusing concoction of sorry and salacity, "obviously you shall sleep in the inner bed, the dry bed, since it was my own stupidity that saw the moor-view bed get wet, having left the window ajar ever so slightly—but enough in a Middlesex blizzard for the snowflakes to come to land on the bedspread and warm themselves to liquid."

"We could move the bed," he suggested, "and seal the window." He hurried over to action his own suggestion, to appear as a man of initiative.

"That will not save the bed for sleeping, I am afraid," Squire said, coming over to place a hand under the fallen bed's top blanket before he could give a first heave. "The soak goes through. No, I shall take the floor."

"Daft idea. We need just…share…the dry one."

"It's hardly big enough for just one of us at a time to have any chance of sleep. Let alone the girth of two men."

"We'll manage," he said, undressing again to show his sincerity and in service to his earlier claim to sleep in the nude.

"If you insist."

Brevity was his way and had worked to his advantage in driving home a decided upon course of action for their first night to be spent sharing a bed. But once both were in the bed, Squire's stated size issue became clear. He had told himself he would make sure their respective naked bits remained… respective. But once in, the reality of two well-formed more-than-boys in the formative romp to manhood not touching was…beyond the plane of mattress available to them. Squire's suspicion about the improbability of sleep also seemed proved in the practice of both being in, under there, together. There were just too many limbs impending on any kind of comfort. But it was warm.

"I can clothe myself," Squire said as the final flickers of firelight gave over to the white dark of a blizzard still building. Squire spoke in apparent reply to his wriggling for comfortable positioning—a Herculean try to keep air between their flesh. When he didn't answer, Squire put it another way: "I can cover up, if this"——thrusting slightly, his bedmate's warmest, soft-meatiest part pressed into him——"makes you uncomfortable."

His eyes adjusted to only just make out the white-lit outline of Squire's Grecian features. He was uncomfortable, but no matter the restlessness, he felt no wish to remove the touch of his bunkmate's nakedness upon him. Rather he felt a rising revelling in it, which sleep only threatened to rip away. "Be comfortable," he said flat as he could, staying still but relaxing into Squire's thrust, "for—for—for sleep, we've a hard day ahead to-morrow."

This gave his bunkmate pause, as darkness consumed the room and gave rise to the carriage of sound of uncomfortable creaks from other factions of the unfinished house. Such rise that made him only want to relax further into Squire's thrust. Some time later Squire said: "Are you warm enough? It's frightfully cold now that the fire's gone out."

"Barely," he said, why he was not sure. Barely warm enough was a false-hood. Were he alone with the kind of undercover heat that he felt in that moment the covers would be thrown back until such a time that the chill of the English night led him to, instinctively, draw the weight of bed coverings over himself once more…probably by that time some several hours after deep sleep.

Squire made a move. And it was to remove any air left between them, sliding an arm…ample, warm, firm…through the gap between his chin and shoulder. All the way until Squire's elbow could bend across his chest…to stretch down and draw him in, deeper. The bed, though only a single, was now amply large. They were the width of one deep-nourished man, at perfect centre with space to spare either side of the mattress—now it was only sweat between their nakedness. "Is this okay?" Squire said.

He did not know how to answer.

Some time later, Squire added, softer: "Does it help?"

"Yes," he replied at last, thankful for the more platonic question.

And like a battle wound wrapped firm and with all the right concoctions of tonic, sleep swiftly followed for them both.

Apparently unimpacted by blizzard drenching, the bed by the window remained made and looked dry come morning. The view was restored, too. And with it the scope of generosity in having had the bed given to him. Many details had been missed on arrival, obscured by the wintry storm. Whited-out. Marsh was building a grand country house in the truest tradition, exaggerated by untruths of frivolous homages to the past; to the ancient Britons, beyond even the most fashionable of countryside faux ruins that the present century had seen erected. And the locale on which the man had chosen to build this age-of-Victoria folly was just as inspiring of the picturesque. He hadn't seen it on the night of arrival, but "Marsh House" sat high on a hill in a hairpin of the Thames. They called it "house" because, well, the whispers were that *Sizar's* was at last getting a vast clubhouse.

Dense woodland ascended the manor hill and sprawled out from its base at three sides, giving the impression of the building being pushed into the river. At its front, facing the water and sheltered from view of neighbouring estates—none of which were evidenced through the woodland—was an elaborate garden raked in stages down to the water's edge. At its middle were stone steps cut into the hill leading to a boathouse where, already he could see, members of his now-crew had assembled. Seeing the others was followed in short succession by a rasp at the door. Squire bed-hopped with all authority-of-knowing, of needing, to conceal something, diving under the covers of the not-slept-in bed as if the door knock was the pistol shot of a starter for an Olympiad final.

It was Kemp Porter—their tutor, though he considered the man more of a coach. Porter barged through with the abruptness of an at-sea assault—not waiting for a summons or even leaving enough space between knock and enter for either of the room's two to vocalise any objection. But lucky for him, Squire was fast. From one bed into the other, with the covers coming down on both their nakedness in sync with the door open; it was a fast-fall curtain call, and even the keenest eye that knew where to look in the shadowed room would have struggled to glimpse anything untoward. From what he had gleaned during the scholarship qualifier, Porter was a sound and difficult to dislike sort of fellow. Much taller than most men, handsomer, too, and muscularly endowed...upper limbs as thick as the lower ones. That Porter's legs were only marginally longer than the arms made biceps appear bigger. His coach's top-heaviness came with a maturity that contrasted his own younger years—though Porter being only, say, five years the medium age of the group's senior. In fact, Porter had much to do with the softening of the image of Marsh as a man among the group, or so he had come to understand via hearsay. Porter had helped mould Marsh into the most-workable head of the bunch. Though his personal experience with the Head of Middlesex so far had been...well...frosty, in all frankness.

He and Squire were to be chastised in their shared room—criticism got in by their coach long before their soles could even touch the wood of their launch into the river. "You boys are late, you've missed breakfast, and the rest of your crew are now waiting for you." Porter spoke with dodging glances between Squire and him, seeming to be sizing up the condition of the bed covers, like a detective inspecting for clues. In this dart between beds, he saw up close how handsome his coach was. A slight incline of the head gave nod to Porter's good looks, a naked under-blanket flirting glance. Porter softened to his look: "Come boys, the shells are in the water." And as quick as the burst-in and examination of the evidence had come upon them, Porter left.

After the sound of footsteps—unnoticed on the approach—had trailed off toward the centre section of the house, he said to the bed opposite, "That was fast thinking."

"I'm a public-school boy, as is our coach there," Squire said. "But times are changing—you can never be sure."

"O' what?"

"Of how a man might...react. To a sight like ours."

All were perfectly innocent, he thought, *all were able to be explained away.*

All that they had done was in simple servitude to surviving the night. Well, to having any chance for prolonged sleep, at least. And they were of the same sex. So—what did it matter that they shared a bed? Yet neither was he that naïve. He had witnessed firsthand the experience of Pipe, an experience that may well have got his friend killed; experience and sordid rumours that swirled about a mate, now dead. *Not that Pipe did not invite it all*, he thought. Pipe had courted such rumour. More than that; Pipe had acted on it, stared scandal in the face like a baby blue groper in a whirlpool with both poacher and shark waiting at the rim of the swell. He was not naïve to the ways of his dead friend; not as stupid—nor as brave, either. No, Squire was right; he settled on this opinion once he had wiped the remainder of sleep from his eyes. Squire had *done right*, by them both. "How's that bed?" he asked at last, to distract himself from further thinking on Pipe and blue gropers and compromising same-sex positions with sharks in the swell.

"Un...inviting...but dry, at least."

'Nother riddle. 'Nother clue, he thought.

"Best we heed Porter's cry. Down to the boatshed, then?" Squire said.

No question, Porter had been genuine. The rest of the Middlesex eight were indeed in the shell waiting when they got down there. Porter waited, too; on the wharf, looking stern and curious. "Good of you to join us, gentlemen," their coach for the row at the end said as they filed into the final two slots in the boat, both at the back. Squire yielded to him, as had become Sqi's way, letting him choose his own placement. He chose to sit at the absolute back, and Squire climbed in once he was settled, sliding into the space between his thighs. Porter watched their manner of interaction with a fascination matching a chameleon anthropologist in the jungle observing a newfound tribe; watched him particularly, he thought; not with impatience, as he expected had been intended to be conveyed by the sternness of Porter's address, but more…and perhaps this was morbid, self-deprecating… but more watched him as a trinket, a curio in a cabinet. An object that didn't belong there yet that this coach might wish to take home and pin behind glass. He admitted in a bashful, to-himself sort of way that he liked the idea of being a pinned curio of Porter's. And the way the handsome coach looked upon him, he liked too. *But!* the time Porter had to entertain curios and for him to consider such entertainment was outnumbered by a consensus of indignation among the rest. It was palpable; reverberating; refracting through him as shell-like sounds might when trapped in a hollered-into clam. He blocked it out, and as for Porter's look: that he relegated to thought-fodder for a privater time.

"Right, gentlemen," Porter said. "Rowing is a bit like——"

As Porter set out the theory of sculling in a scholarly, Cambridge-champion rower sort of way, he allowed his mind to drift… And the felt-and-visual stimuli between his thighs was ample in this aim; for though tightly clothed, the sensation of his place in the boat was as intimate as the night before, by virtue of the company he was in and the watchful gaze of a penetrating coach upon him. Ideal conditions to drift… To carry him off and upstream, north in the direction of Cambridge, where the boy in front, pressed hard between his legs, wanted to enrol. The sight of lines of dark hair that stopped short at the base of Squire's head—these were the banks. The unruly swirls at either side—these were whirlpools that would pull his craft in. How vital the hairs at the stern of Squire's scalp must have been that morning, to stand on end in such a way that would propel the boy to leapfrog into the made bed opposite on an instinct of *we mustn't get caught.*

He phased in and out of Porter's tutorial while adrift. Most defiantly, given this oarsmanship lesson seemed directed at him… A coach-dictation of technique, delivered in a bold continuation of the curio look… The others, the *over there* ones—save perhaps Squire—would probably have seen Porter's manner as disciplinary action. A heightened scrutiny, a taking away of his individual liberty and privacy in light of the trouble he had caused the unit. But it didn't hold water. That private-time thesis crept back in. More than that. He knew Porter was governed by motives more personal than a co-ach's discipline. *Ain't the time*, he thought, pushing private motives from his mind again.

To help push these thoughts from the banks, he homed in on Porter's dictation, which at that point was about teamwork of force: pulling on oars through water; paths in unison of the least resistance. He gleaned what he needed, having the advantage of being at the back with only a master oarsman to watch him. And would pick it up on the way—or rely on Squire to give tutorage later. Once pushed out from the bank—physically out there now—and the instruction further away, coming to him as mediated, through a funnel of Porter-as-coxswain. Well, his mind drifted again... This time to the river itself. The Thames. That all-that-matters artery from London. The Cam regatta for which Porter was training them for would be held in the summer. But the river around them now, the river *he*, was frozen over in parts. Sl-icing through him was perilous, with debris of ice and below-zero water to pose unconscionable obstacle.

The summer seemed so far away here, he thought, especially with the corpse of a worthy contender still so fresh. The corpse of a friend. Yes, the phr-ase had haunted his mind sporadically since the death event. But it was true, Pipe was a friend. Death had shown him that—and that much can happen before long. It was morbid thinking, a grim inner dialogue that drew him back to what was in front of him. In reach. The back of Squire's head, down the lines of a bed-share's neck, to far-apart shoulders and a small waist between his own legs...now sweat-laced in row motion. This is novel, he thought. They had shared sheets for the night, but Squire had been at his back, while he had faced the window. The present view showed him that there was still much to uncover about the boy who yielded the better vantage when left to decide, and, when given the choice, handed over all power to him. This was the way he had come to see Squire. Giving power to him. No, *not giving*. Relinquishing power. Such posturing, such a boy-with-boy dance that also seemed a sparring partner of the entire competition that they all found themselves in. A competition made more curious still by Porter's obvious, exotic-cabinet fascination with him.

All week they were to stay at the house on the Thames: seven days to train and be trained for the regatta at the end. The winter was harsh and especially wet that year. The rain sticking fast to their muscles, achieving body even despite the rigour of their movements. On the second night, all were summoned direct to dinner—much earlier than any were accustomed. Marsh ate at the head of the table, there in presence only. The man's face swollen and stitched like some small girl's first attempt at a floral throw cushion. Was the early dinner a ploy to ensure none slipped away? he wondered. Such plots he would never put past their erratic host; given the haphazard and still-growing Gothic shell Marsh called home. On occasion throughout the eating Marsh rose head, as if in intention to state something…split lips even fluttering, slightly. But nothing sounded, and their host soon turned attentions back to the game on the plate. Marsh also lifted for a sweep at other intervals, of each of the eight, but lingering on Squire especially, whose own head was kept bowed in response. This behaviour was not at all what he had been expecting of Marsh, the man who had much to say on the Brighton sands and impressed upon him a likability that was a breast above the other heads. Their host was vocal then, cordial. And this was the man's reputation, too.

Pipe's death had changed everything, he deduced; clue-gathering of his own that had told him Marsh was, after all, the one to discover his friend's body—before even a detective of Scotland Yard, who'd taken a special interest in the case. Marsh retired early, leaving Porter to create conversation. His coach managed the task but not with any flair. The paired branches of the group nattered among themselves, giving over to only the briefest of responses to inane, coach-chosen topics. Porter's topics were conservative—around respective backgrounds and perspectives on the sport they were being schooled in. Porter left him wanting for a nice natter of his own, with his own half of a boy-pair. But at dinner, with company assembled, Squire, too, left him wanting...head ever-bowed, nothing to say, even after Marsh's departure. Not his bunking mate's way at all. As soon as they had branched off from the rest of the crew after dinner—down the hallway of their wing— Squire snapped back. Like a skeletal key succeeding in a rim lock after an alcohol-fuelled evening of rough-ended ill-fits. *Sqi was in.*

"You're shivering," Sqi said, the first words uttered to him since the whole crew had received their summons to dinner.

He hoped it was a class thing. That Squire was ashamed to show their affectionate friendship in company. Even that his simple nature and second-to-Pipe status embarrassed Squire somewhat...he would have taken this. This reason was simple, proper. "'Tis house—gives me the chills," he said.

Squire smiled; in just a small, half-mouthed way. "It's not the house. It's cold sweat, expelled muscles, wine, and sheer daftness of sculling in this weather; followed by not washing, then eating a dense meal with drinks and nil interesting natter. Bath soaking and sleep are what you need."

He liked being told by Squire what he needed. That was class-related, too; surely, rationally, easily...simply. "Right on it, that is," he said, and shivered again, this time with full knowledge of the source: an apprehension that Squire should follow that statement with a suggestion of solitude.

Sqi squashed fears by barely a space between words: "Shall we go to-gether?" They did and bathed in the same iron tub this time.

Afterward, in their room he asked: "Marsh a queer sort?" The question came in a bath-warmed and wine-relaxed glow, watching Sqi engineer a fire.

"He's a little queer, f'sure," Squire replied, forming gaps with a brass poker in which flames could grow. "But to-night was...out of character of the man I had heard about."

Squire had set them up with a clandestine cellar. Vintage wines his in-bunk-with mate had sourced from the kitchens. It was easy for Squire— moving with an assurance of how large houses worked and an aptness in ambling with command through the service rooms. There was no question of theft, and of all the boys now in the House of Middlesex, Sqi was the only one who was once wealthy. For his companion it was a courtesy to the host to ensure that, as a guest of a similar class, this boy was properly provided for.

"What's y'meaning?" he asked.

"He's been distanced by death," Squire spoke to the maturing flames, the firelight splashes betraying something in the face—what exactly he could not place. "Daresay, we all have."

Squire's manner troubled him: "Some 'f us more than others, eh." He let it sit there, heavy in the air like a moorland fog…

"Has your original head been in touch since Brighton?" Sqi asked.

"Peele? Nah, why should he?"

"Your closeness to…*him*. To Piper. You arrived late together. Why?"

"Held up…someone Pipe knew from London met us at the station, kept him there. I waited for him, so we needed to get the next train."

"Who?"

"An old," he fished for the right word but came up bare each cast, "pal."

"And Peele hasn't troubled you? What about Blunt?"

"Nah—and who's Blunt?"——*Sizar's* used county names for a reason.

"*Yet*," Sqi said solemnly, letting silence slip back and fear shake the voice.

Squire offered no detail on Blunt. It was strange, he thought. As if Sqi had been the one to have been seen arriving late to the beach with a boy found dead there the next morning. He went after his new mate: "How has death pushed you out, Sqi?" He summoned each syllable of his sentence as a clairvoyant would at an all-the-rage-in-this-age séance, with an intent to awaken the airy from the spirit world. And "Sqi" felt right to say aloud now. Intimate—how he should address his companion in words going forward.

"It hasn't…pushed me out," Sqi said still to the flames. "The opposite… *it latches on*, draws me in to it." Sqi was intelligent, perceptive, intuitive… qualities demonstrated by each of the boy's bodily and verbal directives. Sqi's manner told him that Pipe's death had touched with blunt force. "It's late," Sqi snapped away from the flames, as if as the final ditch of a fierce funnel into them, "and I fancy being in the bed nearer the door to-night, if you don't mind." Sqi, who would have ordinarily offered him a choice, took the initiative to skip to the choosing.

"Right you are, we should sleep."

Sqi removed all clothes and climbed into the bed nearest the door. He kept his night-ware on; it was a lie that he preferred to sleep naked, after all, and there was—he loathed to admit to himself—jealousy at sleeping alone that kept him clothed, him now in the bed by the window. They lay awhile in silent, separate beds, save for the dying crackle from the fire. For an hour, it must have been. Sqi might have wondered whether sleep had come for him, but he knew that Sqi lay awake. And when the room was dark as death, when the last light of the fire extinguished, a rustle of sheets into the air like the train of the grim reaper followed swiftly by the fleshy patter of bare feet on the floorboards and familiar flesh being pressed into him. "Is this okay?" Sqi asked once in behind him, their bodies touching again by single-bed necessity.

This time he had an answer: "Does it help?"

"Yes," Sqi replied, pulling him tight—bringing sleep for them both.

Morning row-race training became secondary for him—the whole shot at *Sizar's*, in fact. Secondary to the evenings he spent with Sqi. And he suspected that any such training would have been dramatically more secondary if Pipe had lived. Knowing the fray fibres of his friend as he did, had Pipe survived the pier and therefore not proceeded to Marsh House, he felt it likely he would not have progressed either. Not in the end. In such a scenario, though having proven himself a worthy crew member, some place would have been found for him elsewhere—in the service of Pipe's latest endeavour. Pipe had always taken care of him, afforded him opportunity, but always in tow. Now he was under his own steam. And Pipe was dead…casting his bed-share and host adrift in a mist of melancholy. Macabrely, sharing time there with them—one absently, one intimately—his own mourning seemed…less. As uncaring, unfriendly as it was, he found it hard to wish himself away from Sqi's side.

From pre-dawn to mid-day they rowed under Porter. Sqi was one for the particulars of technique, of learning and applying the correct procedure; while he was more for performance gleaned from experience. A natural at sports, he picked up quickly the base qualities needed to succeed. Not to be the best, not to pose a threat in a serious competition, but with natural qualities enough to prove himself an ample team player. He was an all-trades player, while Sqi was serious, an athlete in a true sense: a stickler for the singular sporting pursuit. And Sqi turned their afternoons over to, singularly, teaching of a different sport. When Porter was gone, they turned themselves to different training, to wrestling, a pursuit in which his bunking-with mate was a champion. They held their sessions on a soft section of the riverbank, down behind the boatshed out of sight of the house and its thousands of glass eyes. It was an alcove bend in the river, where the Thames burst its banks twice a day with the top of the tide, keeping the frost away with the wet and making the ground marshy with its murky waters. It was as close to the malleability of a wrestling-match mat as they were to find, out there, in the Middlesex countryside.

By their third lesson—on the fourth evening at the house—he had a nearing-complete picture of the point of this undertaking, and the stern esteem in which Sqi held their meets. The third wrestle showed the formality of the training, provided a patterned sequence; unfolded the pedagogy to the practice. Sqi had a plan, he came to see. Lesson plans were clear from the first session. That was Sqi's methodical way. But the singular master plan for all their sessions revealed itself to him that fourth night, that third lesson. Darkness started in on the river, breaching the banks like a king tide, sweeping in more wetness than had come the previous nights. The tide not content to stop at the marshy banks, it rose through the gardens and toward the house. They moved their wrestle toward the house but when the burst Thames engulfed the built stone of the formal gardens leaving just the firelight through manor windows like a lighthouse on the storm-swept Cornish coast, this sounded the cessation of their session.

"That first night together—just us," he said as they walked back, the rising water charting a different course for them. A trajectory that would have them pass the boatshed and the path to the house beyond it, new paths that had him choosing words with connotations of intimacy and proximity that were both confusing and deliberate. "Called me y' pick——"

"And told you that the others were a bore, I remember."

"Yeah. But. Y' also said, confess. I wonder…"

"Were you my preference, and the bore-ish character of the rest simply a convenience to cover that up?"

"Yes."

"Yeah."

What the hell happens now? It was entirely too simple an eliciting. Not a confession at all. A mere statement of the facts. But should it have been hard? he wondered as they walked heavy in the wet grounds. They shared a bed and wrestled each day—naked for the former as well as the latter. Wrestling rendered them sweaty and mud-streaked, a mix of sand and ice and dirt on their skin. They wrestled naked. *But!* he went on thinking; this was out more of necessity than some puritanical allegiance to the sport and the conditions of the scholarship qualifier—given their lack of amenities to mud-stain remove any garments they had brought. But…there was pleasure in inhibition-free skin on skin, too.

Returning to the house at only-just dark provided them coverage, as too did the location of said quarters, which were removed, in their own wing; an unused wing of an eccentric gentleman's castle in the sky, in which a domain of their own making had formed. Darkness and diametric accommodations from the rest of the crew and their host and coach were their covers, two conditions they could thank for making their afternoon just-the-two-of-us trainings truly their own. It stood as an advantage of freedom over the majority-crew, he thought. The remaining six, who also lodged in pairs, but in rooms that ran astride each other. There were no private fiefdoms over there.

They haven't the freedom we do, he had come to appreciate.

Then! passing the boatshed that rising water had led them by, a moving, bulk obstruction stretched out across the grass as a silhouette on the lightbox of the storing place for the boats. This lightbox, the boatshed, had been left lit before, sometimes until deep in the night. He knew because from their room he could see it, a sole small barge on the vast black of the estate back, moored at the riverbank—the Thames of which picked up specks of light from the manor if the moon was full, which it was that night. He also knew it was not unusual for light to emulate in a beacon manner, because on the two previous occasions that they had returned to their room by means of stealth—naked and mud-smeared—, Sqi had made a point of altering their two-man convoy to give the light a wide berth. Not possible this night, though, due to the tide...it was as if the boatshed were a spotlight within the confines of an H.M. prison, and each night of their recede was part of a great escape that was only enabled by dodging the light. He was the more partial to risk of the pair, though since arrival he had not much exercised that boisterous side of his character. He flexed it now, breaking formation and setting a course for the window to peer inside. Only to be disappointed with what he saw. Its root being in his recent exertions in the mud.

They had been wrestling for the best part of two hours, were tired and spent—and dirty and cold to the point of ill-health, as addition. They were also both, or so he sensed off Sqi, past the fatigue pressure point. Being in such a state, to peer through the glass of the boatshed was to expect some spectacle much different than the ritual that had worn them out. Like after the purchase of a ticket to a clifftop camera obscura, he was naturally disappointed when what was showing was not a new world, but the same spectacle that had tired them both. Worse. A facsimile of the real thing, a pin-prick picture in a too-bright room. This was his initial feeling on seeing two naked boy bodies entwined. First thought was this: what they had discovered after being forced onto this path by a freak Thames tide was not some tale of intrigue, but two aspiring *Sizar's* boys also pulling in some wrestle training. Except, and worse for it, these two were without the expert tutorship that Sqi-as-champion brought to their makeshift riverside mat. It was a wrestle, no question, a play for dominance of one over the other, of getting on top. But it was fluid, freestyle, messy; and went on much more than a sequence of minutes numbering seven—as he had learned was standard for one period in the game.

The bodies he peered upon were sweat-laced and writhing, with little demonstration of a command of breathing. And watching them confirmed a newly learned critical eye for the sport; yes, missing was what was essential to a professional practice match. He homed in on their faces, to pick them apart. But it was not easy. Their throws were especially entwined; to their credit, these manoeuvres were by his estimation especially advanced ones, if sloppy in their execution. Yes...his esteem for their wrangling ingenuity evolved with the girth of his viewing, as they showed—sloppy as they were—the sorts of takedowns that, he hoped, Sqi was saving for a more senior session of their own lessons. *Yes!* esteem grew with the viewing. Would such moves be as vigorously applied in their own practice? he wondered. He was wistful that they would; these two he was now witnessing had moves more whole-bodied, into-bodied, than anything he had received instruction in so far.

O God, them boys are expert, he thought, and that he did not recognise it as such at first served to only further his reasoning that the boys he was peering upon were performing at a better-though-messier grade. He managed to get a fix on them at an interval when the metronome of their movements reached *largo*, as they lay limp on each other; taking a reprieve. They were Kent men, both. The "III" and "IV," Bernard O'Connor and Joseph Hunt. Of the crew he had observed, these two were the cliquiest—insular in the company of each other, even in Brighton. O'Connor, III, was the brasher, bolder of the two. A typical blood-of-the-Irish type. A simple, rounded face made handsome by a constant smirk and narrowed eyes of disobedience and mischievous disruption. O'Connor was the classic five-eighth of the football team who would easily come in as a second or even first choice for any athletic contest, were it not for a commitment to larrikinism.

Hunt, however, was a classic fourth in the choice-of-one-to-four-in-a-team stakes. A talent, no question. Worthy of picking—younger and more handsome than the Kent three. But not a leader and with a simple character that made him question whether a leader the boy ever would be. Hunt was obedient—a becoming, blond, bit-boneheaded athlete. For all their differ-ence in character, on appearance they could be brothers. Though, as with the character traits between the two, on the question of dominance, of *getting on top*, the winner was obvious. It was O'Connor, and after a brief reprieve, when their faces returned to a blur of wrestle once more, Hunt doubled into a face-down position of must-be-near-impossible recovery from subservience. Only then, in this bent over, bottom position, did the true nature of their wrestle take his focus.

Others…boys other than he and Sqi, it seemed, had founded an own-fiefdom in the Middlesex countryside—and it was not as private.

Now, naked himself, mud-crusted and covered in cold sweat from the rough housing with a teacher of exponential wrestling aptitude…Sqi showed conservatism. Sqi's upper lip stiff with societal etiquette, standing apart in contrast to his own cosying stance. He would not stand back, though; peering through the frosted glass; to see it; to see in…into the boathouse. Taking in every inch of motion.

"We have to leave," said Sqi, the dominant one of his own wrestling show. "*Now!*"

Before he could enquire why, or properly process the true nature of O'Connor's dominance over Hunt—of the method by which O'Connor had managed to pin Hunt's shoulder to the floorboards from behind—sight-lines back to the manor and the steps-descending stride of the housemaster made him heed Sqi's directive to retreat. They ducked down into the darkness of the below-window grass. Sqi gripped his wrist and led them back to the safety of their room. Though he could not help but look back; like Lot's wife from the beginning book…he couldn't resist, and locked eyes with Marsh as recompense for his perverse curiosity.

In looking, he saw: the shadowy, final stage of Hunt's submission wrestle played out like a sinful pantomime. The shadow figures were the show, but he and Sqi sold the tickets. This was why they always avoided the light on the return, as it was a beacon to the house. Their window peep was what drew a crowd, surely—to have appeared as lurking looters.

In looking…in what they saw, they had sealed the advanced wrestlers' fate, drawing authority to them…and Marsh to Sqi and he, too. By looking back, by being unable to resist the forbidden, he exposed them to the lord of the manor, when before they had been just naked shadows.

"*E*very boy here's done it. Ain't nothing but innocent play," he said in Marsh's chambers after being summoned. Chambers, like their inhabitant, that were highly *of the age* and painted-face fashionable—heavily patterned with deep-foliaged wallpaper and furnishings smelling faintly of oil. Marsh was astute; having asked to see them separately, and to see him first. A shrewd move that shook his confidence. *What would Sqi do?* was all he could think.

"I'm not so sure about all that," Marsh said, brow raised even though it clearly pained the man to do so.

O that! Selfishly, in preservation, while under interrogation by the jurisdiction authority, he had thought principally of his own predicament. Caught after dark; naked, sweat-laboured, taking in a spectacle of abomination from a situation of concealment with his lodge-mate in the same state of dirty undress.

"It is open-minded of you to see innocence in that display," Marsh added with exasperation, towing the assumption and seeming to soften by the belief that he had been referring to O'Connor and Hunt rather than himself and Sqi in that plea of innocence. "Perhaps I have misjudged you. You are a good lad. But being a man in my po-osition—I have tied hands, you must understand. Still…what would you have me do?"

Was it possible that his first summons was not as the weaker one, as the shoulder-to-the-mat of the two, but as someone his master wanted to elicit genuine advice from? he held enough hope to wonder. *Protect Sqi*, he thought. It was the least he could do given what their time together had come to mean to him. But…he couldn't condemn the other two either; not after Pipe, who was of the same bent, and whose memory he knew haunted at least one under this roof.

"I ain't see anything but wrestling, sir," he said. "Lewis has been teaching me to wrestle these past few nights. His lessons have been important to me, maybe to make m' sculling suffer. Sorry for this, I'll try harder. But I only saw more wrestling with those other boys. I'll swear it."

Sqi was in there longer, longer by far. Cold crept in and through the room with single beds without his companion. He waited up. He had not much of a choice…sleep since coming here was something shared. And he worried about the distance of it…diminishing further the brevity of his own Marsh meeting.

Sqi entered.

"Thank God," he said. "Why'd ya take so long?" He spoke a little too urgently, he thought, letting the scenario show his anxiety. Their room had driven him there…like a tomb, with the moonlight as the only source of warmth—and a cold companion at that.

Sqi set about attending to the fire that had long passed a languish and said with the encouragement of flames: "It went alright."

"You was an age in there."

"Was I?" Sqi spoke at the register of rarely-pressed recesses of a cathedral organ—sounding dusty and divorced from the whole conversation.

"Yes…" he said, unable to help being caught in the same drift. "I—I—I were worried, mate."

That brought Sqi back. "Sorry to have worried you," Sqi said, chipper again. "But you needn't worry. We have no need to feel shame. Our trespass was merely mild disobedience against the directive to not stay out after dark. Clotheslessness is practically a club requirement and our secretive sporting pursuits pale in comparison to what they were doing."

"I suppose I see." Appeasement swept through, though the biblical parable in Sqi's tone stopped him from attaining relief.

The way he said it must have showed this too…it lured Sqi further, hooking his bedmate's full attention for the first time since the incident. "*Do you?*" Sqi asked, abandoning the fire—probably skilfully enough built to progress to self-sufficiency off its own steam—to leap and land cross-legged on the bed they shared and to face him. Intensity animated Sqi's eyes, glassy and reflective. Beady. Not attractive, but still alluring with their single-focusedness. "Tell me, Thomas. What exactly did you *see?*"

The directness penetrated him; bashfulness pushing out anxiety and rising rosiness up his cheeks instead, like rosewater to the boil. "Buggery," he spat. "But no sin in that." He gave Sqi the truth as he saw it. As it was.

"Time for sleep," Sqi said, and to their separate beds they went. They were both well-spent that night. All sights considered the bed-adjournment was…unfussy, straightforward—in-keeping with their routine. After a time long enough for the fire to start to falter, as its calls for another log went unanswered, Sqi's sheets were thrown back, announcement of an intention to join him in the single bed. Swiftly it was done. From one bed into the other. But there was roughness this time…a bent-on-penetration move in place of an embrace.

It came disjointed rapid——

all part of the single movement into the bed…trying to get into him.

It was desperate. Unskilled. *Dry.* Like a turbine without oil, there was only friction, tearing both piston and cylinder under a steam with pressure that was only building.

He acted fast. Spitting in his palm, reaching behind and between their sweat-laced bodies and grasping Sqi down there, tugging Sqi's length from his entrance with the surprising turning power of a ship's tug. Sqi shuddered under his coating of the head. Firm and throbbing and textured big. And still with a building tension that meant as soon as he slacked Sqi with his fingers, the piston was *in!* fast and all the way to Squire's base.

He cried out. It tore some, Sqi covering his month with a hand, giving him something to bite down on. Breathing became important through it; to last the whole period of the piston's in and out of a seal broken without being run in. It was not okay. It hurt; felt foreign and too-filling and came with a potential for messiness to the sheets that would not be easily cleaned nor explained. But at least it was short, over quick. "I'm sorry," Sqi said at the end, shaking and sweaty, face against his mid-back and still…inside.

"Did it help?"

was all he said.

V
HIGHLANDS

"Can't shake flashes of the face and recollection of the feel of chilled flesh from the beautiful creature of that morning, Porter," Marsh confided to him as they steamed through blizzard snow on a chartered train north to the Royal Highland Hotel in Inverness. The carriages being engine pulled were the "Pullman" prototype; of George Pullman's vision, the industrialist from the New World, that travel by train should be as luxurious as one would encounter on a Cunard or White Star ocean liner—at a time when these companies were themselves looking for ways to make the oceans smaller with larger, faster and more opulent options to cross in. Though the travel times were much shorter, and the terrain to cover much slighter than a transatlantic highway, why should it be any less an "event"?

It was Cohen's time to host, the House of Surrey head of whom had made significant investiture in the Pullman enterprise that year on the Brighton line, with the present prototype poised to proceed to assembly line on British soil by half of the decade to come. A grand hotel, it was, rolling on iron roads. And as with most men of means and the faith—as Cohen was... so devoted that the man should have been of the cloth as well—being pious was made up for in excesses of another regard. As was displayed through the Pullman pleasures the man was introducing to Britain's public, and that they now made passage on to, he had assumed, the second-round contest venue.

As dull as their second host seemed in juxtaposition with the other three game masters, Cohen was not opposed to a good whip in the tail. They were headed to Inverness, but the train that carried them, he learnt from Marsh, *would itself be the venue of competition!* And why not? Was there a view in any hotel on the Isles that could compete with that of this palace on Highlands rails? The course set was through the pelt of snow, past the threshold of what the Roman's considered the end of the known world...was there a better place for the staging of a manly contest?

He was mostly an island in his thinking on whether Cohen's idea was inspired or cruel. His own employer enjoyed the novelty of a train-as-venue, though also regarded it as mean-spirited. To put the tributes to the test en route like this; leaving half of them to not even alight at the terminus; to be sent right on back, without even an unmoving bed for the night. In his near five years in the rôle, he had observed Marsh to be hypersensitive to the plight of the fallen candidates. The man had been predictably eccentric in dealings with him, sporting a liberal mindedness beneath the man's station. A bleeding heart that would have been more at home with the tenor of a poet or philosopher of means, except with a sheltered-ness from the goings-on of the whole of London—a man confined to places where even well-dressed ramblers were required to pay a toll just to pass. With time, Marsh's selfishness had shown through like rotting wood through damp wallpaper. "Matchsticks; first to draw, a chance to choose, to know a match, to draw the short straws. All the matchsticks in my hands, Porter," Marsh ranted. "Goes round n' round in my heart like a relentless, possessed carousel."

He was probably a bit square for the man. Conservatism was bred into him, having come from a father who had done well enough professionally to send him to Cambridge on full tuition; though he never finished, taking up the present post instead. It was a decision that disappointed his father, who ranked athleticism below business. His father's world view made him embrace sport more emphatically, for it was his very own passion, especially when shared with young men along the River Cam...and so were the conditions under which he agreed to join a Middlesex aristocrat as a tutor of sorts, on £50 per annum, the same figure his father had been paying for his education.

He only learned the club was called *Sizar's* after a year in Marsh's employ.

"What will become of O'Connor and Hunt?" he asked his employer, boldly, during a lull in the man's melancholic rant on Piper's pin to the mat.

"Disqualification," Marsh said in seeming disinterest, sights set on the far reaches of see-able white outside, "were it only *up to I*." As Marsh went on, egotism piqued the man's own interest: "And a disqualification *simply so*. But there are other stakeholders to confer with on the matter…other heads, who are pushing for more—more—more judicial courses of action."

Why he found himself on the side of the disgraced boys he was unsure, but on this side, he was: "Surely, as the boys' head, you have the power to decide disciplinary discretion."

"I must tread carefully, Porter," Middlesex said in a tone suggesting irritation at his nerve to question. "An—nd it is a sensitive subject."

He knew the reasons for Marsh's striking at the boys. First, that the boys should be removed because they were caught. It did not matter that what they had been caught doing was more than encouraged through the pairing and room allocations and Marsh's whole damn structure of things. *Pairs, they must be in rooms as pairs*, was the instruction he had been given at Marsh House. And second, the boys should go because they carried on outside Marsh's theatre of intimacy. The rooms in which the boys stayed and washed, he suspected…all watchable from inside the walls—it was for this reason that he always bathed in the dark. In erecting the manor, Marsh had been obsessed with the secret passages and "service quarters" of both castles and other grand country homes. Quarters that he would not put it past Marsh to have been using in all hours of the night; to gaze upon what the man called *personal experiments in team building* the wretched club had brought. Even as Marsh condemned the act O'Connor and Hunt had been caught in, fallen round-one pledge Prett was being bent to same-vein acts.

O'Connor and Hunt; boys of the same team, Middlesex Crew brothers, were facing Broadmoor after Munns and Bishop, originally of the Surrey house, reported their boathouse fuck to their former head at the next Sunday mass. Marsh was also guilty of the boyhunt. Took passionate like and dislike to boys and would not be dissuaded. Lewis and Keeler were two in the man's shadow. As it happened, he struck an instant liking for Keeler in Brighton. *Would I bend Marsh and, if need be, a Scotland Yard detective too, and use the guise of surveillance for an employer to look out for the interests of this boy above the insecurities of Marsh? Mmm, interesting notion that.*

After getting an earful of Marsh woes, he was glad to be out and making his way through the train. The prototype luxuriousness of the carriages gave them a roll on the rails as he imagined the *Mary Rose* would have fared if flung out in a roaring-forties swell—her gunning hatches sealed, to give her a fighting chance. The train—all apart from the locomotive, which was a heavy, solid, British design—was top-weighted with ocean-liner finery but lacking base ballast to bind it to the earth along the London to Edinburgh, East Coast Main Line, and then beyond to Inverness. He bounced off the fine-veneer boards of the main corridor and struggled specially to transit the threshold of carriages, which under weights that were different and ill-uniformly distributed listed to the rhythm of an own northwards waltz.

Marsh had given him little to go on for the Lewis-Keeler stalk; his employer consumed by own-considerations and shaken with a seemingly insurmountable obsession with needs of the self. "Something in the twentieth," he shouted into the snowstorm as he leapt the final threshold to the end carriage of the train. The other tutors relished the out-of-the-way, in-transit qualifier that would free them up for the remainder of the second-tournament time in Inverness: to get to know those who would make up the Surrey Crew and maybe even relax a little. But after Brighton, followed by Marsh House…relax was last on his mind, and buffer time before the Surrey-Highlands serving would have been more welcome.

Voices stopped him in the last carriage. It was a luggage carriage and given the train's prototypal nature was also given over to a cornucopia of luxe interiors. And——*Damn them!*——it should have been silent. He burst in on the boy-sounds compartment without pause or regard. These boys were on his dime, on his neck. He regretted the pact, looking back with anxiety to an encounter at Marsh House in the early hours of the morning following discovery of two boys buggering in the boathouse when, following instructions of his employer, he'd set out to spring upon Lewis and Keeler.

L ast month, at Marsh House... He had been up in-conference with O'Connor and Hunt in the boathouse for most of the night, consoling boys whose into-each-other entanglements had been witnessed. He had spoken with two key witnesses: Munns and Bishop, former Surrey boys, who were making demands for worse-than-disqualification fates for their peers, whose debauchery had been discovered. As if the shame of the sighting and removal from the competition was not enough of a punishment for the poor boys, the Surrey camp was calling for judicial involvement—something that threatened the secrecy of the whole club, and wherein lay the principal concern of his employer. There was talk of Broadmoor as a quieter solution.

After a succession of interviews carried out by his employer already, including of Lewis and Keeler, Marsh instructed him to rouse those boys and find out for himself what the duo saw exactly—an order that was underscored by suspicion from Marsh that Lewis and Keeler were up to their own no good, though without sharing what basis this suspicion had in observable fact. On the topic of all-male "no good" he tended to agree with his employer: there was clearly an intimacy between the west-wing boys. But contrary to his employer's position, from his view hardly any blame could be lumped on the duo, given the ostracising nature of the whole Middlesex countryside experience... Except for groups numbering two, Marsh House could hardly have been called an exercise in team building.

Adrenaline of the early hour and anticipation of what he might uncover behind their door stroked the stag hunter in him. He chose, for instance, not to turn on the newly installed electrical lighting of the hall onto which the Keeler-Lewis dorm door opened. And he chose, too, to tread only along the walls where the iron nails were tightest, rather than in the centre of the aisle where announcement of his arrival was more probable at such an early hour. A nervous sweat moistened him all over as he made passage to their door, with anticipation of what he might find in there. He had full intention to burst on in. To break in the door and allow to pour out any indiscretions of the two of them that he imagined to be going on since arrival.

But before he could act on this impulse to catch, to snare, Keeler made him stop...the thought of Keeler in proximity to the dead boy, more particularly. And with this pause an allowance for privacy and intimacy among boys filled him.

Keeler made him knock.

Crack that twig.

A small, self-deprecating mercy on the moors.

Enough to alert,

to shake off the aim in the crosshairs. To save himself having to make a report back to Marsh or to save another individual in the room, perhaps? Both, probably.

As he had on the first day all three woke in a riparian mansion, he announced himself with a knock and a floor creak then entered. Even with some forewarning by way of slight space between knock, creak and enter, he managed to catch the two this time. It was as he had suspected, but narrowly missed substantiating on first summons. He caught Lewis! Already one leg on the boards when the door swung in, the cover held high, frozen there, like a stag in the forest on hearing the under-boot crackle of twigs from a hunter preparing to strike. The boy flinched, conveyed concern in the heat of catchment, but soon recovered calm; the tautness in the athlete's face straightening to the sternness that he had only ever known. That he could only presume Keeler found comfort in. And with this relax, so came, too, a fall of the covers to the bed, and an alignment back to two boys in single-bedded recline.

"This is most irregular," he said, disliking the choice of words, but impressed in the confident way they were phrased.

To his surprise, Keeler spoke first. "It's cold," the boy said in a voice deep and unaffected. "You look like a military fellow. We're sharing body heat. Tell me, *coach*, what's irregular in all that?"

It cut through him; brought the face he had been thinking of but avoiding into moonlit profile. It surprised him, challenged his assumptions of the dynamic. Of Lewis as the one in control. The strong one. Keeler spoke without any apparent fear, without regard for consequences of the spotting. Okay, yes, that was strange. But what defied all reason to him was that Keeler spoke without shame...being caught in a compromising position so soon after bearing witness to an indisputable display of sodomy. And to have confidence, and challenge to the accusation, even, as well as no shame... It turned him about.

"You're out to-day," he said, skipping over all the exposition he had rehearsed. "We all are. You won't see each other again until the regatta."

He turned to leave but Keeler's voice stopped him. "Round two, the second challenge. Where is it?"

"I don't know," he said to the dark hallway, "none do, none except Surrey."

I shouldn't have said that! It had been coaxed out of him, he told himself, but how?

"You will know, you will be there," Keeler continued.

"Yes."

"Get us there, coach. Both of us. Get Lewis and me both in. Can you do that for me, *Port?*"

His coach, now his Port. How the boy turned him about. He turned back to the room, warm with their body heat, smelling of boy bits and a view of the boathouse from their window. A stench of his own most private moments of a lonely single bed. It was most peculiar. The effect that Keeler's features made on the combination of the face, even in the low light of morning. Keeler's lips were soft, like dough, they sloped gently on each side into a cushioned, resting frown. Eyebrows bold and bushy and pinched at the bridge of the nose protruded over eyes an ashen green. Keeler was a severe boy, stern. Such features would probably only grow brasher with age; but now, they made his boy beautiful.

"Yes," he said against all regard-for-self reason, taken over entirely by a need to please the Keel boy.

I n the Highlands Express… Shoulder to the centre-wood panel and twist of the brass knob granted him access to their speeding-through-blizzard room; into quarters cramped close by the odds and sods of discarded decoration from the train experiment. Part of the host's personal Pullman prototype, a rush through the corridors revealed a different character for each carriage: Parisian wintry plush for one, Tudor classic blacks and whites for another. In the final "storage" carriage, the result was an all-sorts array of offcuts, misfittings and space furnishings. There was not the room for accommodations in this final car—not meant to be. But it would do for two stowaway boys, and service his promise to one of them.

They had made do quite nicely, banded together a bed of sorts from rugs and furs of all dye, fabric and animal. It looked cosy but regal, like the bedchamber for a royal on the Continent, travelling on what he imagined a cabin on the *Orient Express* might look like. It had no headboard, of course, though this was no barrier to invention. For lumbar support, Lewis had padded together what curtain materials were available, while Keeler reclined on the other's front—sinking into Lewis' chest. Such closeness was not appropriate, was exactly what he had intended to freeze in frame with the spring through the door. But they did not move when discovered…

"I could hear you practically from the front carriage," he said in a whisper with all the agitation of a shaken hive. A wholly unnecessary—and probably inaudible for the most part—whisper, falling under the blizzard and the sounds of wheels on rails. *Don't be their footplate. Speak up, you damn fool.* "If you can't keep silent, I suggest you separate for the rest of the journey."

"Won't be necessary, coach," Lewis said, bending forward and taking Keeler along with.

It was not that Keeler was smaller, their frames were nearly equivalent. But Lewis was firmer, in action and in stature. And when Keeler's softer frame moved under the other's direction, he could not help but feel like he was being tugged too. Like Lewis tended the twine that could bend him in any which way the athlete liked. And being called coach made it worse, putting further distance between himself and the two regatta pledges on their couple-made bed...worse when spoken by the wrong one, that is.

"Just remember what we agreed. When we stop, wait until I come to get you, to let you know that all have alighted, then you are on your own. Though why you would want to come in the first place boggles me."

"Of course, we'll behave," Lewis said, reclining with Keeler again as if they were joined at the point of chest and between-shoulder blades. "But——"

"What?"

"Share some insight, coach. It is why, after all, we have come."

"Insight on what?"

"Let's start with the boathouse boys," Lewis said. "Tell us. What will be their fates?"

Damn suspicious, that is. That these two should be so reckless to risk their own places in the summer regatta sunk like iron in his mind; risk the chance at a life-changing bursary to bear witness to the forum where the future of other contenders of a different team was up for contention. Especially, given, he suspected, even the names of the boys in question eluded them. Or more to his challenge point, eluded Lewis.

"O'Brian and Henrys, you mean?" he said.

Lewis' stayed smiling with a sink back further, finding more space for Keeler to sink with. "Naturally," Lewis answered, confirming suspicions.

"Given the circumstances, I don't believe I should comment further," he said. "Wait for me to summon you, remember."

"Please, mate," Keeler spoke up, drawing forward on an individual power. "I know you have taken on risk for this, but we have too. Tell me."

That face. Again. Its haphazard mix—that couldn't age well. But in youth, was, beautiful...how it beckoned him.

"The boat boys, O'Connor and Hunt, *actually*, their fates are collective," he said, with a sigh under the sound of steam from the engine—and for Keeler, he divulged: "Collective and undecided, though it looks like the best they can hope for is disqualification. If they get that they should count themselves lucky. What they did was reckless."

"Reckless, aye. But were it wrong?" Keeler asked, plainly, steady-deep voice, doe eyes under a bushy, furrowed brow.

He seems to genuinely want to know my answer.

Lewis watched them both with an expression that was impossible to read.

Does Keeler realise, he wondered. *Am I that transparent?* He said: "What I think matters, does not matter. It has no bearing."

Keeler replied: "It matters to me."

It was suddenly imaginable what not having Lewis there would be like. Were it just he and the Keeler boy. And this image came as a hot tingling all over: "Well, right, alright then. I am inclined to view the boat-boys incident more as an extension of natural horseplay."

Lewis broke into laughter and responded in a way that was both out of school and showed an above-workhouse class: "You're a study in open mindedness, Porter. I certainly didn't see that opinion coming. I take it few others share your progressive perspective on manners of boy bonding?"

He regretted it, red rising over him like a battlefield rash. "Middlesex supports expulsion but no further action while Surrey is torn between his faith and sympathy for his original tributes, seeking a way for the boys to be treated without endangering the rest of the club. There's talk of Broadmoor."

"And the other two heads? Essex…and Kent. What does Kent think?" Lewis probed, bending forward and by action, Keeler too—as if Lewis' words had grown fainter with the release of what was now known, making closer conversation necessary.

"Essex is keeping out of the matter."

"Naturally," Lewis nodded, a trace of earlier laughter. "And Kent?"

"And Kent…yes, you're keen on Kent, aren't you, Lewis? Well, I—I—I'm not sure. I don't see how he factors in here, frankly."

"Quite," Lewis said, drawing back, laughter all gone and resuming the position that he had found the lad in on door entry.

He turned back on Keeler, feeling betrayed for having been led to let his guard down, and asked as self-preservation (*or is this again in aid of the Keeler boy?*): "I'm taking a great risk here, and there's been a detective sniffing around…has he given you any bother?"

"No," Keeler said, so deadpan it could only have been genuine.

"He's made no attempt to contact you?"

"None."

Damn suspicious, that is.

"Why should a detective be in touch. It was an accident," Lewis said.

He turned to leave, but Lewis stopped him:

"One more thing, coach. The heads, what carriages are they in?"

A look from Keeler led his give-in to hesitation. Again. He told them and left after saying by way of softening: "I'll call in on you after dinner…with some food," more to Keeler, really, before sealing the two back to the private-folly-train bedroom of their own making.

Mason; Edwards; James; Parker. So was the roll call of the Middlesex round-two contenders, lined before him in the dining portion of their county's carriage—fourth from the front. Trains are modern instruments of social ordering, and it was true for this one, too. Only, in this case, augmented by a Surrey world view. The *Highlands Express* was a standard six carriages, but double engine pulled; testament to the absurd embellishment of the Pullman prototype that had been modified to Surrey's heavily evangelical specifications. It was a social showpiece. Carriage one was for Kent, assigned as, surely, a gesture more of prideful admiration than any Christian politeness. Surrey hero-worshipped Kent, that was plain to all. The business of sorting took place in the third carriage, while Surrey's own county occupied the second. This required Kent's own tributes—all sourced, as usual, off the football fields of Cambridge's community outreach program—to pass through Surrey's carriage en route to competition.

At times Kent rewarded Surrey's devotion with tribute offcuts to help make up the Surrey team. Surrey prized such discarded boy bunchings as the least interested in the time demands of recruitment. And when this happened, Surrey would always run as first billing in the Surrey lineup any the man had received through Kent. As had been the case with Munns for the first round that year, who secured a spot on his own team's shell. Middlesex was first up after the tournament car, which he suspected fine-tuned a dual strategy: the near-central arena creating a clear head divide, a teams-on-teams contest—Kent-Surrey versus Middlesex-Essex—, done so by stealth. If questioned, Surrey could have easily argued that the division was a matter of convenience. In such stakes, Middlesex appeared to receive favour, being closest to the action, as did Surrey, naturally, as host of this round. Though even under such a save-face scheme, Essex came last—located just before the storage carriage. The detritus of odd furnishings that Essex and the weakest man's four may have stumbled upon could have given that team ammunition to criticise the quality of the finish on this novel instalment in the contest qualifier; this is if Surrey had cared what the man thought. He let Marsh know his opinion on Surrey's train configuration, though he did not let on about his discomfort with the selection of qualifying pursuit: fencing.

Fencing was not a sport of which he was especially familiar. *Sizar's* heads tended to stay with their chosen combat: Middlesex (Marsh) with wrestling, Kent (Blunt) with boxing, Essex (Peele) with a sprint and Surrey (Cohen) with a swim. The society's history had shown Surrey as the most inflexible to change. The announcement that for the second qualifier the boys would duel by sword was therefore causing somewhat of a sensation, certainly among Essex's tutor and himself. The non-hosting heads, however, settled into the idea, having little personally to lose by virtue of it not being their team that would be formed at the end of the two nights. In fact, he observed, there was generally little concern shown by the heads this round compared with the first. *Good man!* he recalled Marsh exclaiming with the news that fencing would settle the Surrey Crew, *now that's an embrace of the spirit of the twentieth year.*

As the one who in practicality needed to teach it to the Middlesex pledges, he was decidedly less enthused. He saw it like this: The qualifier was the mark of the head who had chosen it. There was a philosophy to it. The qualifying activity was not simply a means to separate the fittest, nor was it—certainly not in Marsh's case—chiefly a means for the hosting head to try and triumph by way of having all four players put forth as the strongest make it onto the final team of eight. No mistake, there was a success in such a hosting strategy, and a pride of practicality, which is why, generally, the rounds would see better selection by the hosts in their chosen qualifier sports—Blunt's best boxers or Peele's best track-and-fielders—being served up in the respective head's sorting rounds.

But, too, there was a pleasure to be had in poaching talent from other houses. Oddly, this seemed to some as the more gentlemanly pursuit. In this case, fresh talent whose talents in the manly pursuits that were dearest to that host could arise in the arena by boys the heads had not themselves selected. *Such a treat*, as Marsh might say on the eve of a regatta with a team made up of prime poachings. And what better example was there than round one of the present year, where Marsh's team—admittedly, mostly rowers—secured just two of the eight Middlesex Crew slots. And more remarkably still, that the boy to display the most natural accoutrement for the task at hand, the rawest display of true wrestling prowess—the kind that couldn't be taught—, would be snatched away from Middlesex as a prize; first from a place on the crew, then from the earthly realm as well.

There were other anomalies to this competition, too. Anomalies that were discordant also with his own experience of how rounds worked with respect to the head playing host. Anomalies that spoke of something in the peculiarity of a twentieth year: The shock of Peele, for example, who offered up Piper and, as second mate to the dead, his splendid Keeler. Not equal to Piper, some ways off Piper's measure. But a raw wrestling talent, too. And wholly, consumingly, compelling… *But why those boys from Peele in that round?* he found himself snagged on. Peele was usually so transparent. That's why in this instance he couldn't reason why the man put forth players for a Middlesex round who were likely to secure spots in the final. And more pressingly the point: how did Piper fall to Lewis? The latter a talent, no doubt, a master of the technique. But with nothing of the rough-edged stamina that were the makings of a master of the game. The death was already labelled as suspicious—something that, judging from Lewis' mention of an accident, showed that the death's suspicion was clearly not known to all. But the pressing suspicion for him presently was one that stretched back to well before Brighton as an arena was even announced and was being embodied now in the novelty of the Pullman contest venue.

There is something of the setting of a stage in all this, as he had told Marsh on the invitation for him to share his thoughts on trains as a sorting venue. In round one it was Peele who shook-up expectation; this time it was Cohen who surprised by departing from convention while at the helm. Cohen was unconventional, certainly; an eccentric, but the kind that was usually knowable. And the last any would expect to stray from expected selection of sorting exercise, let alone venue type—usually swimming at a grand hotel or similar. Particularly strange it was to select an exercise of Germanic extraction; as, though the late Prince Consort had succeeded in importing a good number of German customs into English society, Surrey house was a stickler for the preservation of the home-front manoeuvres. Nomination of fencing may have risen his employer to excitement, but it left him not at all comfortable and with little knowledge of the rules of engagement, nor even of how practising with the four of his house on a carriage amid a blizzard sway may play out. If the surprises of Brighton were anything to guide upon, this twentieth year would be anything but standard and he would need to prepare his house pledges as best he could.

Round two's Middlesex house contenders were all fine enough fellows, if a little too rough, too of the poor house. Nothing of the calibre of the round-one candidates, he thought. Their arms were ample enough to suggest they could, with some training, be turned to rowing; Marsh told him they were selected and offered as gifts for Cohen—and presumably, it would be the same for the other two, too. Or so the Marsh story went. But he didn't buy that. It wasn't all philanthropic motives from Marsh. As he saw it, there was convenience in Marsh sourcing rower-turned boys…it was the man's hobby, collecting boys of a type; like Blunt with footballers and Peele with sprinters, though perhaps Marsh's own notions of modesty prevented the seeing of such easements in the man's own recruiting. Yes, the Middlesex round-two four possessed upper and body-core strength that was aptly and naturally turned to rowing (and wrestling tuition), though fencing called upon less-congruent competencies. Their prospects were made worse by the prepositions of their instructor—being an upper-bodied-muscular athlete, he had no knowledge of the sport other than that it ushered from the Germanic kingdoms...and even on that point he was not certain.

In such an instance, the other tutors often came into play. The others who, in some ways——

strike that——

in most, grappled with greater inter-group estrangement than their masters. Of course, they did: they were echoes of their employers' egos. He had always thought they were even similar in appearance and mannerisms. Cohen's tutor, Simon Brown, was the picture of a provincial vicar. Freckled with ginger hair that was always wet-balmy and hard-part-forced straight at the scalp-line, ending in a crumpled wave at the tip. Brown's face, as with physique, was contradictory. Stern aspects flattening out softness, like a devote Irishman playing to the protestant pull. Fencing was most certainly further beyond the abilities of Brown than his, which was some relief. *Actually!* he figured he was—at risk of puffing up his own abilities too much—best equipped of the four to improvise tutorage of the sport.

Arthur Underhill, that was Blunt's tutor, was a footballer to the exclusion of most else—in body and head. Underhill was a clinical giant, surely, with a head that seemed twice the size of a football, oversized ears that protruded beyond what they should, and a neck that swelled to the shoulders in a gentle gradient that gave little distinction of brain-casing from torso. The rules of football were Underhill's only perceivable claim to fore-planning, the man's brute bodily force, a sole strategy. This turned the Kent house tutor alright to wrestling, for Underhill's competence in using an immovable force upon an opponent—and to Blunt's own common-choice challenge of boxing, where having a head for blows was an undeniable advantage…less so did such characteristics give Underhill a head for a sport of nimble-footedness.

That only left Peele's tutor, the long and gangly Wayne Tanner, of Essex house. Of the tutors, he and Tanner had the greatest tenure—which, really, was not that long…his five years to Tanner's six. Marsh was a stable employer in this regard—all of his predecessors had left cordially and on their own accord, though a penchant for favouritism was creeping in through the most recent appointments. Granted, Blunt's and Cohen's legacy tutors were generally own-accord departures as well—and tended to last three years at least before the demands of their heads exhausted them to the point of moving on. Tanner's longevity in the rôle, he had come to learn from his employer, was a blue moon.

Peele has shown an interest in you, Marsh had told him at the end of his first year, *and may make advances to engage you, to poach you for service to him instead. If he does, I suspect this would be more for personal duties than professional ones, and I would advise caution.*

He had always heeded the advice, keeping his distance. Though Tanner's tenure had proven Marsh's theory flawed—something his employer admitted over port at the end of only his second year:

It seems Peele has found some stay with this one, with Tanner, Marsh had said. *It is the first time in Sizar's history, you know, that Peele hasn't severed ties with the services of a tutor after just one year.*

Before Tanner, Essex house tutors were laughed about as one-season-only boys, Marsh had explained—though on what specific occasion he could not recall. Like a fussy feline, Peele was notorious for becoming obsessed with securing certain boys to run the teaching of Essex house. Peele would pursue the ones wanted relentlessly, sometimes for years…until they would eventually concede and take up the post…by which time Peele had already locked sights on a newer, shiner piece of silvery flint, and dropped the present tutor as soon as a new counsel was confirmed. There was even a rumour, floated on the drift-down gossip of the Kent and Surrey house tutor alumni (who it was rumoured met in a bar in the back alley of Cambridge known only to the exes), that Peele would have the outgoing tutor killed, by contract, to keep the pseudo-man's secrets. Such speak was the stuff of campfires and devil-characterising of "tricksters" like Peele, he realised.

Trickster: or so men like Peele were often called. Those who made feigning attempts to divert attention from their sleight-of-hand, and their partiality to persons of their same sex. The tricks of such men as were carried out in plain sight. He saw such speak as…unnecessary; and felt no appetite himself for further demonising a man who was, while monied, outside the social order—frail of frame and fortitude; frailty increasing of late with scarring to the face, too. And Tanner's longer stay had shored-up ill-regard for idle-character mucking. Tanner had proved a tutor there to stay. And looked the part. Coach matched master's face; was elongated. Like the athletes Peele was most likely to court, Tanner had the appearance of a sprinter, a man in constant envy of the track—with its white lines that made all decisions reflex driven.

He relayed his views on Tanner and the other tutors to Marsh on the train, who made no illusion about why they were elicited:

I shall share your perspectives with the detective inspector in fullness when I am back in London, Marsh had said. *He shall be coming to stay with me, for some time I expect. We have history together, you see, but on that I shall speak no more.* Marsh said it stroking angry cuts on the face—*a mugging in London*, the man had said…a matter on which the detective inspector was also assisting. Marsh had requested the account before the train, after their country training session had come to a premature conclusion: *Prepare your assessments before our next session. Who better to tell the characters of the tutors than an 'ld lad among them?*

It was then that his employer had looped him in—*to be my eyes.* Marsh said that personally there was no reason to consider him a suspect, though the detective inspector would explore all avenues. *He has a theory*, Marsh had divulged in the man's manor on the Thames, that the Piper death was a "statement"; *on what though, he could not be sure*——puffing on cigar——*perhaps the limber lad's trade as a boy whore, or Sizar's itself. The inspector thinks*——Middle-sex had gone on, eyes darting with the dance of the flames in the fireplace of the Grand Hall of Marsh House…a fireplace that was set in the centre of the hall, like the hearth of a Norman castle alone on a barren moor——*that the killer is most likely to be a man who will be on the scene for each step of the whole year, rather than one of the victorious or defeated boys of my first round. And thinking that——* shuffling from a padded chair to the port decanter and refilling the glass, in slippers perhaps too tight and a dressing gown that, really, should have been more modestly fastened——*that*——back in the folds of the chair——*that means four and four in the suspect pool. Four heads and each of their tutors. Now—and yes, he did vocalise this—the detective inspector does not see me as a suspect, and I will go a further step with you, Porter, and declare my faith in you, too.*

Thank you, sir, he had responded.

This "thank you" in the past had served to steal his employer's attentions from the fire-dance long enough for Marsh's eyes to focus and acknowledge him there. *Quite right,* Middlesex had said. *Gratitude, yes. Well, you have been reliable.* Though by this last line the fire had drawn his employer back. *Anyway,* Marsh resumed, *I shall probe the other heads as you, Porter, take charge of the tutors. Though, personally, I feel that there is a simpler solution; daresay among some of the better names of my own Cam crew. The Lewis boy…and from once a good family, probably put up to it by Keeler…* And then the man trailed off, as Marsh often did when hard banked to port, sketching out villains of a muddled mind.

His task was set that night in Marsh's Norman-style keep. He was to canvas for leads among the tutors while Marsh probed for motive among the heads. Meanwhile, of course, carrying out his duties. Quite natural-ly, the amateur murder investigation had distracted his coaching; bent it by the knowledge that one boy he helped smuggle on board this train was under suspicion for the death of a contender from the previous round. Also, that in comparison to wrestling—where bare hands, brute strength and cunning manoeuvring were the tools—this round's manly pursuit utilised actual weaponry. *The choice of challenge does not bode well for Cohen as an innocent party,* he thought, part of him wondering whether another slaying would take place on the *Highlands Express*, this time by sword rather than the bare brute force of hands in pincer. *O yes!* then there was the revelation that Piper was a boy whore. *Quite a well-known one, Porter.* Marsh had said. *By devil, infamous! Though on that I say no more.* How did this all sit with the recent bouts of buggery, he wondered.

P ing! ping! clashing sword strikes rung out through the centre section of the *Highlands Express*, rising above the bass-y rumble of the roll and roar of the train on an iron-blizzard road like frantic fiddles at the climax of a suspense-filled orchestral score. It was early in the sorting but already two from Middlesex house had competed, both making it through to the Surrey Crew. Already his house had matched its home-ground success, which he put down to the favourable bending of the oarsmen-built to the wielding of a sword. He could not give himself any credit, for he had been distracted in training his boys—a distraction that spilled over to his watching them compete. The summons from his head was the cause for his distraction; acting as an undercurrent might on the belly of a boat being rowed; drawing his stroke off kilter, rendering his direction, askew. As the boys had when he watched that naked competition down south, Piper and Keeler drew him in; but this time the mystery of the Essex number one was greater, as he joined the hunt for the boy's killer. Naturally, in his mind, there was a focus on the first round; the one to produce the body. But as with a good mystery, and mindful of another foretelling of the absent detective—that such a culprit will likely strike again—the draw of the search for Piper's killer found more present distractions.

Marsh had clipped his scope to the questioning of his fellow tutors— having enlisted his help to search out a suspect among them—but the pull of the mystery turned his talents to other players, too. To powerful players. To speculate on *Sizar's* heads. These men were beyond his grade...yet they were there, more able in opportunity, and—if the detective inspector was right in intuition—one of them was good-chance implicated, and thus able to strike again. So began a rotary of potential head-guilt in his mind. Starting with Cohen who, just now, was two-for-two through as well. A second Surrey-house win signalled a cessation of the contest and an adjournment for dinner in the rear of the contest carriage. Though it was by no means standard for Surrey house to succeed in sorting contests, there were home-soil advantages elevated by a surprise selection of this challenge that gave Cohen ample chance to select candidates best suited. *No*, he resolved internally as the call of dining started to show effect, *I see no suspicion there.*

He saw little cause to pause on Blunt, either. Admittedly because the man had been the most amicable to him. A sportsman through and through who was known to him, too—from his short time at Cambridge. Blunt had veered from course in the first round by selecting a wrestler as lead: Lewis. But this was strategy, given the predictability of wrestling as the challenge Marsh must choose; and it had worked, too, with Lewis pinning Piper—though how exactly Lewis managed it, he still could not see. It could be said by the same strand of thought that Peele was employing strategy, too; in bringing to the game Piper and Keeler in the first round. But he was soon to discard this line of belief on face value, for Peele was a different head-proposition entirely.

This round, with two in and none through, Essex house was performing true to form. Peele had never won a regatta, and House of Essex "contenders" were scarcely those one would want to form a crew—and they scarcely did. Round one's Piper and Keeler broke from tradition in spectacular fashion— something that, he noticed, quite riled Blunt in the aftermath, who perhaps felt outshone by the stunt. Piper, exceedingly; Keeler, his personal preference, more modestly. That Piper in fact fell first at the Royal Pavilion was near as shocking as the wonder boy's discovery the next day; shocking even to Blunt, the victorious Lewis' head—if Blunt's expression and cold reception to Lewis' win were any signs to tell of the normally unflinching man's state of mind. These were his amateur-detecting observations. But more profoundly from his own world view as a trainer of boys was how exactly Peele had managed to acquire such stock as Piper and Keeler, so aptly suited to that first task. That was the greater suspicion.

With all now assembled and sat down for food at the rear of the contest carriage, he was struck by how unorthodox it all was; for dinner to come like this—when exactly half the contenders still had a fate unknown. Though, he supposed, it was crueller still towards the defeated, the odd one—perhaps two—who seemed to choose to dodge the embarrassment of the meal, given the numbers; gone to hide away, he figured, on a train on which, after arrival, they would be left to return home on. *I should make note of who is missing,* he told himself, *and of the location and accounting-for of all the sabres. Should, well, one end up in the next Piper.*

But set intention did not progress to a plan. After a short sketch of the boys competing did not bring up any to his mind who could be the missing numbers, he let the instinct to catalogue the scene fall to the side. The faces before him were just too new. All he could register was Blunt nipping out for a short time. To use the lavatory, or perhaps in search of the missing number of competitors—either way, not that long really. Slightly longer was Marsh, perhaps, who he knew was prone to a proactive bladder. *None here are in any danger,* he thought, *uncoiling the clue in his mind like it was a brightly foiled foreign sweet. Because there are no other Piper boys among this crew.*

He did not take note of who was missing because, well, there was nothing extraordinary about the group of strangers brought to bear in manly pursuit this time. Other aspects of the present situation failed to grip him, too. Not the train—over-laden with extravagance—nor the body-piercing weaponry could entice his attentions, so why should any of these boys stir the interests of the killer? *Except!* he remembered in a sudden hot flush, for two others he had helped stow away on board, who had direct, intimate contact with the deceased, and who had been standouts of the last competition themselves... and just then he saw them, passing by the porthole glass of the corridor.

There was sizeable delay between the two boys.

Five

full

passes

of the train's length, at least.

Lewis passed first. Ghost-like, appearing to float. Lewis paused at the inner-carriage window, the face glassy, looking in—as if expecting to be looked at. Lewis saw past him, like he wasn't even there, like the boy sought out something else, another ghost in the room. Lewis looked in with empty eyes, dead eyes. After Lewis was gone, he would have put it down to an hallucination, his murder-mystery-ridden mind conjuring up characters for him to chase…

That was until Keeler followed, to make it all spine-tingling real. Frantic and without pause Keeler passed the door. He felt relieved of his senses, like he was at a banquet one thousand strong wherein a battle was raging, and none even noticed. His eyes darted the room, searching for clues that others, too, had seen it—heard the clamour of running feet, at least. But none had seemed to.

He excused himself in a kind of drunken attempt at nonchalance.

He then entered the corridor and commenced the pursuit in the direction of the boys' heading, which was towards the back of the train—where they had made their bed. He coursed through the carriages like a virus through the veins. The blizzard had built to an intensity that, though thoroughfare between carriages was facilitated by a cantilevered bridging section, it shouldn't have been. Were this a standard evening service, attendants would have certainly locked the doors between the carriages. Each time he ventured into the space between the cars he found himself blown back by an unwelcoming barrage of wet blades, tiny shards of ice spun up by the storm and pelted against him. Like warning shots across the bow of a clipper.

They were not in sight. And yet he was sure of their bearing. Something in the dual expressions of emptiness and tremendous adrenaline drove him toward the rear of the train. Through the carriage assigned to Middlesex house then the one for Essex house then the storage carriage, where he had assigned the stowaways—and instructed them to stay put—, right through to the final door of the train. His mad rush to get there made him forget that this was the end of the line. He burst out the door expecting to tread foot on the plate of a connecting carriage.

He found only air instead.

The adrenaline running through him turned to a burn, a hypodermic injection of toxic serum.

But he did not meet his end on the sharp edge of ballast of a stretch of Scottish track. He caught himself on the chain under which his body had almost shot clear through. It happened at speed as an action of pure survival instinct a devote man would probably call divine intervention.

The adrenaline commenced a recede...he caught his breath, his whole body wet and blue from the blizzard blades. Like opium it had reached its high, and with nowhere further to lead him the adrenaline drew back... Sense took its place and with it a condemnation of self—for having been so foolhardy in the pursuit. *But I had been certain*, he thought, as his pulse steadied and the sensation of the below-freezing metal of the chain he clambered to made itself known to the palms that gripped it. He had been sure that this was the destination of those boys' desperate gambit. As he tore skin away from the chain that had saved him, and the danger of a high-speed train through Highlands mountains settled in, he discovered that he was right... this plate at the end of the *Highlands Express* was indeed the terminus for the boys' dash through the train; but in place of two there was now only one.

Keeler prevailed...balled up in the inner corner of a winged platform behind where the door would have swung open when he shot out.

Urgency of purpose returned as he shuffled toward the survivor, knowing what Keeler would say even before the boy spoke.

"Dove right off," Keeler cried, eyes now empty, too. "Out and over—it were a' if the edge were some pier on' a great lake."

Another pier!

Keeler framed the self-murder in a romantic fashion. But the boy's bodily frame trembled with grief.

He took his survivor in his arms, feeling muddy for relishing this moment of intimacy. Since the incident in Brighton—the one where the boy in his arms leapt forward to tend to an injury of another competitor, preventing cauliflower of the ear—he had longed to take the boy in his arms. And though shivering and wet, Keeler smelt still more lovely than he imagined. "I've got you," he said, pulling the neck of his prize into his nostrils for a deep taste.

VI

GRAND

The engine wheezed after a late arrival into Scarborough, whose station was built back from the sea—where he, the detective's deputy, nay fuck-thing, was due half one hour ago. Scarborough as a seaside spot was a dramatic proposition. From the shore the town perched precariously atop limestone cliffs that from their precipice continued in rising slope inland to where this terminus was built. The railway station, therefore, was set back some ways from the waterfront and atop-cliff promenade; locomotives of which had not a liking for gradients so steep. Eager to make up for lost time, he made his way with haste through the sloping streets of Scarborough. They inclined to the sea like river veins toward a multi-fed waterfall. Now fully dark in the town, time creeping on third quarters past the hour of his appointment, he quickened his pace even more—the worn leather of his boot soles slipping on the thin sheet of ice that coated the cobbles.

Scarborough's river streets that inclined toward the sea were empty that evening. Not uncommon this time of year; not unusual for a resort town with the summer season still a distant hope away. Even more so than Brighton, which benefited from London trade, Scarborough was a straight-up seasonal spot of sun and sand, thronged with the leisure classes during the summer, but ghostly in the other quadrants of the year, when recreation was sought on the warmer southern shores. The path to his appointment was a winding one, like again the bends in a river, but the general incline of the passage helped guide his way to where he was going. And as soon as he cleared the block-out of Georgian buildings, the Grand Hotel stood as a scene-filling backdrop—rising up as he rounded the final bend before the cliff-edge promenade and lit up like some mighty liner teetering on the brink of oblivion, at the edge of the known world.

Teasingly close to tumbling off the limestone cliffs and into the sea… but equally a building so impossibly, immovably large the Grand was, so as to command a force all of its own. It pulled the sea into it, perhaps with the enlist of the secret services of the moon, which that night had been consumed by the gloom of an icy, unseasonably frigid spring. The Grand Hotel was the town's latest landmark; even so, there was an ancientness to its entrance. Three arches, the centre the largest, were the portal to its inside. This entrance was less a welcome than a gateway into another world. What townsfolk there were about in this spa town in its off-season, seemed to congregate at the Grand entrance.

What drew them out of their dwellings that night? he wondered.

It was as if they were called upon to watch some nocturnal spectacle: sparks of light, or the launch of a new ship. These locals lined the peripheral of the freshly cobbled street that fronted the entrance of the Grand Hotel. But encased in the crowd, it surprised him to find, were less local-looking folk. Could only presume, of course, but they appeared to be prostitutes and the destitute, pulled from the triad of the industrial heartland cities of Manchester, Sheffield and Leeds. From their faces, they appeared to have… floated in, possibly, from the Russian industrial port of Novorossiysk…drifted in on the incoming tide…caught in the current of this grand building and drawn to something indescribable amid the frigid nights of a cliff-side town's *something's off* season.

It rrreeks of home, he spoke under his breath, so softly that it may have only been audible in his mind. A stench of the spiritual realm; something within which he had been developing some interest of late. *Zerrre be spirrrits herrre*, he added, a ripple of the spine and a spit upon the cobble stones. He waded through the bumbling non-gentry to ascend the stairs toward the panelled glass that would fold into the Grand Hotel, doing so with trepidation like one might at the threshold of some sacred burial chamber. Careful not to stir some invisible hex across the line of its opening. Columns rose each side of his ascent; these were—to his untrained eye—a confusing mix of Classical and Gothic styling, and ornately scrolled; they accompanied him like trees would horse-drawn transport through a trek to a tucked-away country manor house—not quite in-keeping, somewhat alien. The drifters—those otherworldly, whorish folk that had been brought in by the tide—bobbed together at the base of the flight like swollen-dead toad fish. Smelly and off-putting, and potentially poisonous to the touch. He felt their sunken eyes on him like the judgment of a primitive-island-parish congregation at the arrival of a chaplain who the tribe did not trust being versed enough to be there. It was pure projection, of course—he had only got there by offering himself as a buggery orifice, after all.

I'm whorrre, he said with a wicked smile that tempted a hexing.

Now that he was being sent to perform in some more public-professional function, he felt the full phoney. These bobbing beings, if they even existed outside of his fevered vision—he had conjured up stranger manifestations before—were there surely to point out his not-meant-to-be-there failings. They carried to him feelings of being one of them even as he pretended, under instruction of his benefactor, to be something else. His London life had been one built of his tight body and talent for bending men to tend to his needs. He hadn't banked on snagging a detective who would give him a real job to do.

Zey see thrrrough me.

On climbing, the Grand Hotel drew his eye skyward toward the rush of lit-up rooms with lights that shrunk toward the top and into the starlight. Nearest above him, carved upon the keystone of the central arch was an anchor with its roping entangled, a clam shell at its top and, above that, at the summit of the Grand Hotel's entrance decoration, Poseidon's trident. Strong and stern as a seaman's cautionary tale, of the monsters of the deep oceans that land-dwellers relegate to myth.

Is varrrning?

He paused under it. In the dimly bright night of a spring arrival, he saw the face of foreboding there. In the lantern light, stood under the arm and flukes of an anchor forming an angry chin, a rope-caught-upon-shank forming a moustache and a shell in the shape of a crown. The brain is trained to see faces in inanimate assemblages of shapes; it is its way of making sense. And sure enough, here was Poseidon himself. In his reckoning, Poseidon's trident was the one element of the central entrance arrangement that stood for one thing and one thing only: beware, treacherous waters ahead.

What am doing herrre?

But before he could give serious thought to abandoning a mission that would see him adrift well beyond his depth, a figure definitely there stepped in front of his path——

"You a guest at this hotel?"

He fumbled before his accuser in porter's dress. He sort of wobbled there, under Poseidon's warning, as if by sheer nervous movement he might extract some sympathy from the smartly-dressed doorman before him. But then he remembered his directive and retrieved from the frayed fold of his trouser pocket the coin he had been given—the passkey! When he presented it, flat in his palm, it was more in the manner of a beggar at a banquet than a man in receipt of the silver to grant him access to a secret club's gathering. But it was legal tender. It sprung the porter into action like a coiled character after feeding through the slot of a pier-head penny arcade. The porter opened the Grand Hotel's world up to him. Stars were replaced with the sparkle from crystal in chandeliers. It felt as spacious as the sky in there, and much more opulent.

"May I, sir?" the porter said in a tone much different, and palm open to his bag.

Head still skyward, he must have nodded, as the weight from his borrowed tan baggage was relieved. Check-in was a blur made easy by the presentation of coin once more and guidance to a sea-view suite on one of the upper floors. The hotel was the largest brick structure in Europe and only young, erect just a few years before him. And its history was not something he knew. The impression he got from being in the building, however, rubbed upon him at least a sense of the weight of it. It was a symbol of Empire and of a whole new mode of moving about. A megastructure for an entirely original concept of travel—to a place…to stay, for leisure. It was big; a cliff itself built on a cliff. Outside his window seagulls flew, as white above storm clouds, which were even darker than the night. White was also down below, atop high-seas waves that looked like just the ripple of the banks of a placid lake at this height. And just on the horizon, rain of an encroaching mariner's nightmare brewed, its edges creeping in like a lighthouse-engulfing fog.

"You're the new tutor then?" an uninitiated voice said, swept in from behind. This voice was deep as a foghorn and came with the first lashes of rain against the pane. He spun 'round, startled, defensive…and trapped by the figure filling the door frame of his room. It was a serious lapse not latching the door.

Is danger alrrready.

He surveyed the suite for something with which to arm himself, but save for the hard edges of cumbersome furniture, everything else within was of bold colouring and soft finish.

"Who vants to know?" he said, best feign of fierceness while still looking for something sharp. "You no Marsh man."

The man before him, handsome and broad and tall, he now noticed, was about twenty years junior to what Marsh would have been.

"And how would you know?" handsome and broad and tall—— H.B.T.——said as advancing on the suite, sealing the escape.

"Bekause meet him," he said, not mentioning the observation that this man before him was much too young…and more handsome, broader and taller than the man known as Marsh he had met on the train from Brighton.

"I see…" H.B.T. said, bringing the bulk of athletic body closer. "And quite the impression you must have made on this Marsh—to make him send me instead."

H.B.T. stripped the space between them like the air was sweat-stained sheets of a hard-ridden bed.

"He tell you why am herrre?"

"*To spy!*" H.B.T. spat, looking about like there may have been a person hidden somewhere among the hardwood furnishings of the suite. "Yes, he told me. You're the detective inspector's inside man." Now all space between them was sucked out, they stood toe to toe; H.B. coming in at a full heads height of *T.* over him. "Well"——breath coming now like a freshly snipped cigar, musky but sweet——"you're more of a boy, really, aren't you?"

Zis one ought be detective.

"Pardon?" Just seconds after meeting, H.B.T. had the handle of him; could *hear* even his below-breath thoughts. And knew how to wrangle him just so, in each which way. "You lucked out," H.B.T. added, looking past him through the window to outside. "Like Tanner next door, yours is an absolute sea view. You wouldn't catch sight of land even if I was to dangle you by your ankles arm's reach clear of the hotel walls."

"And vill you, be danglin' me?" he asked earnest.

It was a fair question in his estimation. H.B.T. certainly had arms of the girth that would be capable. "Maybe later," H.B.T. responded, leaning in close enough that noses touched. "For now, best that you come with me."

Starting at the crotch and plugging buttonhole by buttonhole up to the clavicle, H.B.T. bound him up by the coat. The coat had a tear just below the shoulder, where the wet had seeped through the cotton of his shirt and to his skin. H.B.T. pressed palm to the spot. This touch told him that this man knew...about Glass...about his companion rôle with the detective...about Marsh and about Glass' disinterest in pursing the old flame. In touching the wet cotton to his flesh, H.B.T. was telling him that there was knowledge of him as the jealous link between two men.

"I've got a witness for you," H.B.T. said taking his hand and tugging him from the room without any allowance for protest or response.

Like the mass of the man into the room, H.B.T.'s hand...B.H.E.—big, hard and enveloping—took his own clammy offering through the maze of the leviathan lodgings.

"I zhought only Marsh knew me vas koming," he said, their hands still joined, eyes locking as H.B.T. consulted a floor plan halfway up a flight of stairs with a view of the dark sea.

"Ah yes, well, there's your first lesson then, my Eastern mate. Tutors also know at least as much of the goings-on in their own house as their heads do."

"You tutor zen?" he asked, settling more now into the rôle that he had been assigned. "Potter?"

"Porter, but close." Porter gave him another smile that he thought said, *but you knew that, that was a test.* It wasn't. His talents had always lay in the flesh of male recognition, and not so much in their naming. Though he liked that Porter thought that. "For now, I'm still the tutor," Porter went on, "just until Marsh can find a suitable replacement…or until he's willing to risk Prett being on the scene. There's a killer about, you know."

He should probably have been taking notes of the key players. But didn't, believing himself to have enough to contend with already. "This tutoring, it pay verrry well?"

"£50 per year."

It seemed to him an incredulous figure, surely on par with the salaries of the professional classes. Though, truly, he did not know.

"It's only a side hustle for me."

"You leave? Rrresign?"

"On the contrary, Eastern mate. I've been called up! Surely you knew?"

"What?"

"It's tradition. Whenever one of his own can no longer fulfil his duty in the final, for whatever reason, the tutor steps in. Forfeiting his position as help to play for a spot in the club. The rule was set up as a sort of test of the competence of the training. The tutor gives up his paid position to put his principles into practice."

"If you arrre rrreplacement. What am I herrre forrr?"

"Come mate, surely you've sleuthed at least that. You're my tutor!" Porter tugged him into tow again, resuming their snaked course through the hotel. "It's all cricket," Porter called back when at speed. "And you'll have me to steer you straight. It's just a farce, remember. You're not actually the tutor… you're hunting for clues."

The Grand Hotel was a hedge maze without apparent exit. As at sea, so was the case on land: a vigilant fear of fire. Though buildings, like ships, were gravitating to more heat-retardant materials such as iron and brick, they were also upping the stakes in terms of what was conceivable, and such castles in the sky were now often design-pegged by precautions. In the case of the Grand Hotel, Scarborough, this meant numerous detached stair cavities that anticipated access for fire squads in the case of threat. But which also, as a secondary advantage, imbued these structures with a maze-depth awe.

"First time in Scarborough then, Cox?" Porter asked, no longer having hold of his arm but now instead coming up in the nearest wake of his walk, pushing him along through the flexing of a near-tangible cushion of air between Porter's crotch and the small of his back.

"Da," he said, struck by the sound of his name—he had not disclosed it.

"O that's alright, Scarborough's a place of firsts," Porter said, darting him down a cascade of stairs and onto a corridor in the direction of the station end of the hotel. "England's first resort, Scarborough. Its restorative spa waters of which not only turned its fortunes but rose it from the ruins of revolution. Do you know your history, Cox?"

Porter touched off his arm to guide him off on a fork and through to another corridor at another level within the building. What level number up from the street he could not tell, the hotel being as long below street level as it was above, sloping down the cliff-line to the sea like the hull of a monster ocean liner.

"Not much," he said short, the novelty of being thrust forth like a carriage on Isambard Kingdom Brunel's long-since-failed atmospheric railway, run thin.

Porter touched his arm again, by bicep this time, to come about and stick him on a path for the rounding of a final bend that led them back to a landing atop the stairs of the hotel's main foyer. He looked down on reception with its commotion of travellers, some checking in or out, with great trolleys stacked high with animal-hide articles—some of shades whose species he could not trace. Looking down there, all manner of living animals roamed; from shin-high terriers come down from the hills up north to the giant grey furs of wolf hounds, he imagined, from the fine terraces of Dublin.

"She's always bustling, the grand dame," Porter said. "Even now in spring, when it's all dead outside."

He knew enough of the ploys of handsome men to recognise this statement as a stall. Porter's eyes not really looking at the fur-laden ladies from Scottish and Irish cities nor their furry companions. Handsome eyes that, he knew, were searching for something, someone, in particular. That Porter had him tucked in stead while surveying and speaking served as affidavit to this fact.

"Come along then," Porter said after several sweeps of the foyer.

"It von't alvays be easy, vith me," he said, resisting for a second then giving in.

It seemed to tickle Porter. Was it the way he spoke, his Eastern tongue? Or the syntax? Slightly off…tinny to the ear?

"Wouldn't dream of it," Porter said, that handsome grin again. "I prefer it hard *vith you*."

Porter seemed to seize the this-time-it-will-be-though suggestion in his threat to carry on leading him by arm through the foyer, out of the Grand Hotel, across the cobbles of Scarborough—wet and smelly from dung and piss of horses and tramps—and into another hotel: that other dame of the Scarborough seaside. Less bold but a street-up more refined: from Grand and into Royal Hotel. The mass of vagrants that had been there to crowd him on arrival had completely dispersed. Either entirely imagined or scared off by Porter…scurrying back into damp crags of the town like crabs—both possibilities of which he found equally ghoulish.

The Grand Hotel was a symbol of Victoria—crudely so. She was even built as a "V." The Royal Hotel, however, reflected the Regency, a time of decadence and princes in proxy rule. Not Victoria of Britannia as matron of a growing Empire, nor an Olympus statement. Porter-led, still by arm, but with a relaxing urgency—of grip and of pace—they tore up the hotel's atrium staircase, its dome full gold guiding and insular English excess, to a room on the top floor, at the corridor's far end. The room was small, in the cavity of the ceiling, and opened with a key. But it was not the size that mattered, rather what waited within: a boy his own age, strange looking for certain, but a beguiling combination of doughy cheeks and stern-and-frowned brow with sharp cheekbones.

A boy who, at the sight of him, lunged at the door.

"It's alright—I've got you—you're still safe with me," Porter said in short-but-softer-than-the man-spoke-to-him succession.

Still.

It caught his ear in much the same way that Porter caught the strangely beguiling boy.

Tightly.

Determined.

It was a hysterical display. The way the boy thrashed feebly in ample arms; boy-fringe frantic, like the fins of a stingray into the sky from shallow waters. But it worked. Porter's arms swallowed the boy into submission like a knitted blanket around a small child.

The room offered sea views, but they were the in-ceiling kind that probably only Porter would be able to appreciate without needing to resort to pointed toes.

"One 'f 'em Brighton crew, I take it?" he said, directing his query to Porter—the boy's keeper, it seemed.

Porter nodded, a jerk of the boy in his arms acting as further confirmation.

"Herrre vith yourrr own monies, vithout Marsh man knoving?"

"It's alright, trust me." That was what he thought Porter whispered to the boy before nodding and guiding the boy to the bed, where Porter sat the young one down and then explained by backstory the tale of "Marsh House" and "Lewis"—the latest dead, who took a swan-dive plunge from the *Highlands Express.*

"Porter herrre is only one what knew you verrre on boarrrd vith Levis?"

The boy, now known to him as Keeler, nodded—brow furrowed but cheeks and mouth soft, relaxed.

"And you verrre also only vitness of zat boy jumping?"

This time Keeler looked to Porter first, before then nodding.

"And you'rrre back now. Why?"

"It's no good," Porter chimed in, "he won't even tell me that. Just that he needed to be here, something to do with making sense of why Lewis did it."

"Why arrre you——"

"Why is he helping me?" Keeler spoke up, soft but with spite and all by only slight flutter of supple, pink lips.

It was his first chance to laugh with sting in a knowing way, and he seized it: "Zat I know."

Keeler gave little away, even after his sting.

Could the boy be so naïve about the spirit of Porter's generosity? he wondered, Porter's fidgeting and cheek-reddening in his sideline confirming selfish intentions toward the boy.

"Why brrring me herrre?"

Porter was, visibly and by reply, much more comfortable in responding now: "That one's easy," the cushion-of-crotch-air bravado of the seasoned tutor's cockiness restored. "It is my only window... Marsh had planned on meeting you himself. He was there, in fact, with an aperitif at the bar in the Grand's foyer, anticipating your arrival. He was excited, even; for the opportunity to meet with the detective-inspector's deputy from Scotland Yard, who would help settle all this unpleasantness and to whom he could share his theories. Until, that is, he—and by he I mean you——"

"Da."

"Until you arrived. I was at the bar with Marsh at the time and, well, Marsh scurried away and assigned me to the task of settling you in. A liaison with you that, I suspect, will last for the length of your stay with us."

"Why vould yourrr master give me to you."

He had been perfectly deliberate in his choice of descriptor, which provoked a recoil in Porter. "He is not my master. But rather was my employer, and I am the only one he can entrust his embarrassment to. Embarrassment that you were...not what he expected, because he has met you before and by seeing you whatever illusion he had built up for himself regarding what sleuthing with a Met deputy would be like has been dashed—and this I should note from a man who flicks from one illusion of fancy to the next like each were a unit in a pack of a corner-side cardsharp's tossing of a deck. Where was I? *O yes!* seeing you shattered that illusion of what Met deputies might be like, as it did whatever fantasy he had of assisting your own employer with this investigation."

"I'm not prrroud," he said. "Glass is my master herrre. Glass has told me about Marsh man...I'm much happier having ended up with you. You know zis Marsh vell?"

"Well enough after five years, and enough to say that I vouch for your instinct on me as the better to deal with...and while he isn't my employer anymore on account of me stepping in for Lewis, I remain on hand during the transition, and, of course, to help you with your rôle."

Their exchange had become a power play, like a rapid-fire chess match where the upper hand changed sides with each slide of a piece in their board of discussion. Porter held the floor for now; not chequered but carpeted in emerald overlaid with a golden pattern. Porter eyed him up from a position of wide-footed athleticism, with a strong-straight back, arms defined with hands clenched at big buttocks. Keeler pushed Porter off kilter, he could see. He preferred the man dominant, and so was pleased to find the man he'd met in the Grand Hotel returning slowly to form in the heat of their conversation.

He had found before—and hoped to again now—that backing down in front of strong men showed itself as the best method of advance: "I'm not..." he searched for the words that would further lower himself into submission, "not—not—fit forrr purrrpose. I vouldn't know firrrst zing about koaching. I've played sporrrts, but no technique."

Porter unclenched the hands at buttocks, slouched even—at least as much as the man's strict physique would allow—and took advantage of a pause in his submissive speech to sit on the bed beside the beguiling-strange stranger.

O yes, he thought, the question of the boy who had become lost in their exchange. Porter and the boy bedded, he went about addressing them both: "But, although I not exactly in Met Police employ—as it sounds like Marsh might know, and you, surrrely, arrre astute enough to also—, I do have job to do herrre, as do you. Orrr at least you feel zat you do, otherrrvise you vould not have prrrodded me herrre, in such underrrhanded fashion, to meet vith zis boy. Orrr, morrreso, I suspect, to bearrr vitness."

And it was the checkmate, or the stalemate, whichever chess-match metaphor summed up best the coaxing of a soon-to-come honest explanation from Porter to the key question that troubled him: why did Porter feel the need to draw him there, to the boy, as the first port of call for his duties as companion-cum-undercover detective?

That Keeler was familiar with the dead boy whore even before Brighton served as the starting point for Porter's explaining why he had been tugged there—much to Keeler's clear disapproval. This was followed by description of more activities of Marsh House and the Keeler/Lewis connection, on to the sordid discovery of sodomy between O'Connor and Hunt that, between all there assembled, seemed less sordid—though why it was such a scandal was well understood.

Factoring Lewis into it all was the lingering mystery. The Lewis leap was known to his master, yes. It was what had drafted him in as deputy, in an undercover position. But that there was another Brighton boy present for it, this was novel. And the more he listened, the more it became clear that the key person of interest in all of this—all this of which, of course, was the Pipe death—, the key witness for the case that had obsessed his detective inspector...was not Lewis, nor Marsh, nor Porter, but the silent boy on the bed, front row for it all.

This strange boy beguiled a link between them all. *This vas gift.* Keeler as mate to two dead, and witness to the leap. And here again, for round three, hiding in the wings. It was the only nugget of intel he needed to convey back to Glass to allow the detective to get on with enquiries. But why was Porter handing it to him, even without him needing to search for it? Especially when Porter, clearly, cared so deeply for the boy? The irony of seeing Keeler as a boy—even though Keeler and he had probably only months in the difference of age, and he would never re-gard himself as a boy—was not lost on him. But still, something called up in him at this thought, as aside as it were. A ping of intuition, of something not right.

A detective hunch…a clue, even. Right, resolved, he thought. *"You!"* he directed to Keeler, "close, perrrsonal associate vith tvo dead men, who while konnected zemselves vith each other, verrre not konnected in same manner as you vith zem. I kan underrrstand why you vould feel anxious about diskoverrry, at rrround thrrree. *And you!"* swinging on Porter, "zank you forrr handing me someone to question, zough firrrst question I have is forrr you, and why after all trrrouble you have gone to, to prrrotect zis boy, you vould choose now to kast off any trrrust zat might have been nurrrturrred betveen you."

Keeler's look at Porter confirmed his reading of the boy's hurt feelings—perhaps he was cut out for detecting, after all.

The boy—whose features had been, at introduction, stern and angular around the eyes, but soft and fleshy around the lips and the cheeks…softened, all over. Like the parting of a clam shell, spread to reveal inner iridescence. Vulnerable, betrayed, and now pervious and hurting all over.

Porter—quite again as a surprise—livened at the sight, looking into Keeler like the boy were a pearl, and they were alone in the world.

"I seized the opportunity for you," Porter said to bed companion.

Porter's manner told him this statement was not as a response to his playing-detective question, but as a private declaration to bedmate. And Porter said it smiling, as-jovial, like one would in setting out the genesis of some marvellous gift.

"When Marsh bowed out," Porter went on, "and having freed myself from the responsibility of his employ——"

A freedom, he thought, won by the Lewis self-murder.

"——and knowing how desperate you are for answers…well, I took this as your chance. *This one* here," no eye contact, just an inclined head, "I recognised right away."

"Da," he chimed in, but Porter would not let him contour the melody.

"Not recognised as an individual, but as a type. He's like me: a substitute, brought in because, for some reason—no doubt embarrassing and deeply personal—his own employer felt the need to sit this one out."

Keeler's eyebrows angled again, bringing strange more into beguilement. "Can we trust him?" Keeler asked, with an intensity, a charisma that felt a first for that meeting; but still, softly as an on-edge clam.

"Don't you see?" Porter said, taking the boy's hands. "It don't matter whether he can be trusted or not. Get your answers on the investigation so far and let me worry about getting you…getting us…away after."

He had to hand it to Porter. It worked…this ploy. He answered every question Keeler put to him through Porter as proxy. Though Keeler did not get much really, and so the ploy yielded little profit. In fact, the whole exercise was probably more illuminating for him than it was for them on the bed, which made the use of him easier to take. He knew, actually, little.

Glass was obsessed with finding the killer of the Pipe boy and tying in Pipe's killer with a ribbon of some kind of deeper meaning. But so far as he could tell, Glass had very little to go on, and was intensely cagey with the whole affair. Pipe had consumed his master. In fact, the only time he had seen Glass since Brighton counted once, when the detective had summoned him to meet, for lunch at the Cock in London, 201 Fleet Street, just the night before, where Glass had set out this assignment. They had made sordid shake on the agreement on top of sheets of a room at the Grosvenor Hotel on Buckingham Palace Road, which was why he was late and did help assure him of his currency in the investigation. Late…on accord of having to return to his Glass-appointed apartment, across the city, for clothes and a wash-off of the night's agreeing-to. Glass, though vigorous enough in the appetites of their fleshy re-acquainting, was starting to wane interest-wise, and so he had no qualms now in divulging the little that he did know; given, as he saw it, he had given up a job for a meal ticket that likely wouldn't last long. Perhaps there would even be a quid pro quo to be had with these here bedmates… or among the other men more powerful that this queer tournament had brought into lodgings beside his.

"He zinks it's prrrobably one of fourrr old ones, heads, y'know, zat did in zat boy; zough has not narrroved it down much frrrom zat. Zat Marsh, yourrr man, vas…less likely in his mind—mostly, I zink, bekause detective doesn't rrregarrrd him vith spine forrr it. Zey had dalliances zose tvo, Glass and zat Marsh, I'm surrre of it. And deep-rrrememberrred dalliance it must have been, too, if Marsh fobbing me off on his ex-tutor vas as drrramatic as you make out."

Porter nodded, a verification that he really did not need.

"I'm pleased vith how it's turrrning out, zough: zerrre be much morrre juice at zis end, and Marsh sounds like intolerrrable sod. Anyvay, back to it. Ah da, I mean…it must have been deep-rrrooted, zat dalliance, bekause, you see comrades, frrrom what little I do know, it only Marsh zat sees some sense in zinking zat murrrder and suicide should be konnected. It vas on his insistence zat someone should be sent to Skarrrborrrough. Zough zat zat someone should be me, it seems, vas vorrrser state of cirrrkumstances."

"Why not come himself, as a detective of Scotland Yard?" Porter asked.

"Glass claims zat me being underrrkover vill be morrre frrruitful. But I zink he doesn't vant to be back…also prrrobably vants to avoid Marsh."

Porter seemed to see something in what he said that he himself did not.

"I go now," he said abruptly, leaving Porter to his playmate and taking hurried-but-small strides back to the cobbled channel between the Grand and Royal Hotels. Careful not to fall on the slippery-steep incline to the clifftop giant hotel, about to pass a small curio shop at the base of the Grand next to the funicular——

It went black behind his eyes. Like in Murmansk at the deep bay off the Barents Sea, where as a boy on his bicycle he'd sometimes black out when the seagulls, fat from the cold of the northwest, would sweep down and hit him from behind, in protection of a gull chick.

After black he saw red. The Grand, that biggest-in-the-civilised-world mass was so newly mortared that its laid bricks were not yet weathered at the edge, giving him several painful cuts as his face was pushed into them and his trousers yanked over his rump. No similar care as shown before to undress him was shown to his long Johns. So thinly worn and yellowed that it took no effort at all out of his assailant to pry a hole over his own, with just a finger and thumb of the less dominant hand. The dominant one grating him over the brick sharps like he was a smelly cheese being shred over a pasta mound. His face felt hot with the graze, like he often got on his knees as child.

Then his hole was momentarily warm. He knew it well,

ah, ze feel of phlegm. To be spat on!

So familiar a sensation as to calm him mid-assault like a thumb in the mouth. But the calm soon broke, as he was broken into. Any healing he'd stolen since the taking of a detective's sovereign was instantly undone with the shuddering into him of a spit-slicked, tip only of a big, big dick. Biggest in county big. So engorged and already throbbing with the rush-up of seed. All weight was now on him as the brick abrasion spread down his neck and over his chest. The man on top of him bucking like a bull before red—starved and stabbed and shaved-horn sharp, driving the blow into the cloth-holder home.

He was denied any rhythm in the rape, just a single plunge, like a sword to the gut, jerked at the hilt.

"Am whorrre," he said, tooth and brick edge through his lips. "*Port in me.*"

"Fuck!" Porter cried, staying weighted against him.

But then his brilliant attacker——

pulled out. Spewing seed across the bricks, over his legs, on the piss-stinking ground, all crevices except his whore own.

He cried out himself. Denied any compensation for the pain.

Seed continuing to be wasted down his trembling leg, Porter keep weight upon him, like the iron of a printer's press, grinding his Russian-runt face into the Grand with a whispered tale of the *Bullingdon Club.* Another club of university connection…this time a dining club of Oxford. There's no member's fee, but if you want to play, if you want to join in on the fun of privileged vandalism, of trashing hotels and taverns in which members would meet, you needed to be prepared to pay the proprietor for their silence.

"If you want to smash up my yard, boy," Porter said. "If you want to wreck my chances with Keeler by your loose suggestion of what *this*," replacing the space where agreeable meat was with the bone of fingers, "could be for me, best you be ready to reimburse me for the damage."

He wailed, fallen on the ground, licking the piss-scented seed he was sorely denied.

S eed he had missed out on seeped his ravaged long Johns; draped down
each inside leg, the material warm and thick like spoiled herring soiled
by being left out too long over wire in the spring sun. Porter bound him
back up in trousers, his face was torn and peppered with brick crumbs, but
Porter carried on like this was how he should look, explaining as he limped
hole-broken back into the Grand that for this round their host was Mr Blunt
of the House of Kent, who *likes to play by his own rules*. The rules this time
were as follows: there would be no pre-challenge training within the houses.
Instead, contenders and tutors would assemble, together, on night one, for
a combined course in the chosen masculine pursuit. Festivities and get-to-
knows were to continue through the night, then the tournament was to commence with first light, with boxing partners chosen by Blunt based not only
on the impression of contenders at the crash-training course, but how the
young men had happened to impress upon their host in the socialising that
followed group sweat. That the masculine pursuit would be boxing was about
the only carryover for the Kent-Crew sort that year.

Porter relayed the Kent house rules like they were a script for a newsreel,
which, really, they were. In fact, Porter had the script in pocket: a handwritten
Blunt note to each tutor that set out the terms of the instalment this time.
Porter had received it because news of the Lewis death had not yet got out to
the club executive or anyone other than Glass and Marsh, and so Blunt had
no way of knowing that, in fact, Porter was tutor of House of Middlesex no
more. This was how Glass wished it to stay. Should Lewis' leap turn out not
to have been self-inflicted, keeping it secret might help to *flush out* any suspect
parties. Porter explained that the keeping-secret of the Lewis leap suited the
man, too, as it also kept Keeler away from it; freeing Porter to sleuth around
for answers to individual questions about Lewis and Piper, while not swirling

my boy into the Scarborough scent. "It's a late training," Porter said as they winded through the richly red-carpeted halls of the Grand Hotel to his room in the upper floors of the for-Victoria, V-shaped, brick monstrosity of a building. "Starts at midnight."

Already, through the windows of the staircases, he could see that down on the beach fires were being lit in pits dug in the sand in the square of a boxing ring. He paused at one landing to watch as the fourth fire erupted, shouting embers up high into the frigid air. That the flame looked big, even from high up in the building on the cliff, when all else down there—including donkey ride sheds and left out bathing machines—splayed out as mere specs, sand-grains against the large, rock-licks of the fire pits, spoke to the flair for manly display in a Blunt affair Porter had signposted. "I hope ya up for a late night," Porter spoke in his ear as their breath fogged up the view of a beach ablaze.

He waited for Porter to attack again or even mention what happened. To make it more real than the tingling pain could. But he was denied. "I vake up at night," he said as prod to the predator inside his withholding penetrator.

"In that case," Porter went on, lips grazing his earlobe then leading him away from the window and back down stairs in the direction they had just come, "best to the bar instead, to meet and break the news to the other tutors that you're their new chum. I'll stay with you for a few rounds, to make sure you behave, before heading back to someone that matters."

It was half the hour past ten by the time they entered the bar of the Grand Hotel in Scarborough, giving him enough time to wipe his visible wounds. While it ran just a flight of stairs up from ground level, the bar opened onto a seaside view more befitting a cliff. *Better zan cliff*, he thought, as he took in the floor-to-ceiling, wall-to-wall vista; better because it was high enough up that all of the Scarborough foreshore, harbour, spa building and castle were spread out before him, but not so far up that all definition was lost…no in-flight sensation of a seagull that was his room's view. "First lesson of coaching," Porter said, towing him from the entrance to the three shapes seated and drinking as silhouettes against the view. "We tutors always meet for a drink on the first night before sorting. And we do it alone-together." The last part came late, and only just audible above breath as they reached the three.

"Who's he?" a gangly one said. *Probably coach for fruity one of Essex*, he guessed, recalling the notes on house heads from Glass that did not extend to the boys of their employ, though his master had suggested that tutors would likely resemble their heads. Gangly eyed him up in a wave of contradictions: aloof elitism in the twisting of angular, pinched lips; and bitter appetite in the eyes—glassy and salt hungry.

"Gents, let me introduce, Mr Sergei Cox," Porter proceeded without Gangly acknowledgment. "Do mind his appearance."

"Tutors only, Porter. You know that," said another, the biggest. Towering even Porter, broad of body and voice and neck with bullish features that were wide and a little misshapen after contact with other men, similarly built. Hard contact on and off the playing field…or so was how he built Biggest up in his bent mind. *Blunt's man*, he thought, *has to be*… That left the last to be claimed by Surrey house and sat there as a love child of the two others: muscular enough, but with a quiet conservatism, like a new priest in the fresh throes of the cloth, having first drinks after graduating from the seminary. His eyes returned to the biggest of them, the latest to speak. The one who spoke with disinterest, as a statement of fact. He liked Biggest the best.

"Quite right," Porter said, "in which case, perhaps I should not stay for a drink after all. You see, Cox here is the new Tutor of Middlesex, I'm merely on hand for his transition."

Biggest remained disinterested, downing drink and indicating by nod to Quiet Conservative that, yes, you should indeed fetch another.

Gangly straightened up, lips snaking a smile to match the hunger of the sickly man's stare. "That so? Fascinating," Gangly said, teasing with touch the stem of a grape alcohol. "Take a seat then, Sergei—I smell a story. Porter, perhaps fetch your successor a spirit, as he has some catching up to do."

As Porter wrangled spirits for them both—as a true military-minded man, gin was the order—introductions were made. He was right: Gangly was *Tanner of Essex*, the talking monopoliser whose type he disliked, an angular, sneaky disposition. Biggest was *Underhill of Kent*, disinterested in getting to know him particularly, which he liked…always had preferred the company of disinterested men. *Arthur Underhill*, he committed Biggest's full name to memory; a look of the New World about him, of New York...too broad for Little Olde England. *Da, morrre disinterrrest to interrrest me*, he thought, so loudly in a spirit fog that this time it may actually be audible. And then there was unmemorable one, the Surrey tutor—Quiet Conservative. This name he did not catch, seeing the third as just background to the two who counted—in the cases of death and sweet flesh.

Porter bowed out after three gins, sometime after eleven, to sneak back to "my boy" in the Royal Hotel. Porter had been a solid wingman, with an off-stage brutality that was becoming. Porter cordially skirted the topics of gossip that gangly-Tanner sorely sought while in the bar, which proved helpful. Surrey's unmemorable one retired one drink after Porter, and big-Underhill looked set to pull out soon, too. But the spirited get-to-know had rushed confidence over him, and he resolved to make a play for Biggest to stay. It would take some spillage of juice, he reckoned. Tanner was unshakable, so stayed privy; an annoyance for sure, but perhaps Tanner could be useful, as a buffer, to the unfolding of this do-stay-Biggest story. "One of zem Middlesex Crrrew is dead. And yourrr little club herrre's rrrules mean zat Porter takes spot of him. Marsh'll need him new help, but I'm not him. I'm frrrom Met Police, herrre to rrreporrrt on situation frrrom kontext of Pipe kid." Biggest now 'lil more interested, Underhill got them more spirits while Tanner, pain-fully predictably, grew hungrier for the detail. "It makes me of use to zem, zat," he said in response to Biggest's surprise that he was from the police. "My forrreign charrracter, not what you expect, niet?"

But Gangly was more keen on a probe of the first reveal: "I'd heard that rule, but never thought it actually a thing. So, Porter is...*out*, essentially?"

He downed his Biggest-delivered spirit in one gulp and was damned if he was to continue any further attentions to Gangly. *Me'll dirrrect intrrrigue of me own tale, zank you.* Gripped by gin, homing in on Biggest to make the man stay in the bar of the Grand Hotel that had views closer to the breaking waves of the beach than any of the rooms, he lunged into the suspense of an undercover London junior detective's assignment. "It kould just as easily been one of you, what killed him. I'll need to do questions."

Biggest continued to come about as he unfolded the story of the search for the Pipe boy's killer. "Straight up interesting matter, that," Biggest said. "And happy to yield to questioning. I have some case questions myself."

The Marsh brush off combined with Porter taking him to Keeler had freed him to take an own direction—after all, Keeler's hiding there and presence for Lewis' leap gave him a fresh-cut scent to take back to Glass. *Just stay back and observe*, Glass had instructed. *Niet fun forrr me in zat*, he thought-said, full of gin, between rounds. *Why vould I listen to man who so feeble-headed he kould not kome himself.* He would develop his own technique. Detecting was, after all, an infant profession. Still mocked and fear-mongered in the papers for the reckless consideration these men held for class. Charging criminals from across the spectrum in a same manner, as if with no regard of standing. Well, his background was of the lowest status, yet in this grand bar, with, well, now one expert athlete above his station hooked on his story...he would pursue rather than observe. But before he could go in pursuit hooking the biggest one, Biggest was back at the bar and Gangly had the table: "What do you know of the dead whore?"

Nix was the answer, but he said nothing.

"I ask because I suspect that you, nor your detective, have much of an inkling of the boy's sordid origins, or"——looking about the bar like this part was the most dangerous tattle, and they were both at the threshold of whether or not it would leave lips to manifest in voice——"*the particulars* of my own dear head's rôle in bringing the threepenny upright into civilised company."

He stayed wordless, partly because he couldn't grasp all of the lingo at the speed with which it was delivered; assaulted by the verbal onslaught—Biggest remaining at the bar. *Kome back!* he thought.

Gangly continued at incredulously quickened a pace: "*Boats!* well, clippers specifically—that's Peele's gambit. He's come into a new one, snatched from possible piracy after the collapse of the China tea trade. Well, not collapse so much as squeeze out, as the Suez Canal has snuffed out his Chinese chances, bringing steamships—much more fuel-efficient now, you know—into viable, vying competition. Clippers can't compete with steamships on the route anymore and, well, my man's all about the clipper: so it's now other markets he's

after. Down underneath markets." It had all been said in one rushed batch,
Gangly turned towards the bar where Biggest was receiving drinks. With Biggest set to return to them at any moment, Gangly dragged breath for more:
"*But mutiny!* well, Peele saw opportunity to buy up more clippers after China,
one clipper in particular, among the latest of the tea clippers. He plans to ply
it on the Australia route, for wool, and thinks that it is in with a chance of being the fastest there. But before all that, after China, while in the coal service
of Shanghai and Japan, and jute with the New World and Manila—hectic
times!—before this there was murder from first mate and captain mutiny. I
know 'cause I was there, aboard in the Java Sea. There's speak of an inquiry,
in New York of all places. Probably next year, it looks like."

Lost, Gangly tore his attentions back with "*Shipboard whore!* well our dead
London whore, you see. That one spread his filth at sea and not just along the
Thames. I saw it firsthand, on this clipper. After the first mate had murdered
a seaman, after the master had helped the man escape then threw himself
in the sea after a three-day fog in a becalmed Java Sea, after this I boarded
with Peele. It was at this time that the purchase of such a vessel was the best
price. Peele doesn't mind a few dead men if it'll snag something special. My
master is expert at seizing the initiative of a ship in peril. By the time of the
captain's leap, all left to sail the clipper were four tradesmen and apprentices
numbering six."

Tanner's voice suddenly slowed to a near-dead weight in water, like all
wind had abandoned sails and all light had left the bar save for the flicker of
distant shipping, leaving only stale, hot air between few words: "We. Found.
All. Huddled. In the hold. Ten of them, ten that were registered with the clipper. But there were eleven bodies down there. Ten in a huddle in the shadows like lepers, with one more unlisted sailor in the middle, naked as you
like. The ten like-lepers had lesions to match, and shunned the light like
rats, while the one in the centre was unblemished. Peele scooped up the naked one and abandoned the rest. Thinking that the boy had luckily escaped
from the scourge of *the Java Sea diseased ten*. But do you know what I think?"
Tanner said, tracing bumps across a diseased face that, too, seemed to shun
the candlelight. "I think that boy was the cause of it all, and that those

poor bastards down there, pressed with the rats into the damp down-under-neath nooks, were trying to get away from a wretched creature that none knew from whence that thing had come. *Dead!* all of them. Before you ask the fate of the ten"———scratching at the sores now, secreting pus mingled with dull-coloured blood———"and the boy survived without the slightest symptoms, though remained a carrier…best to be avoided…of which most found out too late. Should have known, really. The clipper's figurehead, you see, is of that witch from Rabbie Burns, that cautionary tale to men to take care with any who appear scantily clad, or in this case, turn up hole and whore-pole out. *Burns!* indeed, and much more than the tail of a man's horse! And no Blue Riband for guessing which witch whore I might be referring to here."

"Pipe," he whispered.

"Maybe there is God," Gangly said with a drunken nod, "a God after all, and he lives at the pierhead in Brighton. Well done, *Cutty-sark!*"

"What a load of dollymop muck, Tanner," Biggest said. "We all know where you got *those scabs*, and it wasn't inside the cargo hold of any clipper."

It was desert-water relief to have Biggest back, the hard-to-grasp delivery of the Tanner fever-dream tale along with its teller's scratching that made its subject matter even more horrible. Biggest seemed to consider whether to sit or not…deciding in apparent disgust at the display on a drink down—including one presumably for Tanner—and setting the remaining glass in front of him. "Interview me first," Biggest said, then left the bar.

Left him to lust long in a fog of spirits for some stock of Biggest within. He got up shakily. "Umm, wherrre is rrroom wherrre Underrrhill sleeps."

Tanner, either oblivious to his disinterest or too proud to show offence, answered promptly: "He's out-to-sea facing, left of Brown. Room 249."

Brown, zat was it! "Da," he said, downing the gin that was the last liquid he needed and getting on the pursuit, leaving the least coach-y of coaching tutors to finish a drink alone and bleeding, too, as the story of the diseased siren creature of a fallen tea clipper formed like an oil on water—a second-in-command story to relay to his own master. He left the bar in pursuit of Biggest and hungry search now of a life-giving reward for his broken hole.

VII

BEEHIVE

tchy, his rod down there twitching and raw. Scuffed. Sandpapered with some whore's disease, he was sure. He woke early with this sensation, Keel nestled in the pit of his arm. He was not unfeeling about the down-there unease, though this care was not for the whore who he'd used but for Keel, who he'd wanted to be the first on his rod. He consoled himself with the knowledge that Keel was broken. If he had to guess, he would say that in the musk of his pit was the first good night's sleep Keel had had since Lewis' *Highlands Express* leap... *Fuck off!* he thought. As he did each time Lewis entered the mind. He shoved the boy away, off his brain and back into the snowy ravine the rival had dove in to. As if by transfer of touch, Lewis had been haunting his dreams each night since the *Highlands Express*, except for the one just passing, where the whore who took the name Cox had appeared. "Cox," clearly a pseudonym for someone as severely Russian in appearance and tongue. The Eastern boy cut a peculiar deputy, and a stranger still bedfellow of a Met Police detective. *O yes*, he had thought on meeting the boy, *I know*. Knowing that made punishing use of the runt easier to reason away.

What was left of the storm of the past night raged on, sea spray lashing the windows of their attic room in the Royal Hotel. Like it was the window of a kitchen in a cottage attached to a lighthouse on a rocky outcrop at the shelf of the North Atlantic—rather than a hotel room situated a cliff and street back from the beach. Blunt had cancelled the beach meet when the storm hit, at well after the eleventh hour. The Yorkshire coast was proving itself viciously unpredictable that year. The beach had washed itself away as a feasible arena to practice, though Blunt, around midnight, had fashioned an alternate arrangement, in the beach-view restaurant, several floors below the bar where he had drunk among former colleagues. He had intended to attend, until Keel made the request that he stay. Receiving it was a relief in part, which saved him the need to insist himself, and further frighten Keel by sharing his own anxieties around whether it was wise to have made the introduction at all—they gained some insight, granted, but by no means enough to have warranted the risk.

Cox had turned out to be of little flesh nor mental consequence, of no real knowledge or stake in the investigation; his risk-taking had told him this much at least. This fact helped him honour Keel's wish for him to stay, though he felt a strange guilt for leaving the foreign boy to fend forth alone. More likely, he wanted to make sure that runt remained corked about his down below use of. Call it a foreboding. The dreams he had of Cox were shadowy, the boy running alone along the Scarborough foreshore like a tsar being pitch-fork pursued into exile. They were manifestations of his failure to harbour any compassion for the boy. Vivid enough that at dead-low dark, once Keel was in a sea-swell-cabin sleep, he had taken advantage of a lapse in the weather and ventured over to the Grand Hotel—it being close to two hours into a new day by that stage. He called by Cox's room. There was no answer and he learnt from Surrey house's Brown—who his knocks had disturbed—that Cox had not shown up at the restaurant for training at all.

It did not bode well.

He called by the hotel bar—it was empty. Then by reception, where on request the bellboy accompanied him back to Cox's room to gain entry. It was empty and the bed, not slept in. He called in on Brown again, but to no benefit by way of leads. Brown invited him deep into the suite—much larger than his own. Brown's suite had a clipped view of the sea with a solid vantage of the coastline, from which he caught sight of a broad figure making a perilous return to the Grand Hotel over the Cliff Bridge towards South Cliff;

oddly shaped and near swept off feet against the assault of rain, which was by this stage an unending wave. The sight unnerved him...why, he could not place. He didn't mention the figure to Brown, perhaps because it was so haunting a figure he feared it might be conjured up by lack of sleep and a carryover of nightmares, and if so, Brown would certainly think him mad.

No! he thought in later hours. *The figure was real.*

Perhaps the reason the figure in the storm perturbed him so was because it served as reminder that he needed to *make a move!* The break in the weather had long since broken back and were he to have a chance of getting back to the Royal Hotel in one piece, and past the night porter before access was barricaded against the storm—if this hadn't happened already—he would need to *move now!* And so, he left Brown and asked the bellboy to lock up Cox's room again. Loyal service to Keel's needs was enough to appease with wishful thinking—all would be well-sealed with Cox. So, self-deception corking his conscience, he headed back to Keel, getting into the Royal Hotel in time and, he believed, without being seen. Meanwhile, the poor weather had risen to dismal again, it swept through the harbour and up the walls of the Grand Hotel as he left it, as if a real threat of tearing the building off its moorings, to pull it out to sea.

The rain was heavy come daybreak, too, when the fighting was scheduled to start. Not heavy at all like that of the early dark hours, but still with enough bite that you would—under normal conditions—never consider doing anything out in it, let alone square up and box an opponent for a spot in a club of gentlemen most secretive. But. In comparison to the register of the rain throughout the night, this morning was calm, and Blunt seemed most resolute with daylight that the display of masculine pursuit would go ahead, Scarborough hail or high water. He had gone by Cox's room again before dawn, but still, the Russian boy was not there. Though surely had been and was now on the beach in the calm-by-comparison-but-still-storm rain, ready for the start of the boxing, he consoled the regretting pit in his stomach. And so headed down there, where the qualifier went ahead as scheduled, at first light, on the South Sands. Weather be damned—it was all true Kentish tradition.

As he stood in the rain watching the boxing, one thought stayed with him: he could have used Cox's trench coat, seeing as the boy wasn't…using it here. The rain was so heavy it formed a mist. One that was eerie. Most mists are eerie, granted, but this one carried in with it reminiscence; of the Brighton Sands, that day at the start of that wrecked year's sorting, when he had seen Keel for the first time. This day, the boxing matches played out in squares marked by singed sand points—now sand pools—of the night before. Playing under hundreds of the Grand Hotel's seaward-gazing glass eyes, the storm had brought in seaweed to outnumber the spectators, who were gathered 'round the match like haggard soothsayers. They were joined by the crabs who, on account of the weather, went about their scavenging of the weed for bits of fish-flesh and other meaty chunks…undeterred and as they would normally, when crabs would have run of the place.

The crabs were bold. Not to be pushed to shore shyness in weather that was theirs—not when there was carrion to be had.

More salaciously than Cox missing the match was that Marsh missed it, too. Brown told him that Marsh had been in appearance the night before. In force for the midnight firelight training. Yet now missed the main event that morning. Rudderless and further disadvantaged by Blunt's selective pairing, not one Middlesex house boy succeeded in boxing. Nor did any of Essex house's boys make it through—a point less surprising—, making it four and four for the Kent-Surrey alliance. Meanly, he was glad of it. Had he really been so unhappy in Marsh's employ that he would be glad in the man's house's ill-fortune? Or was there something else in there? An ego, perhaps, which wanted to see the quadrant falter without his leadership? Among those *in there* feelings were thoughts of Cox and what might have become of the boy. What might have led a wet Russian to abandon a spy front so wholly ate at him the most as the mist took foothold of the beaches. Tearing up a sense of dread, like the sight of the crabs worming over the lumps on the beach—nipping and devouring, weed and dead meat.

"Mr Porter," called a boy through the mist, timed as if his anxieties were written in red in the white that surrounded him. "Me beg y' pardon, sir, but you're needed down at th' Spa."

Once definition had come by his side, he recognised the messenger as the bellboy from the Grand Hotel's main entrance. Seeing the boy out there, blonde hair blackened with wet, rain running through the channel of a once-neat part, made him fear what message could be so urgent as to bring this boy out in cold-catching weather.

"Needed, you say?"

"Yes, sir. There." The Grand bellboy pointed along the coast to the observation tower beside the Spa building, the latter a Joseph Paxton statement of High Victorian splendour. Not as high nor as splendiferous as Cuthbert Brodrick's Grand Hotel, mind, but of a magnificence still to command a pull all of its own. The tower the boy pointed at was still a Paxton, but of less appeal. Italianate, in the pretence of the southern resorts and their "Riviera" ambitions. As a beacon he found it false, and tawdry, and angular, and not near touching on the Englishness of the other two buildings' embellishment.

"Who needs me, boy?" he asked in annoyance, as shelter from dread.

"A detective, sir."

Cox, he thought, relief rushing through. "Sergei Cox?"

"Don' know, sir. A detective, with Metropolitan Police, for a matter urgent, was all 'em told me."

He followed the boy back up to the Grand Hotel's reception. Time had lapsed while he was watching the crabs, and the rest of the crowd had gone by his messenger's arrival. He could have made his way to the Spa via the seawall promenade, it appeared to have been the most direct course. But he opted instead to return with the boy, back to atop cliff street level. The bellboy knew the best way, as such lads could always be trusted to do—to be intimate in short cuts and passages most direct through warrens as imposing as the grandest hotel in Europe. Sure enough, the route led back to the cobbled street of St Nicholas.

The route had taken them into the Grand Hotel at the earliest convenience, via a service door in the base of its substructure; an unassuming door concealed from sight through which he gained access to the deep belly of the building. Its secrecy reminded him of the cathedral cavities in each abutment of Brunel's Bristol carriage bridge that, accessible by iron doors of similar non-consequence, were located below the start of embellishment and which, even now, not so many several years after the bridge's opening to service, had been forgotten so much that even Bristolians believed these towers to be solid stone, rather than tombs of construction that could and were entered by workmen—as one workman on the bridge that he had once...runwith... had told him about one late evening of their run-in.

Bellboy deposited back at reception to dry out, he took the boy up on an offer of a coat to use. What he was given was hardier than the one he had on. It had been handed in to lost and found but was unlikely to be claim-ed on account of it being damaged. Coated up, he set out across the Cliff Bridge and along the South Cliff promenade-up-high, in the direction of Paxton's tower. He was headed toward Olde Scarborough Town—old in spa water, restorative bathing terms; but not ancient, like the curtain walls of the castle on the opposite headland. Some ways after the bridge he was stopped by a closed gate at a tollhouse at the entrance of the south shore promenade. It was not normally shut, and certainly not usually manned by boys dressed in the Grand Hotel's uniform. Simply stating his name was all he needed do for them to let him pass—confirmation that he had indeed been sent for. This confirmation added to the churn inside him as to what this summons was all about—the likelihood that Cox was behind the initiative rubbed thin. Also thinning was the rain, to be replaced by a further roll in of mist from the storm still raging at sea; it swelled around Paxton's tower like a king tide catching a lonesome river barge unawares.

He slowed his pace. But like a bather caught in riptide, reached Paxton's pavilion soon enough. Jarringly for a visitor approaching the landmark for the first time from the Grand Hotel, from above Paxton's pavilion scalp— that bit of the building that ran flat, far lower than the folly-embellishment at the top of the façade—was betrayed something of the building's inner workings. There was an ugly extravagance from this vantage: of piping and technological machinery, rather than the intricate carving of fable figures in stone. How he felt about the ugliness, he could not place. It was what it was, it was necessary to the function of the centrepiece of the Spa attraction. A building that encompassed all the latest conveniences, like the combustion principles that had delivered him to the place at speed and on rails. *It's not the ugliness I dislike,* he decided in haste of need for some resolution, after an evening and dawn of decided indecision. *It's me not understanding the mechanics of it, the reason for its horrid functionalism.*

Beyond the above-Spa view—and by Spa he encompassed, as Scarborough did, the source of the waters around which a resort was built, together with the building—he gleaned some sense of the history of the place... The pavilion was the second on the site, replacing Henry Wyatt's 1839 turreted building that was splendid but too small. Paxton was righted the provision to rectify the site's necessities with a design that would hold its own.

Porter was not privy to the site's provenance...much less had he any knowledge of what might become of the place. He just had a sense. As naggingly noxious as the notion was, he had an inkling...an idea: of ill fortune on and of this site, built in grand style to encase restorative waters. This pavilion would surely hold its own; whatever mass of interest the Spa might spring, stopped only by the fiercest of fires, perhaps, he wagered inside. And on that tinge of foreboding for reckoned ruins to come, he arrived at the crest of the stairs to the Lower Promenade. The stairs were past the pavilion, but before the tower—that had been his yardstick for the journey there, and for whose future, too, he harboured only ill feeling.

Looking again from above, his gaze was drawn down the saw-edge sweep of steps to stone and then sands and then the misty sea.

And it was down there.

On the lower platform that he was confronted with another sight of ugly beauty, putrid perfection, on a bottom pedestal of promenade.

It was

so clear,

even after 237 steps

and through a razor,

rain-hail downpour.

It was Cox.

B alled up. Cox was an it-mangled mess. An island of brokenness with its own defiant tower where mist swallowed the base of its mound. Like a stream eroding shattered shells under the shelf of a boulder broken off of a cliff, Cox was stripped and doubled back into a ball. Most grotesque was that it folded the wrong way. Instead of being bent over at the belly, its body was coiled a reverse way at the lower back, forcing the ribcage to protrude most perversely. Twisted like a sochniki pastry. Like a gymnast's backflip gone gruesomely awry, Cox's pelvis pointed skyward, manhood erect. Erect and as vital as any of the splintered bone protrusions that marked its unnatural bodily trajectory. Reaching out; like organic markers on a sundial. Its erection the mass of its Everest, while the lowest ebbs of it got lost in the mist…underwater, it seemed, until he descended to its level. Its face, cobble pressed and between the smalls of its knees, no doubt disfigured further than any Grand-wall pressing, but thankfully out of sight, lost underneath the weight of it, like the mossy underside of a grand garden statue. Dante's sculpture divine.

"Mr Porter," a voice from behind in unison with a hand on his shoulder.

It posed a double-senses startling. The person-once-known-as-Cox, now a mangled it lump of corpse, was troublingly not without aesthetic contemplation…such an inhumane assessment that had distracted him from the four figures for company, down there with him. Actual men. Distinguishable as clothed and unbroken at the spine.

"Um, I…" He couldn't get the words out, corpse-Cox demanding of his full attention. "Ye—ye—yes," finally ripping himself away. "That's right, and this is Sergei Cox. I knew him."

"Quite. Know that. I'm the one who sent him and then sent for you."

This response was sufficient to make him focus on the breathing body of a man, who spoke words rather than hellish bodily torment. *It's detective*, he thought, as much a question as a realisation. The confusion was compounded by the man before him being not what he expected. It was queer seeing Glass, given the brief Marsh had given. Glass looked younger and more enticing, more virile than he had envisioned. It was queer because Marsh was, probably, more handsome a man; the detective being somewhat thin-lipped and bulbous eyed. But Glass was more youthful, more relatable, more of a fleshy—an uncomfortable adjective in the present context, but there it was before him—form. Peele was clean-shaven too, but on the detective, which he understood was a requirement of the profession, rather than effeminacy being anchored to the absence of hair, it made a mature man in Glass. He and the other tutors were clean-shaven also, as where the competitors. So, Glass seemed with them more. He stammered a little in how to respond. Finally coming out with: "You're the detective, then?"

"Quite," Glass repeated, the man's eyes that seemed to both search for and arrive at a finding in the same glance.

"Ahem," came a second figure, voice familiar. "Sorry for exposing you to this, Porter. I told Oscar here that you were of no consequence to this," gesturing to the backwards roll of Cox, made tawdry through Marsh's offhand, "but he was so insistent. A bit lost in his investigations, it would seem to me."

"Thank you, Mr Marsh," a wide-eyed Glass said, the cuttingness of the address clear on Marsh's face. "But I'm afraid you've left me with little option but to involve this young fella in this mess. For which, Mr Porter, I do apologise."

"It's alright," he said. "Well, actually…" turning, taking it in, "it's not."

"Quite," Glass said, the same searching/arrived-at eyes.

"I feel sick about all this. I've never seen death before; well, in passing… on the streets, of a destitute. But never anything like this. It's just such a queer statement, seeing him posed like that…it rattles me."

"As it should, my boy. I'd be questioning your sanity if it didn't."

Glass moved queerly around the mound, he thought, eyes fixed in the arrived now.

"But I'm alright to assist you with your inquiries…in any way I can. More than alright. In fact, I insist on it. I owe Cox that at least," he said, resisting the urge to scratch the meat under his trousers.

"Quite," Glass said, back to being distant. "I can and do appreciate that, Mr Porter. And you're happy to bend to questioning now?"

"Yes."

Glass nodded, jotting a note in the pad cradled in the small of the detective's right hand. "Good lad. Willing co-operation makes for a much easier job, a happier me, and I can make the process easier on you, too," Glass said. "Nay need to ask what I must out here in this, nor to put you to unease having to speak with poor Mr Cox in sight—yours or mine. It seems to have affected you somewhat, not surprising given the extreme gore of the death——"

"Moreso its st—st—staging," he chimed in.

"Quite," jotting down something again. "It has me too, Mr Porter, I don't mind squaring."

"Thank you, and yes, somewhere out of the weather and more away from here would be welcome. I'm yours for the morning, detective."

"Quite?" Glass said, right brow animated.

"Yes—I'm no longer in Mr Marsh's employ, you see, and so will return to Cambridge by steam train this afternoon. So—lead the way, detective."

"Detective inspector, Porter," Marsh butted in, inserting a third body in their two-fold.

"Detective is fine, Mr Porter. Or Oscar—if I may call you Kemp."

This time it was Marsh whose eyes widened to taken aback.

"Please," he said, squaring onto Glass so as to specially exclude his former employer from their sphere of discussion.

"Right then, it's settled," Glass said. "I have just the place to take you— warm and where I can gain some insight from you. It should not take all of ya morning. Wait here a few minutes, will you, while I make arrangements for Mr Cox's transport somewhere out of the elements? Won't be long. Then we'll head on."

Transport!

The word struck him as a trifle unkind and clinical. But necessary, he supposed, given the poor thing's present condition. He was no undertaker, but the beyond-breaking points of Cox's contortions would mean a logistical calamity of concealment that no normal casket was up to.

Glass went about instructing three boys at police disposal; too young, he believed, to be up to the task of moving Cox's mass somewhere out of the weather. How they would manage it, and why Glass thought for a minute they would be up to the task was on his mind when Marsh rolled over him like sharp rain: "I may no longer pay for your privilege," Marsh spat, face in so close that the brush of moustachioed bits pricked his chin—Marsh being shorter than he, but mustering up intimidation in the moment borne of a jilted man with nothing to loose. "But I still expect you to keep mine. He and I have history, Porter. And that is a man set on pinning someone for all this. That someone won't be me, so I suggest you tread carefully. Oscar is playing detective because I let him, you would do well remembering that." Marsh was veiling something with this threat, though whether it was a warning or a plead, he couldn't say.

"Right, that's sorted," Glass said, detective body put between he and Marsh so that the space where the detective's lip fibres would have been had they been left to grow were even closer to the touch than Marsh's moustache.

Over Glass' shoulder he could already see that the three Grand Hotel boys—they couldn't have been older than fifteen—had already wrangled a horse-drawn wagon from the sands, brought it broadside of Cox's mound, and were fashioning ropes to bind the former boy, now an *it*, in preparation for hoisting from one surface to another. The wagon even had a crane-pulley system fitted, more typically used for the careful raising and placement of delicate stone. Was it resourceful respect, coincidental fortune or—and this final idea he most suspected—a detective's clear directive that had led the boys to locate an instrument that would enable Cox's death piece to be relocated without pry from the promenade?

"Let's go to that some-place-warm, shall we?" Glass said, pushing out his morbid thoughts on transport.

Leaving Marsh out in the cold, Glass charted a path along the Lower Promenade towards the Grand Hotel. The rain had stopped but the mist had bellowed. They waded through it like the rudders of gondolas on the lake in the Underworld, bound for Hades. When the beach came, they took it, passing through where the houses of Surrey and Kent had triumphed at first light, past the Grand Hotel that towered disinterested-yet-at-the-root-of-it-all over them, to the harbour where the detective pulled them back on to stone and up a narrow street, rising crooked away from the sea...to and in front of a dockyards inn named BeeHive. The air of a halfway house about it—its doorway, tall and narrow, much narrower than a domestic dwelling—BeeHive's entry was tacked on to the building—built on a slope—and practically at its corner, in the mouth of a pinched alleyway.

BeeHive was in the direction of uptown but hidden, more in-the-gutter than the main thoroughfares of the harbour. Its corner met with the corner of Scarborough Post Office, so the immediate surrounds of it were respectable enough—something that only served to make it stand out more. Like the torn and soiled lace of a night-mistress whose frock—once fashionable, when swiped from a lady's railway station trolley's trunk—now betrayed in its tattered hemming a more sordid tale. And like said mistress, BeeHive sat there at its corner of Main Street and alleyway, as a honeypot for passers-by. It had not been imaginable to him that the detective could have such a place in mind to conduct interrogations.

Perhaps we will head on, he thought.

But no, sure enough, Glass stayed stopped out in front. "This will be just the honey for you, and me, too," Glass said, ahead of sweeping through.

He held a time before following. To assess what he was headed in to, ahead of the heading into. BeeHive Inn's sign above its threshold was the most assuming aspect of it. About the inn from proprietor "H.Sellers" was scribed: *Within this hive we are all alive, Good ale will make you funny, If you are dry as you pass by, Step in and taste our honey.*

And he did, up four steep steps that met him immediately as a hurried explanation of the narrowness of the entry; into BeeHive to be interrogated by a detective on the hunt for Piper's killer, and now with one body more.

R emote in any drinking company offered, inside was more a dull hum than a buzz of energy. It was not legal for drink houses to operate all hours, but the appearance of some of this establishment's patrons told him they had been there since night. "Get that in' ya, Kemp," Glass said, setting down a pint of lager for each of them at a place picked out by a window.

The spot Glass chose was a booth on a sort of between-floors landing of the hive. They faced each other, though Glass was looking out and down the lane they had come up, looking out and over the boats of the harbour. These boats had also drawn a great number of women in their hour-glass petticoats to watch the sight. They clinked glasses and took a long swig each. His swig was especially long, more than double the detective's. The frothy brew was so cold it clamped his teeth, but he was thirsty enough to ignore this, eager to alleviate the affairs of that morning via alcohol that he stopped for nothing, not even breath. The shock of death made him a boy again, putting him back in the drink halls of his first flush as a failed Cambridge undergraduate.

"Now," Glass said, smiling then serious, at the sight of him with a more than half empty pint glass after only one sip. "Suppose you start with the story of how you came by that coat."

At first, he wondered if this might be some form of detective ice-break-ery. The coat had been on his mind, he might even have glanced at it absent-mindedly as he waited for Glass to arrive with their drinks. He had been about to cast it off, being balmy inside it on account of the full fires in the warren of a man's watering stop. But the enquiry was no innocent get-to-know; Glass, it would seem, felt that enough detective time had already been wasted in buttering him into BeeHive. It was straight in with the detective's hard line of questioning. "*It's Cox's!*" he cried, the shock of discovery taking the wind out of what would have been a shout.

"Yes. It is," Glass said, the detective's features twisting into a devilish sort of delight. "And he was last seen wearing it heading out of the Grand in the dead hours of this morning. So, I have to ask: how did it get to be over your body?"

His mind went blank. *Where did I get it?* Suddenly, having found himself under hard probe, he couldn't remember even his name. He took another swig, though that was probably the last course of action he should have taken. *Why didn't I clock it as Cox's?* he thought, now turning on himself. Still blank, he played with the frayed threads of the gash across the coat's shoulder that should have given the coat's owner away to him immediately. Caught, is what he felt; by the honey-gold of lager, caught wearing a dead boy's coat. Then the mist cleared. *Because of the damage!* "It was offered to me," he said after too long, eyes shot out the window, focused on the boats.

"By whom?"

"A boy."

"Which boy?"

It would have looked suspect, looking elsewhere, like he was plucking his story fresh from the sea. "The one that works reception at the Grand"—— but the boats were necessary, they helped him focus on the events, on getting his account out straight. "He's the bellboy, this boy, I t–think. The one that springs into action whenever you come or go."

"All of which I can make sure of. Verify, you understand."

He turned back to face Glass, rose his lager for a final drain down to the foam. "I know," he said, then returned to the boats.

"How did the bellboy come by it?"

"It was handed in. Lost property."

"Why hand it over to you, and so soon after it had been lost? What if someone should come to claim it, what would happen then?"

The questions were all good, sharp; precise enough to prick implausibility from his tale. But he was no longer worried. So long as he stayed sharp and precise himself…so long as he stayed with the boats. "He had other garments there, he told me. Ones that were much longer since lost, but none that were as apt as this one with which to weather the storm that morning. It's a hardy coat, this one," playing with the frays still. "It's of the East. And besides, the bellboy felt it was unlikely it would be claimed."

"Why was that?"

"On account of the damage...which he noted with me, but which I did not recognise at the time as the distinguishing marker of Cox's coat."

"Yes, and..."

"And on account of where the coat was found."

"And where was that?"

"Outside. At the Spa-facing point of the hotel. At its apex. At the sharp point of its 'V.' Like it had been discarded rather than lost."

"Interesting."

"Is it?"

"O yes. Most interesting." Glass, too, downed the last of lager. "Will you have another, and I'll explain?"

"I suppose...y–yes, yes I will," he said.

"You needn't worry, Kemp," Glass said some minutes later with the setting down of another round of lager. "I don't suspect you. To wear the coat of the man he had killed when summoned to the scene of the crime... No killer would be that careless. And I can tell by the shape of you that you ain't a careless man."

"In that case," he said, tearing his sight-line from the Scarborough harbour and to the detective seated opposite. "I don't mind mentioning another detail relating to this coat, not noticed at the time, but which now, I realise, is no doubt significant."

"O yes?"

"You say Cox was last seen wearing this coat, leaving the hotel?"

"Yes, some time after midnight."

"Well, I witnessed it returning."

Glass bent over the second-round brew like a boy would a fire in the woods at a critical point in a campfire ghost story. "You have my attention. Go on, Kemp," Glass said, dip pen poised over note paper, dropping blots of black on the off-white page like a squid suspecting attack. "With as much precision as memory will allow. Take ya time now."

"Since you will no doubt verify my account with the bellboy at the Grand's reception——"

"——naturally, I will——"

"——I would prefer have it on the record now that I was in Cox's chambers well after 2 am this morning."

"Can you be any more specific on that?"

"I can't, but the boy who gave me this coat should be able to. He was the only one working reception at the hour I came, so needed to call for a replacement while he left the desk. He would have made a note of it—if he knows his job's worth."

"Right, excellent. And he accompanied you up to Cox's room?"

"Yes."

"Let you in and remained with you for the duration of your time there."

"Yes."

"Very good. But what cause had you for wanting to gain access to Cox's bed area in the first place?"

"A genuine one: concern for…him. He had missed the boxing training session held in the restaurant. I called by his room, there was no answer, and so sought assistance from reception."

A third round of drinks arrived at the table from the innkeeper; only too delighted, it seemed, to be plying drink to gentlemen at this hour. Brew to upright men, rather than doubled-over remnants of the past night—no longer in any condition to consume. "Cheers," Glass said, bringing their glasses to clink, "now this is where I am going to drill you on the facts, Kemp, because from what I have heard already, there were many key players missing from that training session."

"Quite," he said, welcoming the interrogation—though somewhere inside cautioning himself not to get swallowed up by the alcohol honey, for there was still the matter of his other hotel, in which was his boy of true concern and who he was determined to keep out of it.

"Three by my count," Glass went on. "One so-called house head and two tutors meant to be coaching: Middlesex—I mean, Mr Marsh—, Underhill and Cox. And yourself, too. You were missing."

"I take issue with you there, Glass," returning his pint to the table harder than intended, spilling some of the third brew over them both.

"Call me, Oscar, please," Glass said, wiping trouser pouch with a handkerchief retrieved from breast pocket. "You're not a suspect. Actually, as of now you're my star witness. I just...need all the facts."

"Very well," he said, turning back to the harbour and its several more boats to calm himself. "To explain my absence: I felt it necessary not to attend, to give Cox a chance to, as you say, coach on his own, as he would need to do for the final round of this tournament when I would not be there. Before the scheduled training, I brought Cox along to drinks with the other tutors—a ritual on the first night of each sorting—, where I stayed with him for a time before leaving him there with the other three, deliberately again, so he might get accustomed to fulfilling the rôle without me present."

"All perfectly logical," Glass said with the manner of a man whose determination to keep the peace between them was plain.

I can use this, he thought. "If I can add, with all due respect," he said, taking his chance to steer Glass away from a logical next question of where he was when the boxing training took place, or where he went after leaving drinks early...the one part of his story that could be his undoing, placing him somewhere outside of the Grand Hotel. "From my perspective, Cox's absence was the only absence I should have concerned myself with, and therefore the only person I would, naturally, have sought to check in on. And it was only when I did, go that is, to check on him and how the training went, that I learnt that he hadn't been there. Further, it seems—and I am not a detective, but this is still as it seems to me—that even from an outsider, Cox is the only absence that is curious here."

"O yes? Please, show the man your work."

"Underhill, as Kent tutor, I expected to be secretive. Blunt and his boys always are on a Kent turn. In fact, it would not have been suspicious to me if Blunt's tributes were absent either, on account of his quarter not wishing for any inkling of their strategy or the nature of their technique to seep out in a mere training session. After all, unlike my former employer, Blunt favours strategy and self-advantage over the fairness of chance and would have known well the abilities of his own team. The training session, therefore, was Blunt's opportunity to observe the candidates of the other houses. Whereas Marsh would draw lots to determine sparring opponents, Blunt sees them all in action beforehand, and pairs up opponents to suit his home's advantage. He keeps a tight leash on his 'coach' during sorting, too, Underhill of whom, bless him, hasn't the same head for strategy. Perhaps he was instructed to stay away?"

"That is most useful, Kemp," Glass said, the distraction seemingly serving its function, the detective's scribblings now several pages over from where the bar-drinks part of his story had been jotted. "And how about your former employer, why was his absence not suspicious?"

"To the contrary, a head missing training is highly suspicious—this morning's tournament, more so, I might add. But when one knows what we know," he said, raising his glass so there could be no missing his second meaning, "Marsh not being there is hardly surprising."

"And what is it that we know?"

"Cox," he said.

"You believe he was jealous of my deputy?"

"That is manifest. It seems a safe assumption that Marsh was still shall we say *processing* his disappointment at receiving that boy instead of you, compounded by the fact that Cox was someone he had already met...and not as part of dealings with the Met. Even someone as arrogant as Marsh would be inclined to read himself as being outdone by the boy."

Now it was Glass who seemed keen to stem further questions along a particular line of the inquiry. "Yes, well, I'm not sure I follow you there, but moving on"——flicking back through notes...he hoped, not to arrive somewhere near the after-drinks question. "Ah yes," Glass said, clearing throat. "I need a clear account of your movements, Kemp; a mere formality, you will understand."

He felt the harbour pulling him back like a rock anchor slipping through the sand. But he resisted the boats this time so as not to betray a tell even more than he had already. "Of course," he said.

"If I can pick up on something you said...ah yes, here it is: You said that it was only when you went to check on him that you learnt Cox had missed training. How exactly did you learn this, if he was not there when you checked? And why did you feel the situation serious enough to fetch a boy from reception to gain entry to his room?"

Again, it was sound questioning that, no doubt, the detective felt exposed a flaw in his story. He was relieved that the true blemish of his timeline still eluded Glass, and knowing that time was short, that the morning was almost away—and with it his need to stay much longer—, he seized the question as an opportunity to draw out the time he had left. To distract the detective from getting to any other apparent inconsistencies in his story. "Sounds like you may have collapsed two separate events there," he said, going on to explain that entering Cox's room with the assistance of the boy from reception came only after he had attempted to check on him, and that it was when he went up that first time on his own that, after knocking, Brown emerged and told him that Cox had not been seen all night.

"Did you try the other two doors in that part of the hotel?"

"I did," he said, "but there was no answer from either, and so I assumed that Tanner and Underhill were sleeping and sought the assistance from reception."

The strange South Cliff-leaving man seen from Brown's room wearing Cox's coat—a man, it chilled him to realise, who was probably Cox's killer—captured the detective's imagination. "The man you saw, how big would you say he was?"

"Difficult to say. Not tall, ill proportions. He was oddly shaped, broad."

"And you saw the man from Brown's room, you say. This room, it was, you would say, well-appointed?"

"Yes, much larger than mine. Though the one next to it, the one for Underhill was the same size but with a much better view."

Glass' brow bunched in the manner of working something out.

"Don't look too much into that, Oscar," he said, buttering the detective up. "Naturally Underhill would have a better view than Brown, it's the hosting house's privilege."

"And your house, how did it fair with views?"

"Well, I'm technically a contender now, so fair for me. But the rôle of the Tutor of Middlesex: rather well indeed."

"The room assigned to Cox, you mean?"

"Yes."

"Room 250?"

"Sounds right, though I couldn't be certain."

"And the room of the last coach?"

"Tanner?"

"Yes."

"Right next door, and better than Cox's."

"251?"

"That I definitely don't know. But a sea view, absolutely. Tanner made quite the point of that."

Glass nodded, then retrieved from the rear of the detective's notebook a diagram of the tutors' floor of the Grand Hotel and slid it before him.

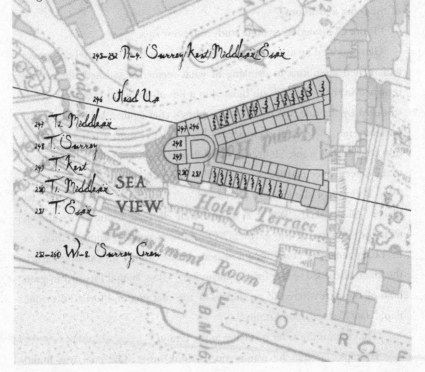

Blotchy black scratchings on this diagram showed the housing for tutors and round-three pledges, with room numbers and even a key. Glass' key had tutors as "T.," with a "T1." and "T2." for Cox and him, respectively. Pre-boxing-sorted pledges were marked as "P1-4." and those who would make up the Kent Crew as "W1-8." "I had our boy at reception mock this up for me," Glass said. "The Kent Crew were transferred to sea-view rooms following their win, with mountain view for the first night and sharing arrangements for P3 and P4 Essex and P3 and P4 Middlesex in rooms 233 and 232. Larger rooms 238 and 237 were for P1 Kent and P1 Surrey, while 259 and 260 were reserved for W1 and W2 Surrey, who I understand were formerly known as P1 Kent and P1 Surrey. All pledges were to remain on the same floor with the coaches. The four heads as they call themselves were in the same rooms as their respective coaches, just one floor up and so are not shown here—though one room, 246, was set aside for head use. Study it for me, take your time now. And tell me, does it correspond with your experience of the room allocations?"

"It does," he said after some study and brew sips.

Glass nodded again, tucked the diagram back between notebook pages and turned attentions to drinking in what seemed a satisfied silence. He returned to the boats. As sails bloated in a full-of-sun wind akin to toad fish stranded by the tide, the feel of a dead boy's coat against his body pressed questions into the unsettled crevices of his mind, like mortar roughly packed into cold-porous stone. He traced the violent frays of coat damage, gripped, as the detective seemed also, by the terrible possibilities of its previous wearer. "Was it clever of the killer to abandon Cox's coat, or to take it in the first place?" Glass asked. "Was it as an elaborate distraction and concealment, as is the function of the garment? Or was it a reckless improvisation? A necessary means of concealment of gore on the clothes, for example, which the killer discarded at the first opportunity?" Glass leaned forward to grab hold of the part where the two halves of the coat met and turned over one flap: "*Aha!* You see, blood stains."

"That means the killer is staying at the Grand?"

"Perhaps...or that he wants you to think he is. The coat was found outside, so it could have been a clever attempt by the killer to suggest he was a guest—achieved without the need to get past reception, which as I'm sure you too have discovered is near impossible for a non-guest."

"True. But surely it's as simple as the killer not wishing to be seen in the hotel wearing Cox's coat?"

"Content to walk through covered in blood instead? No, my friend, there is careful calculation in the leaving of that coat where it was found, I think." Glass was more proper-tongued in detecting speech and furious notetaking, he noticed. "You have been most helpful, Kemp. There are few men untouched by bias in this affair. Unpolluted by the hand of other forces. Even Stew Boy, your employer. We knew each other as boys, as you seem to know. Even with him I have to be careful with what detail I share."

"Prett," he said, but intended only to think.

Glass nodded grimly: "The well-spoken pretty boy from the stables? A confidence trickster of the highest order, I'd wager."

"Will you warn your friend?"

Glass stayed grim as the detective's head changed course: "In certain matters, Kemp. With certain affairs, men cannot be made to see sense. And I cannot risk isolating our Stew Boy any further. I must put the pier first."

His own intimacy with the power certain boys could wield led him to wonder about Glass and the case. "*The pier's* getting much police time. Why?"

"What is the boy's pull of a detective inspector from the many murders of the capital? When there's Jack ripping his red trade throughout London?" He nodded. "He stands for so much more. He could be the undoing of so much more." The detective laid out a gambling-in-the-gentlemen's-clubs tale. Surprisingly learned on the subject given Glass' lot in life that would not permit access to these spaces. What he knew of *Sizar's* seemed timidly compared with the stories of "high play" in the gentlemen's clubs that stood to-day in the public eye, with dealings that went on off the streets of St James's. Though he was really not privy enough to the goings on inside *Sizar's* to call whether the club was same or different from the stories of the detective—*a place in the regatta at the end could change that!* But it was possible

Sizar's gambled just as brutally. "Have you heard the story of the sunken-ship bet?" Glass asked. He shook his head. "It comes from the account of Horace Walpole and tells of a Mr Blake of *White's*. Blake betted 1500 pounds that it was possible for a man to prevail under the sea for twelve hours. For the bet he hired a daring fellow, desperate no doubt, and sunk him in a ship." Glass left it to hang, the boats of Scarborough all in white as backdrop.

"What happened?"

"Neither fellow nor ship ever resurfaced. But Walpole writes that another ship and another fellow would be 'tried.' Of course, never with the sinking of the assassin himself, Mr Blake, but instead another wretched fellow torn off the streets. And this is just the surface of it, just one of the stories that have found their way out and on to the public record."

Was this murder? he wondered. Certainly such "crimes" are of the least interest to the magistrates and lawmakers, and perhaps Detective-Inspector Glass, too. The deaths bet on were of vagrants in games of human sport that euthanised vermin off streets spewing with the crimes of the ungentlemanly masses. *Right?* And because those betting were probably lawmakers and magistrates, too, murderous gambling maybe showed an above-God's-vengeance arrogance of these men. Was *Sizar's* just one more of these? Maybe the Piper death was all one big murderous bet, after all. Maybe that's why it's drawn unusual interest of a Met Police detective. Maybe Glass is pursuing the case to untangle something of clubs, to bring the whole rotting lump of them down.

"On m' way now to inspect Cox with a pathologist," Glass said as his eyes skipped between the safe-in-harbour boats. "Seems you cared for him, certainly went out of your way to check up on him. Tragically, at exactly the time when he needed someone most." It stung a shred, itched him still, *down there*, and Glass seemed to take note. "Care to accompany me, to see him again? Perhaps to gain some closure from the shock of this morning?"

It was a monstrous suggestion, the very thought of seeing the runt's mutilated corpse again, in more clarity…it turned his stomach, stocked with lager. "Yes," he said in bitter spite of himself. A damned-man's leap in his trousers at the pressing thought of seeing the mass once more.

O ff the cobbles and moved under the streets of Scarborough, Cox
was housed at unrest on a slab-pedestal of the Royal Northern Sea
Bathing Infirmary—a building located partway between BeeHive Inn and
the Grand Hotel. *The infirmary suits Cox*, he had crudely thought on approach;
built of a red brink and at a time commensurate with the Grand Hotel, but in
the Italianate style, like Paxton's Spa Tower, where the Russian's death pose
was shaped. And a grotesque shape it was, without the mist or rain to mask
it. Especially being lit that way, by candlelight, like the darkest conjurings of
a séance—a monster of lowest order and darkest pagan science. They had
entered direct from the back of the building, where the wagon that Grand-
Hotel staffers had loaded Cox onto had also delivered the broken boy by.
They ventured down into the bowels of the infirmary. As he descended the
slope that the death wagon had travelled, he could not help but see horror in
the bed quilts lumped on the earth beside the horses.

Taken from the hotel's stocks. To any passers in the town for the transit there, seeing the velvet-covered lump, steadied by two boys riding up
there with it, and one more at the reins...those lucky onlookers would
not have thought twice. And had they; stopped, that is. To ponder...what
might be passing them. They would most certainly have assumed it to be
a bureau under there, from one of the sea-view staterooms, bound for a
woodturner whose workshop was in Olde Scarborough Town, who would
work up a repair for a collapsed pigeonhole compartment, or an urgent
replica carving and reattachment of a front leg, perhaps. Never would
they have attuned—even in the most unsavoury of imaginations. Never
would onlookers be mindful of what mutilation of a young man quaked in
the musk underneath quilts that had adorned many a bed of the grandest
hotel in Europe.

"It's sculptural," the drafted-in coroner—a Dr Henrik, as formerly introduced—said encircling Cox. "I only arrived here some minutes before you both, so my assessment of young Mr Cox's state is still...evolving. I beg that you bear with me." Henrik spoke in a manner of unravelling Cox, like the corpse were a fine Egyptian rug, found in storage in a tomb.

It made him queasy, the way the doctor worked.

"Quite alright, doctor," Glass said, stepping back into a shadow in the room, "don't let our presence distract you from your work." Glass continued quietly to him from the shadows, "The good doctor here attended to the pier boy in Brighton in the winter just passed. His insights into that body and what we could glean, investigative-ly, from his condition were most useful. I sent for him direct this morning, via telegram, and he was gracious enough to travel in on the first train."

Perhaps it was the damp and shadows of the place making him suspect, but the good doctor did seem to have, he thought, gotten to Scarborough rather soon after the death, even if on the first train.

The doctor cleared throat, perhaps indicating that the detective's voice was audible at a level that caused distraction...or, perhaps, for a different reason. "You were right to send for me, detective inspector," the doctor spoke up, projecting to the shadows as well as the lit portions of the room, like a professor to an auditorium of medical students while stood over a cadaver. "First, because I am suited best to deliver medical juxtaposition of the Piper and Cox corpses. And second, and on this point is why I assume you have brought your guest here—Mr Potter, was it?"

"Porter."

"Yes, as I said, Mr Porter here, you trust his discretion, so I speak free?"

"Yes, yes. Both those, boy," Glass said re-joining candlelight.

"Well then, gentlemen. It is fortunate indeed that our good detective inspector here had the foresight to summon me, rather than entrust this examination to a local coroner. Fortunate in the first instance because I can save you time by stating with every confidence of medical training that *this* before us is the product of a crime and a criminal entirely different from the Piper case, and further—and I would stake my professional credence on this fact—that the two cases should be considered as distinct and only coincidentally connected to misfortunes of this so-called gentlemen's club."

"And second?" he spoke up, stepping forward to join Glass' side, buoyed by BeeHive brew, the detective's vouching for him and an at-the-pressure-point *need to know* what a man with medical training could make of such a macabre entanglement of a once boy.

"Second, Mr Porter, it was cunning of the detective inspector here to summon me as none of my colleagues, I believe, could stomach such a sight of a boy defiled as he is…which would disqualify them outright from the true depths of this poor boy's desecration."

"Put your faith to one side please, doctor," Glass said, "speak medically."

"Ah, indeed I must, detective inspector, for what has been done to this boy is, medically speaking, utter deterioration of the body…soul removed."

"Alright, doctor," Glass said, approaching Cox with the detective-forensic angle. "Let's expand each of your two points in turn. First, connection with the Piper case: I admit that this before us, poor Cox, marks a radical escalation of cruelty and mutilation. And from my experience, could hardly say it was the same man. Yet, and I am no doctor, my professional past seeing the products of the criminally insane has taught me that an escalation of the criminal mind is not unusual. In fact, it is most common."

"I am, nor do I pretend to be," Henrik said, stepping up too, like a competitor to the plate of combat, "an alienist, one turned to trying to make sense of the needs that drive men alienated from their moral core. But, on what I see here—and even if I were to accept a sharp escalation of criminality…the gradient is simply too steep for me to link the two cases. The deaths are too different. In fact, they are diametrical."

"How? Enlighten us, doctor."

He thought Henrik a quack the way the man relished Glass' esteem. Though he too was desperate to hear…

"In every way," Henrik said, grasping the open socket of the tweed vest the doctor wore, poked out of a stinking-stained leather apron, "but I will only relay a few. Let's work backwards, shall we, as is the method of any forensic investigation, whereby we reverse-engineer the damage to the flesh, to arrive at the cause of death—and in your case, detective inspector, so continues a further reach back, to weapon then motive then, for all our sakes I hope, the perpetrator. Cox himself points the way through his back-broken death dance." Henrik looked to them with a toothy grin, like a cat with milk-coated whiskers proud of its own cleverness. "We start with decay," the doctor went on, pressing a finger to Cox's raised pelvis, which wobbled in response...so unsavoury, like a month-old trifle. "Piper was fresh as a kept-alive catch when I examined him: flaccid and pink, even, with no rigidity. Cox, however, has discoloured already at a rapid pace, far beyond what I would expect given the low temperatures death occurred—I presume—in and in which the body remained left out. He does not present as a corpse kept on ice." The man, crooked and wicked in the eyes, was right, Cox was already discoloured to a purplish black, and parts of the boy bloating with decomposition. As Cox thawed in the comparative warmth of the infirmary's fire-lit basement, he even thought he could detect a smell to the lump of flesh in front of him... more like what a week-old whale beached on the rocks would give off.

"That is indeed a striking physiological anomaly between the two boys, I agree," Glass said, much word-smarter, *"yet!* what bearing this has on the killer or any connection to be drawn between the two deaths, I do not see."

"Ah!" Henrik retorted, with the elation of an excitable professor whose pupils had taken his lesson-plan trajectory. "But I disagree most strongly. In fact, I chose to start with this physiological point because it reveals most about the motive and mindset of our latest killer, medically speaking." Henrik circled Cox, poking the former boy at various points in the breakages of its body, like a fairground performer keeping spinning plates turning for show. The result was a wobble of decay with a momentum all its own, and a treatment of Cox as rotting meat, which was all the boy now was...such regard disgusted him, turned him sick, *down there.* "I am willing to accept," Henrik continued, stopping the poking now that Cox moved off a momentum all of its own, like the convulsions of a dead-but-still-twitching spider, "that Piper is...remarkable. Even the most scientific of minds would have been struck by the indefinable, spiritual, beauty of that boy. *But!* it was not all his makeup that made him stay fresh in that way."

"What are you trying to say?" Glass asked.

"It's simple. The modus of their deaths are contrary to each other. Piper was killed with passion, whereas this boy"——Cox still convulsing grossly on its backwards broken joints, the penis rigid, *rigor mortis* seemingly having instantly on-death set in——"was slain with utter loathing. This one was slaughtered worse than even an animal is. In slaughtering an animal for food, care is taken not to damage the meat. There was no care shown this boy, his flesh was torn and damaged on purpose, to advance decay."

Glass gave a look that said the detective knew he had a train to catch, and then spoke in summation: "I have to say that before this happened, I was comfortable Piper's death could be kept separate as a fit of passion."

"And what I'm saying," Henrik said, reanimating Cox's death dance, on the second time as an inhumane, unnecessary, boredom-driven spectacle, "is that this latest death should only lend credence to your view on the first. You see, I've been looking long on the Piper case, and doing some reading on it, too. Did you know that in corners of the Orient, British explorers have encountered deaths so peaceful that they mimic meditative states? Bodies that are dead, but have no signs of decay? Suspended death; or life, in hibernation. These cases are always tied to forms of spiritual pursuit, life-long pursuits of calm. Piper, I think, stayed fresh because his death occurred in the throes of passion. Piper was killed by someone who loved him, that I am sure of. The frightfully reverse of which is true here. Here there is only hatred." After a full encompass of the slab, Henrik went on: "It is just as well that the boy's face is broken and buried under itself, for were we to see it, I believe, it would convey the complete terror of a full consciousness of the carnage its body would endure."

Having given away more of the morning, and into mid-afternoon, than he had intended, he took this window to make his excuses. As he ascended to the street, Henrik moved to other points of difference between the two cases, the next of which he overheard in a clipped way as leaving. The next point stayed with him all along street level…Glass asking whether, on the matter of leaving an inside deposit, down there, Cox differed, too. White-hot fear coursed through him. *I pulled out, didn't I?*

A nxious; death a ballast to the mind, he shuffled along the Scarborough foreshore, his back to castle ruins and slow enough—though this had not been his intention—to give Glass time to finish up with Cox and come upon him a way up from the infirmary; just before a turn into the town on a shorter route that would have led him back to the Royal Hotel. The sight of Cox's brokenness flashed in the black blinks of his eyes, while Glass was recruiting again. This time, he was the one the detective wished to deputise into danger. Glass assured he'd be chaperoned as precaution against a fate similar to Cox's...this time. Glass sweetened the call with an offer of accommodation in central London. He said he'd consider it and let the detective know of his decision before leaving Scarborough that day, though the truth was that no consideration was needed—it was a lifeline in what had become an untenable arrangement, being now out of employ.

Keel was in bed and asleep when he returned. No matter what the time of waking hours, sleep was all Keel ever seemed to be doing now. He had no patience for it after that morning, after what he had seen—after the state that the boy he once knew as Cox had wound itself up in. After being forced to bugger the dead boy on account of ill-affection from the living one he'd sacrificed so much for. "Get dressed, check out and head to the station," he ordered, "and here," tossing his wallet, what was left in it being all the money he had to his name, "use what's there to book us a compartment on the afternoon train to London."

Keel seemed much more chipper, being bossed about was apparently a tickle. Certainly, more chipper than the dominant dreading disposition that he had become used to. The prospect of a train into London, especially, rather than a return to Cambridge as originally planned, seemed to delight.

For the train journey, they ended up staying separate. It was by necessity… of the company of Glass, who, elated that he had taken up the offer to deputise, decided to head back early as well, and take the chance to fill him in on the case so far…

"While I respect the good doctor's position," Glass said as early signs of the capital smudged into view, "every detective instinct in me tells me that the Piper and Cox cases are linked."

Glass spoke through assistance from a notebook that seemingly contained all the detective had learned from the investigation thus far. An amateur he must be judged, but the detective seemed to have very little clarity in the case. But he tended to agree with Glass' instinct on the two murders: there must be some link between the deaths, however tenuous. Certainly, too, a single killer is better to stomach than two, and much more than a few in cahoots.

"I can only assume that Cox uncovered something in his capacity as an investigator," Glass elaborated, "a likelihood that, let me assure you, I take with the gravest of responsibility. He should not have been left alone the way he was. And when you are out there, in the field, shall we say, I will be with you. You will be in no real danger."

It gnawed that Glass likely made similar promises of no physical harm to Cox. Nibbling at him also was that Glass had almost certainly been in town when Cox was killed…this town presence was not spoken of. But he knew that *of course the man must have been…to arrive on the scene so promptly.* Even the good doctor, in his knowledge of the trains to this part of Yorkshire, seemed to arrive to inspect the body in suspiciously good time. He held his tongue, staying silent as Glass sketched out what had been gleaned—detective-ly speaking. Setting out the statements of the four heads, of whom, it was clear from his notebook glances, Glass seemed to regard as the only likely suspects.

Glass used a handwritten list of names given by Marsh as a reference throughout the discussion. While remarking on the sentimentality of Marsh not striking out the losses of Piper and Prett, even with the impermanence of a pencil scratch, *Lewis*, as the boy had a tendency to in this game so far, snapped grim reality back.

Splatter pen in angry strokes over Marsh's neat list was Glass' hand, crossing Prett and Piper out first, followed by all the pencil crosses, now in ink. Then came the noughts, the winning names. From it a disturbing game of noughts and crosses came to the fore, with the names of two dead written angry-large by the detective at the top right. The sad game brought on silent melancholy in the detective, who was probably contemplating whether what was now in black and white before them could possibly be a coincidence. And if not, how such an outcome could have been orchestrated. Melancholy the detective must have been, because the man wrote "Pipe" rather than "Piper." Connotations of the first dead as a *pipe boy* scratched somewhere inside him. *The Pipe* boy. *Why is that so familiar?*

"Tell me, Porter," Glass said at last, finger tracing the names in Marsh's hand to the right of where the detective had written angrily and large. "The night of the Lewis train suicide—that was amid another round, and therefore, the boy should not have been there, I presume." He nodded slow, wanting for time to think. "Any idea why he was?"

"No," he lied.

"Or of any other round-one boy who might have been on that train."

"No," for the second time.

Glass watched him intently. It burned like the guilt Judas may have felt when questioned of knowledge about some man in particular. "Any, unusual absences, you might have noticed?"

He leapt at the chance not to lie a third time under questioning: "There were missing pledges from dinner, but I couldn't place them. Marsh stepped out, and so did Blunt. Blunt longer than expected, though only slightly."

Glass nodded, an air of a detective thinking things through, tapping "Blunt" of Kent, the head between the two dead, and the man's tutor, "Underhill," too. "You swim, Porter," Glass then said.

"Yes, it's a requirement. All the tutors do."

"Why?"

"It's Cohen's favourite sport. A common pursuit to have to teach."

"But Peele can't swim. He told me so when I interviewed him."

"Neither can Marsh," he said with a shrug. "Doesn't need to teach it."

"How about Blunt. Can he?"

"O yes, he's as expert as Cohen."

Glass continued to tap the angry ink in that same thinking-through manner. Seemingly sad-satisfied enough to study the game between them in silence for the remainder of the trip back to London. Perhaps he should have been studying this too. But he went the opposite way, his preferred way, pushing Lewis out…to focus on thoughts of what to do with Keel when they arrived. It was the more pressing matter, in his mind—as damned a man as the thought made him feel. That, too, he pushed into a ravine in his mind.

By London he was no closer to a good man's resolve. He would be sure to make full use of the accommodations Glass was offering, though he was not yet sure whether he would himself be staying there, nor whether he would hold up his end of the bargain with the detective. A bad man he had become indeed, he felt. Seeing Cox as he had. It had reshaped his priorities, and any appetite to continue further with this investigation and the club by which he was no longer employed…well, resolve to have any further involvement was ebbing away, pushing from a page that also bore the name of a boy he had shielded, but whose rôle in it all was spine-crumpling close to the bone.

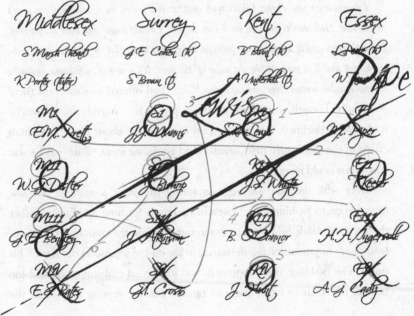

*D*etective-Inspector Glass' conditional free board was for a fourth-floor flat in a ramshackle wooden tenement perched precariously on the docks down from the Tower of London; so precarious a position, in fact, that once inside the one-room space, the whole structure seemed to sway away from its foundations and toward the Thames—under only the motivation of their weight. That the building was off kilter was shown by the window with their view...of the murky water, when they should have had a view of the muddy bank opposite. Walking down from London Central Station, the dwelling was, decidedly, on the wrong side of respectability. Both in build and in the other boarders—all halfway boys, all of whom were only marginally more respectable in appearance and mannerism than those who made their burrows from the slums that surrounded the building.

I should warn you, Porter, Glass had said on the train, *the accommodations aren't second-rate. Hell, they're not even third-rate. In fact, I would wager that there are parts of London's inner streets that are more peaceful to lay your head. But the place is dry, for the most part, and it is safe, despite the noise of the area. It's a sort of safe house, actually, for my London errand boys and informers.* Glass had offered to show him there personally. Though, mindful of meeting up with Keel outside the station, he had politely declined, and dredged up some excuse about meeting Cantab chaps in the city centre first, which could go on for some while—as he was sure Glass could imagine.

Even with the due warning, on seeing the place a man of law saw appropriate to let him lie in—even in exchange for time and favour rather than coin—, made him want to storm right back to the station. To head out from there in pursuit of the detective, to lay on the scoundrel the size of his mind. The building, from approach, was like soiled crab traps, stacked too high at the Thames edge, about to tumble into the flowing filth under the weight of scavenging rats; and such a fate would have been relief for civilised eyes. But Keel's rapture at the place softened him. It shocked him, was the truth. How a boy that shattered, so wholly stupefied into ill-ableness could arrive at such a place of vagrant muck of sight, sound and smell—of the absolute grubby sole of a city. *To liven here.*

"This is an ace place you've scored us here, Port," Keel said as floorboard rot threatened to give way under them. "And it's all ours, did you say?" *Port in me!* Keel must have been jerking him about, he thought. Gearing up to strip him back for the sordid situation of the lodgings he had secured them. He thought this until Keel persisted in praise past the point of any conceivable pull back, continuing to find space to grow there. "Come here, Port," Keel said, perched on the sill of the one window in the single room with one bed, a table with two chairs and the greased-in kitchen of a navvy bachelor. *There is a beauty to it,* he conceded, at Keel's side, as long boats of all heights and widths lit up with lanterns plied their trade into factories and out to ships. "I live around these parts," Keel said, "used to, I mean. Never did manage m'self a Thames view, though. Was always lodging some ways back that way," pointing further into the wrong end of London.

Out of Brighton, out of Scarborough, out of society proper. He felt especially out of calibre with Keel now. There was a beauty in what Keel saw, but was it a beauty for him? And one that would suit for the two months before Peele's go at sorting…to which, he wasn't even sure he would help the detective out in—and if he didn't, he would feel no guilt, after seeing this set up. "Listen, Keel," he said, drawing his companion's attention from the Thames.

"Yes Port?"

He felt like he had made his mind up, seen through the fantasy of masculine competition to the stark realities of poor London docks life. But the move in of moon and lantern light made it harder. Unfairly, these sources put sparkle in Keely blue eyes: "I–I'm not sure I can stay with you…here," adding that last bit because, in the saying, clearly there was no way he was letting the boy go, only now succeeding in keeping Keely blue eyes.

Keel took his hand, no dent in enthusiasm. It made him wonder whether what he was saying was understood. "Come with me," Keel said. Out of the room—without closing the door—Keel pulled him, down the stairs of the ramshackle wooden house, into the night, onto the rotting timbers of the dock, then on…out of the slums of the wrong side of the Pool of London, past its Tower, and along and along and along, until London Bridge.

"Time please, mate," Keel said, acting most out of character. Light-stepped. Jolly, even.

"Ten minutes to midnight."

"Marvellous. On to the bridge, then." *I will miss the last train*, he thought, yet continued to go light, allowing Keel to tow him out and on to the bridge. "Come along," Keel said. Still easy to tow, he now moved with Keel to quicken their flight across the bridge. They called it "new" London Bridge, the third by that name to make the crossing. But of course, to him, it was old. It was also the busiest. The most congested strip in London, he reckoned; even nearing the midnight hour, when the toll to cross was much cheaper and tramps, pickpockets and other vagrants were generally able to slip along it without spending a penny—to ply their night trade. *We're among the underclass then*, he thought, non-toll-paying night-crosses. "Time, mate," Keel repeated, this time at the bridge's apex.

"Near-on midnight."

"Near on? No, no, that won't do. You strike me as a man of strict London timekeeping."

Which he was. "Alright, if it's that important to you. On my mark it will be two minutes to twelve."

"That's better."

"Mark."

"Moment of truth time, Porter," Keel said, dropping grip of him to grab hold of the lantern post instead and vaulting the barricade to land on the narrow shelf of decorative sandstone—fast-flowing Thames facing. Keel's hand then came back and outstretched. "Joining me?"

He looked about, then instantly cursed his own self-consciousness. The bridge was bustling, but none on it paid Keel's vaulting any attention. He grabbed Keel's hand and followed. "Now one to twelve," he said, checking his breast pocket, pre-empting the question.

"Almost time, then," Keel responded, clamping his hand a bit tighter—letting go of the anchor point of the bridge lamppost pole. He turned to face Keel. The flicker of the lamp flame of the lantern above together with the moon in a cloudless night shimmered Keely blue eyes again like unfair, splendid sapphires. Keel leaned in: "Do you trust me?" said so intimately soft, lips grazing his ear.

"Yes," he answered as a reflex.

"Then on my mark," Keel said, still ear brushing, but hands dropping to rest on his waist. "At midnight, *stay with me.*"

He didn't need to check his breast pocket now. The minute had been so painstakingly long that he felt that each second was etching itself somewhere in the alcoves of his soul. It was obvious what this was.

A pact. *Is this how it went with Lewis?* he wondered. How wilfully he had given over to it. How reckless he was in his affections, even after he had threatened to leave—because he had? He did not understand the significance of on-the-strike-of. Part of him wanted to tilt them over now, to be done with it. But gently, Keel held them both there. On the sidelines of Keely blue eyes, he could see the churn of dark and dirty water, and when the inevitable final second came before Keel's mark...well, he felt it coming, somewhere deeper, beneath the proximity of his breast pocket, under their very feet, as together they left the bridge.

The capital's river was not that far from the stone bridge deck. Death was not a guarantee, though had it been that might have been a comfort. For the waters down there, in addition to being freezing, were also fast-flowing, with the putridity of industrial debris. He did surprise himself, however, with the way he went about the bargain. There were no pinched-shut eyes, no frantic final verbiage, no after-the-fact fatal remorse. He stayed focused on the blue pool of Keel's sapphires as the bricks, stars and waters of London somersaulted around them.

It was peaceful.

Instantaneous, almost.

No pain, and in the end...

there was white.

VIII

PALACE

Vicious intrigue behind this place," Glass said in a roundabout queer sort of fashion in lieu of hullo. The detective had caught him among the dune weeds, Birkdale Palace Hotel coming into form from the beach, the waves to their backs. "Sinister story its bricks tell."

Two months had passed since the fall from London Bridge. It seemed more like a year ago on account of all that had happened, but all up there was only some six months since Brighton—when the whole drama had started—and now, the dawn of the summer and the eve of the final regatta. Birkdale marked the last sorting round, headed this time by the House of Essex. In exchange for his assistance on the case, Glass had allowed him— *with his girl, if he had one*, the detective had said—free board in an apartment on the Thames. The offer had seemed serendipitous at the time, providing a temporary solution to his lack of employment and the caring for Keely, his boy. Even if, on leaving Scarborough his patience for rolling-Keely-gloom had been wearing thin.

Glass had come good on a promise not to call by, enquire or in any way other make impression on the apartment on the water in the Pool of London that was, no sugar-coating it, a cesspool. Just as well the detective had not visited, for the man would not have happened onto a welcome reception, given how rapidly the situation had changed following arrival…how dark it had all become. And what came out after a fateful fall from the bridge. Were it not for a sense of owing it to Keely, to his boy's memory, he would never have come to Southport at all, nor probably have stayed in the tenement on the Thames after hauling himself from the water after the fall.

"Hullo, detective inspector," he called over his shoulder. He shouted it, really, to be heard over the wind and surf.

"Oscar, please."

The Palace Hotel was built only four years earlier and already the stubborn pretensions of its position were showing themselves. In and yet out of Southport, in Birkdale. With no train or tram or reliable road access, it was cut off, on the headland—calls already coming in constant for an extension of the line to bring visitors closer to its doors. There was a more direct means of reaching it from the station and through the town, but he opted to head direct for the sea, then to reach her from there. Doing so was part of a hoping, beyond hope as it turned out, that he would manage to avoid meeting Glass again outside the formality of the activities to come. That he would put off a bit longer questions about how he had got on staying in that apartment on the Thames.

They were cursed to find each other, it appeared.

Glass now caught up and hovering at his side, he continued his approach to the strange proposition of this hotel; off the flats of the beach, through the reeds of the dunes and onto the greens of the Birkdale Palace Hotel grounds where grand lodgings stood starkly separate, south of Southport. Here, conversation was easier, and Glass seized the chance to return the unease by sweeping him up into another story of intrigue: "*It's built backwards!* her main entrance, her state rooms, all her finery face inland rather than out to sea. And word is that this was a mistake, an oversight of the builders in interpreting the plans of the architect, who was not on-site to oversee its construction." Glass spoke more formally than he was used to, like the man was not a detetctive anymore but a local historian giving a haunted-Southport tour.

"It does seem strange," he said, taking in the flat back of the building while his own back was flat-facing the sea.

"Stranger, too, given the architect is now dead."

The straight-in sinisterness of the story unsettled him, but he made attempts to sound nonchalant: "O?"

"Suicide, according to Sandgrounders, which is what Southport folks are called. Though," with a slap on his back, "that could just be what they tell superstitious Londoners." The slap-back *snapped back* Glass into a mode of address closer to what he was expecting. "Good to see you, mate. How'd my little flat work out for you? Not too awful, I hope."

Eager to avoid the topic of the Thames, he allowed some interest in his tone and clung to local folklore: "What do you make of it?" he asked as they came around from the back of the building to arrive, yes, unmistakably at the frontispiece, which one would normally expect to face the sea. "Do you see any merit to the story?"

Glass seemed satisfied enough staying with the ghosts, and slipped back again into a mode of a man much different: "It's possible, I'd say. Architects and engineers are not as hands-on with the process as they once were, you know. Simply can't afford-a-be. Juggling all those projects, not just here but abroad now, across the Empire. Spread that thinly, they are. All competing to out-price and outperform each other. I mean, you can see how such a mistake could happen. Even with the detetcive branch, at a senior level sometimes these men oversee a whole case without ever *seeing it*, if you know what I mean. Mistakes may lessen with experience, but the stakes are that much greater the more senior you get…and were a mistake as monumental of this one to happen, well…the ruin and embarrassment of the architect, to whom all responsibility would reside, would be…crushing, wouldn't it?"

It was deeper than he wanted to be getting in to, especially given the macabre business that had brought him to the place. Distraction from the Thames or not, he'd do what he could to keep matters light-hearted. So, he pulled back to a steady calm, saying simply as they entered the hotel: "It makes for a good story."

But Glass was bent on the deep. "Aye, suppose for some it does. Tragic if it's true; throwing himself from his mangled creation like that, tying him to what he'd ruined——" Glass then said fast, slicing through the man's own statement like the story had ensnared, towing the detective down a stream to no place good. "It can't have hurt occupancy. Already this place has a reputation as a portal to the spiritual world, you know, something which is sure to unsettle our church-going Cohen. Cox had an interest in such things. I find intrigue in it, too. Right up my street, ghost stories." They stayed silent after that, moving through check-in and to his modest room at the rear of the hotel with a kind of ghost-like float themselves. Then Glass said: "I shall rely on you, Kemp," a sea view before them, "to help make those final pieces fit. It's almost complete, mind you—just some final due diligence before I reveal, wrap up and depart."

He stayed at his window, watching Glass return to the green to meet up with Marsh on the rear lawn, and them head on together down to the sea. He did not envy his former employer, the nature of the words Marsh had for the detective of which he had some idea. The men soon disappeared into the view. Sea mists had found him there once more. The same as from Scarborough, it felt like, creeping up the beach and over the hotel, to leave specks of salt on the window. Though a new room, as with the whole hotel it felt tired under the weight of heavily layered fabrics and brightly patterned wallpaper and carpet. The room felt older than it was.

He had come to Southport with a story a man should tell a detective. A crucial testimony. The first solid break in the case that revealed a key suspect. He had wanted to avoid meeting Glass before Marsh had *the talk* he now watched…before what he was now witnessing could come to pass. This is how he wanted it in case this evidence was compelled to leave his lips too soon. Thankfully it hadn't. Even with ample opportunity while alone with Glass in the open dunes of Merseyside to tell it, Glass' story of a young grand seaside hotel's superstitious start stuck the evidence in him like a cork, scaring him from any inclination to be forthcoming with the man.

It wasn't that he believed it, the story, the suspicions…more that the position of the hotel was undeniably unnerving, threatening even, to best-laid plans. It had pushed him off centre, given a ghost to the final act of a *Sizar's* sorting. "One should never turn their back to the sea," he said to the empty room, his breath bringing its own inside mist to the salt-speckled glass.

lmost exactly two months previous... White and soft was the fall from London Bridge into the Thames. Painless and warm, too. Death was, truly, as the evangelical preachers promised it to be: *a sweet relief*. Instead of the mucky freeze of the black Thames at midnight, impact was straight into the clouds. With Keely there with him, too. It was soundless at first, as they lay strangely stargazing while in the clouds. In a sort of perfect, upside-down other world. "You took that well," Keely's voice broke in, piercing heaven's silence. Other sounds, mechanical sounds, flooded in afterwards. "Landed good, too. With a little in-air guidance from me. But still, you stayed loose, let the tumble happen, to land flat as an egg on a fry."

His senses swept away the disorientation.

Hearing, then touch—the cloud, though pillowy enough to soften impact, was not atmospheric, but rather of this world, and therefore, much coarser. *Smell* caught up then. They hadn't impacted with the Thames, as a threshold up into the sky, but instead were only far more closer to it now than on the bridge; its odour made proximity inescapable, that smell was unmistakable to any man who had spent a time in the capital. He could now *taste* the salty putridity of its contents, too, splashed in squalid droplets across his lips: as spat-up by a vessel of industry.

He was waking to reality, a sensation similar to the return to consciousness after a fainting spell. Something that, as a keen wrestler, he was not at all disfamiliar with, having blacked out many times while in another man's hold. Disorientation of space and time, starting to focus.

Then lips.

Soft and wet, pressed his own. As if a raid on his regaining of his senses. Surface at first, and then...something wetter and deeper. Keely venturing confidently into him.

213

Any comfort he had in going into the white without rigidity left with the kiss. On the surface of it, his shock at lips on his own seemed absurd. They had slept together, each night since the *Highlands Express*. He had held this boy in his arms through sleep, and weeping, often until the latter subsided into the former. *Fuck!* he'd fucked bloody the Russian runt. But never before had he kissed *one that matters*. And it was also, embarrassingly, everything-ly, his first kiss. And it was heavenly. Beyond what he would have died for——

Keely broke it off, severed the wet everything. "I love you," Keely said, elevating everything further. "It's a cotton barge!"

The former ill-registrable for now, the latter adhering his base senses into the fullness of the scenario he had found himself in—Keely cosying into his armpit, like his lover would often at night. He wrapped Keely into him. "I——"

"Hold on," Keely hushed, another abrasion—or escalation?—to the perfect moment. "This second part is the painful one." *Abrasion.* Keely gripped hold of his forearm, securing it around waist like his limb were a life vest. "Deep breath now, and don't let go," Keely said with a wink and roll of them both across the cotton top, to the edge and over, into the Thames.

The river hit him like the death of a disbeliever, a black oblivion of blistering coldness and foul water. So stabbing-ly cold that when they resurfaced in the stirred-up wake of the cotton barge, he had to scream to get the shock out of his lungs, to let air into them again. Keely, turns out, was the life vest in this event, towing him and a ballooned bag he had not noticed 'til now to the edge of the Thames. Keely had timed the roll expertly, bringing them out just in front of the Tower of London's Traitor's Gate. Long since disused for the purpose of transferring prisoners of the state, it was at that time open and under refurbishment for the restless appetites for intrigue of Londoners...but that night offered refuge for them both, out of the cold.

"I know you love me," Keely said, as stripping him of his clothes and his boots and wrapping him in a blanket that his lover retrieved from a crevice back and undercover of the entrance into the Tower. "But I couldn't bear to hear you say it, just before I was to put you through *that*."

Why Keely had put him through that at all was the natural response. But instead, he said: "How long have you known?"

His teeth had been chattering through his speak, though settled down quick in the warmth of the blanket. There was no spice-coating it, it stank there, and the blanket was an absorber for all the foul odours of the London liquid run-off. But it was warm, and though a little mouldy, there was no dampening his spirits. Keely stripped naked as well, then climbed into the blanket with him. Keely inserted so hips were cushioned by his thighs, and Keely's back reclined on his chest. "Thinking on it now, I feel like I must have known from the start, at Brighton," Keely said. "You were the only one out of the lot of them not solely fixated on Pipe." Reading his silence Keely explained: "*Pipe* is how I knew 'im."

"Ah yes, well, see, I didn't realise that. You are not wrong, certainly the fascination was palpable with that boy, no question. But for me, you were the most interesting of the two, the way you sprung into action and tended to that nasty case of could-be cauliflower ear. That clinched it for me, then and there. And you turned more heads than mine, too."

"Maybe, but yours stuck in its turn, and from the start. But to give ya the God's honest, I realised it in the country. Sorry for waiting so long to say it, my lovely Port."

"Why tell me now? Because I threatened to leave?" He did not mean it the way it came out, as defensive as all that.

"Yes, though not to make you stay. Ya should, leave that is. But I wan' ya to know, when y'do go."

"Why do you think I should leave?"

"Because where I see a future, possibility, you see squalor."

"I'm sorry."

"Nah, don't be. You've looked out for me this long, kept me safe. Isn't it about time I did the same for ye?"

"What was all this, then?" he asked by means of reference to the whole Thames affair, pulling Keely into his still-wet chest.

Keely let out a belly chuckle: "That was cruel, won't it? Though you proved your love to me."

"You were testing me?"

"Nah…though you were tested in the process. It's meant as your farewell, to show you that there's no need for you to worry about me, here."

"Truly? By hurling us both into a barge then into the Thames, and now here, in a cavity under a medieval prison gate? It's had the opposite effect, I'm afraid. No way I'm leaving you now. Hell man, I thought that was a suicide pact!"

Keely roared into a whole-body laugh, spread from recesses of the belly. It was just about the most foreign sound he could ever imagine being attributed to the boy in his arms.

"You laugh, but no sane man could call me hysterical in my logic given what happened with Lew——"

He cut off himself, but too late. The reference to their late third party was conveyed, stopping Keely's laughter cold. He hated himself in that moment. For allowing his frustrations with the whole affair along the river to ruin their moment and silence the only sound of elation he'd ever heard from the boy he loved.

Boy. Loved.

Two concepts he never before dared place beside each other. Fond of, certainly. Cared for, sure. Consoled, even in a brotherly, bed-ly, in-arms intimate kind of way; that he could justify. Indeed, these were the entire manly foundations on which the club through which they had met was built. But love? And then to ruin all that. "I'm sorry, my love. That was cruel, and I never want to be cruel, not least to you. Truth is, and you'll think I'm broken in the brain for saying this: I was willing to die to-night. I do anything for you." And he kissed the wet crown of Keely's head. The Thames water was vile and the smell of it was everywhere, but wrapped in their blanket, the cavity at Traitor's Gate at the bottom of the Tower of London felt like their fortress, and his lips, on any part of Keely—as he abandoned any conservatism left in him—held for him nothing but sweetness. "What say I fire-up our stay"——teeth tinny-clapping as he said it——"and source a hot bath for us, in which you can tell me what to-night has been all about?" And Keely kissed him again, as would become their preferred way of agreement.

B y god! it was remarkable what a love statement could do for a man's head. After a journey in from Scarborough with the detective in his ear and thoughts of not continuing on with Keely, to encounter the station of these accommodations as—Keely had him pegged—squalid in his estimations…to now, after the trauma of the Thames, together with the adrenaline of a thought-fatal dive from London Bridge still fresh as opium through his system…to be back there, together, naked, warmed by a fire and with fresh water in an iron tub. It was, no mistake, the best kind of heaven.

They assumed the same position as at Traitor's Gate, Keely wedged into his thighs. The iron held the heat and was close enough to the fire that the steam continued to rise. He never would have thought it possible—not by the state of activity around the unstably-leaning building when they had arrived—, but it was quiet now. The only sound came from the crackle of carbon in the fire, and the lap of hot water against iron and bodies in the bath, stirred by the slight adjustments into each other as they found incredulously more comfortable melts. They slept intermittently there, warm and bonded to each other like bolts through iron sheets. The blue of the full moon a hue on their bodies, as the fire warmed-red the water of the bath.

"Pipe taught me that," Keely said, nodding to strewn-out cotton drying by the fire. "He were always finding ways of getting ahead. His methods were ever a little mad, and never free of risk. 'An enterprise without risk yielded no reward worth having,' he used to say. We'd known each other since we was boys. I worshipped him, all of us did. Every boy here working 'round the docks. But he seemed to have more tolerance for my hero-worship than the others; letting me tag along with him on his gambits, which took us just about all abouts of London, so it did. And these pool 'f London parts was always where we ended up last."

Dawn was near, the fire approaching its final embers, and water starting to cool—steam no longer rising. That was alright, since the cold blue of the moon had warmed to an orange of pre-morning. He was tired, but alert, in that weird hinterland of awake and asleep, hope and a not terrible but reflective mute despair. This was the space wherein confessions were made.

"Pipe had no shortage of admirers," Keely went on, "and had grown quite tired of all the attention. Nah, wait, that ain't true. He craved it, needed it there always, but had become, recently…and 'twere recent, for, for the longest time, he seemed content just to knock about, getting through life a bit easier on account of looks. Until we arrived 'ere, that is, to settle. It would be, about two years, maybe a little more, but not more than a few months more. It were here, not much more than two years ago that Pipe, coming-a-age, started wanting for more. *The Pipe* of the papers were born then."

The fire had died, and the bathwater had fallen below the room's temperature. Knowing the significance of Keely's speech but also his own responsibility to them both as now-lovers, he folded Keely forward, alighted from the bath himself and scooped Keely up—the one he loved was, after all, a lean and slight-framed young man—and carried him into bed. Drying them both in the sheets, then casting all top sheeting aside and wrapping himself around Keely as covering, drawing up a folded-down blanket as ballast. Keely remained silent throughout the transference, amiable to it. Until the feather-down-lined heat off the blanket warmed both their bodies to the same entangled wetness of the bath, which is when Keely continued.

"'Money, status or power,' Pipe told me one night several years back over smoked salmon he had scored off an Atlantic fisherman. 'Everything else, *like this*,' he had said, holding up the tail of the fresh catch, 'is small time. It's time now to get serious.' I didn't get what he meant when he said things like that, until I started seeing less of him and he started moving 'round more. 'An army of gentlemen's companions,' that's what he called his business. But really it were just whoring, or so I thought, until he came back one time. To this building, yeah, after a weekend out of th' city. I know now that he had been with Mr Peele; and like just about every man whose touched him, Peele promised him everything. But Pipe were proud, too, never one to rest solely on his looks; he were no fool, he knew he wouldn't have this pull forever. And so, a spot on Essex's next sort were what Pipe asked for instead of payment; the first spot. And he got me a spot, too."

Not all of this was a surprise to him, Peele was notorious for giving slots in the club's lineup to boys the indiscreet man favoured…and quite often, those who Peele aimed to keep silent through the arrangement. Pipe was different, of course, the boy had real talent, a genuine justification for being there. *And was infamous! O yes, the pipe.* That was something that, to his knowledge, had never happened to Peele before, certainly not in the time that he had been a tutor at *Sizar's*. The sleuth inside him wondered whether it was this talent that got Pipe killed. One of those murderous bets in a gentlemen's club. Certainly, the shock of Peele bringing to the tournament such a rare thing, a raw talent, was palpable throughout the first round.

"Why did you go to Brighton, my love?" Even before it came out, he was unsure about the last part of his question. They were doing things that, he knew, men were not meant to. But…such sentimentality; was that a step too far off from social acceptance, even in the society of just them two?

"He were a perfect sort of creature," Keely said, seemingly undisturbed by the term of sweet affection.——Taking the initiative, he kissed the bone behind Keely's ear.——"Not human," Keely went on, still unaffected, "and when he wanted you somewhere, with him, it were impossible to resist it. The bastard had a siren's pull. You'd happily ruin yourself for 'im."

Dawn was here. And it was welcome, for they were on their own time now. But the weight of Pipe was still wedged between them, as was Lewis, and, privately, Cox too, keeping away any kind of unadulterated happiness. But he was determined to shove on. Selfishly, to learn…what Keely knew of what happened to Pipe in Brighton, what Keely had learnt from what Lewis knew, and exactly the circumstances with Keely's last companion. He could not bring himself to categorise Keely and Lewis as lovers… But learn he wanted to, of what Keely had experienced in the lead up to what ended that night, round two, in a leap from the *Highlands Express*. "It's time," he said, recalling the bridge and running of a midnight gambit he had thought would mean the death of them both. "Tell me what happened on the train."

S *outhport's Birkdale Palace, present day…* Even from his second-floor room,
beyond the green and into the mist-muddled dunes where Glass was
striding back to the hotel, he could read a fallen face. He knew then that
Marsh had kept true to word and followed through with their agreement:
that Glass would be given the chance to conclude the investigation, but would
do so in a clipped capacity and never to be given alone access to any of the
competitors, nor be permitted to speak with *Sizar's* heads a second time, and
to only be able to interview the tutors if Marsh was present. Unsure what
Glass' next move would be; that is whether the disgraced detective would
agree to the terms, resist, or abandon the investigation all together, he headed
downstairs to the Birkdale Palace Hotel's lounge, its "bay windows" facing
queerly inland, to the town proper.

Knowing the tutors' tradition of meeting for a pre-tournament drink,
Peele had made allowances in the schedule. But as the sorting would take
place when the Southport sun is still high and on the first day of arrival,
and Peele being Peele…in place of spirits or lager even, in the bar or dining
room, their host had reserved the Palace Sun Room for a High Tea. "It's
unorthodox, I know," Marsh said to the assembled tutors, arriving a short
time after him, "but I'm afraid I find myself somewhat at a loose end, and
I thought perhaps I might join you all for tea. With all that has gone on this
year, I feel I have quite neglected my social function with you."

Essex house tutor Tanner, who was pouring four cups of Russian Caravan
tea, was self-appointed convenor of the affair, nodding first to Marsh and
the stated intention to join, then to the server who had just delivered two
tiers of cakes and cucumber sandwiches, indicating the need for an extra
service. There was an awkward silence that followed as the four tutors,
each as different as the four seasons, and Marsh waited for the tea to cool

sufficiently for the sipping to begin. "So, you're back with us then, Porter," Tanner said as soon as each present had taken a sip—as way, it seemed, to twist the dagger of awkwardness of his being back among tutors at tea with his former employer. "I——"

"Temporarily," Marsh broke in, asserting in a way that aggravated awkwardness. Marsh was not all without social graces, however. And did then soften the air: "I asked Kemp to stay on until a suitable replacement could be found. And he graciously has agreed."

"I see…" Tanner said, absorbed by the chance for gossip and already finished a first cup, clicking middle finger to thumb at the server to, this time, pour a second cup in the host-tutor's stead. "So—nothing has changed, then? Porter will still compete in the regatta as a competitor?"

"O yes," Marsh said, "it will be a first, but it is in the rules, and we need rules now more than ever."

"Hear, hear," said Brown. From the rumours he'd been hearing, he suspected this support was in reference to the enforcement of rules of competitor conduct, rather than rules of the game—showing Brown's dogged commitment to seeing two more members of the Middlesex Crew removed from the row at the end.

"Having you is a pleasant surprise," Tanner said, a seeming determination to stick to one controversy at a time. "I thought you might have left us when you didn't return to Cambridge. Living somewhere God-awful in London, the last I heard. So, that's reassuring to hear you will still compete. 'Twill make for a more interesting race, with you there. And——"

Tanner sprung erect at the end of the chair, teacup mid-rise to mouth: "Pardon me, but this is a private function," Tanner called out in that way the boy-man often did: effeminate and elite, flourished with a roll of the eyes to an inner-imagined circle.

"Sorry I'm late, gentlemen," Glass said, ignoring Tanner.

"Do we know you," Tanner shot back, holding as host. "I saw you lingering by the door, for an age. By your look I thought you were a server. I thought to stop, but then I thought: *no, that's the stance of a server.* You should have interrupted me, sir, if indeed you are something more."

Glass looked between him and Marsh with a perturbed grin: "I see you haven't announced me, then?" He went to get up, to join Glass' side as deputy, as was their agreement. Glass gestured for him to stay. "Best you sit with the rest, Mr Porter," Glass said, stern, relegating him from deputy detective to suspect again. *Marsh had indeed told Glass, then,* he thought. *Probably even named me, too, though he had said he would leave me out of it!* He shot a glance Marsh's way, whose active avoidance of eye contact confirmed his thinking. It was a relief, really, like the breaking loose of scaffolding around an under-restoration ruin. It exposed the old structure underneath for what it was. No artifice, only actuality. Exactly what was needed at this stage of the game. "I'm Detective-Inspector Oscar Glass, of the Metropolitan Police, investigating the deaths that occurred this year at your club's events. Your club head here assures me of co-operation."

"Thank you, detective inspector," Marsh said, more than a little flustered. "I was not sure when you would be down. I was just about to inform the boys here of your arrival and our promise of co-operation with your inquiries when you, well, arrived."

"How do you take your Russian, detective inspector? Your tea," Tanner said, still seated, teapot elevated, folded over at the waist—the actual server having shown initiative by delivering another cup and saucer. "I'm being mother to-day."

"White with two sugars," Glass said. Everyone else sat silent and awkward in that men-at-tea kind of way. All save for Tanner, who seemed to enjoy serving again. Brimming. Handing a full cup to the detective. "Thank you," Glass said, taking a sip then launching into a laying-out of the facts, staying standing to pace in front of the seated assembled, like they were all one great big corpse, and the detective was first on the scene, gathering clues like they were crowns out of a wishing fountain: "Three deaths, three murders, from self and other hands, of both cold and hot-bloodedness, of calculated cruelness and passion. Under a pier, off a train and at the Spa."

It unnerved him to think on Lewis' death as a form of murder. But, he supposed, that's what it was. Still, *curious for a detective to lump it in with murders of the cold-bloodied kind,* he thought. *And was it in passion or of a cruel heart?*

"Murder by other hands is the simplest of these types," Glass continued, "but it be the most important, too. I first saw no need to hassle yous boys with an ask for answers, I laboured under the assumption of innocence that, as underlings, you had no press on decisions of the men you served. Recent *incidents*, however——" Glass did not single him out when saying this, but it was clear in the way the detective put emphasis on one of the words that reference was being made to the conversation with Marsh that morning "——have shown how silly my thinking was. And so, having already asked at length your masters, I must now ask yous *what I must know*. Ideally, this would have been done one by one, which I might add would have saved yous some embarrassment; but petty vendettas boys, these have forced my hand. We'll turn today on the latest killing, because time is short for me and detecting work must start at the end. My askings are few. I have already asked of your masters about the passion kill, and to focus on the latest death has me asking yous about a boy who was known to me. Speaking of what is known, I ask yous names first. All I have on paper. But only one of yous I have a face to match."

Running through each tutor in turn, Glass got confirmation of name and house to whom that name was engaged, starting with Tanner. Glass then flicked back through the same notebook as was at Scarborough to where— he could only presume from what came next—were minutes of their own meeting at BeeHive Inn. "Yous assembled considered," Glass said, "we start with the last time yous four were like this, plus one more—the victim—at the bar in the Grand Hotel, Scarborough."

"How delightful," Tanner said, reclining and crossing legs, in more the manner of a maiden than a man. "I do enjoy a good whodunnit."

"Do you, indeed, Mr Tanner?"

"O indeed, *I do!*—and Way, please!—all the plot twists and unsuspecting shady back dealings. More tea?"

"Go on."

Tanner topped Glass up without offer to any of the others assembled. "O yes, and the ends are always my favourite. No matter how clever you think you've been in picking the clues from the red herrings and setting out your theory of who did it, there's always some last-minute revelation, which unravels all your sure-as-sure conclusions. Marvellous fun, whodunnits."

"Yeah. Well. The work of detecting is a bit more formalised than all that. Ta for the tea, but ya stay silent now until spoken to." Glass took a short sip of the tea, making a scrunched-sponge of an expression, like it had the essence of citrus rather than Russian Caravan, looking into the cup as if—all this talk of liking twists in a whodunnit—Tanner may have just slipped poison into it. Glass returned the saucer with cup to the High-Tea table with a force that shook the other porcelain pieces in its company. Tanner puckered up, too, going that way his peer often did when rebuked by a man the tutor found distinctive. Which was pretty much every man with him, he thought earnestly and without maliciousness. "Your skin," Glass said to Tanner, "looks terribly…sore."

"You needn't worry, detective. I'm not contagious—not in tea service, at least," Tanner said with a perverse wink. "And you might as well know, since you're bound to ask. I contracted it in service to my host."

It had all the ringings of a crack in the case, but instead of pursuing it Glass turned on Brown. "You left first from the Scarborough bar, right?"

Brown quaked immediately under the question: "N–n–no," without any bass to the exception. "Porter did."

Glass grinned, seeming to congratulate self-cleverness. "Very good, Mr Brown," Glass said after checking the notebook. "That was what we detectives call a control question. It was a test, of both a current statement——" *Mine*, he thought. "——and of your own use to me as a witness." Brown looked in no way put-at-ease, twisting hands in crotch in the manner of wringing out a dishcloth. "Ya passed, Mr Brown," Glass said with a pause after, though there was little visible change in Brown's discomfort. "So, Porter bows out, then you, right?" Brown nodded. "Need words, Mr Brown."

"Ye–es," Brown whispered, more air than speech.

"And that was the last you saw of Cox?"

"No. Well, yes, I mean——"

"And you started out so well. What one is it, Mr Brown?"

Despite Brown's clutched crotch-hand turning white under pressure, there was no stopping the nerves borne of a detective's scrutiny, spreading down and up the rest of Brown's body. Marsh's mouth opened, possibly to offer assurance, but Glass shot his former employer down with a stare carrying all the stone of Medusa before any utterance could be made. "The last I saw of him was at the bar, yes, that's co–orrect," Brown blurted at last. "But I did hear from him again, or rather, I heard him, some time later, talking with Underhill about going down to the Spa."

It was as instantaneous as a land mine, with Underhill and Glass in the crosshairs. The look of disdain left Glass, smacking itself on Underhill's face. In the wake of its blast, Glass' features were transformed; a transformation mythical in magnitude, like Jason stumbling upon the Golden Fleece among worthless tourist trinkets in the back of a two-penny jumble while on provincial-spot holiday. "*Quiet!*" Glass barked, though no one had spoken. "Ya going great, Mr Brown. Do go on."

He thought it strange that Glass had not made any notes yet that session. *A revelation such as this!* of which, he thought would have sent a detective's pen a'scribbling. "I me–ean, what I thought I hea…" Brown stumbled, eyes in crotch again as speech trailed off into the inaudible.

"Did you hear any voices other than Underhill and Cox?"

"No."

"Come now, you've gone this far. None at all?"

"Well, not until much later, when Porter came by."

"And when was that?"

"Around two thirty."

Glass nodded. The verification of his story not seeming to impress on the detective much of anything. "And you?" Glass said, turning on Tanner.

"I wondered when you'd get to me," Tanner said, who had remained uncharacteristically mute since the rebuke from Glass.

"Did you hear anything?"

"What Simon says checks out with my experience of the events. Though, I'm not sure even I—Arthur and I being by no means close—would have pushed him over the edge in quite so spectacular a fashion."

"Speak plain, Mr Tanner. Did you hear the voices of Mr Underhill and the victim and did you, *listen now*, did you hear exact mention of the Spa as their meeting place?"

"Yes," Tanner said eventually, giving time to thought. *Tanner always was*, he thought, *the calculated sort*. "I heard both boys," Tanner continued, "and mention of the Spa as where they said they should meet. More specifically, at its God-awful phallic tower thing." Brown nodded, eyes still caught by crotch, the damage done.

Outside the inland-bay windows of the tearoom Cohen stood with Surrey house's four tributes plus those of Kent, overseeing their warm-ups for the race due to commence on the strike of five that evening. Blunt was elsewhere, as the man often was during preparation for any rounds of the tournament other than Blunt's own. Both heads of house were unaware that a long-held house alliance was being coached into betrayal over tea. As one alliance came under threat, another one was taking unusual form. Marsh, always the hands-on kind, had asked Peele to oversee the warm-ups of the Middlesex house four, which was taking place on the green behind the hotel, overlooking the sea, out of sight. "Where were you when all this was going on, Porter?" Glass asked, breaking through his faraway thought of four from his own house, without a tutor to coach nor head to guide, dragging him 'round the building and back to tea, to face explaining a gap in his own testimony he had feared Glass might find.

"I was in my room," he said quickly, rehearsed. This was the truth, he was in his room, just at a different hotel.

"You hear anything?"

He looked to Underhill, who had the expression of a man before the gallows. "Nothing. I was asleep."

"And that's why you missed training?"

"No, having introduced Cox to the other tutors, I thought it best to allow him to stand on his own feet. Sleep was secondary to this." Glass seemed satisfied enough with that, and so his thoughts drifted back to outside, to training, to pledges, and as it often did those days, to Keely. While he drifted towards the unseen sea, Glass homed in on Underhill, looking ready to strike.

O*n the Thames, back in time...* He was in the dither between dark and wake. Dawn and sleep. Made worse by new surroundings and exploits of keeping his coach. It was a ploy with Kemp, the stunt on the Thames; an insurance policy in excitement engineered to make Port stay. He did love his coach, he thought at least. What is love anyway? Not least: what is love between two men? What struck him was how the stunt spun on impulse. A swift snap out of complacency, taking Port's kindness for granted to decide upon a flight of danger and trust display. It was an action not of him, this rattled the most. He would have normally let Kemp go. Pipe, however, would have taken the entrapment route. Pipe, ever looking to routes of survival, would have seen this man as the harbinger of useful protection, which his coach was...but Port was more than that also.

Kemp was right. It was time to tell; time also to use keeping tactics that were, by degrees, more genuine. And a place of their own—albeit borrowed—away from the crime scenes of secretive clubs gave rise to the perfect prospects for telling. Tiredness helped him start to talk, taking him back to a time with a man he should have been more forthright in trying to keep. *I am haunted by him*, Squire had said, as ghost, in a derelict west wing to the back of his memory of their time together; orphaned and isolated in Marsh House...his memory caught in the threshold between Pipe and Squire's leaving him. The fire had died in the place with Port on the Thames as the confession came, carrying him back to Middlesex county, when the fire had died also.

In a daze of not asleep, not waking, the two timelines folded onto one another, like bound pages in a book—collapsing chapters in his life over and onto each other. *I was at his side when he died*, he heard in his mind so loud it might well have been in the bed with them, in the voice of Sqi in the manor.

"'I were at his side when he died,' he confessed to me, in Marsh House," he then said aloud to Port in London. The manor memory; vivid, so vitally there; came the first night Sqi had spent inside him. Right afterwards, in fact; as an outpouring, like the release of a valve, of everything ever pent up, swirling within Sqi and pouring now out of his own mouth as a similar forbidden essence from himself. He had to censor himself now. Slow the stream of recall from one realm into the next. Stop himself from relaying to Port—holding him naked in the present—how he had felt in the moment of cathartic confession in the past. When Sqi not only held him, but had recently filled him with carnal exertion, too.

"'After the match, Kent were fixed on Pipe,'" he relayed to Port, filtering out the soreness and intimate swell from the surprise attack. Keeping the fleshy parts of that period out of his story prompted pause for thought on what it was, exactly, he and Port now shared. Is this the extent of it? Naked, bodily sweat embrace, with sweet kisses? Washing the heated parts of his time with Sqi from his story made that place where soreness was in memory... twitch. A pulse down below and between cheeks that was so primordial he was sure he felt a returned signal in the limp loins of Porter, pressed sweat-laced in the crevice of his base. Or maybe that was just a wish for something more physical from his too-sweet coach.

"'Piper was good, a raw-talented, naturally national champion,'" *he relayed to Port, speaking as Sqi.* "'So good, and so quick to fall to fatigue at the end of our match that many—Blunt among them—were left to speculate about whether he had thrown it for coin or other incentive.'" He relayed to Port the truth that Blunt and others had suspected. That Pipe threw the match and had done so as part of a plan to use Peele's infatuation for a secured income. It all started when Pipe went to one of Peele's recruitment rounds at the man's castle estate. As was not unusual, Pipe took the initiative without being invited—in fact, Pipe wasn't even known to Peele then. It had been through one of Pipe's "runner boys," used on a racket that involved agile sprinters lifting valuables without the need to have studied the craft. After a nip into the fashionable parts of London, the runner boys could simply outrun any police pursuit, and disappear into the warren of tenements on the wrong side of London. One of these runner boys had, in a shining case of charity and fool fortune, tried the trick on a track 'n' field ex-champion, who now coached at *Sizar's*; it was Tanner. Tanner secured the introduction to Peele—a man who favoured the criminally down-trodden...in the respect that such boys were more bendable to persuasion, and easier to silence when greased with money. Pipe's runner boys also worked as telegraph boys for the London G.P.O., and plied whore trade in brothels like the one on Cleveland Street. Profitable for *the Pipe*, but high risk.

So, Tanner facilitated Pipe's entry in the race, via the introduction of one of Pipe's runners. Tanner could not have known the butterfly effect it would have. Naturally, the runner sprinted back to Pipe, relaying information on the recruitment weekend, in which Pipe saw opportunity. Recruitment at Castle Essex was a debauched display, and almost immediately of seeing Pipe, Peele wanted the boy to live-in, at lodgings on the castle estate. But there were a few of those already, and Pipe did not much fancy that. Pipe formulated a plan with Peele to take on a ceremonial rôle, as house coach, with a more sizeable remuneration than previously offered to those in the position...this was done on much the down low...were Tanner to have learnt of it, this planning would have been met with flamboyant objection, and recourse for unsavoury and unmanly backlash. Pipe had been perfectly forthright with him about the plan as it had formed. Peele would have Pipe as frontrunner for round one, as Marsh always chose wrestling as the manly pursuit—Pipe's prize sport. Pipe was an amateur, had no time for learning, let alone accepting any rules of engagement, yet still, was the best.

The plan was, as Pipe had explained it to him: simple. Pipe would perform. Put on a show of strength and manly talent against an opponent—which happened to be Lewis, a worthy match. It would be a match that would come down to the last round, with Pipe, on balance, demonstrating a potential far more compelling than the opposition, though falling in the last throes. Pipe had, he recalled, relayed the plan with complete confidence. Pipe was cocky like that, sure of own abilities to the exclusion and expense of all else. He was there to soften the blow of Pipe's triumph, to at least suggest Peele had by some systemic measure, upped the game more broadly. The upshot for him, Pipe had said, was a shot at the win. And if he lost, well, Pipe had always found a way to look out for him.

After the thrown match—he continued to recall, lying in the London arms of Port, in body only…in everything else, *back there, in that bleak-Brighton winter*—there was a dinner for the winners, while the losers, muscle sore, were ushered through tunnels and into waiting carriages, back to the Royal Hotel for a stay again in the dorms of the night before…this time with only half there, and extra body space as reminder of their shortfall. It had gone to plan, of course. Without fault line. Pipe had been proved the star wrestler, inexplicably out in the end. And he had shored up the illusion that Peele, somehow, had sourced some strategy-selection skill through strong candidates, well two at least, rather than usual Essex house boys, who were accustomed to running, but athletically useful in just about nothing else.

He remembered Pipe walking out proud, as his friend always left a theatre of exhibitionism. All eyes on Pipe, teasing the audience's gaze, but never returning it. Though he knew the plan, had been told it plainly enough that this outcome should have seemed straightforward, he remembers a desperate longing for Pipe to look back and see him. Even though, rationally, there was no reason in that moment to feel this rush of want for a look… But the look never came. Vaguely now, he can recall Porter by his side as he tended to that case of could-be cauliflower. Running with Pipe had required him to pick up a thing or two about tending to injuries—a way to keep himself useful.

The deeper he went into the past, the more the present started to fade…

Blunt couldn't let it rest, Lewis had told him, and now he told Porter. *So, after dinner, with me in tow, Blunt and I headed to the Royal. Pipe was not in the communal accommodations. His bed was made up and his bag was gone——*

"Gone?" Porter asked, pushing in, *out of time.* "That's curious. Stolen, did they think?"

"He didn't say," he said, thinking deeper. "One of the others staying there had thought he had seen a man down the hall with it," he recalled from the detail Sqi had relayed, "though the boy couldn't be sure."

"Could this witness describe the bag?" Porter asked, distracting him further from his recall of the memory of the confession.

But the answer to this question needn't be plucked from his recollection of Sqi's recount. It was housed in the halls of his own memory. "I remember it," he said. "There were loads of bags of that sort about. It were not all that special. Smart, mind, above what Pipe would have bothered buying himself, and above any of the other competitors' purses. But nothing of the craftship of your bag," he said to the dawning corner of the room where "K.P." in upper-crust leather was embossed on a bag that stood tall over his own rucksack. "Your usual run-of-the-mill professional overnight bag, I guess you'd call it—tan, I think it were."

"Were there signs of forced entry?" Porter followed up quick.

He went silent. The answer was that he did not know. And recollection was broken down by the irritation of constant interference.

"Sorry," Port said, kissing his earlobe this time, with a pinch of teeth as a finish. "I interrupted you."

Port had.

And it had quite taken him out of the country and into the capital again. Tired as he was, it was not unpleasant to be back. In his coach's arms. *I like it here better*, he thought, *more comfortable, tender…less sore.*

"You were saying that Lewis and Blunt called by the dorm."

"Yes."

And he floated back into the Middlesex countryside and the voice of Sqi… One of the other non-qualifying Essex house boys suggested—Essex three, or was it four…does it matter? One of them suggested, quite offhanded yet smugly, that we might try the bar for Piper, after the shame of the fall. It seemed a sound enough logic, given the circumstances. And Blunt was no less keen on locating him, so we headed to the bar…on the way, we spotted Piper in the restaurant. Alone, with a fine feed—oysters and crab, it looked like; oysters all gone, crab waiting on the plate. Not the meal of someone who had just blown the opportunity of a lifetime…not the meal of any workhouse boy. Anyway, he refused the rematch—refused to give satisfaction, to make sure, you see, that I had qualified using skill rather than being allowed to win.

Piper seemed disinterested, even in the offer of money from Blunt—quite a large sum. Oddly, I was the one to bring him 'round; in the end, he said he'd wrestle me again just for the crack.

"Squire," breaking back into the bed in London, as teller of the tale, "his details of the rematch were sketchy. I knew enough of Pipe, what he were like, of his way 'round others, not to press Squire for more. Pipe could be cruel, and not without knowing it. For him, cruelty was a sport, especially with those who *felt things* for him. It were a power play for him. I didn't press Squire for details about how effortlessly Pipe had embarrassed him. Pipe had done it enough times to me in our wrestles, and that were as, supposedly, pals, and without messy details like earnings beyond whoring to consider. But as bad as Pipe had been about it, Blunt were worse. And what Squire held back from saying about Pipe's way after dominating him in a wrestle rematch, he wholeheartedly poured into me." He stopped short of sharing that this came in the form of semen poured with a surprise assault, the outcome of which he felt was still somewhat engaged inside him.

"'Kent went strange,' that was how Squire told it to me," he said, in bed, in London. "Now not only had the rematch confirmed suspicions one of *Sizar's* heads had that the lead from Essex house were a star wrestler who had thrown the match, but that he had shown it, with refusal of payment, pushed the man from curiosity to a whole different level...one of being cheated by Peele or whoever had planned the whole thing. Although only a competitor, a freshman to the game, Squire seemed so...serious. He allowed himself get caught up in a feeling of what it meant to be a 'one' in the game, and to fall to another one, and sly selection like my Pipe mate."

He knew that Port got it, understood the dynamics of Blunt's ways and the whole society as a dysfunctional, druid utopia of ideas.

His coach confirmed all this via a sad silence.

"Blunt were livid by the trick, Squire told me, insisting on wresting with Pipe himself, and not only making a fool of himself in the process, but injuring his leg as well. Blunt then sent Squire off, saying something along the lines of that he was glad he hadn't saved him for his own host round. And, I reckon, went to sleep. But Squire headed downstairs."

Slipping back to being slipped in by Sqi... I went to the bar and committed to drinking away what money I had on me. I must have been drinking a whole hour before he joined me. We were the only two left in the bar. Piper sat with me while I drank. He didn't say anything, didn't try to console me or talk on a different topic. He just gave me his company.

"Bed time, mate," Piper said when I'd finished my second drink with him there—two after how many others before, I don't know. "Come, I'll walk you back."

He left me to stumble from the stool at the bar and after him. He did not wait, powering forth down the steps onto the Promenade and askew a little, onto the planking of West Pier, knowing I would follow.

Newly erected and opened just a few years earlier, I had not the chance to visit West Pier before this, nor had any of the other lads been there yet, making Brighton's second pier a mystery that night.

Unlike the Chain Pier, famous across Britain, Brighton's second attempt was more slender yet also, strangely, more rigid—with something of the railways about it.

I was much less lucid than Piper. I slurred some words after him about the pier surely being closed, as the first tollhouse approached. But he ignored me.

Didn't even glance back, just marched his way along the pier and, jumping the bars beside its two tollhouses, proceeded all the way to the head, leaving me to slip and stumble after him.

West Pier was Eugenius Birch-designed, the finest designer of piers in Britain; and this one, many said, was destined to mark the finest of them all. Though that night, in the blistering blow-in from the south, with the little lantern lighting that was left to burn from the last to attend to the structure, Sqi had implied there was more menace than marvel to the arm that extended the two of them out and over the waves.

The thrill of a pier walk was this sensation of walking on waves, causing much trepidation for the majority of its custom, who had no faculty to wade beyond standing height themselves. And although Lewis was a fine swimmer, competent to tread water, alcohol impaired every move across the wooden planks of the Birch counter-lever.

It felt wrong, not because we shouldn't have been there, but like there were something in those waters that would grip us tight and drag us under, even if Piper, sober, was as able a water-goer as I.

When I got to his side, he had an expression that haunts my dreams the most: like he had already jumped.

He looked into the water below, brown and white-wash tipped, like it was the most intriguing and terrifying thing he had ever seen.

"Swim with me," he said, to me I assumed—though he spoke to the sea.

It wasn't a question, or a request. It was a statement of telling...of knowing, that I would.

He stripped himself, and then turned his hands to strip me.

We shivered together under the moon.

He seemed an intoxicating mix of fearful and fearless. It was yet another example of how better than me he was. Even full of drink, all I felt was cold fear, focused on the crude brown of the churn of tide around the iron pillars below. I felt no desire to push through it, and yet, when the word "Jump!" came hot in my ear...

I did.

He didn't laugh at my foolishness in jumping. He stayed stern. Of course, knowing that I would.

But as soon as I was in the air I knew that he would not jump in, too.

He would leave me there.

It was so cold I couldn't breathe. Like I had forgotten how. The currents were an indefatigable force that caught me in the cruel brown of their tide. The mud sands were dozens of feet below me, but it was so rough in there that I could feel their grains grasping at me.

I felt sure that I would drown, and that the Piper had left me to...this felt confirmed when I heard footsteps above, along the pier.

It was comforting thinking of Piper leaving me, that he was not there with me, for no matter how strong a swimmer he might be, he would surely be beautifully broken were he to join me, and I had no wish for him to see me fail in endurance again.

With him gone I would be free for a sweet let go, for the seabed sands to take me.

But just as I was about to let myself slip below, he was there, next to me, in the water. But far heavier.

He hit and sank without a pause.

The water didn't even slow him. If anything, it made him weightier. Rushing into him like a hull of iron.

I dove down after him. I pushed all the air out of me until I was sick and my lungs burnt, but it was not enough to make me deep enough to reach him. He was gone instantly.

I couldn't reach him.

My attempt to save him got replaced with a wish to die with him, near him.

But I wasn't good enough even to drown with him.

I woke up on the shore being shaken by that bastard Blunt.

Then again the next morning, back in the dorms. Blunt said later that he had collected our clothes and threatened that I'd be blamed if word got out.

I told him about the footsteps, but he insisted it was an accident.

I asked for Piper's clothes, but Blunt said he'd burnt them.

I couldn't have any piece of him.

"We conjured up a Gothic fantasy about that house," he said, back in London in the out-of-character tenor of a writer of the age. "I know now I were his bridge with Pipe. *His Piper.* I were a poor substitute, but something. Sqi became obsessed with every detail of the night, including why Pipe was going back to the Pavilion, and the man who made the steps. Whether it was Pipe pacing, or the devil himself come to push him in. I knew the answer for part of it: that it were to Peele that Pipe were headed, that it were part of the plan. But I kept it from him, I let the mystery continue, so he would keep me with him for it.

"On the train he told me he loved me, right after you left us. So…I told him the truth. He locked me in the cabin and went in search of Peele, or Blunt, I'm not sure who—maybe both. Someone whose would give him further answers, someone whose could match the footsteps to. I don't know what he found out, whose he spoke with, but he learnt that it weren't an accident…he learnt about the detective. That Pipe were murdered…that he had been under him when Pipe's neck were crushed. That he were drunk and of no use of help, even had he still been on the pier. This meant, I reckon, that I no longer were enough of a substitute for him."

He thought telling Port all that would make him want to cry.

But getting it out of him had been enough of an outpouring. The only wet parts were those Port-touching. Holding on to the story, like Sqi seeking Pipe's clothes, had been a way of holding on to the memory of Sqi—of Pipe too, probably. Now that the story was out, he clocked on that he never had any part of Sqi—and certainly not of Pipe—to hold on to in the first place.

L *ate afternoon, present day at Birkdale High Tea…* Underhill sat silent, pale and tight as Glass ran through particulars of tutor whereabouts at Brighton and the rôle of tutor-coaching in the recruitment of challengers, according to the notes the detective had made. Glass skipped over the revelation that Cox had been led to the Spa by one of them—unquestionably the deepest break in the case so far. *He's doing this on purpose*, he thought. *He's making him sweat.* And it was working, he could see the tension ratcheting up in Underhill like the pressure in a silty riverbed caisson, up and up, red rising in Underhill's face like a bad case of the bends…up and up until the bubbles in the poor man's veins became too much. "I want to make a confession!" Underhill erupted with force and a rattle to the Russian Caravan tea service.

Glass had been verifying other parts of his testimony from BeeHive Inn with Tanner—who recalled also seeing the strange figure on the bridge, but from Tanner's own room window—when Underhill's blurt out came. Queerly, Glass appeared annoyed by the interjection. "O goodie," Tanner said, retrieving an overturned teacup and pouring another serve, switching from disinterest in the topic of Pipe-as-absolute-Peele-obsession to the titillation of Underhill having lured Cox to the site of a grossly grotesque demise.

"I thought you might," Glass said, a brush of annoyance aside, notebook stored away.

"*Now!* and privately," Underhill said, folded in like a defeated heavyweight boxer whose knockout blow had come to the gut. "Please."

"I will need a witness," the detective said, "but certainly, I see no reason for any more company being privy to what you have to say than one. The rest of you can go—I have everything I need now to finish up this case."

"Porter," Marsh said, "go with Brown and Tanner, ready the boys——"

"*No!*" Underhill cried. "If another has to hear it—I want it to be Porter."

"Very well," Marsh said, hurt plain at Underhill not wanting the *Sizar's* head present. "Oscar, I'll call for a carriage to take us to the pier. Assuming, that is, you still wish to attend?"

"Yes, now leave us," Glass said waving Marsh away, "before Mr Underhill loses his nerve."

There was reluctance by some to leave, especially Tanner, whose upset at not getting to bear witness to Underhill's confession was selfishly palpable. When it was only three men in the room, the only sounds that remained were waves breaking in the distance, calls of challengers training on the foregrounds of the hotel, and Underhill's own laboured breathing—a man he could never imagine leaking from the eyes seeming set to surprise him.

"It works to your favour to get ahead of this, Underhill," Glass said, sitting for the first time that session so the three of them faced each other on the same level. "There have been other testimonies that have placed you with Cox that night, so best that you tell the man your account now."

"A vicar?" Underhill whispered.

Glass nodded and went on: "You've my ear, Mr Underhill."

Underhill was a big bulk of a fellow. The kind of immovable man whose every part seemed devoted only to the simple-yet-commanding task of expanding into and holding space. He felt wholly disconcerted, therefore, watching Underhill attempt to speak, but not be able to. Like an infantry soldier teetering on the brink of charge into a battle whose enemy odds were so inhumanely stacked against them. Having been asked to stay, to bear witness to Underhill's statement, he felt a consuming instinct to comfort, to take Underhill in his arms and calm the shudder that ripped through his former colleague like a livewire shock. So that the words of the man's confession might come more easily.

"I didn't kill 'im," Underhill said when the movement of the man's lips rose to the task of speech. "But what I need to confess is as bad, if not worse." Underhill looked to Glass for reprieve, but the detective gave away nothing. Glass would make the fellow say it. "I buggered 'im," Underhill said, mean and anguished, like each word was a distinct tribal poison. He rose red at the reminder of what he had done to Cox as well. Like Underhill was a ghost sent to drive him mad and confess himself. Like an arrowhead torn from Underhill's breast, it was clear that the confession had to come out. But brought with it further damage…torn ligaments and profuse bleeding, coupled with infection and a couldn't-be-worse expression.

Glass did not look at all surprised: "And you're confessing this because"——leaning in close——"you want justice for Cox? You wish to repent your actions?"

"No," Underhill replied, self-loathing pronounced enough that no apparent offence was taken to Glass' tone. "Because we were…disturbed."

"It is a depraved act."

"*No!* someone came by right in the middle."

"So you…"

"I pu–ulled out and fled. By that time the training was already under-way, and I didn't fancy running into him again that night, so I went to a bar instead."

"BeeHive Inn?"

"Yes."

"One of the only bars open at that hour, I reckon. And, unluckily for you, close to the local vicar's residence."

Underhill straightened up a little, like the detective's knowings on things might offer some hope, after all.

"The proprietor of the BeeHive told me the local vicar has been making threats to have the bar closed for disturbances to the peace…one man's peace. Threats often silenced through free ale, I might add. And unlucky for you, it was while at the bar that you were approached by him and the man made certain demands. Am I right?"

"Yes. He said he had seen it all from the bushes. The whole Sodom sin affair, until it was…interrupted."

"And what did he want from you?"

Underhill's frame was the first to shake, followed by speech. It was difficult to watch. Like a should-be-sturdy canal boat jerking along a crossing due to some unknown crippling to its structure——a crack in its rudder, perhaps. Then, straight after the appearance of these hairline fractures, all self-loathing broke loose. Underhill had done so well to have kept it in until this point; but like the bursting of a dam, his former colleague had sailed past breaking point. Underhill's breaking made for a tremendous roar and outpouring of pent-up water within. Underhill didn't weep, the man wailed, hysterically, like one pushed so far into depths of grief that the only bodily response was a variant of possession. "To see me...finish," Underhill said, spittle and nose sap running as unconfined as the man's tears. "He said it was the only way he could absolve me of the carnal sin. A form of catharsis, the sick bastard said."

"And he offered himself as a vessel for the absolution, I assume?"

"Yes," a bit calmer now, but tears still coming, "he had...he had me...do it with him...in his vestments. Fortunately, I had enough drink left in me to be able to go through with it."

"And you finished?"

"Yes."

"Where?"

"...*in him.*"

"And you're sure you didn't finish in Cox?"

Why is he asking that? he thought with a horror all his own.

"Yes, I'm sure."

"This is important, lad. I need to know this. There was no trace of your stock in the boy, you're sure now."

"*Yes!* I was far from close."

But it's alright, I didn't either, he calmed himself. *Won't find any trace of me in the poor runt. 'M saving that for Keely.*

"Alright, good. Then what did you do, after finishing off with the vicar?"

"Went back to the bar and continued drinking, until morning, when I was needed on the beach."

"And you didn't return to your room, or go looking for Cox?"

"No."

"So why confess? No trace of you at the scene, other than the witness, and the vicar seems unlikely to go to the authorities given how thick in it he is as well and that——"

"The vicar did the deed too!" he spoke up. Out of turn, clearly, by the look on Glass' face—he'd found himself transfixed by the salaciousness of it all. *I'm as bad as Tanner*, he thought, sinking back into the softness of the High Tea settee, wearing his best sorry-I-interrupted expression.

"Quite right, Porter," Glass said once—again—annoyance with him subsided. "But let's allow Underhill the space to tell his story."

"I thought so, too," Underhill said, "as I drank 'til the stars started to fade. Told myself that my dealings with that vicar were behind me, after having gone through with his disgusting demands. He"——looking about like further clarification was needed on the dastardliness of the sexual encounter——"made me *whip him*, and degrade him with words...while I did it to him. Anyway...I thought that, at least, it was all behind me. But before we left the Grand, and this was after Cox was found, as I came down with my bags and with Mr Blunt, the vicar was there, waiting for me in the lobby. I made my excuses to my boss, something about attending a service while I was here. He had no issue with it... Anyway, when alone, the vicar said that under the circumstances, now that the boy he had seen me with was dead, I should need to continue my penance with him, or else he would be compelled to tell the authorities what he saw."

Glass stood abruptly up, like all on the matter was now settled: "I would call that bluff were I you, Mr Underhill. But besides...you would face disgrace, maybe worse, just to be rid of this vicar and his hold over you?"

"I would, sir," Underhill said, for the first time that teatime in the mode of address that he had come to know the man for: assertive and backed by bulk. "I'd sooner go down for it than get into it with the likes of him again, and at least maybe I can bring the devil down with me."

"I see..." Glass said, just as Marsh appeared at the doorway.

"Carriage is here," Marsh said, eyes lingering on the scene of them like it was the reveal of a West End drama that the club head, nosy as ever, was desperate to be a part of.

"Right—I'll be right there," Glass said. "Thank you, Stew Boy," Glass added, softer, which had the effect of moving Marsh on. Glass sat again and put a hand on Underhill's knee: "It's a good thing you told me."

Underhill was slumped and apparently un-listening.

The detective went on, even softer now: "I *know* you didn't kill Cox, and your account gives you an alibi that has already been confirmed by the innkeeper. As for this vicar, he actually gives you an added alibi, given that I have already questioned him and he confirmed that Cox was alive when you left him. And more crucially, that Cox retained his coat—something this vicar who stalked you back to the Inn confirms. So that rules you out. As for this man of the robe's threats, I wouldn't heed them nor him any further notice. He can't touch you anymore. Such matters have a way of sorting themselves out an–nd, I can promise you this, the matter of what happened with that vicar, and Cox for that matter, stops with me." Glass raised Underhill's chin so that their eyes met: "That vicar won't be troubling you again. You hear me, son?"

Underhill nodded, a broken figure still, but with glimmers of shocked relief seeping through, like a man overhearing a death-row pardon order.

"Good man." Glass looked set to leave, before something switched in the man's expression, leaning in close instead. Voice and way with words changing, as he'd noticed before. "You're a fine man. Strong. Don't let lesser men take advantage. Many men do what you have done, and most of them are lesser men than you. Take ol' Stew Boy, one of your club 'heads.' I knew him when he was a *King's* boat boy at Cambridge, while still wet in long John L. Sullivans, *when I'd rip the arse out regularly to use him.*" There was an unravelling about the detective's eyes that unnerved him. "I was rough with the *King's* boy in the mud, and the boy in *King's* had liked it rough. He was a privileged little fuck, that one. And I enjoyed roughing him up because I was a bigger man than him. A better man. Something that Stew Boy's now trying to feel a bit of by running this little club. But he'll never be a man like I was, and certainly nothing like you. I know how this club all started, boys. It's rooted one day by the boatshed when Stew Boy moaned, *after he had moaned*, about not getting a look in at *White's*, or any of the others. He was spectacularly unpopular. 'If you don't like the rules. Why not be a games master?' I'd told him. Starting a club wasn't what I'd meant. Last thing London needs is another gentlemen's club. I hadn't meant anything, really. I was in the high of release of having half buried the boy. The rains had been especially harsh that June, you see, and Stew Boy had visited me dressed in his graduation gown on the banks of the Cam when I'd said it."

Eyes more crazed now, speech sharper, too. "I had buggered him so hard into the marshy edge that the *King's* boy had choked a bit on some mud. After the first gasp, I had even rolled his face in so it was full black, held it there, too. Until he blew Cam-side bubbles. Couldn't swim, our Stew Boy, y'know. And the cunt calls himself a rower! He was a weak little bitch's pup, and I'd have said anything just to shut him up. He was not good for much of anything, that one. Nothing he put his hand to. He tried the French horn. I used to find it a laugh hearing him squeal as I fisted that *King's* boy's own French horn. You know, the gape *down under*. It was more in key, I tell you." A calm came over Glass now, face and voice returned to an expected register, as if wheedled out of possession by thought of some pleasant place. "You're strong," Glass said. "Don't throw that away. Goes for you too, Porter. Right, that's me then." A slap of Underhill's knee then the detective was out the door, to disappear out of sight through the foyer.

He stayed with Underhill, them both in a state like a water-soaked shock-wire. He was determined to let his former colleague—never a friend, though—make a move first. He wanted to ask Underhill why he was trusted as a witness, but resisted this temptation to talk. Instead, he put his hand on Underhill's thigh, more intimately placed than the detective's touch. Nothing crazy in it, though nearer the groin on a part meatier. *I won't tell* and *don't do anything foolish*, the squeeze was his way of saying. Maybe something of *I'm in your same boat, too*, about it.

They sat together silently for probably one quarter of an hour after Glass' departure, with just around half one hour to go before Underhill would be needed again, out on the green, with Blunt, for the start of the race. After Lewis, whose self-harm of the highest order seemed to come on as sudden as a storm cloud at sea, in the silence he found himself wanting to shake Underhill and urge the man not to self-punish any further. To take this stage to at least try to make Underhill feel better about the man's lot.

Yes, he should speak up, he resolved. He shouldn't keep his silence, not when Underhill had specifically called upon him to be there. He opened his mouth to speak——

"Porter," Glass cut in from the door before he could rouse his resolve to the level of sound. "All's forgiven. Just so you know. I'll see you at the pier, I expect. Underhill, Cox's killer will be revealed soon, and that vicar won't be able to hide behind his vestments forever. Take care of yourself." And Glass was gone. Glass had spoken with such finality, such crystal resolve that he could only assume the case had been solved...and that invitation to the pier was to learn at last who among them had done it. Glass pushed the invitation to the pierhead upon him like a tugboat nudging a liner through a channel on a navigable course out to sea. *Must go!*

Evidently also reflecting on their situation, Underhill took the thigh-hand he had rested there. "Thanks, Kemp," Underhill said, shaking it. "You're a good friend." Underhill's voice was still masculinely cavernous. It rung out with a bellow. But also, in that tender moment, was softened...like a declawed bear's embrace.

Keely had taught him about grief, and the voice of his lover inside was telling him now that the better course was to sit with Underhill without comment, and just touch him, gently, as a commitment to keeping his new friend's story safe. And calming himself about his own lot in Cox. Keely's inner voice won out, delaying his curiosity to race to Glass' on-pier reveal or to speak a word. Sitting and holding Underhill's hand took him over. Underhill, like Lewis, had laboured under the ill-compassion of Blunt. In the silence following confession, with quiet company and a light touch, Keely's wisdom was on show. Underhill seemed to be...returning to form through his touch. "Listen to the detective," he said as he broke connection with Underhill's inner thigh some minutes later, "care for yourself." *Take care* had been the phrase that initially sprung to mind, though he filtered it out for its undercurrents as a threat. And then he left, for the foyer, with full intention to head direct to the pierhead. Underhill did not stay at High Tea, his new friend left to return to duties. In the foyer an attendant from reception bearing a telegram came out to meet him.

Unclothed, back in time on the Thames... Shillingless, he came alive with Port in London. The leap from the city's bridge had been a reformation, and now that Port had committed both to the faith-jump and to the declaration of a shared love, they could set about building a new world order—away from Marsh, with Sqi at rest and Pipe, remembered, always there, somewhere, but kept to the past. At least that was his hope... Having no money helped them start over on an equal footing. He took to odd ends to earn feed for them both, fishing and manning market stalls, and turning his hand to just about anything else that was going. It stank eternally there, by The Pool, scents that rose with the encroach of summer. But they were happy. Even Port, back turned on all the privilege of public-school upbringing and daddy-paid Cambridge tuition; he knew Port was happy there, too. Along with happiness, the months brought revelation. And while he plied the same trades Pipe had taught him, around the docks and on the many bridges of the Thames, to keep them fed and even afford some nights out, Port kept their keep in other ways, holding up an agreement to assist on the Pipe inquiry, even if it wasn't in a way the detective would have welcomed...

"That man you was with at the station," he had said the morning after their Thames swim, at a cafe aptly named "Traitor's Gate" that had views of both the bridge and where they had come ashore. "He's the detective working Pipe's murder?"

"Yes, *why*?" Port asked over coffee and pastries paid for with last monies.

"I know 'im."

"How?"

"He were Pipe's lover." Port looked as shocked as a society highflier after first wallet snatch. "He nicked Pipe for whoring," he went on, "originally," using coffee sips as dramatic pauses. "Before them came to an arrangement.

244

It explains why we're staying where we are. Our room's in a whorehouse for boys. Ain't sure whether it still runs as one…though based on some familiar mugs about the joint, I'd say it does. Plus, Glass be the reason we missed the train to Brighton. Pipe confronted him."

"Did Glass see you at the station? Now or then?" Port asked desperate.

"Nah, I know how to keep m'self hidden."

It was the foundation of an in-it-together realisation, and breakfasts there at that table on the Thames then became a once-weekly affair for the two months in which they were in residence in a whorehouse whose affiliation with the Metropolitan Police was, early on, unknown.

Port remained committed to the pursuit of truth while they stayed there, which began in that first week with a visit to police offices where Port had expected to call in on Glass, only to be told that the former detective had taken early retirement. Naturally, he reckoned, it could have all been a ploy by the police; detectives were a threatened species, and often needed to move about without recognition, in a city where they made many enemies. So, Port resolved that a visit to Marsh was warranted; of whom, bitter still from Cox along with a continued brush-off of attempts to have Glass visit, agreed to use society connections to verify whether, in fact, Glass held appropriate authority to act as investigator in the case.

Glass didn't. Furthermore, Marsh's connections revealed that the former detective had left the profession with disgraces that involved abuse of power to solicit sexual favours with boys across the city. The situation was a sensitive one, as Port's investigations uncovered. For, the deaths the phoney detective was investigating were real, and from the two-month talks with the best sources inside the police force, Port learned that Glass had managed not only to fool those in the club into thinking the investigation was legitimate, but to keep the deaths a secret from authorities, too. Feelers Marsh put out, gingerly of course, returned no trace of any investigation of the murders of Marty Piper or Sergei Cox. Neither had been reported missing. Cox was not believed to be the boy's real name and though *the Pipe* was a household name, the boy's legal name was not known to police either. The Brighton and Scarborough boy bodies were firmly off the police radar.

Port edged toward the expectation that Glass could well have been motivated by a genuine pursuit of justice for the Pipe. The former detective was once intimate with the famous whoring figure, after all, who might not receive—being a criminal orphan boy whore from the docks—the right kind of attention from the investigative bright lights of Scotland Yard, were the death reported. Working on this basis, Port and Marsh formed an unlikely alliance and decided to allow Glass' investigation to run its course. On the eve of the final sorting round, to take place at Birkdale in Southport, it was decided that to service different priorities—the protection of the club on one hand and the pursuit of truth and justice for the dead on the other—Port and Marsh would work to see Glass' investigation continue to its conclusion, but with clipped wings; the latter as safeguard against the possibility that Glass was the man responsible for the boy deaths of that year.

To-day in Birkdale… A telegraph from London sent him racing from Birkdale Palace to Southport Pier. As it happened, only some half hour ahead of when the final-round pledges were due to proceed along the same path. Glass was sat alone at the pierhead, a steamer having not long pulled away, picking up with it whatever wanderers had been there before. Marsh and the other three were at Madame Tessy's Tea Room just short of Glass. The four heads of *Sizar's* were bunched at a table meant for the tea drinking of two; Marsh and Blunt tracked his approach to the former detective like a coast-watch spotlight locked on a dangerous-cargo barge attempting entry into a harbour—flying flags already distrusted. He came up out of breath on Glass, who apparently knew it was him and did not turn. "I think it's true," Glass said, as much to the air between pier arm and the steamer out to sea as to him, "about that architect jumping to his death. After having got his creation that backwards. After letting the plan get away from him that much; was there anything other he could do?"

"He could have blamed the builders and his contractors?"

"Ah, you see, but he couldn't, and no others would have blamed them either, not really. It was his responsibility to oversee it. No, there was no other way...after it had been done, once his creation had gone awry; there was nothing left but to jump from it. There's a poetry in it."

"As a detective, I would have thought you would be the last chap who'd regard poetry in death," he said, sitting beside Glass, joining the sleuth watching the Southport steamer shrink on its course towards the Ribble and Alt Estuaries.

"Before this case, I think I would have agreed with you on that. But no, not now. Take that pattern of noughts and crosses that emerged from Stew Boy's list of the Brighton wrestle boys. A detective mind would see that and think, *must be something in it! Must be a clue!* It was pure coincidence, that pattern. I *knew* it was, but still I pondered over it. How poetic is that? Even Lewis' suicide. It seems out of place, doesn't it? But no, look closer, and there's a rhythm to that, too. The lad might even have inspired others. A ripple of death. Just the week following there was a poor bastard thrown from a carriage crossing that new Tay Bridge, the one that replaced that almighty engineering fuck-up from *Sir* Thomas Bouch. Bouch needed to take responsibility for the design of the first Tay crossing. What was the lad who landed in the Tay from Bouch's replacement taking responsibility for, I wonder. Whatever it was, he was taken so quick by the current, so we'll probably never know what led to it. That's poetry in ravine-splat and river-sweeping action, my friend! Neither bodies recovered, by the way."

He wouldn't allow Glass to distract from the case at hand. "Speaking of patterns, there is something that has been bothering me. Two things, really. First, your real reason for being in Brighton when *the Pipe* died. O yes, I see things too. And second, why you sent a boy in to do a job you were more aptly positioned to do yourself, at Scarborough."

"Time is short, Porter. Ask me directly."

"Where were you the night of the Pipe's death?"

"Killing him," Glass said.

*E*arlier that same morning on the Thames... He had been left with lucid instruction on the day that Port took the early-morning service to Southport. He was to use whatever funds they had saved to find temporary lodgings elsewhere in London and transport their belongings to those new lodgings that same day—as after all they had learnt, and with all that would likely unfold in Southport, Port could not be certain whether staying in the accommodation given to them by Glass would be tenable for much longer, and were Glass' involvement in the case as sinister as what was now seeming possible, there could be imminent danger to them. He had never met Glass up close, though Pipe had spoken of the man often, being of the view that the detective was harmless. But he would follow Port's direction to each point. It would prove a welcome distraction throughout the day, he told himself once Port had disappeared waving into the steam of a Southport-bound train.

How quickly as a pair they had accumulated items to decorate their room. A sketch from a street artist of barges plying the Thames pinned to one wall. Several potted plants from the market sellers in Smithfield—helping to patch from view rotting wood holes. Even a broken pew from St Magnus the Martyr that he and Port had rescued from the rain one night following drinks down by the bridge; to carry home, mend, adorn with cushions and then use each night to recline on in front of the fire—often Port reading, while he rested on the rhythm of Port chest...content just listening. In merely two months they had put down roots and built a modest home for themselves. He had never done that before. Never acquired more than what could be stuffed in a rucksack. Never saw reason to, nor wanted to. Never ached for home.

Providing for them both had opened up a renewed purpose for him— selling of cotton plucked from barges on the Thames being his most profitable venture. In savings, they had enough to stay comfortably somewhere secure in London for probably near-on a month. Secure, but significantly back from the Thames and the stockpile he had tucked into cavities in hidden, up-and-under parts of Traitor's Gate. That day, therefore, as part of a transfer of belongings, he would need to transport the cotton he had remaining. Down along the Thames and to the front door, where he had paid a local lad to watch over the growing pile of their home furnishings. It was their nest egg.

Mornings, down around the whoring-trade parts of the docks, were the best times of day to move goods—being when the whores were sleeping-off their trading of the night before, and their trades, tucked back in their guises of respectability. The morning also brought with it light, which he needed to put into action the plan he had for the movement of his cotton. Rubbish was rife along the Thames, especially in the little alcove in which their ramshackle two-month home had been built. Filth collected, pooled and bubbled-into-decay in the stagnant section under their building, partially concealing the point of entry for his planned transfer. Like the catacombs of Paris, the Thames was riddled with cave systems that connected with cellars under the structures built along its edge, predating the rebuilding of the city after fire and other strife to the superstructure.

This building once used its cellar for the side hustle of alcohol plucked from shipping docked in the Thames, where it was sold on at underworld rates, often in concert with the more organised outsourcing of flesh. Clearly, Glass' stake in the building had disrupted this old model, and the service entrance into the cellar from the street did not appear to be in use anymore. This worked to his advantage that morning for, he knew, unlike many such cellar entry points that branched off the Thames, this one did not have iron-bar obstructions, and, assuming the space had not been cleared out completely, several wooden rowing boats were stored under there. He knew this because Pipe had often assigned boys under sway to make use of these crafts; to smuggle back out some booze, when Pipe needed to loosen the cogs of a shifty customer, a gonna-tell lawman or just for personal parties.

London is sinking and the Thames is notorious for bursting its banks after heavy rainfall. This, coupled with Pipe's fear of the water and its want

for him, including an acute distrust of caves that flood—like this particular
man-made one, which would flood right up to and through the between-parts
and nail-voids of the floorboards of the ground floor—meant Pipe kept well
clear, and often sent him, like Pipe did with the cotton, to man the boats. So,
he was familiar with the space. Access would normally be from street level,
down the cobbled incline that was large enough for a carriage pulled by two
horses, to load up and transfer out sizeable crates of ale. But in low tide, as
it was that morning, access was also possible from the river, via a drop down
and swing into the inlet. To those who did not know any better, it just looked
like a cut-out in the stone at the edge of a recess in the Thames wall.

Sitting on the wall just over where the entry manoeuvre would happen,
he then did the drop 'n' swing as soon as that section of the foreshore was
clear of the odd stumbling drunkard. Taking the initiative at low tide meant
landing in the cavity under the cobbled promenade into water that ran up
to his knees. This cavity was cut into the wall like a port in the hull of a
ship, the stone beneath it continuing solid to the sooty bottom of the river—
navigable at low tide, engulfed and kept hidden at high. It was the perfect
place to stow perishables—the water supply keeping the chamber chilled,
light not escaping to show its secrets due to a hairpin bend a half dozen
feet in from the Thames, which led to another corridor that opened into the
cavity below the building.

Summer was the best time to retrieve boats from here. The weather was
stable, rainfall was low and flooding uncommon. This summer had seen the
city struck by heatwaves, making it one of the driest on record. It left the Thames low and its pollutants particularly pungent. The stench hit him as soon
as he rounded the hairpin. It struck him broadside like a blacked-out barge
at night on a fast-flowing river. It bumped out all the general filth smells of
the Thames, until just its one category of choking foulness was amplified,
like through the bell of a tuba, low and guttural. It was a different genome
of decay, heavier in the air, bodied like a gas, its molecules so weighed down
with rot that they could not escape the cavity bend, to the relative freshness
of the aboveground city. Like the divide between fresh and salt water, this
odour was kept inside, like the ballooning bloat of an ungutted fish.

He could pinpoint the smell as soon as he entered the cavity. It was no longer a storeroom of ale, a place for keeping boats:

this is a tomb.

He would have left the cavity to its decay, abandoned the boats and the chance of collecting the cotton down at Traitor's Gate, which he had planned to pass off for rubbish in the waterproofed sacks he had stored them in. He would have pulled out...were it not for the light—its sources so numerous that at first he thought the cellar on fire. It was on fire, in a way. Hundreds of tiny, red candle droplet fires. The candles were so numerous, so built up over time, that the cellar had lost at least one foot of clearance, as candles were placed on the top of the wax of those burnt out before them.

It's a chapel of death.

He waded in via a channel that led from the Thames, through which boats were once launched. Every base surface other than this body of water was white, the wax ragged like the wash of a storm wave at the shore, deceased wicks leaving behind uncountable mounds that rose and dipped into the channel like stalagmites and stalactites in a secret, ancient cave where monsters lurked. At the end of the channel, where the wax rose highest, and the light was its most concentrated, half in the water, half out, was an iron, square-hulled boat, just the length of a man.

Blue and beautiful and perfectly preserved;

    it was Pipe.

He should have ran.

Should have been horrified at the shrine.

But he wasn't, couldn't be...for in death, as in life, Pipe was a creature of unfathomable beauty.

He should be rotten, he thought with a measure of envy, as he came to stand over his dead idol.

But Pipe remained fresh...statuesque.

Blue, but with a blush of pink, too.

In iron,

    naked,

        on ice.

He touched him, he had to. Pipe was soft, like having had just died that day. He checked for breath, but there was none. Pipe was dead sure enough, but defiant to the order of things. He went in close. *No, he doesn't smell.* But the smell was everywhere, it overwhelmed everything. Terror-in-realisation came when movement caught his eye. But only just, in the far reaches of the damned chapel—the one corner of the space where no candles found light. Where the wax steeply sloped like a dune to a gyrating object. *A machine?* was his thought. *Some kind of generator?* Some combustion engine perhaps, used to produce the ice needed to keep Pipe fresh. But as his eyes focused...found definition in the dark, it was clear that this object was organic. The source of the rot: a body, broken and backwards, bent and grotesquely wobbling under the onslaught of desecration.

The water kept the rats away,

but not the crabs,

they came in on all tides,

all angles of the walls,

in and out of the water.

The wretched corpse on which they fed rattled and shook them off with a momentum all its own; but not enough to stop the tearing of putrid flesh, which hung from the frame in ribbons. It was Cox. Not that there was any-thing left of *the outsider to all this* to suggest identity. There was no humanity in that discarded corner. No light, no iron vessel to keep the poor thing in. No ice, no care, except from the crabs that tore at flesh. He backed out the way he had come in, daring not to turn his back on the broken thing. His being there had disrupted the crabs, and therefore the rhythm of the corpse. He would not turn his back, for he was certain that if he did, the object in the corner, so discarded, would scurry after him like a monster crab who, having only known misery, must now inflict it on others. He vaulted back to the London levels. Shaken but set on a course back to the station and for the next service to Southport. While waiting to board, he sent a telegram from the station marked urgent and addressed to "Kemp Porter, Birkdale Place Hotel". Hoping it would reach his lover in time. It read: *Boys found. Who we thought. Dont approach. On way.——T.K.*

egs-toughing closeness, presently at the pierhead… Glass' confession came eyes
to the sea, a solitary tear escaping the one eye visible in profile. Glass
spat it out, like the bursting of a caisson, like holding it in any longer would
crumble the already cracked man's entire structure. "I didn't set out to kill
him," Glass followed up with, softer, seeming relief that the words were out.
"But the death was just too…perfect, for him. Too fitting. He was always going on about how he knew the sea would claim him. He wasn't afraid of it.
He welcomed the want. That's what he was like. He courted the want of
dangerous things." *Southport had shown itself to be an unstable place*, he thought as
a mist on the horizon rolled in, eating the steamer. "He was plying as a *shake
lurk* when we met, around the navy docks at Greenwich. Posing as a shipwrecked sailor. He was obsessed with the sea. He would even taunt it each
time a storm rolled in, dangling on the edge of a bridge or pier or break
wall. I found it wild and weird and beautiful, like every part of him…I always knew he would stay young forever. I often wondered whether he was
the lad of the sunken boat bet I told you about, come back to the surface
with no rich man the wiser while also, at the same time, staying down there,
living-dead underwater."

Glass spoke like the words had been delivered a thousand times before,
like a eulogy whose meticulous rehearsal was marked in the folds and anno-
tations of the paper it was scripted through. "When we met, I was working a
case and, foolishly, having had a few side-hustle boys by that time, saw him as
one—albeit the prize one—that, like all the others, I could control. I saw his
scam as something I could swindle him with. I would have done anything to
sleep with him; I chose the threat of prison in his case. When he submitted,
he was just playing along, allowing me to think I was the one in control. That
I had him, that he was mine. To threaten him, I needed to follow him. And

that's how I found out I'd found *the Pipe!* It's then I tried to win him. I thought an allowance and a place to live in the city would make him give up whoring and stay with me, make him grateful. To think I could tame the Pipe was as stupid as thinking anyone could tame the sea. Making me think I could was his gambit. And he was expert at it."

He became aware that there was movement on the pierhead. Peele, ever the club showman, had stirred up commotion for the arrival of respective house runners along to the finish line, parallel to the teahouse, running a ribbon the winner could sever with first chest. And a crowd was beginning to swell, and chatter to rise to the level of the gulls.

But Glass was a man in confessional, set on a path. "I lost my job because of him, my reputation, any prospects of gainful future employment. I became obsessed with him, to the exclusion of the others. Boy whores, who I had run-ins with previously, but had cut off after meeting him, who banded together to bring me down. I argued they were informers. But these boys must have learnt something from me, for they had evidence that they were much more than that. When I asked them why they did it, they said they were jealous of him. He had that effect on people, everyone seemed to love and hate him. Hate always came, usually when he saw no use in you. I kept his secret though. Because I thought I could still use it to have him.

"I didn't end up with nothing. I had property, including a building he had whored in. But he did not stay long there; I'd fuck other than a roof to offer him after the scandal, and he soon met someone who could provide a better life for him, who I now know was Peele. I followed him, first into the country and then to Brighton, on the same train. He caught me following on occasion. And sometimes tried to shake me off. He missed the private-though-on-the-public-timetable train to Brighton because of me. That was to my advantage, as I could follow on a service on which my presence wouldn't have been questioned. I let slip to Stew Boy about the time of the train in the heat of our joint time with the Pipe on the beach—it plagued me, that slip, that Stew Boy might realise I was on the same train as him. Though worry was needless: Stew Boy is too self-obsessed these days to be attuned to any compromising circumstances other than his own.

"I think Pipe liked it. Liked me knowing, holding it over him.

"He taunted me, like he would a storm. Thinking that he was safe as long as he kept his distance, didn't wade in. But I wasn't going to let him go. I'd never tell, but I'd never let him live with a man either. He'd never turn his back on the sea. He didn't trust it. Thought that its want for him was so strong that, the moment his back was turned, Poseidon himself would rise and claim him…he shouldn't have thought that my want was any less."

Glass broke sight with the unseeable horizon, the mist running now, consuming crags of the Merseyside coast like the Severn bore—the pier in its sights.

"I saw him there, naked on the pier, back to me, facing the sea—it just made sense. There was poetry in it—giving him to the sea would just take one push. I came up behind him. He had never looked so perfect than he did that night, white and reflective against the moon, his muscles bulging, like all of them had only just been engaged. He had a very distinctive odour, utterly intoxicating, too sweet for a boy: thyme with highlights of rose. And once I was in it again, I knew that pushing him was not enough. I needed to claim him myself, before the sea. And so, I grabbed him by the neck. I'm not all that strong, but I was that night; like everything I felt for him, every impulse was in my grip. He didn't resist me, even as I rose him up and he started to crackle between my palms. 'You're mine,' I whispered to him as he bucked and seized. But even then, he didn't permit me fear in his eyes. He was… impossibly…unfeeling toward me, even as I snuffed life from him. And when he went loose, when he was finally relaxed and limp in my grasp, I let the sea have its go."

The first breath of mist had reached them now. Cold and salty, latching to their skin like uncountable barnacles to the pole borings of the pier.

"At first, I felt relief. I slept that night for the first time in months. But as soon as I woke, I knew that I couldn't let the sea keep him. I had taken the pile of clothes from the pier before I had left. It was only come morning that I realised another man's clothes joined his…but with no sign of a second body or, later, news of anyone missing…that confused me. I thought I was done for when Cohen and Blunt and Peele spoke of seeing a man on the pierhead.

But they mustn't have recognised me. They were too interested in implicating each other to see anything of that night in my shape."

And saving themselves... he thought. *Blunt lied about burning the clothes.* "Blunt was rather agitated about my question of whether there were any other boys unaccounted for, now that I think about it," Glass said, as if his thoughts were written in the mist. "The train told me that I couldn't take the risk being seen with anyone else from Brighton, and that Pipe was travelling with that Keeler boy. I had no way of knowing whether Keeler saw me during the confrontation with Pipe, or any other time—I'd never seen him myself, Pipe kept the boy hidden from me. This was why I sent in Cox, not knowing who the other set of clothes belonged to. They were of a good cut, so I suspected they may belong to one of the tutors—that's why I avoided yous lot, until Cox's backbend forced me to show my hand...only in a limited way at first, only to you. And I had no way of knowing whether I had been seen by Keeler. Had any recognised me, it could all have been over. I had put coin in Cox, you see, so he was mine to use."

Just as well I didn't put my stock in him, too, he thought brazenly, part to test whether Glass was a mind reader as well as murderer.

"The Pipe had many followers, you ain't get that kind of press in London without a network to help you rise above the average whore. But he saw Keeler as his protégé—though he never told him so. He was very protective of him. The clothes were a kind of souvenir. But they were nothing without him, and since it was my hands and not the sea that had taken him first, I came back in the morning to claim what was mine. Running into Stew Boy was a surprise, it shook me. I hadn't known that he was bound up in it all...I hadn't known there was a club beyond Pipe finding a benefactor in the country, though I had a whiff of *Sizar's* already from the lips of my other whores. I thought Peele was running something like what had been the set-up on the Thames that I took over. A boy brothel. And you know, after all I've come to learn, I'm not sure that this club is far off that. You look at me queerly, but I know gentlemen's clubs. And this one is the worst kind. Perverse. Not a real club at all. As that crude fuck Tanner—watch him, you hear!—poured out tea instead of coffee in that damned folly hotel, I knew."

Glass was becoming increasingly crazed-cryptic as the confession rolled on. The man seemed to be of two halves, two different men. Different tongue for each. Different breeding, walk of life. "That *Sizar's* men drank tea rather than coffee. I'd made note of that on the *Pullman Limited Express* because it spoke of a misguided principle against *White's*. *White's* had its start in coffee, you see, what diarist Mr Samuel Pepys calls 'the bitter black drink.' Know your history, Porter. I do. Quite simply, during the reigns of Charles II, coffee houses were the only means of public expression. This was radical thinking at its start. Before the printing press was in existence as we know it to-day, it was in the coffee houses that men got news and got to discuss it. *Heresy!* and something in need of quashing by Royal decree—actually! Kennett's 1706 history of England recorded that a royal proclamation was needed *because in such houses, and by occasion of the meeting of disaffected persons in them, divers false, malicious and scandalous reports were devised and spread abroad, to the defamation of his Majestie's Government, and to the disturbance of the quiet and peace of the Realm*. The attempt was made in 1675, by which time the freedom of tongue in coffee houses was so enjoyed by enough classes of men that outcry stopped the proclamation. And the coffee and chocolate houses thrived, with some 2000 of them spread through London and Westminster by 1710, and open to all men, except the very poor."

Whereas in Birkdale Glass' eyes had gone a bit crazed, at the Southport pierhead the man was now full possessed, with a spewing of facts so precise it was as if any humanity left in the man had been exhumed to be replaced only with the dusty contents of a forgotten tome. "As these meeting places grew, they became flavoured with the tastes of the men who congregated, inviting many proud and pungent varieties like the coffee beans of the most exotic reaches of Britain's Empire. Military men met at *Young Man's*, clergymen in St Paul's Churchyard at *Child's*. O yes, many were politically motivated gatherings, with the Whigs at *St James's* on the street of the same name, with Tories assembled nearby at *Ozinda's*. And it was around this same area of the West End that *White's* got its start, out of gatherings at the White's Chocolate House, where the order of the day was as a meeting place for men of fashion, to sip, smoke and share the finest company.

"Bigger than the clubs that would hold these men, the coffee houses that brought the likeminded together for the first time founded this idea of a *public sphere* in its richest brew and intercourse between men that was most civilised. Only when, at the most fashionable of these black-drinking spots did the best-connected start—like Eve in her dalliance with the Serpent that led Adam to shame his nakedness—to concern themselves with who might be among them...the magistrate who might be sharing free thoughts on liberalism over a black brew with a man one day, who he'll need to sentence for moral impropriety the next... Only then did the clubs descend into awfulness, and hence the coffee clubs went private, *White's* being the best-surviving earliest of these—skimming the cream of its clientele to form the first member's list of the "Club at *White's*," all men of spectacular means and leisure and very well connected, of course. Through refusal of the bitter black charms of coffee as a simply Whitest objection, rather than freeing masculine intercourse, *Sizar's* and its men are nothing more than limp-wristed pourers of Russian Caravan. But you want to know more about my forever-fresh boy, don't you, Porter?"

He felt the impulse to flee like every cell of his skin was a cliff-top fire in a nation's early-warning system. *What does the story of gentlemen's clubs have to do with any of this?* But the need to know kept him there.

"Initially, on seeing Stew Boy again after all these years, I felt at first like there might be something to be salvaged in me and his knowledge of me, which forced me to play the part of the detective. But that was only at first. The once-tasty Stew was gone, and years of built-on frivolity only served to focus me on getting back *my boy*, and to learning who was to blame for taking him from me. You see, Porter, that night, before going to the pier, he had visited me. Walked right up to my room. He had known I had followed him there. He had liked it. He even let me *finish with him, in him*, for the last time, he said. That's where he was when Peele went looking. Getting my stock. And letting me finish in him sealed it for me. No last time was ever going to be enough, even in death. That's why I needed him back, and what did I learn when I got him? That while he was full when I left him, he had cleaned himself out afterwards. But why? For who?

"As soon as I heard about the regatta, *I knew!* By God, yes, he had thrown that match! Nothing would have got him into a boat that close to the water. Taunting the sea from a bridge or break wall was one thing, but being in it like that, adrift. He would never have allowed it. And so, my investigation began, to learn who he was going to visit that night after me, had I not taken him at the pier. Who he'd cleared himself out for and who he had thrown the match for. Blunt showed that he had some part to play in it when he let slip on the train that Pipe was naked, also with his mention of West Pier. None of that he would have knew if he wasn't there… Blunt may not have been all I had thought him to be at first sight. But he was plenty guilty. Bets were placed, I'm sure of it. And, mark my words, Blunt carried enough boy blood on the hands. Then of course, Peele was centre to it all."

Glass was not speaking to him, not really. He needn't have even been there to hear it. Glass was speaking to the sea and the place were water claimed its own at pierhead…albeit a different pierhead entirely.

"Once I got him home and we were alone, I searched inside him my-self more deeply, to be sure. But he had voided me. And so…I added myself back."

"Why are you telling me all this?" he said at last, unable to keep the shake from his voice.

This time Glass spoke to him directly: "Don't you see? Because it's solved—I have my answers! I know those who helped take him from me. And now that he's lost to me again…it's time to wrap up."

Cold fire spread through him with the realisation of what *lost to me* meant.

"That telegram from your mate, you see," Glass said without needing to, "it was delivered to me first."

Before he could react. Before even the pins of panic had pricked all the way through him at the terror of realising that Glass was now, as the man had been since Brighton, one step ahead, the fallen detective was on foot and up and balanced atop one of the giant cleat horns where the steamer had moored before being swallowed by the mist. And as the winner—of Essex house—pierced ribbon by chest, Glass swung into the detective's final act.

Y ellow-white faces watched as a single skyward shot stopped the running of things, bringing silence to the pierhead. "I'm the killer," Glass
announced to the assembled with the beam of a ringmaster, "but yous were
instruments that led to deaths. Caused more deaths, too. So, let's share blood
of two of yous around. Have blood on yous hands as there is on mine."

Before any had time to decipher what the crazed words might mean,
the fallen detective had buried two bullets. In Peele then Blunt, a shot each
to the gut. Chaos followed, with shot men doubled over, grasping the entry
point, plentiful blood on the hands of both men. The pledges, frozen in a
heading toward the end of the race, turned on their heels and ran for town
instead. They were followed by any others who had turned out to witness,
along with panicked screams, all of which were base to the shrill cries of
Peele, writhing on the seagull-soiled boards. Cohen had fled, Brown close in
tow. Underhill stayed, applying pressure to Blunt's wound. Tanner stayed,
too, but was in apparent shock and knelt at Peele's side without adminis-
tering aid. They were all that remained at the pierhead. He went to Peele,
applying pressure to the wound. But his attentions were still drawn to Glass,
the mist now a wall at the crazed detective's back. A sign of Glass' complete
madness was that the man seemed relieved, elate even. Paying no notice to
those just shot. Glass looked at him and said: "There was poetry in it." As
Glass said it, mist rose up to claim; but Glass did not let it engulf him fully,
not before the revolver was in the man's mouth and the trigger pulled.

The mist went red,

　　just a shatter of a second,

　　　　before it took Glass to be claimed by the unseen sea and crept
back itself in the direction of the now out-of-sight Southport steamer.

It had all the theatrics of *the end*.

IX

THE CAM

Even the most rain-hardened Londoner was caught by surprise that afternoon when the clouds opened in a once-in-one-hundred-year deluge. The downpour washed out the sewers of the Thames and broke its banks, emptying the chapel of both its sacred and profane shrines. Pipe's "boat" shouldn't have floated, but somehow its iron found buoyancy, carrying the beautiful creature through the channel into the Thames then away from the city and out to sea. The boy was last spotted by a naval lookout from white chalk cliffs in the Dover Narrows—that great strait of shipwrecked sailors, where it is believed the beautiful creature finally went down into one of those ravines under the sea. Generations of gentlemen's clubs to follow would place bets on whether the undead creature stayed fresh at the bottom of the sea, complete with some failed attempts to find him in copper diving dress. All of which, so far, had ended in the depths claiming those who ventured in search of the forever-young man under the direction of coin.

In another anomaly of nature and brutal, unfair treatment, Cox got stuck in the tomb, only to be flushed out and over the streets once the floorboards of the house buckled and the whole wretched structure came down. *It*, that twisted, twitching mass of bones and rotten remnants of flesh made its way back into the Thames and was spotted being carried upriver, all the way to Trewsbury Mead, where the Thames gets it origin in dried-out streams that were turned into mud by the rains. Having nothing left to offer in terms of a feed, it went still at the start of the Thames and was beached there. It would be seen by many ramblers, who mistook the mangled mess in the mud for dredged bog branches, and so left it there forever: unburied and unclaimed.

Glass' pier suicide coinciding with the collapse of the man's horror whorehouse on the Thames captured the imagination of the penny papers as a welcome sideshow to the Ripper murders and made simple the job of the true and present Scotland Yard detectives in tying both murders to their deviant former colleague. This outcome suited *Sizar's*, too, to tie up the scandal neatly and separately from them, their operation's viability being in the balance, like a wounded, stalked stag after the gut shots of two out of the four of their executive branch. Theirs was a club in survival mode that, far from celebrating twenty years of running, was left limping on, to ensure that its extant sizars had enough of a future to see through even that year.

In self-shooting, Glass had laid out a convenient conclusion to the case, one with merit in motive and evidence that dissuaded any entertaining-of further inquiry by rendering it an unneeded drain on police resources and invasion into the private lives of respected society gents who, let it be remembered and as the Met Police told all the papers, were the victims of Glass' sick-sodomite vendetta. "Oscar Glass is guilty here, wholly and singularly," the Scotland Yard Commissioner declared to reporters assembled in Southport within a week of the mist being painted red. The Whitechapel murders were in full swing and no closer to any kind of resolution. There was no appetite for a multi-murder case gaining a foothold out of London, especially a case that would give opportunity for reporters to reveal that failure to achieve a break in the Whitechapel case had in fact given the disgraced sodomite detective the break needed to run amok at the English seaside. The beautiful creature of the penny-costing dreadfuls was notably Piper *not* "the Pipe" of London boy whore fame. No reporter made the connection, leaving many to think the Pipe simply retired from criminal life.

There was plenty to pin both murders on Glass by. When faced with a photograph of the dead man, other lodgers due to sleep in a dorm with

Piper the night of the boy's death identified Glass as the one they had seen in the corridor carrying the boy's bag, of tan and matching another bag Glass owned, and had travelled with, both of which were found in the man's London apartment. Cox was Glass' lover, too. And the boy, poor and of Russia, snatched from an honest-paid job, was bent into service to Glass under the pretence of a position with the force the man no longer had any authority to offer—the Commissioner remarked. And, on the subject of no authority, there was the matter of the house on the Thames, possession of which Glass had taken during time as detective and from which both bodies were seen to be carried out by the storm and along either which way of the river—though neither were ever recovered.

There, at the time of what would become known as the Great London Flood of '88, was spotted a young man, a crooked man. First seen being flushed from the basement of the building and onto the cobbled streets, then again down at the river access point, with a cane, trying to stem the escape of the two corpses, to divert their contrary parade through Greater London and beyond. The man, identified as a Dr Henrik, acting coroner from Brighton, was later apprehended. Henrik, denying any suggestion of involvement in either death, did confess to aiding Glass through the replenishment of ice and light for the vigil, while a raid on the assumed sodomite coroner's Brighton accommodations revealed that Henrik had taken to collecting other corpses as well.

"For scientific purposes only," Henrik told the magistrate at a subsequent hearing. "*That boy*, Piper, he was a question that had never been posed by science before." Although all the other corpses Henrik collected had died not of the man's hand—being spring and summer Brighton drownings— appetite for judicial blood spill led Henrik to be found guilty of being an accessory after the fact in the Piper case, and an accomplice in the case of Cox. It was a save face for Scotland Yard, Porter thought at the time, having met the man and not believing that Henrik had any part in Cox's death. Blaming Henrik was also a convenient explain-away of the escalation of the brutality and the complexity of the death pose that was Cox. At the hearing, Henrik's colleagues, when shown the sketches of the Cox body the man had made—verified by Grand Hotel bellboys from Scarborough and London spectators along the Thames the day of the flood as being *that grotesque*—did testify both that one man could not possibly have effected such distortions unaided, and that Henrik's notes of both killings—also in evidence— betrayed a deprived, deviant mind. Henrik was hanged by the neck until death within a month of Glass' self-execution, closing the case.

He found it unsatisfying in the extreme.

Cox ate at him…

Right from the moment he had first suspected some involvement of Glass, with Keely's sighting at the London Bridge Railway Station. Through his amateur investigations that followed…in which Pipe always fit in with his findings,

while Cox,

in turn,

was…

adrift.

Pipe was, in the puzzle of the beauty's death, as in the boy's life, a piece of perfect symmetry. A passion kill all the way through; and Glass, broken and consumed, was *all the way*, too—so total in a logic for extinguishing life, and in keeping the body of a slain obsession afterwards.

But Cox was imperfect,

as a person

and a victim

and a corpse.

And Glass, clearly, did not confess to killing both.

Naturally, his annoyance with Cox as an ill-fitted piece doubled when Glass self-shot and, after arriving back to the Birkdale Palace Hotel, he found that Glass had left for him *the notebook*…in his room, on the window-sill; rested upright like in the display of a London booksellers. The gesture made him think back to and about their conversation on the train to London from Scarborough when Glass had asked him to deputise to help solve the case.

Is this what he meant?

W arming themselves waterside, Cambridge was at its most stupen-
dous in the summer, especially so come the day of the regatta on
the Cam, less than one week after Henrik hanged—showing the sun did not
care of such things. The event fell on a midsummer Sunday, when students
were on leave of their studies; it was the same day each second year, a standing reserve date the club had of the river for their amateur row race. He and
Keely had opted out of their places on the team, as announced to Marsh
in Southport and in exchange for staying on in an interim capacity to train
up Prett as the new tutor and coach of Middlesex. He had also secured a
promise that O'Connor and Hunt would be permitted to compete, as would
be possible with a pardon for their misconduct. Marsh agreed, with the other
heads too preoccupied with recovery—of health and friendships, the latter
concerning two in particular, after Cohen's abandonment of Blunt at the
pier—to fight it.

He and Keely stayed in London after Southport, in a place of their
own. Against the odds of what they both would have thought financially
feasible before Southport, the place they found was on the Thames, further upstream, nearer the rebuild of the Palace of Westminster. Though
short staying in their own abode, the new start had shown itself to be
sound thus far. It was a comfortable new start for them, paid for by inroads he had made en route from Southport with his father, including
an agreeable acceptance for officer training at the Royal Naval College
in Greenwich, a referral that Underhill—through some former-employer
campaigning of his friend's own—had made possible as way of repay-
ment for a debt Underhill felt was owed. These agreeable opportunities
would see them graduate with a degree without needing bother with a
Sizar's stay.

Underhill, also seeking separation from the club, had secured a reference to study at Greenwich, too, as part of a severance agreement with Blunt—in whose best interests it was to keep onside an outgoing tutor during a year of great scandal. 1888 was the year *that other place*, Oxford, added "boycott" to its dictionary, so a wariness of the power of the downtrodden to bring down powerful men through poor word of mouth was at its height that year. He and Underhill…he and Arthur, had become friends, and now socialised often in shared anticipation of the start of their naval training the following year. He could see himself coming to rely on Arthur in the years ahead, especially as Keely turned mind to possible careers; the trades that Pipe had taught Keely, as Pipe had only been all too aware, of which were a young man's body-game.

It was Arthur who had convinced them to travel to the Cam. *To spectate*, Arthur had said, *to send the bastards and their follies off from a nice picnic spot.* He had needed Arthur's belief in the idea of going right up until they reached the university grounds by hansom cab from Cambridge Railway Station. Once there, with Keely and the warmth that made the Cam swimmable again; its banks adorned by young day trippers, dipping into the river via ropes tied to trees whose bloom was still in full swing; once all this was shown by the summer sun: then he was on board with the benefit of a send-off. But…bittersweetly, because he felt in some deep uncharted way that this would be the last time he returned to Cambridge. Certainly, the last time as a young man.

After taking Keely on a tour of his old lodgings in *Jesus College*, they returned to Midsummer Common where Arthur had lay out a rug, upon which was a basket with sandwiches and wine, for them to watch the start of the race. The outcome of that year's regatta would be out of their sight-line, which suited him. Cambridge was both familiar and changed in this final visit; the sight of the rowers readying to set off—those whom he once coached among them—was both routine and indescribably wrong. Was it because, he realised with sudden obviousness, this was the first time since Brighton that all suspects had been assembled…save for one?

Glass had killed the Pipe. That was known. But equally known—albeit to he alone—was that Glass did not kill Cox. He was resolute about that fact now, seeing them there, the Brighton Crew plus the heads and tutors—three on the Midsummer Common included. It was like suspect lineup. He was also resolute in Glass' instinct that the killer of Cox was at Brighton; was connected...not necessarily to Pipe's death directly but bound up in it some way. He needed to make a choice, now, in the next few minutes while sight-lines were open: before Cox's killer slipped away...again.

He flicked through Glass' notes like a tropical fever through a soldier, finger on the trigger. *What have I missed?* It must be there, he reasoned, somewhere in Glass' hand and his own experience of events with those of his own company—many of which, after all, he had kept from Glass. The Pipe backstory as told by his lover. Keely's rôle and place at Lewis' leap. All pieces still with edges heartbreakingly incongruous to each other. *Another approach*, he thought. *Try a different angle.*

To the side of his thinking, Arthur was conversing with Keely about the liberal transformation that Cambridge had undergone within the last generation, about the formation of a Royal Commission in 1850 and about the statutes of one Queen giving way to another, of Elizabeth to Victoria; about the upset this had caused among the old guard and the rise of socialism under the Prince Consort. All set-dressing for the formation of a secret club to try and preserve the romance of centuries-old traditions at a time when an institution that had long run itself and set its own learning agenda was under siege by the meddling of the church and state in Masculine affairs. And all while in London mateship mattered more than any tradition, when mates had clubs of exclusion. The side-of-thinking story proved central to his own progression of thinking, piquing a puzzle piece in him.

Church. The vicar. Another witness.

Glass held true that the scandalous Scarborough vicar—blackmailer and predatory boy-bugger elicitor—would be of no further bother to Arthur. He now knew that in the time before heading to the pier, when Glass was intercepting Keely's telegram and set-piecing the notebook in his room, the man was also arranging a telegram of the detecting variety: to the Scarborough Borough Police tipping them off to the vicar's penchant for late-night vigils of sodomite sin atop the steps at the Spa where the body of a young man and good-chance-whore from the East had been not long ago discovered. The vicar was caught in action at the spot that same night, and the vicar's accommodations raided, wherein incriminating evidence was found...blackmail materials, or so he came to read. The vicar's downfall had been helped by policemen knowledge of complaints against BeeHive Inn, where such men of the badge drank free, and of the vicar's inability to bring a countercharge against Arthur—having failed to learn even a new intended blackmailee's name...the details of the gentlemen staying at the Grand Hotel at the time of the Cox murder being a closely guarded secret among hotel staff and authorities, even from predators of the cloth.

They were interrupted, he thought, circling a progression to unlit paths.

The vicar may now have been out of the picture. Gross indecency it looked, which carried two years' hard labour; that was before further investigation revealed diddling of altar boys and getting caught with a local fisher-boy tramp—the lad-in-lure being honey used to ensnare the vicar, with the help of the BeeHive and police, who had mutual drink-related benefit from having the vicar out of town. A life off the streets was the result. But the vicar had proved useful to his newfound friend, in a roundabout way. The vicar had taken much from Arthur and left his friend with scabs that were only now starting to scar; but Arthur had gained something valuable from the profane vicar, too. Arthur had a compelling alibi, which also meant, in his mind, that the testimony Arthur provided could be trusted.

Arthur didn't finish. Neither did I. Progress. Pieces finding fit for the first time. Glass' insistence that Arthur confirm there was *no finish* in Cox when they were caught in flagrante slotted into Henrik's case book, finding of seed in the body of Cox. *Someone else finished the job. Not the vicar, who Arthur later finished in...no, Cox's killer buggered him first.* That led to another piece: *Cox's coat!* And to another: *The figure on the bridge! So oddly shaped. Not broad! but a tall man bent over?* And another: *Seen from Cox's room...with a sight-line of the coast.* He was getting close with sight-lines, he knew it. Like a weary, storm-battered captain in a fog, spotting the shadow of what could be the entrance to an at-last harbour. *O yes, at last!* he could taste the salty resolution of the case.

*T*ime for the starting gun close, he held the clues in his mind like salty-plump oysters in the mouth, various promising pockets…close to the popping. As he held them, he also flicked through Glass' notes of witness statements, knowing as he did that the final piece and its click-together with the entirety of the puzzling case was near. In the softening white of the not-yet-known, next to him, Arthur and Keely's words went through his approach to the end like a seaweed-weighty wind. "Why are them lined up like that?" Keely asked at the periphery of his puzzling, as comment to the crews' arranging into formation, in single file upriver, one ahead of the other rather than side by side.

Arthur seemed only too delighted to explain. "Because our regatta runs as a Torpids, rather than as an Eights. It goes back to when Marsh and the others were rowers. They weren't good enough for the main team, so rowed in the 'Torpids,' which originated in Oxford, on parts of the Thames that were too narrow for normal side-by-side contest. Around the time the heads were rowing as Torpids, there was a strong second-order mentality. Those in the Eights often weren't allowed to race in the Torpids as well. It was seen as the lesser sport. Yet still, in some cases, Torpids were seen as 'feeders' for the Eights, and their boats as 'nurseries' that would supply future talent for the main-event college races. It's a more interesting race, more hands on, less rules…like Marsh's take on wrestling, I guess. It runs here, on the Cam, at a part wide enough for the Eights, where the Eights are run, but where Torpids is chosen instead. It's *Sizar's* ethos of class-less in-clusion on the basis of the best masculine talent. And a cracking watch…"

Keely; lovable, lumbering under any detail, Keely; looked wide-eyed, not quite in comprehension. *He should-would have known all this had he not been too occupied by Lewis between his legs during our trainings at Marsh House!* he thought on the sidelines—then pushed it aside to join the mound of thoughts of Lewis already piled.

Arthur, still delighted—still someone he should emulate in matters of same-sex interaction, he thought—, spoke plainly and with patience: "It involves bumping the rear of the boat of the crew in front."

Keely laughed, handing out sandwiches, "Any excuse to do it arse ways, aye?"

And. That. Did it.

The mist cleared and all the pieces found their place. The oyster burst.

It's all backwards!

That was the detective's-own clue. The whole story of the Birkdale Palace Hotel, Glass' final words and who they were directed to. Who the man was *looking at!*

He darted the faces in the boats, and yes, sure enough. Among his own twist-arm substitutes, there was another…a different *tutor* filling in for a missing team member. *Was it another death?* A type of murder that one would not normally think of as murder. Another Lewis? *That tutor* who had been so interested to hear about his own substitution for Lewis…whose own job was under threat from Pipe…Pipe of whom would never have raced, couldn't have faced being in a boat where water was as much splashed in as staying out, but who must have had plans for employment beyond proving able-bodied-ness, knowing as he now did how Pipe had obsessed about prospects beyond the flesh. The missing link was there, looking right at him. Always had been. *How had I missed it?*

Glass had not cared for Cox, not really. Certainly not enough to have passion-murdered the relative stranger. Not even enough to hate the Russian; to break the poor boy down so utterly, mangled like the failed iron of a pleasure pier…reduced to a thing of inhuman ruin. Glass had kept the body, but not cared for it. Stored it only, probably as penance to the shrine the former detective had erected to Pipe. Glass neglected Cox, allowed the poor thing to rot. *Why did he keep Cox if he wasn't going to make use?*

Another piece revealed itself, as if Glass was sat there beside him and overturned his palm to reveal the reason.

There

was

poetry

in

it.

Glass was talking to the killer in those final moments. *Looked right at him* when Glass said it. Monster-of-a-sort to monster of a different entirely. Cox's killer was monstrous in a more malicious way. The reasons to dislike Cox— rejection of advances, i.e.,—were mild; and to kill Cox, he was now seeing, were cruelly...pragmatic. An only broadly necessary kill. On the *rejection of advances*, submission was achieved in the end, though force was required. He hypothesised: The killer, having heard firsthand of the Underhill rendezvous, had turned up to training but left early via the restaurant exit that led onto the hotel terrace...similar to the portal he had been led back through by the Grand Hotel's bellboy. Those boys were all-too willing to give away the monster building's secret easements, but to keep tight-lipped when needed—as the vicar found out. The killer had then travelled along the beach to interrupt and scare off a peeping witness, cloaked by dark. *Yes! the vicar again.*

Still hypothesising, though it all seemed so clear now: The culprit would have then made advances on an unsatisfied and unspent Cox; Cox of whom, he suspected, would have been bitterly disappointed at the vicar stopping a nowhere-close Arthur from leaving a trace. Especially after, *he knew*, the Russian whore had been denied some seed already. *Cox had been most upset after my withdrawal.* As on edge as Cox must have been, as eager and any-caution clouded by hotel-bar spirit as the boy was, Cox still, probably, resisted...given the diseased donor on offer. *Cox had no sores!* Even inside ones, *he knew*, so would not have risked getting some. So, rejection. All facts that led to Cox receiving the lesser, unwanted killer-seed...*after the fact.*

Once spent, resentment would have set inside the killer, leading to the dismantlement and display of Cox as violently as to represent the killer's distaste and jealously at the affections Cox courted...inclusive of those that Pipe— the main event, always—also captured. In the end all this was, also, not really important. Such was the tragedy of the Cox affair. Cox was merely a test run for a later, *necessary* murder that would have the killer installed as a member of a Crew. As reaction to an inevitable, in-time removal of a head's favour as tutor. And he had been present for the most important clue…though it had been forgotten due to Glass' lacklustre notetaking during the high-tea interrogation. *A figure seen on a land bridge from a room with only sea in sight.*

He had it all backwards, they all had. *Betting in the gentlemen's clubs?* That wasn't the red herring of the whole Pipe affair. *Glass knew that, he did shoot Blunt remember!* Lewis may have jumped, but someone led the lad to it. Some high-stakes bet drove the boy from the *Highlands Express.* Blunt hadn't the money of the others, *Blunt even coaches at Cambridge for Christ's sake!* And Keely's tale made clear the man's anguish around the wrestling match. *A win from a lad Peele selected! Imagine the odds on that.* But if you had inside knowledge on the candidates…if you thought the win was a sure bet, even against a known champion. Big odds there. Worth staking an entire estate on, that is. *To know a match, to draw the short straws!* No, betting wasn't the red herring. Glass knew that—bets had caused the deaths of non-club members before and did here, too. It was the *more deaths*, the ones after a detective's own kill. That's what could entice the intrigue of a true detective. Even a disgrace-retired one.

Nothing about Cox mattered, not even the motive for the runt's death. Cox's function was a misdirection, a freak show carnival side attraction. *That murder was itself a red herring.* An opportunistic kill, and practice session; a throwing-off the scent, for a later, more subtle kill. Probably one more in line with Lewis. As Glass said, the poor boy's self-murder had *inspired*. It veiled a murder-proper, to fly under the radar of suspicion, that would need only *a gentle push.* Hiding in plain sight in the shadow of the pointlessness of Cox's ruin; to appear like a collapsed iron pier. A *Sizar's* hopeful who jumped from the replacement of Bouch's own engineering fuck up, perhaps, or——

The gun fired! Three shots, as was tradition for the start of a rowing race. Three gunshots, like on the pier. The detective in his ear: *As that crude fuck Tanner—watch him, you hear!—poured out tea instead of coffee in that damned folly hotel, I knew.* The killer to have eluded him now had a name. And he shouted it at the Cam. His Keely and Arthur stood at attention. He shouted it——

But the race at *The End* was already underway.

Printed in the USA
CPSIA information can be obtained
at www.ICGtesting.com
LVHW031818201123
764261LV00075B/78/J

9 780645 555332